Faith

STORIES

Faith

STORIES

EDITED BY

C. Michael Curtis

A MARINER ORIGINAL
HOUGHTON MIFFLIN COMPANY
BOSTON • NEW YORK
2003

For Reverend Joseph S. Harvard

FIRST PRESBYTERIAN CHURCH
DURHAM, NORTH CAROLINA

....

Faith is the substance of things hoped for,
the evidence of things not seen.

—HEBREWS 11:1

ACKNOWLEDGMENTS

THIS BOOK would not have come to be without the patient and diplomatic resolve of Julia Livshin, who managed permissions and attended to a daunting series of details; the cheerful efficiency of Heidi Pitlor, Houghton Mifflin's editorial emissary; the steadfastness of Charles Everitt, longtime friend and literary agent; and the astute research assistance of Kathy Crutcher and Bruce Fudge, two *Atlantic* colleagues whose careers are just beginning. Thanks also to Elizabeth Cox, the substance of things hoped for, and seen.

CONTENTS

ix INTRODUCTION

ELIZABETH COX 1 *Saved*

GABRIEL GARCÍA MÁRQUEZ 13 *A Very Old Man
with Enormous Wings*

MARY GORDON 20 *The Deacon*

NATHANIEL HAWTHORNE 38 *Young Goodman Brown*

✓MARJORIE KEMPER 51 *God's Goodness*

HANIF KUREISHI 67 *My Son the Fanatic*

JOHN L'HEUREUX 77 *The Comedian*

JAMES A. MICHENER 90 *Voyage Four: 1661*

YUKIO MISHIMA 99 *The Priest and His Love*

JOYCE CAROL OATES 114 *At the Seminary*

EDNA O'BRIEN 131 *Sister Imelda*

KATHERINE ANNE PORTER 150 *The Jilting of
Granny Weatherall*

REYNOLDS PRICE 159 *Full Day*

TOVA REICH 169 *The Third Generation*

RÉMY ROUGEAU 189 *Cello*

SALMAN RUSHDIE 207 *The Prophet's Hair*

WILLIAM SAROYAN 220 *Resurrection of a Life*

ISAAC BASHEVIS SINGER 230 *A Night in the Poorhouse*

✓KHUSHWANT SINGH 241 *The Mark of Vishnu*

AMY TAN 246 *Fishers of Men*

ALICE WALKER 254 *The Welcome Table*

DALY WALKER 259 *I Am the Grass*

JESSAMYN WEST 277 *Music on the Muscatatuck*

KATE WHEELER 290 *Ringworm*

313 BIOGRAPHICAL NOTES

INTRODUCTION

THIS BOOK BEGAN to take shape almost immediately after the publication of *God: Stories,* its partner-in-reflection. Several stories in the present volume could not be included in the earlier book, both because I ran out of room and because they seemed, somehow, not to fit. Once *God: Stories* was published, and reviewers began to tell me what I had failed to consider in putting it together, I began to realize that I had missed a number of mind-broadening possibilities. In choosing stories rooted in Protestant, Catholic, and Jewish traditions, I had unwittingly excluded more than half of the world's believers.

Faith: Stories, at least in part, is an attempt to close this gap. And while such an attempt to be inclusive necessarily exposes the limitations of the exercise, this book attempts an encounter with spiritual traditions unremarked in its predecessor. I've included two stories — sections of novels, as it happens — that touch on matters fundamental to Quaker traditions and lore; other stories concern Hindu, Islamic, Buddhist, and Confucian values and ideas. While none of these stories intend or accomplish a full appreciation of the traditions from which they arise, they do underline instructive truths about the strength and transformative power of diverse faith experiences.

Faith, of course, occurs in many forms, and with various consequences. We tell ourselves we need to believe in something beyond our own basic wish for survival and comfort, and readers should not be surprised to find here a scattering of stories about the stare-down between rationalism and steadfast faith in sacred agency. Hanif Kureishi's "My Son the Fanatic" and Salman Rushdie's "The Prophet's Hair" are examples. The same might be said of Khushwant Singh's

"The Mark of Vishnu" or Marjorie Kemper's remarkable "God's Goodness." In some stories faith is disorienting, even crippling, while in others it provides a gentle and unexpected respite from the hard realities of lives taken over by pain and disappointment.

God: Stories was intended, among other things, as a resource for reading and assessment by church groups like the one at the West Concord Union Church, in Concord, Massachusetts, where many of its stories were discussed well before they reappeared in book form. *Faith: Stories* will, I hope, extend that exercise, and its broader range ought to invite a conversation about ways in which faith commitments both divide and strengthen us.

C. Michael Curtis

Faith

STORIES

Elizabeth Cox

....

Saved

W HEN JOSIE WIRE walked down to the front of the
tent at a revival meeting, her friend Alice was with her.
The words of the preacher had stirred their hearts, and
for weeks afterward they spoke of nothing but being missionaries in
Africa. Alice would be a medical missionary, Josie a regular one. Both
girls were twelve, though Josie would turn thirteen in June.

"My dad thinks we'll change our minds later on," Alice told Josie.
"He says just wait till we get interested in boys."

But Alice was already interested in boys, and Josie dreamed of them
at night. "I can't imagine changing our minds, can you?" said Josie. "I
mean, I have seen pictures of Africa. I've wanted to go there even before I knew about God."

"I'm just saying what he told me," said Alice.

Alice's father was a neurologist who lived in a big house where Josie
loved to spend the night. On Saturday mornings Alice and Josie sat at a
table in the dining room with sun pouring through the long windows.
A Spanish woman named Rosa served them eggs and bacon and hot
cinnamon rolls. She said, *Por favor?* if she didn't understand something.

Josie liked to try to talk to the Spanish woman. She liked to imitate
her accent, and flounce around the kitchen copying Rosa. Rosa wore
skirts that made her look like a flamenco dancer. She told Josie that
she had grown up in Barcelona. Once Josie had walked into the
kitchen and seen Alice's father standing next to Rosa with his hand
on her shoulder. Rosa was barefoot, her head down, and she looked
beautiful. Alice told Josie that Rosa kept some magic beads in a box
by the sink.

"And whenever Rosa prays," said Alice, "she rolls those beads around in her hands."

After that, Josie stole one of her mother's worst necklaces, and when she prayed she held the necklace, rubbing each bead hard. Josie's family did not have servants, had never had them. Her own father taught history at a private school, and her mother, until recently, had worked as a clerk in a downtown store. Mrs. Wire had stopped working a few months before, and money was now tight.

Alice lived in a posh neighborhood, though it was situated not far from a housing project. The girls enjoyed walking into the poor section to give dollar bills to children or beggars. Their parents did not know they were doing this. Each Saturday since they had dedicated their lives, the girls gave away their weekly allowance to poor people.

"We've got to stop giving all our money away," said Alice. "We don't even have enough to go to the movies anymore."

"But I don't mind staying home, if it's for a good cause," said Josie. She felt that her dedication was stronger than Alice's, and wanted Alice to feel the way she did. "There are so many people who need us."

"Like who?"

"Like that lady we gave money to today, and others who hang out in bars. People like that."

"We can't do anything for those people," said Alice.

"*Maybe* we can." Josie began to thumb through the phone book looking for the number of a bar called the Wagon Wheel. Each time she thought of its name, her blood grew excited. The bar was located not far from where Josie lived, so she passed it going to school, or to town. She grew silent trying to look inside, trying to see what was going on. On this Saturday night she suggested to Alice that they find the number and make a call to someone at that bar.

"What would we say?" asked Alice, putting her own finger on the words in the phone book. For the first time she looked excited about Josie's idea.

"We could just talk. Whoever answers, we'll just ask them about their life. It'll be good."

Since the idea was Josie's, she had to make the call. A man with a gruff voice answered.

"Yeah. Who is it?" The man was used to getting calls from wives checking up on a husband.

Josie couldn't speak.

"Hello?" said the voice.

"Uh, excuse me," Josie finally said. "To who am I speaking?" She tried to make her voice sound gravelly and older.

"Who the *hell* is this?" the man said.

Josie tried to hand the phone to Alice, but Alice wouldn't take it. "My name is Josie." She was almost shouting. "And I'm calling to see if you are a saved person or not."

"Is this a joke?" the man asked.

"You have to answer if you are saved." There, she said it. Josie could hear the tinkle of glasses and wild music in the background.

"No," he said. "I'm not." He expected a punch line.

"Do you *want* to be?" she asked.

"What does it mean?" the man asked prudently.

"It means *everything*," said Josie, and smiled at Alice. It was working. She and Alice grew excited at the idea of their first prospect. "You won't have to worry about anything, like if you're going to heaven. Stuff like that."

"I'm not ready to die anyway," the man said.

"I mean when it's time, then you will go to be with the angels instead of to — *you* know."

"What do I have to do?" The man sounded mollified.

"You have to love Jesus," said Josie.

"Okay," the man said quickly.

"Really?"

"Yeah." The man hung up.

Josie dialed the number again.

"Yeah?" said the voice.

"Listen," said Josie. "That was mean. I just wanted to ask you about something and you hung up on me."

"We musta been cut off," said the man. "How *old* are you?"

"I'm fifteen," lied Josie, excited that the man who was *not* saved, and probably drunk, was asking her about herself. She did look fifteen. She had breasts and a deep curve at the waist; her hips moved out like little hills. She and Alice had both developed figures that were catching the eyes of boys, and men. Alice had even begun to go to the drugstore with Boog Barnett, who was the handsomest boy in the eighth grade. Boog said words like *piss* and *damn*. Sometimes Alice repeated the words. She let him put his arm around her waist and buy her Coke floats. Since her interest in Boog had accelerated around the same time as their being saved, they had talked almost as much about Boog as they had about being missionaries.

"I bet you're pretty," said the man. "I bet you look like some of the students I used to have in my classroom. What's your name?"

Josie told him her name, and said she had a friend named Alice. She and Alice shivered with the thrill of talking to a strange man on the phone at ten o'clock at night. They had not expected anyone to be friendly. "What's yours?"

"Samuel Beckett," said the man.

"That's nice. That's a nice name," said Josie, mouthing the name to Alice. "I think I've heard of you."

"I don't see how."

"What do you *do?*" Josie asked.

"I used to be a teacher but got fired."

Josie grew silent.

"I probably taught little girls like you. You don't sound so little, though." He spoke his words as though he were proffering a gift.

"What do I sound like?" she asked.

"Like a young woman. I'm wondering what you look like, though. What kind of hair do you have?"

"What do you mean?"

"I mean is it long or short, and what color is it? I'm just trying to picture what you look like."

"It's brown," said Josie. "It's kind of curly."

"Well," said the man. He was waiting to hear more.

"I thought we were talking about whether or not you were saved."

"I said I wasn't."

"But don't you want to be?"

"Depends."

"Depends on what?"

"On who's saying it. I have to hear something like that from somebody I can trust. I have to be sure the person's telling me the truth. Are you telling me the truth?"

"Oh, yes. My friend Alice will tell you too. She'll tell you the same thing. We work to*gether.*"

"I don't care about any Alice," said Samuel Beckett. "I want to hear about *you.*"

Josie tried not to look as pleased as she felt. Over the last couple of weeks, Alice had spent more and more time with boys, and Josie had been left alone in her quest to be faithful. She thought Alice was being drawn away from God, and Alice kept saying that you could like a boy and *still* like God. Josie didn't see how.

"I bet he's old," said Alice when they hung up. "I bet he's old and decrepit."

"He didn't sound it," said Josie. "He sounded real nice."

"How nice can he be, him being in a bar?" Alice folded back the bed and fluffed the pillows. Each of them had two large pillows on their bed. At Josie's home each person only had one pillow. It occurred to Josie that the reason Boog Barnett was asking Alice out was because Alice was rich. Alice said it was time for bed and they should say their prayers now.

"Do you think God likes jokes?" Josie asked.

"I don't know," said Alice. "Why?"

"Sometimes when I pray I tell him a joke. I think he likes for me to. I bet not many people do that." Alice said she was tired. But they talked for a while about what their life in the Congo would be like, until there came a long silence when Josie asked Alice a question about native rituals. Alice didn't answer.

"You asleep?" Josie asked, and the lack of an answer made her feel alone. Josie prayed silently for the man in the bar. Then she prayed to be sexy like the woman from Barcelona. She also prayed for her mother, who seemed to be crying all the time now.

Over the last year, whenever Josie came home she might find her mother in the kitchen with her head on her arms, crying. So one night the week before, Josie asked her brother if their parents were going to get a divorce. The next day Mr. Wire reassured Josie that she need not worry about divorce.

"Did James tell you I asked about that?" said Josie.

"Yes," said Mr. Wire, "and I wanted you to know that your mother's sadness is about you. She worries about you, and the operation that's coming up."

A few years ago Josie had been diagnosed with aortal stenosis, and would need an operation on her heart. The operation was scheduled for August. The doctor had explained how the procedure would be performed, but he had waited for Josie to be older, stronger. Josie thought about what the doctor told her, but she hadn't worried until she saw her mother's sadness. Every night she prayed that her mother would stop crying.

On the next Friday night Josie and Alice called the Wagon Wheel again to see if the same man would answer. He didn't, and the harsh voice who spoke to Josie hung up on her. She called back, remembering the persistence of the disciples, and asked for Samuel Beckett. She tried to make her voice sound older by lowering it. She heard the gruff-voiced man call out the name "Sam Beckett?" and a long pause. When he returned to the phone he said, "Nobody here by that name," then, "Wait a minute. Here he is."

"Hello?"

"Samuel Beckett?"

"Yeah."

"It's Josie."

"Well, I recognize your voice. *Pretty* Josie." His voice slurred against itself. *"Pretty baby."* He sort of sang her name. "I sure think you oughta le' me see ya."

"Why?" said Josie. She didn't want Alice to know what he had said, but she had blushed and Alice was saying, "What? What did he say?"

"He wants to meet me," Josie mouthed. Alice sucked in her breath.

"I think if I meet you I'm more likely to see whether I wanna be safed. You could tell me what's like, and maybe I'll be confinced."

He did not sound like someone who had ever been a teacher. "Well," said Josie. "I wouldn't be able to come *there*. I'd get in trouble if I did."

"We could meet in the park," he said. "Would you meet with me in the park? You know how the benches have numbers on them?"

"Yes."

"You could come to Bench 23."

"I would bring Alice with me," Josie said, but Alice was shaking her head no. "I mean, if I come, I would bring Alice."

"Sure," he slurred. "Alice is a *pretty* baby too." He hung up, and Alice and Josie argued about whether or not to go to Bench 23 during the coming week.

"He didn't say *when* we should go. Does he think we're just gonna go and wait every day?" Alice said.

"I don't know."

Alice and Josie went to Bench 23 on Monday afternoon, but no one was there. Alice was relieved. They waited almost twenty minutes.

"We probably ought to get home," Alice said. "My mom will be worried."

They called the Wagon Wheel again the next weekend, but this time on Sunday night, and Samuel Beckett answered the phone. His voice was clear, not slurry.

"Hello?" Samuel Beckett said.

"I waited for you at the bench," said Josie. "I waited on Monday and you didn't come."

"I'm sorry about that," said Beckett. "I'm afraid I was drunk. But I'll meet you this Tuesday afternoon," he said. "That's my day off. Did you know that I got a part-time job as bartender? I think you're bringing me good luck."

"I *am?*"

"I might turn into a believer yet." She could tell by his voice that he was smiling, happy.

"Really?"

"I'm busy now and have to go, but you meet me on Tuesday at two o'clock."

"I don't get out of school till three-thirty."

"Four o'clock, then."

"Is it still Bench 23?" Josie asked.

"Yeah," Sam said.

"I'm not going with you this time," said Alice. "I have cheerleading practice."

Another thing that was coming between Alice and Josie was the fact that Alice had been selected as next year's cheerleader. She was cheerleader, plus she had Boog Barnett. Josie had only one boy interested in her — a guy who was good in math class. Fred Jacks had body odor and his hair was long and unruly. Every time she looked at him she wondered if someday in the future he might look good. She had seen pictures of Cary Grant when he was young, and thought how unappealing he was. She wondered if Fred Jacks could turn out better than she imagined.

On Tuesday morning Josie wore a red sweater and a navy-blue skirt to school.

"You're getting so dressed up today," her mother said. Her mother's crying had lessened and she was becoming even cheerful, but sometimes the cheerfulness felt forced. "What's the occasion?"

"Just felt like it," said Josie. Her mother smiled.

"That Freddy Jacks is just as smart as he can be," said her mother. The first half of the day dragged, but after lunch, English class and social studies went by quickly. By three-thirty Josie was leaving the school, walking toward the park. Alice was not with her.

She saw Samuel Beckett sitting on Bench 23. He was tall, even sitting down he looked tall. He was thin and wore old pants and a clean shirt. His hair was combed, and Josie guessed his age to be about forty, though she couldn't tell for sure. She hoped she looked older than her thirteen years, and imagined she would have to admit that she had lied about her age.

"Well, you certainly look older than fifteen," Mr. Beckett said upon seeing her. "If you are Josie, I would have said you were sixteen or seventeen, at least."

"Thank you." Josie sat on the bench where he had scooted over to create a space for her.

"I brought my Bible and some religious tracts." She handed him the tracts, but her hands were shaking. "You can keep those."

He slipped the papers into his shirt pocket and thanked her, but kept his eyes focused on Josie's purse, which hung from her shoulder. His eyes were bright blue and his face thin. He did not have a beard, as she had imagined, but was clean-shaven. Josie had expected him to look scruffier. He was actually handsome. He had a low, calm voice. He sounded like a teacher now. His words were not slurred, though the whites of his eyes looked bloodshot and watery, as if he had been crying for a long time.

"So what do you want to tell me?" He was going to let her begin. He was going to listen to whatever she had to say.

"I don't know what to say," Josie began. Then she thought. "When I got saved in April, I had to walk up to the front of the tent at a Billy Graham meeting. I walked all the way."

"Did that scare you?" he asked.

"A little bit, but afterwards I felt so different. Happy, you know? I want to make everybody else feel that same way."

"I'm not sure you can do that," Mr. Beckett said. He laughed and touched her arm, the arm that held her purse, and Josie jumped. She pulled away from him.

He took a strand of her hair and pushed it behind her ear. Josie's heart leapt at his touch. What awakened in her made her body collapse inside and she grew sweaty. Her breasts felt at attention.

"Now, what do I have to do?" he asked. "There's no tent, no long walk."

"Well," said Josie. "You have to want it yourself. If you don't *want* it, it won't work." Her voice was unsteady, and her hands shaky. She felt she was doing the Lord's work, and that this was how hard it was going to be. She thought about what it would feel like if this man kissed her. She pursed her lips as she had seen women do in the movies. She felt older, sexy. She felt wild, and held tightly to her Bible.

"Maybe you don't want to be saved," she offered. "Some people just aren't interested. I have a brother named James, and he doesn't care a thing about it." Josie put the Bible on Sam Beckett's legs, and he looked down at it as though she had dropped a stone in his lap.

"Why not?" he asked her.

"James likes being bad. He thinks that if he's saved he can't be bad anymore."

"That's probably not true," said Mr. Beckett.

"I don't know," she said. "I don't think you can *want* to be bad."

"Sometimes you can't help it, though," he said. "I mean the wanting."

His words were so exciting that Josie felt trembly. His eyes grew bright looking at her, and she thought she saw his mood change. He gave her back the Bible.

"Come with me," he said, and offered his hand to lead her away. Josie followed him into a section of the park that led to a stream. She tried to walk the way she imagined Rosa would walk. She tried to pretend that she was Rosa. When they were in the trees, Sam looked around, then he put his hand on Josie's shoulders and turned her toward him.

He leaned to kiss her forehead. For the first time Josie could smell him. He did not smell like her brother, or her father. He smelled the way she imagined Africa would smell. He had the odor of fur and ground. She loved his smell.

Josie did not try to squirm away but stood very still and let Mr. Beckett run his hand down to the small of her back, over her bottom. She let him touch her breasts and thought that this might be the only man who would ever touch her. If she had her operation, and if something went wrong, then this might be her only chance for love. She let him roam around her body at will. Then he moved her toward the ground until he was almost on top of her. He looked at her for a long moment, and Josie couldn't tell what he was thinking. He looked sad. She could feel a stiffness in his groin that Alice had told her about.

Alice had laughed when she told how Boog Barnett had gotten stiff at the drugstore.

Sam Beckett was kissing Josie's forehead and cheeks, but he had not yet kissed her mouth. Josie had never been kissed on the mouth, except when she was seven, and that boy had moved away. She didn't count that as a kiss, and wanted her mouth to be kissed now. She thought if she could be kissed that maybe her operation might be put off again, until after Thanksgiving, after Christmas. But when she turned her mouth toward him, Mr. Beckett stopped abruptly.

He moved to get up. "You are very young," he said.

"*Por favor?*" said Josie. She wondered if he had realized that she was not yet fifteen.

"You know, Josie." Beckett spoke, confused, but taking charge of himself. "You shouldn't be so willing to trust people."

"I don't trust people," she said.

"Anyway." He brushed some dirt off his arms. "I'm thinking that maybe you brought me good luck."

"Why?"

"Because I got a job after I talked with you."

"I thought you said you were a teacher," Josie questioned.

"I was. But I lost that job, and when I was out of work I just drank more than ever. I lost everything."

Josie kept wondering if he might take her money. She had ten dollars in her purse, and she thought he might take it all. "Are you poor?" she asked.

Mr. Beckett said nothing.

"Maybe you could get back your job," said Josie. "I mean, I bet you were good." She was trying to think of a way to bring back the fervor of his previous attention, but he already seemed through with her. She didn't know what had gone wrong.

"I really was a good teacher," he said.

She could see him tear up.

"Mr. Beckett," she said, and opened her hand to him like offering a small bird. His hands were large and warm. He didn't seem old at all, and for once in her life Josie felt richer than Alice. "I have a secret," she told him.

Josie decided to tell him something she had not even told Alice, though Alice would have to know sooner or later. "You want to know what it is?"

"I guess so." Sam Beckett was smiling, but his smile seemed impatient now. He wanted to leave. "I don't have long," he said.

Josie could not believe she would tell this man what she was about to say. She licked her lips. "Four years ago the doctors found a hole in my heart, and on August 10, they're going to operate. So when I have the operation, they don't know if I'll come through it or not, so that's partly why I decided to be saved. Because if I'm saved, then maybe God will let me live, you know? And then I can go to Africa, which is my main dream. Do you know there are animals there that people don't even know what they are?" She paused to take a breath. "And if I do *not* come through, then I figure since I'm already saved I'll go to heaven and look down on everybody, watch what people do. Maybe I can watch you, what you do. Maybe you will look through a window one day and see me there."

Her story jangled this man, visibly made him jump, and he looked at Josie Wire for a long time without speaking. He looked at her as if he were not seeing anything, but instead was seeing someone he used to know.

"How did they know about the hole in your heart?" he asked.

"I would get so tired, and blue in the face," Josie said. "My face turned blue, and my lips." She looked at Mr. Beckett. She wanted him to kiss her again. She wanted him to kiss her on the lips.

"I have a secret too," Sam said. He would give this girl the truth. "My name is not Beckett. It's Hunnicut. Bob Hunnicut. I was just teasing you when I said Beckett." He covered her hand with his.

Josie didn't think that was much of a secret, and said so. "That's more like a lie," she said.

He lifted the Bible from the ground and held it.

"I think I might like to look at this book," he told her. "I might like to read it myself."

"You would?" Josie could hardly help from asking. "Does this mean you might hope to be saved?"

"I think it *does*," he said slowly, and held out his hand. Josie shook it, pumping Bob Hunnicut's arm hard.

"I can't believe it!" she said. "Wait'll I tell Alice."

Josie began again. "Listen, my daddy's a teacher," she said. "He teaches at Webb School. Maybe you could get a job teaching there."

"Well," said Beckett/Hunnicut, "I think I better take care of that matter myself." He stood and the length of him amazed Josie.

"You got to have *faith*," said Josie, and she stood up facing him. "*I* have faith. I am going to go to Africa someday, and see everything. Have you ever been over there?"

"No," he said.

"Listen," said Josie. "Would you kiss me? I mean, before you leave?"

Bob Hunnicut leaned over and meant to kiss Josie's forehead, but Josie at that moment turned her mouth to his mouth; and her first thought, after he kissed her, was that kissing was overrated, that it didn't feel like anything. He walked away.

As she went toward the edge of the park, Josie couldn't decide whether or not to give him all her money; but as she opened her purse he was gone. She did decide, though, to keep the secret about her defective heart a while longer. Alice did not need to know yet. If Alice knew the truth, they could not plan to go to Africa. Josie Wire loved dreaming about Africa. She kept that dream inside her. She would love the smell of it there. She already knew what it would be like.

Gabriel García Márquez

....

A Very Old Man
with Enormous Wings

TRANSLATED BY GREGORY RABASSA

ON THE THIRD DAY of rain they had killed so many crabs inside the house that Pelayo had to cross his drenched courtyard and throw them into the sea, because the newborn child had a temperature all night and they thought it was due to the stench. The world had been sad since Tuesday. Sea and sky were a single ash-gray thing and the sands of the beach, which on March nights glimmered like powdered light, had become a stew of mud and rotten shellfish. The light was so weak at noon that when Pelayo was coming back to the house after throwing away the crabs, it was hard for him to see what it was that was moving and groaning in the rear of the courtyard. He had to go very close to see that it was an old man, a very old man, lying face down in the mud, who, in spite of his tremendous efforts, couldn't get up, impeded by his enormous wings.

Frightened by that nightmare, Pelayo ran to get Elisenda, his wife, who was putting compresses on the sick child, and he took her to the rear of the courtyard. They both looked at the fallen body with mute stupor. He was dressed like a ragpicker. There were only a few faded hairs left on his bald skull and very few teeth in his mouth, and his pitiful condition of a drenched great-grandfather had taken away any sense of grandeur he might have had. His huge buzzard wings, dirty and half-plucked, were forever entangled in the mud. They looked at him so long and so closely that Pelayo and Elisenda very soon overcame their surprise and in the end found him familiar. Then they dared speak to him, and he answered in an incomprehensible dialect with a strong sailor's voice. That was how they skipped over the inconvenience of the wings and quite intelligently concluded that he was a lonely castaway from some foreign ship wrecked by the storm. And yet, they called in a neighbor woman who knew everything about life and death to see him, and all she needed was one look to show them their mistake.

"He's an angel," she told them. "He must have been coming for the child, but the poor fellow is so old that the rain knocked him down."

On the following day everyone knew that a flesh-and-blood angel was held captive in Pelayo's house. Against the judgment of the wise neighbor woman, for whom angels in those times were the fugitive survivors of a celestial conspiracy, they did not have the heart to club him to death. Pelayo watched over him all afternoon from the kitchen, armed with his bailiff's club, and before going to bed he dragged him out of the mud and locked him up with the hens in the wire chicken coop. In the middle of the night, when the rain stopped, Pelayo and Elisenda were still killing crabs. A short time afterward the child woke up without a fever and with a desire to eat. Then they felt magnanimous and decided to put the angel on a raft with fresh water and provisions for three days and leave him to his fate on the high seas. But when they went out into the courtyard with the first light of dawn, they found the whole neighborhood in front of the chicken coop having fun with the angel, without the slightest reverence, tossing him things to eat through the openings in the wire as if he weren't a supernatural creature but a circus animal.

Father Gonzaga arrived before seven o'clock, alarmed at the strange news. By that time onlookers less frivolous than those at dawn had already arrived and they were making all kinds of conjectures concerning the captive's future. The simplest among them thought that he should be named mayor of the world. Others of sterner mind felt that he should be promoted to the rank of five-star general in order to win all wars. Some visionaries hoped that he could be put to stud in order to implant on earth a race of winged wise men who could take charge of the universe. But Father Gonzaga, before becoming a priest, had been a robust woodcutter. Standing by the wire, he reviewed his catechism in an instant and asked them to open the door so that he could take a close look at that pitiful man who looked more like a huge decrepit hen among the fascinated chickens. He was lying in a corner drying his open wings in the sunlight among the fruit peels and breakfast leftovers that the early risers had thrown him. Alien to the impertinences of the world, he only lifted his antiquarian eyes and murmured something in his dialect when Father Gonzaga went into the chicken coop and said good morning to him in Latin. The parish priest had his first suspicion of an impostor when he saw that he did not understand the language of God or know how to greet His ministers. Then he noticed that seen close up he was much too human: he had an unbearable smell of the outdoors, the back side of his wings was strewn with parasites, and his main feathers had been mistreated by terrestrial winds, and nothing about him measured up to the proud dignity of angels. Then he came out of the chicken coop and in a brief sermon warned the curious against the risks of being ingenuous. He reminded them that the devil had the bad habit of making use of carnival tricks in order to confuse the unwary. He argued that if wings were not the essential element in determining the difference between a hawk and an airplane, they were even less so in the recognition of angels. Nevertheless, he promised to write a letter to his bishop so that the latter would write to his primate so that the latter would write to the Supreme Pontiff in order to get the final verdict from the highest courts.

His prudence fell on sterile hearts. The news of the captive angel spread with such rapidity that after a few hours the courtyard had the bustle of a marketplace and they had to call in troops with fixed bayonets to disperse the mob that was about to knock the house down. Elisenda, her spine all twisted from sweeping up so much marketplace trash, then got the idea of fencing in the yard and charging five cents admission to see the angel.

The curious came from far away. A traveling carnival arrived with a flying acrobat who buzzed over the crowd several times, but no one paid any attention to him because his wings were not those of an angel but, rather, those of a sidereal bat. The most unfortunate invalids on earth came in search of health: a poor woman who since childhood had been counting her heartbeats and had run out of numbers; a Portuguese man who couldn't sleep because the noise of the stars disturbed him; a sleepwalker who got up at night to undo the things he had done while awake; and many others with less serious ailments. In the midst of that shipwreck disorder that made the earth tremble, Pelayo and Elisenda were happy with fatigue, for in less than a week they had crammed their rooms with money and the line of pilgrims waiting their turn to enter still reached beyond the horizon.

The angel was the only one who took no part in his own act. He spent his time trying to get comfortable in his borrowed nest, befuddled by the hellish heat of the oil lamps and sacramental candles that had been placed along the wire. At first they tried to make him eat some mothballs, which, according to the wisdom of the wise neighbor woman, were the food prescribed for angels. But he turned them down, just as he turned down the papal lunches that the penitents brought him, and they never found out whether it was because he was an angel or because he was an old man that in the end he ate nothing but eggplant mush. His only supernatural virtue seemed to be patience. Especially during the first days, when the hens pecked at him, searching for the stellar parasites that proliferated in his wings, and the cripples pulled out feathers to touch their defective parts with, and even the most merciful threw stones at him, trying to get him to rise so they could see him standing. The only time they succeeded in arousing him was when they burned his side with an iron for branding steers, for he had been motionless for so many hours that they thought he was dead. He awoke with a start, ranting in his hermetic language and with tears in his eyes, and he flapped his wings a couple of times, which brought on a whirlwind of chicken dung and lunar dust and a gale of panic that did not seem to be of this world. Although many thought that his reaction had been one not of rage but of pain, from then on they were careful not to annoy him, because the majority understood that his passivity was not that of a hero taking his ease but that of a cataclysm in repose.

Father Gonzaga held back the crowd's frivolity with formulas of maidservant inspiration while awaiting the arrival of a final judgment on the nature of the captive. But the mail from Rome showed no sense of urgency. They spent their time finding out if the prisoner had a navel, if his dialect had any connection with Aramaic, how many times he could fit on the head of a pin, or whether he wasn't just a Norwegian with wings. Those meager letters might have come and gone until the end of time if a providential event had not put an end to the priest's tribulations.

It so happened that during those days, among so many other carnival attractions, there arrived in town the traveling show of the woman who had been changed into a spider for having disobeyed her parents.

The admission to see her was not only less than the admission to see the angel, but people were permitted to ask her all manner of questions about her absurd state and to examine her up and down so that no one would ever doubt the truth of her horror. She was a frightful tarantula the size of a ram and with the head of a sad maiden. What was most heart-rending, however, was not her outlandish shape but the sincere affliction with which she recounted the details of her misfortune. While still practically a child she had sneaked out of her parents' house to go to a dance, and while she was coming back through the woods after having danced all night without permission, a fearful thunderclap rent the sky in two and through the crack came the lightning bolt of brimstone that changed her into a spider. Her only nourishment came from the meatballs that charitable souls chose to toss into her mouth. A spectacle like that, full of so much human truth and with such a fearful lesson, was bound to defeat without even trying that of a haughty angel who scarcely deigned to look at mortals. Besides, the few miracles attributed to the angel showed a certain mental disorder, like the blind man who didn't recover his sight but grew three new teeth, or the paralytic who didn't get to walk but almost won the lottery, and the leper whose sores sprouted sunflowers. Those consolation miracles, which were more like mocking fun, had already ruined the angel's reputation when the woman who had been changed into a spider finally crushed him completely. That was how Father Gonzaga was cured forever of his insomnia and Pelayo's courtyard went back to being as empty as during the time it had rained for three days and crabs walked through the bedrooms.

The owners of the house had no reason to lament. With the money they saved they built a two-story mansion with balconies and gardens and high netting so that crabs wouldn't get in during the winter, and with iron bars on the windows so that angels wouldn't get in. Pelayo also set up a rabbit warren close to town and gave up his job as bailiff for good, and Elisenda bought some satin pumps with high heels and many dresses of iridescent silk, the kind worn on Sunday by the most desirable women in those times. The chicken coop was the only thing that didn't receive any attention. If they washed it down with Creolin and burned tears of myrrh inside it every so often, it was not in homage to the angel but to drive away the dungheap stench that still hung everywhere like a ghost and was turning the new house into an old one. At first, when the child learned to walk, they were careful that he not get too close to the chicken coop. But then they began to lose their fears and got used to the smell, and before the child got his second teeth he'd gone inside the chicken coop to play, where the wires were falling apart. The angel was no less standoffish with him than with other mortals, but he tolerated the most ingenious infamies with the patience of a dog who had no illusions. They both came down with chicken pox at the same time. The doctor who took care of the child couldn't resist the temptation to listen to the angel's heart, and he found so much whistling in the heart and so many sounds in his kidneys that it seemed impossible for him to be alive. What surprised him most, however, was the logic of his wings. They seemed so natural on that completely human organism that he couldn't understand why other men didn't have them too.

When the child began school it had been some time since the sun and rain had caused the collapse of the chicken coop. The angel went dragging himself about here and there like a stray dying man. They would drive him out of the bedroom with a broom and a moment later find him in the kitchen. He seemed to be in so many places at the same time that they grew to think that he'd been duplicated, that he was reproducing himself all through the house, and the exasperated and unhinged Elisenda shouted that it was awful living in that hell full of angels. He could scarcely eat and his antiquarian eyes had also become so foggy that he went about bumping into posts. All he had left were the bare cannulae of his last feathers. Pelayo threw a blanket over him and extended him the charity of letting him sleep in the shed, and only then did they notice that he had a temperature at night, and was delirious with the tongue twisters of an old Norwegian. That was one of the few times they became alarmed, for they thought he was going to die and not even the wise neighbor woman had been able to tell them what to do with dead angels.

And yet he not only survived his worst winter, but seemed improved with the first sunny days. He remained motionless for several days in the farthest corner of the courtyard, where no one would see him, and at the beginning of December some large, stiff feathers began to grow on his wings, the feathers of a scarecrow, which looked more like another misfortune of decrepitude. But he must have known the reason for those changes, for he was quite careful that no one should notice them, that no one should hear the sea chanteys that he sometimes sang under the stars. One morning Elisenda was cutting some bunches of onions for lunch when a wind that seemed to come from the high seas blew into the kitchen. Then she went to the window and caught the angel in his first attempts at flight. They were so clumsy that his fingernails opened a furrow in the vegetable patch and he was on the point of knocking the shed down with the ungainly flapping that slipped on the light and couldn't get a grip on the air. But he did manage to gain altitude. Elisenda let out a sigh of relief, for herself and for him, when she saw him pass over the last houses, holding himself up in some way with the risky flapping of a senile vulture. She kept watching him even when she was through cutting the onions and she kept on watching until it was no longer possible for her to see him, because then he was no longer an annoyance in her life but an imaginary dot on the horizon of the sea.

Mary Gordon

....

The Deacon

N O R O M A N C E H A D been attached to Joan Fitzgerald's entering the convent. She wasn't that sort of person, and she hadn't expected it. A sense of rightness had filled her with well-being, allowed her lungs to work easily and her limbs to move quickly, removed her from the part of life that had no interest for her, and opened her to a way of being in the world that connected her to what she believed was essential. Her faith, too, was unromantic; the Jesus of the Gospels, who was with the poor and the sick, who dealt with their needs and urged people to leave father and mother to follow him — this was her inspiration. Yet when she thought of the word *inspiration,* it seemed too airy, too silvery, for her experience. What she had felt was something more like a hand at her back, a light pressure between her shoulder blades. The images she had felt herself drawn toward had struck her in childhood and had not left the forefront of her mind: the black children integrating the school in Little Rock, the nuns in the Maryknoll magazine who inoculated Asian children against malaria. The source of their power was a God whose love she believed in as she believed in the love of her parents; she felt it as she had felt her parents' love; she believed that she was watched over, cared about, cared for as her parents had cared for her. She had never in her memory felt alone.

Her decision to become a nun, her image of herself as one, wasn't fed by fantasies of Ingrid Bergman or Audrey Hepburn. By the time she entered the Sisters of the Visitation, the number of candidates was dwindling and almost no one was wearing the habit except the very oldest sisters in the order; she'd been advised to get her college educa-

tion first, and by the time she entered the order, in 1973, only two others were in her class. After twenty-five years she was a school principal
in New York City and the only member of her class still in the order.

They joked about it, she and the other sisters, about how they'd
missed the glamour days, and now they were just the workhorses, the
unglamorous moms, without power and without the aura of silent
sanctity that fed the faithful's dreams. "Thank God Philida's good-
looking, or they'd think we were a hundred percent rejects," Rocky
said, referring to the one sister living with them who was slender
and graceful, with large turquoise eyes and white hands that people
seemed to focus on — which she must have known, because she wore
a large turquoise-and-silver ring she had gotten when she worked on
an Indian reservation in New Mexico. Rocky and the fourth sister had
grown roly-poly in middle age. They didn't color their hair, they had
no interest in clothes, and they knew they looked like caricatures of
nuns. "Try, as a penance, not to buy navy blue," Rocky had said. They
seemed drawn to navy and neutral colors. They weren't very interested in how they looked. They had all passed through that phase of
young womanhood, and sometimes, watching her Hispanic students,
and the energy they put into their beauty (misplaced, she believed: it
would bring them harm), Joan nevertheless understood their joy and
their absorption, because she had been joyous and absorbed herself —
though she had wanted to make things happen, to change the way the
world worked.

All the sisters she lived with had the same sense of absorption.
Rocky, who had been called Sister Rosanna, ran a halfway house for
schizophrenics and was now involved in fighting the neighborhood in
Queens where the house was located. "They want us out," she said, always referring to herself and the psychotics as "us" — believing, Joan
understood, that they were virtually indistinguishable. Four days a
week Rocky lived in the halfway house; the remaining three days she
joined Joan and two other sisters — Marlene, who directed a home-
less shelter, and Philida, who was the pastoral counselor at a nursing
home. They shared a large apartment — owned by the order — on
Fiftieth Street and Eighth Avenue. They had easy relations with the
neighborhood prostitutes and drug dealers, who were thrilled to find
that these people, whom they called "sister," seemed to have no interest in making them change their ways.

They could have been almost any group of middle-aged, unmarried

women who made their living at idealistic but low-paying jobs and
had to share lodgings if they wanted to live in Manhattan, housing
costs being what they were. But at the center of each of their days was
a half-hour of prayer and meditation, led in turn by one of the four of
them. They read the Gospel of the day and the Old Testament Scriptures; they spoke of their responses, although they didn't speak of either the texts or their thoughts about them once they had left the
room they reserved for meditation. This time was for Joan a source of
refreshment and a way of making sense of the world. If anyone had
asked her (which they wouldn't have; she wasn't the type people came
to for spiritual guidance), she would have said that this was why she
loved that time and those words: they were the most satisfying consolation she could imagine for a world that was random and violent and
endlessly inventive in its cruelty toward the weak.

Unlike the other sisters, including Philida, Joan had always been too
thin. When she thought about it, she thought she had probably become stringy, and her skin, which had tanned easily, was probably
leathery now. Perhaps her thinness and the coarse texture of her skin
were traceable to her anomalous bad habit. Joan was a heavy smoker.
She'd begun smoking in graduate school, the education program at
the University of Rochester. Her study partners had all smoked, and
she had drifted into the habit. She had wanted to persuade them —
and herself, perhaps — that they didn't know everything about her
just because she was a nun. Nuns didn't smoke; everyone knew that.
But Joan did, though she had tried to quit. The women she lived with
didn't allow her to smoke in the apartment; they had put a bumper
sticker up on the refrigerator that said SMOKE-FREE ZONE. And of
course she didn't smoke in school. She went over to the rectory to
smoke.

She was the principal of Saint Timothy's School, at Forty-eighth Street
and Tenth Avenue. Once all Irish, it was now filled with black and Hispanic children. Joan was proud of what Saint Timothy's provided. She
knew that she suffered from what one of her spiritual advisers called
"the vanity of accomplishment." She knew she had a tendency to believe that she could do anything if people would just go along with her
programs, and she made jokes about it, jokes on herself, jokes she
didn't really believe. When she made her last retreat, which was run
by a Benedictine sister, the nun urged her to contemplate the areas of

life that were unsusceptible to human action, the mysterious silences of God, the opportunities for holiness provided by failure. She tried, for a while, to center her meditations the way the Benedictine had suggested, but then concluded that this was a contemplative's self-indulgence; she was in the world, she was doing God's work in the world. There was work to be done, and (was this what she had grown up hearing described as "the sin of pride"?) she could do it. She had long ago given up heroic plans and dreams, but she could make her school run well, and she could give to children — who often didn't have it elsewhere — a place where they were made to feel important, where things were demanded of them, but where they were valued and praised.

Though Joan was frustrated and vexed by the poor quality of many of her teachers, she believed that the children got from her and her staff a quality of schooling they could never have gotten in the public schools. She came to understand that many of the teachers were at Saint Timothy's because they wouldn't have been tolerated anyplace else. She put up with most of them, because at least they created zones of energy and discipline. She drew the line, though, at Gerard Mahoney. Gerard had been teaching seventh grade at Saint Timothy's since he left his seminary studies, in 1956. Joan was sure he'd been thrown out, not for bad behavior or any spiritual failure but simply because he couldn't make the grade — not then, not in the years when the seminaries were full to overflowing. God knows, she said to herself, nowadays he would probably be ordained. But they'd sent him home, to his mother, who had been the housekeeper at Saint Timothy's since, Joan once speculated to Rocky, Barry Fitzgerald was a curate. Mrs. Mahoney had been there when Steve Costelloe arrived, fresh from the seminary, thirty years earlier. Steve had been the pastor at Saint Timothy's for the past fifteen years. Gerard's mother had died twelve years ago, after a long illness, when Gerard was fifty-two.

Joan and Steve got along, which was more, she thought, than a lot of women in her position could have said. Essentially, Steve was lazy; his saving grace was that he understood it. He was a pale redhead, with freckles under the gold hair that grew on his hands; he was going bald; he had broad shoulders, but then his body dwindled radically — he was hipless, and his legs (she'd seen them when he wore shorts) were hairless and broomstick-thin. He had a little pot — whimsical, like something he carried tucked in his belt, a crystal ball he tapped his fingers on occasionally, as if he were waiting for messages. He was incapable of saying no to people, which was one reason he was universally beloved. Saint Timothy's was a magnet for people who had nowhere else to go; Steve was constantly cooking up vats of chili (his recipe said: "feeds 50–65"), and some unfortunate was always in the kitchen.

Often someone who had no real business being there was found to have moved into one of the spare bedrooms; the rectory, built for the priests, was nearly empty. It housed only Steve and Father Adrian, from the Philippines, who giggled all the time; when faced with the desperate situations of junkies and abused wives, he would say, "Pray and have hope," and giggle. Sometimes Joan and Steve said to each other — thinking of the hours they spent counseling people in trouble — that Adrian's approach might be approximately as successful as theirs, considering their rate of recidivism. In the Philippine parade he'd been on a float, playing a martyred Jesuit. His brother, who had contributed to the construction of the float, blamed Father Adrian for their failure to win the prize for best float. "You were laughing when they hanged you," he shouted at his brother. "That's why we didn't win." "I couldn't help it," Father Adrian said, giggling. "The children made me laugh." Steve was happy to have Father Adrian, because he was willing to take the seven o'clock mass, and Steve liked to sleep late. Joan suspected that Steve was often hung over. He was in good form by noon, for the larger mass that served the midtown workers, who came to him on their lunch hour and usually, she guessed, went back to work refreshed.

Problems arose when Steve felt that one of the people in the rectory rooms ought to be moving on; then he would come to Joan desperate for help. She would summon the person in question to the office (not in the rectory, of course, but in the school, next door) and speak firmly about getting a hold on life and going forward. Some of them just ignored her, and stayed on until some mysterious impulse sent them elsewhere. But a few of them listened, and that was bad: it encouraged Steve to ask for her help again, and she couldn't say no to his unhappiness; he was as hopeless as a hopeless child. She often said that the one temptation she could not resist was to try to fix something when it seemed broken and she believed she had the right tools. More often than not she felt she did.

Steve was dreadful with money, and a terrible administrator. He was saved by his connections: people he'd met when he played minor-league baseball, or when he sat in the Sky Box at the Meadowlands because someone had given him a Giants ticket, or people whose confessions he had heard on an ocean liner while he was a chaplain on a Caribbean cruise. Once a year Saint Timothy's would have a fundraiser, and somehow he'd be bailed out. He left the administration of the school to Joan, allowing that she was much better at it than he, and saying, "Just don't get our name in the papers, unless it's for something good." He had no stake in proving himself the boss, and she was grateful for that; when her friends ran into trouble with their pastors, it was because those pastors resented a loss of power. Steve wasn't interested in power; but Joan believed he was genuinely interested in the welfare of his flock. When she was angry at him, because he had foiled her or screwed something up, she thought he was interested only in being universally liked, and that he'd become a priest because it gave him a good excuse for not being deeply engaged with human beings.

In the end he'd backed her up about Gerard, whose shortcomings were impossible to ignore. When she walked down the hall past his classroom, the sounds of chaos came over the frosted-glass pane above the door. She had taken to making random visits; the sight of her in the doorway quieted the kids. Pretending she was in full habit, pretending she was one of the nuns she'd been taught by, she could stand in a doorway and strike what her mother would have called the fear of God into any class. Even the rowdy seventh-graders — the boys who could have felled her with a punch, the girls who were contemptuous of her failure to get the knack of feminine allure — even they could be silenced and frozen in place by the sight of "Sister" staring down at them, as if from a great, sacral height. It couldn't go on.

She talked to Gerard first. Gerard smoked too, and she saw to it that their cigarette breaks in the rectory coincided. She asked him — gently, she hoped (though she'd been told that she wasn't tactful and lacked subtlety) — if things were going all right in his class. He said, "As well as can be expected." She had to hold her temper. Expected by whom? she wanted to say. She said that keeping order among adolescents was difficult, and if he wanted to brainstorm with her and some of the other teachers, she'd be glad to set something up. Then she looked into his dull black eyes, eyes that seemed to have been emptied of color and life and movement, and thought that if there was a brain behind them, it, too, would be inert and dull. No storming was possible in or from that particular brain.

She wasn't someone who thought much about people's looks (whether people were good-looking wasn't a judgment she made about them), but Gerard's looks annoyed her. It was as if he had sat passively by and allowed someone to push his face in; the area from his cheekbones to his lower teeth was a dent, a declivity, a ditch; his lower teeth jutted above his upper ones like a bulldog's. Something about the way his teeth fit made it difficult for him to breathe quietly; he often snorted, and he blew his nose with what Joan thought of as excessive, and therefore irritating, frequency. His ears were two-dimensional and flat, like the plastic ears that came with Mr. Potato Head kits. His clothes were so loose on him that she could not envision the shape of his body. He wore orthopedic shoes, and she imagined that he had a condition no one talked about anymore, something people didn't need to have, which he just held on to out of weakness or inertia. Gerard had flat feet.

He said he was doing just what he'd been doing for forty years, and it seemed to work out all right. He mentioned that one of his earliest pupils was already a grandfather.

She wanted to say to him, What the hell does that have to do with anything? But she was trying to keep in mind what would be best for the children. She suggested breaking up the class into focus groups; she suggested films and filmstrips; she offered him more time in the computer lab. They didn't actually have a computer lab; it was a room with one computer. But Joan thought that by calling it "the computer lab" she would encourage everyone to take it seriously. Gerard, remarkably, was more skilled with computers than most. She imagined him honing his skills alone in his apartment, the one he'd lived in with his mother, playing game after game of computer solitaire, or computer chess, or some other equally solipsistic and wasteful pastime. To whatever she suggested, he responded, "I guess I'll just go on doing what I've been doing. It seems to work out all right."

She was slightly ashamed of her glee when Sonia Martinez, the mother of Tiffany, one of the smartest girls in the seventh grade, came in to complain about Gerard. Sonia Martinez said that the children were learning nothing; that she wanted Tiffany to do well on her exams and get a scholarship to one of the good high schools, Sacred Heart or Marymount; and that Tiffany was going to be behind if she stayed in Gerard's class. She mentioned her tuition payments. You've got to be kidding, Joan wanted to say. Parents paid Saint Timothy's a tenth of what was charged at private schools — less if they were parishioners, which Tiffany's parents were. She didn't like Sonia Martinez, who was finishing a business degree at Hunter College and worked for the telephone company, whose children were immaculately turned out, who was obviously overworked and naturally impatient. But she admired her tenacity, and she knew that Mrs. Martinez was right. Sonia Martinez threatened a petition by the class parents.

"Just wait on that," Joan said. "Give me a little time."

Sonia Martinez trusted her; she said all right, but the semester was ticking on, and the placement exams came early in the fall of the eighth-grade year.

As Joan walked over to the rectory, she felt the liveliness in her bones. A salty, exciting taste was in her mouth, as if she'd eaten olives or a salad of arugula. She thought that if she tried to run now, she could run easily, and very, very fast. She felt no concern for Gerard; she told herself that his job was no good for him either, the way things were, and anyway he was sixty-four; the time had come for him to retire. If Catholic schools were going to have credibility, they would have to have standards as high as those of other private schools. They had to get over the habit of thinking of themselves as refuges for people who couldn't make it elsewhere. Anyway, she told herself, I'm doing it for the students. They're my responsibility. My vocation is to serve them.

This is what she said to Steve, who, of course, said she was overreacting, that Sonia Martinez was overly ambitious, that they had, in charity, to think of their responsibility to Gerard, who had been with the parish all his life.

"So we have to forget our responsibility to the children we are pledged to serve?" she said.

"It's one year of their lives," Steve said. "This school is his whole life. It's all he has."

When she talked it over with her friends, Rocky — who because she dealt with schizophrenics was in an excellent position, she said, to deal with the clergy — suggested that she tell Steve that Gerard probably wasn't happy: dealing with chaotic, aggressive adolescents couldn't be pleasant. Joan should think of something else for him to do.

"What, what can he do?" asked Joan, who was wishing more than ever that their apartment wasn't a smoke-free zone. "He's a complete loser."

"He must be good at something."

"He can't even read the Gospel properly," Joan said. "Didn't you hear him last week — 'When Jesus rode on his donkey into Brittany'? You were the one who had to dive under the seat and pretend you were looking for a Kleenex."

"Everybody's good at something. What's he interested in?"

"Smoking."

"Didn't you say he did computers?"

She understood at that moment why people believed so literally in the Holy Ghost, in the purges of fire. A heat came over her head; her own wisdom was visible to her. She would put him in charge of the computer lab. That they had no computer lab was a minor problem. She had been reading about how obsolete computers sat around in offices. She would get Steve to schmooze up his executive friends for donations: Steve would get free lunches, the gift would probably be a tax deduction for them, and they'd think they were buying a few years out of purgatory.

Steve, as she told her friends afterward, fell for the scheme like a ton of bricks. Within a month they had six computers, none of them new but all of them workable. Gerard was more adept at the technology than any other teacher in the school, but so were most of the students. After he'd given the teachers some minor instruction, he had little to do but sit in the corner, watch the teachers and the students work, make sure the switches were turned off at the end of the day, and occasionally dust the keyboards. Everyone was happy — especially Sonia Martinez, who was doing a paper on computer literacy and minority advancement. One of Joan's friends, who taught education at the college run by their order in Brooklyn, was able to pump up one of her students for a stint teaching seventh grade. Joan knew this wouldn't last: the good young teachers left because they could earn more elsewhere, or they got married and then pregnant. But for now things were much better. She hardly saw Gerard except when their cigarette breaks coincided. When she did, she congratulated him on his new job. He said, "We are all in the hands of the Lord."

She wanted to smack him.

*   *   *

Steve told her that the parish was going to celebrate Gerard's twenty-fifth anniversary as a deacon.

"What the hell does he do as a deacon anyway?" she said. "Besides mangle the Gospel?"

"He brings communion to the sick, though sometimes he gets lost and wanders around midtown with the Blessed Sacrament. To tell the truth, he doesn't do much. But it means a lot to him. His mother was heartbroken when he was sent down from the seminary. I think the old pastor really pushed for his deaconate. It's a good thing. Or, as my grandmother would have said, 'It does no harm.' And sometimes that's the best you can hope for."

She wanted to say to Steve, It's the best *you* can hope for, but she held her tongue.

"We're going to have a little party. We'll have mass, and then wine and beer and pretzels and chips in the basement. Can you organize the children?"

"To do what?"

"Have them sing something?"

"What do you think this is, *The Sound of Music?*"

"Come on, Joanie, give me a break. I'm stuck with this."

"So I provide the entertainment?"

"Entertainment — you? Do you think I'm crazy? Just the organization. That's more in your line."

Joan was surprised at how much what Steve said hurt her. But she determined to forget it. She asked him who was going to be in charge of the food and the decorations. "Marek," he said. Marek was from Poland; he had been an accountant there, but now he wanted to be an artist. He was living in one of the spare rooms at the rectory. He was supposed to be the sexton, and to do odd repairs, but he was as bad at that as Gerard was at reading the Gospel. She wasn't hopeful about the food and the decorations, but one of the things she had learned was that if she tried to do everything, nothing would get done well. It's not my problem, she said to herself; she would forget about the food, the decorations, what Steve had said to her, and concentrate on the children and their song.

She chose the littlest children, who still loved any excuse to perform. She herself had no musical talent; she had hired Josie Myerson, a niece of one of the sisters, who was getting a Ph.D. in music, to come to the school once a week to do music with the children. The girl was energetic and talented, and what she did, if inadequate in its extent, was at least first-rate in its quality. Josie, who was plain and misunderstood by her mother, looked at Joan with a hopefulness that made Joan uneasy. Soon, she expected, Josie would talk about wanting to enter the convent. Joan would discourage her; Josie was too neurotic, and the last thing the order needed was someone who joined because she couldn't make it in the larger world. But Joan knew how to use her power over Josie when she needed to, and she needed to now. Josie taught six of the girls and six of the boys the song "Memories," from *Cats,* which she thought would be appropriate for a twenty-fifth anniversary. Then they would break into a Latin medley, including dancing, which would make them all happy and lighten the tone.

Steve announced at the beginning of the mass that it was to be said in thanksgiving for Gerard's ministry. Most people, he said, didn't understand the role of the deacon. He could do all the things a priest did except consecrate the Host. His ministry was in the community, and he was of the community; Gerard certainly was, having lived here, on the same block, all his life. Joan was sure that almost none of the parishioners had any idea who Gerard was, other than that he was funny-looking and often made mistakes in the reading. Nevertheless, they applauded him when Steve called for applause, and because it was a Sunday, enough people were there to make the applause sound genuine and ample.

Just after communion Joan went downstairs to determine where the children should stand; she didn't know where Marek would have put the tables, and how she would accommodate the arrangement. When she turned on the light, her heart sank. Marek had done nothing to make the place festive. On one long table were two boxes of Ritz crackers; a slab of cheddar cheese on a plate; some unseparated slices of Swiss, the paper still between the slices; a plate of dill-pickle spears; a bowl of green olives; two bags of potato chips; and a bag of Chee-tos. There were two half-gallon jugs of red wine, a bottle of club soda, and a bottle of ginger ale. Two dozen paper cups, still in their plastic. A packet of napkins, also wrapped. On the four pillars that supported the ceiling were taped white paper plates with the number 25 written on them in blue ballpoint.

Desperate, Joan ran upstairs to the rectory kitchen for bowls to put the crackers and the chips in. Frantically she unwrapped the paper cups and unwrapped and spread out the napkins. She ran upstairs again for some ice and looked for an ice bucket; unable to find one, she emptied the ice trays into a large yellow bowl. When the children came downstairs, she told them to stand in front of the food table; somehow, she thought, they made the whole thing less dispiriting.

She'd been worried that there wasn't enough food, but only three adults came downstairs from the church: Father Adrian; Lucinda, the Peruvian housekeeper; and Mrs. Frantzen, who had taught in the school until her retirement, fifteen years earlier. Then Steve came downstairs — he was always surrounded after mass, and had a hard time getting away — but said he could stay only a minute. He had a baptism in Westchester — one of the assistant coaches of the Knicks had had a baby, and no one but Steve could baptize her. He told Gerard he'd take him to Gallagher's for dinner — that he'd be back at five. "You too, Joan," he said, running out the doorway. "You'll join us too." He didn't wait for a reply.

She told the children they could eat what they wanted, and they dived for the potato chips. Their activity was a welcome spot of color, because no one had anything to say. They kept congratulating Gerard, and saying what a wonderful thing the deaconate was, and how wonderful it was that he had served the parish all these years, in all these ways. No one said what the ways were exactly. Mrs. Frantzen said how proud his dear mother would be. Father Adrian offered a prayer for the repose of Gerard's mother's soul. The children sang their song but skipped the Latin medley. Father Adrian and Lucinda drifted upstairs. Mrs. Frantzen said she'd have to be going.

Gerard lingered while Joan collected the food to take upstairs. She supposed that eventually Marek would get around to it, but she much preferred being busy over trying to think of something to say to Gerard.

"Well, Gerard, it's quite a day for you," she said, with a false brightness that turned her stomach.

"I count my blessings," he said. She could think of nothing else to say. He helped her carry the leftovers up the stairs. She thought of the upcoming dinner at Gallagher's. She thought that Steve had selected the restaurant because the management knew them, and because they could smoke there. She rarely thought about drinking, but she planned that as soon as she sat down, she'd order a Scotch and soda.

*   *   *

When she got to the apartment, the other sisters were watching a video of W. C. Fields's *My Little Chickadee*. She was glad to take her shoes off, settle on the couch, and join the laughter — much too raucous, they said happily, for a bunch of nuns. It was three o'clock. At four she'd have to get ready for dinner, and at four-thirty she'd leave. But she had time to watch the movie. Marlene had made chocolate-chip cookies, and Philida was putting coffee Häagen-Dazs into their blue-and-white ice-cream bowls.

"Now, this is heaven," Rocky said. "Forget eternal light and visions of unending bliss. This is it."

"Ten years in purgatory for blasphemy," Marlene said.

"If only this weren't a smoke-free zone," Joan said.

"If only you weren't trying to kill yourself," Rocky said.

"All right, all right, I'm sorry I brought it up," Joan said. She thought about how Fields's cruelty was delightful, and wondered what it had to do with Gospel generosity, and decided that it had everything and nothing to do with it and she should just relax. She wondered what W. C. Fields would do with Gerard. He certainly wouldn't be going to Gallagher's with him. Or maybe he would. For the steak and the Scotch.

At four-thirty the phone rang. It was Steve, from his car, or from the highway beside his car. He was waiting for a tow truck. He wasn't going to be able to get to the city by five. They'd have to go on without him; he'd be there as soon as he could.

"Don't do this to me, Steve," Joan said.

"I'm not doing it. It's in the hands of God, Sister."

"God has nothing to do with it. Just get here. Can't one of your rich friends lend you a car?"

"I'm in the middle of the highway. I have to deal with this first."

"Just hurry. Just go as fast as you can."

"Aye, aye, sir," he said, and clicked off.

When she told the other nuns what had happened, Philida was suspicious. "I'll bet he's sitting in someone's rumpus room and just said his car broke down."

"Steve wouldn't lie."

"Steve takes care of Steve."

"And a lot of other people too. You can't say he's not generous, Philida."

"When it's easy for him."

"I'm just not going to think about it," Joan said, angry at Philida for making things more difficult. "It's impossible enough as it is. Will one of you come with me? Steve'll pay for it. Or probably no one will pay. The people who run Gallagher's are in the parish; Steve probably baptized all their kids."

"Joan, if you had a choice between dinner with Gerard and watching *The African Queen* and ordering in Thai food, which would you choose?" Marlene asked.

"In solidarity with a sister, I'd go to Gallagher's."

"Solidarity is one thing; being out of your mind is another. Offer it up, for the poor souls," Rocky said.

"This is community life? This is my support network?"

"We'll keep the movie out for an extra day, so you can see it tomorrow. The community will pay the late fee."

"That's Christian charity at its most heroic."

"We gave up the virgin-martyr thing years ago, Joan. Hadn't you heard?"

She had what she thought was a brilliant idea. She phoned Gerard and explained what had happened to Steve, and asked if he'd like to put off the dinner until another day, when Steve could join them.

"But then it wouldn't be my anniversary," he said.

"Well, it could still be a celebration."

"This is the day of my anniversary," he said. "No other day will be that."

She gave up. People's wanting something so much often wore her down. She very rarely wanted anything for herself enough to try to force someone into giving it to her. Gerard wanted this, and like a lot of people who had very little else in or on their minds, he had plenty of room for a stubborn will to grow in.

"Great, then I'll meet you at Gallagher's," she said. She couldn't remember when the prospect of anything had made her so sick at heart.

Slabs of beef hung from hooks in the restaurant window. On the pine-paneled walls, behind the red-leather booths, were pictures of New York sporting, political, religious, and show-business figures from the 1890s to the 1950s. Diamond Jim Brady, Fiorello La Guardia, Jack Dempsey, Yogi Berra. Stiff-looking monsignors beside men in fedoras and coats with collars made of beaver or perhaps mink. An age of easy, thoughtless prosperity, a slightly outlaw age, of patronage and conquest and last-minute saves from on high. She thought how odd it was that she liked this place so much, since it had nothing to do with the way she had always lived her life — was the opposite of the way she had lived her life. Yet she didn't feel out of place here; she felt welcomed, as if they had made an exception for her, and she liked the feeling, as she liked the large hunks of bloody meat and the home-fried potatoes and the creamed spinach, more than the Thai food the sisters would be eating, more than the cookies they would devour while they watched the film.

"So, Gerard, it's a great day for you," she said with what she hoped he wouldn't notice was a desperate overbrightness, masking her terror at the fact that after she said this, she would have nothing to say.

"I thank God every day of my life. I count my blessings. Except I have to say I was a little disappointed. None of the old students came. I thought they'd come. The celebration was mentioned in the parish bulletin."

"Oh, Gerard, most of the old students don't live in the parish anymore. And besides, you know how busy people are."

"Still, you'd think at least one of them."

"I'm sure they were at the mass. You know how shy people are to come to anything after mass. Catholics simply weren't brought up to do it."

"I was surprised, though."

He wouldn't let it go. She felt, at the same time, hideously sorry for him and angry that he wouldn't accept the ways out she offered him. Did he have any idea how horribly he had failed as a teacher? Was today the first news of it for him? If it was, her mixture of pity and dislike was even stronger, though equal in its blend.

"I'm surprised Father Steve went off to the baptism. You'd think he could have found a substitute."

"I think it was a very good friend."

"He's known me for years."

"Well, you know, Steve, he always thinks he can do everything. I'm sure he'll show up. You know his way of pulling things off in the end."

"It's a very important day to me."

"Of course it is, Gerard, of course."

"It was a great blessing, my being called to the deaconate."

Yes, she wanted to say, a job with so little to it that you couldn't screw it up.

"My mother was very upset when I was sent home from the sem. I just couldn't cut it. The pressure was very tough. I think these days they'd say I had a nervous breakdown."

Suddenly she wondered if she had to think of him in a new way, as someone with an illness rather than with a series of bad habits. She didn't know which she preferred, which was more hopeless, which less difficult to bear.

"My mother wanted a son as a priest more than anything. All those years being a housekeeper in the rectory. I really disappointed her. I just couldn't cut it."

"I'm sure you were a great comfort to her in her last days."

His dull eyes brightened. "Do you think that's it? Do you think it's the will of God? That I couldn't cut it at the sem because if I had been a priest, she would have been alone in her last illness?"

"I've heard you were very devoted to her."

"I took care of her for fifteen years. It was a privilege. It was a very special grace."

"Well, then, you see," Joan said, not knowing what she meant at all.

"Still, I was a big disappointment to her. There was no getting around that. And I was disappointed today, that so few people came. Next to my investiture, it was the most important day of my life."

Gerard began to cry. The waiter hovered behind them and then disappeared. Joan wondered what on earth people in the restaurant imagined was going on between them, who people thought they might be to each other — this unfortunate-looking old man and the underdressed old maid across from him.

She tried to give her attention to him, not to think of the waiter or the other diners, not to be mortified at the sight of this man — he was an old man, really — crying, trying to light a cigarette.

"Sometimes I just don't know what it all means."

A wave of anger rose up in her. Anger toward Gerard and toward the institution of the Catholic Church. What was it all worth, the piety, the devotion, if it left him crying, struggling helplessly over an ashtray? Seeing life as meaningless. At least it should have provided him with sustenance. He had missed the whole point; he had taken only the stale, unnourishing broken crusts and missed the banquet. She was angry at him for having missed the whole point of Jesus and the Gospels, when he had been surrounded by them every day of his life, and angry at the Church for having done nothing to move him.

"Surely, Gerard, you know that you are greatly beloved."

He stopped crying and shook his head like a dog who had been fighting and had had a bucket of cold water thrown on him.

"I appreciate that, Sister. I appreciate that very much. That's why even Father's not showing up is the will of God, I think. I always thought that of all of them, you were the one who really cared about me."

She felt sick and helpless. How could she say to him, I wasn't talking about me, I was talking about God. He was looking down at the tablecloth; his shoulders were relaxed, not hunched and knotted as usual. He lifted his head and gave her a truly happy smile.

"You see, you were the only one who cared enough to notice what I was going through. Everybody just let me go on teaching, doing a terrible job, giving me class after class to screw up. Do you think I liked it in there? I was just afraid of losing my job. It's all I have, coming to the school."

"There's the deaconate — you could make something of that."

"I'm not very good with people," he said. "But you figured out what I was good at. You looked at what I was really like. You saw that I had a talent for computers. You paid attention. That's what caring really means. You were the only one since my mother who cared enough to tell me I had to improve. Everybody else thought I was hopeless. They didn't want to look at me, just kept me around so I wouldn't be on their conscience. You really looked, and you found my gift."

Turning computer switches on and off? she wanted to say. Dusting keyboards? Turning out the lights and locking the door?

"Now I know I have a real place, a place where I'm needed, and it's all thanks to you. That's the kind of thing Jesus was talking about."

Oh, no, Gerard, she wanted to say, oh, no, you're as wrong as you can be. Jesus was talking about love, an active love that fills the soul and lightens it, that draws people to each other with the warmth of the spirit, that makes them able to be with each other as a brother is with a sister or a mother with her child. Oh, no, Gerard, I do not love you. You are a person I could never love. Never, never, will I feel anything for you when I see you but a wish to flee from your presence. She prayed: Let me stay at the table. Let me feel happy that I made Gerard happy. Let me not hate him for his foolishness, his misunderstanding, his grotesque misinterpretation of me and the whole world. She prayed to be able to master the impulse to flee.

But she could not.

"Excuse me," she said, and ran into the ladies' room. In the mirror her eyes looked dead and cold to her. She believed what she had said to Gerard, that all human beings were, by virtue of their being human, greatly beloved. But the face she saw in the mirror did not look as if it had ever been loved, or could ever love.

She looked in the mirror and prayed for strength — not to make herself love Gerard but to sit at the table with him. Only that.

He believed that she loved him. He believed that she had his interest at heart, when all she cared about was keeping him from doing damage to her children, whom she did, truly, love. Only Steve had prevented her from throwing him out on the street. Steve, who, she was more sure than ever now, was relaxing in Westchester.

The poor you always have with you. She heard the words of Jesus in her head. And she knew that she would always have Gerard. He was poorer than Estrelita Dominguez, thirteen years old and three months' pregnant, or LaTrobe Sandford, who might be in jail this time next year.

The poor you always have with you. She thought of Magdalene and her tears, of the richness of the jar's surface and the overwhelming scent of the ointment — *nard* she remembered it's being called — and the ripples of the flowing hair. She saw her own dry countenance in the greenish bathroom mirror. She combed her hair and smoothed her skirt down over her narrow hips. She returned to Gerard, who had been brought a Scotch and soda by the waiter.

"On the house," Gerard said. "I told him we were celebrating my anniversary."

"And you, Sister," the waiter said. "What can we give you? A ginger ale?"

"Just water, please," she said. "A lot of ice."

The waiter was an Irishman; he'd be scandalized by a nun's ordering Scotch. She didn't want to disappoint him.

Nathaniel Hawthorne

....

Young Goodman Brown

YOUNG GOODMAN BROWN came forth at sunset into the street at Salem village; but put his head back, after crossing the threshold, to exchange a parting kiss with his young wife. And Faith, as the wife was aptly named, thrust her own pretty head into the street, letting the wind play with the pink ribbons of her cap while she called to Goodman Brown.

"Dearest heart," whispered she, softly and rather sadly, when her lips were close to his ear, "prithee put off your journey until sunrise and sleep in your own bed to-night. A lone woman is troubled with such dreams and such thoughts that she's afeared of herself sometimes. Pray tarry with me this night, dear husband, of all nights in the year."

"My love and my Faith," replied young Goodman Brown, "of all nights in the year, this one night must I tarry away from thee. My journey, as thou callest it, forth and back again, must needs be done 'twixt now and sunrise. What, my sweet, pretty wife, dost thou doubt me already, and we but three months married?"

"Then God bless you!" said Faith, with the pink ribbons; "and may you find all well when you come back."

"Amen!" cried Goodman Brown. "Say thy prayers, dear Faith, and go to bed at dusk, and no harm will come to thee."

So they parted; and the young man pursued his way until, being about to turn the corner by the meeting-house, he looked back and saw the head of Faith still peeping after him with a melancholy air, in spite of her pink ribbons.

"Poor little Faith!" thought he, for his heart smote him. "What a wretch am I to leave her on such an errand! She talks of dreams too. Methought as she spoke there was trouble in her face, as if a dream had warned her what work is to be done to-night. But no, no; 't would kill her to think it. Well, she's a blessed angel on earth, and after this one night I'll cling to her skirts and follow her to heaven."

With this excellent resolve for the future, Goodman Brown felt himself justified in making more haste on his present evil purpose. He had taken a dreary road, darkened by all the gloomiest trees of the forest, which barely stood aside to let the narrow path creep through, and closed immediately behind. It was all as lonely as could be; and there is this peculiarity in such a solitude, that the traveller knows not who may be concealed by the innumerable trunks and the thick boughs overhead; so that with lonely footsteps he may yet be passing through an unseen multitude.

"There may be a devilish Indian behind every tree," said Goodman Brown to himself; and he glanced fearfully behind him as he added, "What if the devil himself should be at my very elbow!"

His head being turned back, he passed a crook of the road, and, looking forward again, beheld the figure of a man, in grave and decent attire, seated at the foot of an old tree. He arose at Goodman Brown's approach and walked onward side by side with him.

"You are late, Goodman Brown," said he. "The clock of the Old South was striking as I came through Boston, and that is full fifteen minutes agone."

"Faith kept me back a while," replied the young man, with a tremor in his voice, caused by the sudden appearance of his companion, though not wholly unexpected.

It was now deep dusk in the forest, and deepest in that part of it where these two were journeying. As nearly as could be discerned, the second traveller was about fifty years old, apparently in the same rank of life as Goodman Brown, and bearing a considerable resemblance to him, though perhaps more in expression than features. Still they might have been taken for father and son. And yet, though the elder person was as simply clad as the younger, and as simple in manner too, he had an indescribable air of one who knew the world, and who would not have felt abashed at the governor's dinner table or in King William's court, were it possible that his affairs should call him thither. But the only thing about him that could be fixed upon as remarkable was his staff, which bore the likeness of a great black snake, so curiously wrought that it might almost be seen to twist and wriggle itself like a living serpent. This, of course, must have been an ocular deception, assisted by the uncertain light.

"Come, Goodman Brown," cried his fellow-traveller, "this is a dull pace for the beginning of a journey. Take my staff, if you are so soon weary."

"Friend," said the other, exchanging his slow pace for a full stop, "having kept covenant by meeting thee here, it is my purpose now to return whence I came. I have scruples touching the matter thou wot'st of."

"Sayest thou so?" replied he of the serpent, smiling apart. "Let us walk on, nevertheless, reasoning as we go; and if I convince thee not thou shalt turn back. We are but a little way in the forest yet."

"Too far! too far!" exclaimed the goodman, unconsciously resuming his walk. "My father never went into the woods on such an errand, nor his father before him. We have been a race of honest men and good Christians since the days of the martyrs; and shall I be the first of the name of Brown that ever took this path and kept" —

"Such company, thou wouldst say," observed the elder person, interpreting his pause. "Well said, Goodman Brown! I have been as well acquainted with your family as with ever a one among the Puritans; and that's no trifle to say. I helped your grandfather, the constable, when he lashed the Quaker woman so smartly through the streets of Salem; and it was I that brought your father a pitch-pine knot, kindled at my own hearth, to set fire to an Indian village, in King Philip's war. They were my good friends, both; and many a pleasant walk have we had along this path, and returned merrily after midnight. I would fain be friends with you for their sake."

"If it be as thou sayest," replied Goodman Brown, "I marvel they never spoke of these matters; or, verily, I marvel not, seeing that the least rumor of the sort would have driven them from New England. We are a people of prayer, and good works to boot, and abide no such wickedness."

"Wickedness or not," said the traveller with the twisted staff, "I have a very general acquaintance here in New England. The deacons of many a church have drunk the communion wine with me; the selectmen of divers towns make me their chairman; and a majority of the Great and General Court are firm supporters of my interest. The governor and I too — But these are state secrets."

"Can this be so?" cried Goodman Brown, with a stare of amazement at his undisturbed companion. "Howbeit, I have nothing to do with the governor and council; they have their own ways, and are no rule for a simple husbandman like me. But, were I to go on with thee, how should I meet the eye of that good old man, our minister, at Salem village? Oh, his voice would make me tremble both Sabbath day and lecture day."

Thus far the elder traveller had listened with due gravity; but now burst into a fit of irrepressible mirth, shaking himself so violently that his snake-like staff actually seemed to wriggle in sympathy.

"Ha! ha! ha!" shouted he again and again; then composing himself, "Well, go on, Goodman Brown, go on; but, prithee, don't kill me with laughing."

"Well, then, to end the matter at once," said Goodman Brown, considerably nettled, "there is my wife, Faith. It would break her dear little heart; and I'd rather break my own."

"Nay, if that be the case," answered the other, "e'en go thy ways, Goodman Brown. I would not for twenty old women like the one hobbling before us that Faith should come to any harm."

As he spoke he pointed his staff at a female figure on the path, in whom Goodman Brown recognized a very pious and exemplary dame, who had taught him his catechism in youth, and was still his moral and spiritual adviser, jointly with the minister and Deacon Gookin.

"A marvel, truly, that Goody Cloyse should be so far in the wilderness at nightfall," said he. "But with your leave, friend, I shall take a cut through the woods until we have left this Christian woman behind. Being a stranger to you, she might ask whom I was consorting with and whither I was going."

"Be it so," said his fellow-traveller. "Betake you to the woods, and let me keep the path."

Accordingly the young man turned aside, but took care to watch his companion, who advanced softly along the road until he had come within a staff's length of the old dame. She, meanwhile, was making the best of her way, with singular speed for so aged a woman, and mumbling some indistinct words — a prayer, doubtless — as she went. The traveller put forth his staff and touched her withered neck with what seemed the serpent's tail.

"The devil!" screamed the pious old lady.

"Then Goody Cloyse knows her old friend?" observed the traveller, confronting her and leaning on his writhing stick.

"Ah, forsooth, and is it your worship indeed?" cried the good dame. "Yea, truly is it, and in the very image of my old gossip, Goodman Brown, the grandfather of the silly fellow that now is. But — would your worship believe it — my broomstick hath strangely disappeared, stolen, as I suspect, by that unhanged witch, Goody Cory, and that, too, when I was all anointed with the juice of smallage, and cinque-foil, and wolf's bane" —

"Mingled with fine wheat and the fat of a new-born babe," said the shape of old Goodman Brown.

"Ah, your worship knows the recipe," cried the old lady, cackling aloud. "So, as I was saying, being all ready for the meeting, and no horse to ride on, I made up my mind to foot it; for they tell me there is a nice young man to be taken into communion to-night. But now your good worship will lend me your arm, and we shall be there in a twinkling."

"That can hardly be," answered her friend. "I may not spare you my arm, Goody Cloyse; but here is my staff, if you will."

So saying, he threw it down at her feet, where, perhaps, it assumed life, being one of the rods which its owner had formerly lent to the Egyptian magi. Of this fact, however, Goodman Brown could not take cognizance. He had cast up his eyes in astonishment, and, looking down again, beheld neither Goody Cloyse nor the serpentine staff, but his fellow-traveller alone, who waited for him as calmly as if nothing had happened.

"That old woman taught me my catechism," said the young man; and there was a world of meaning in this simple comment.

They continued to walk onward, while the elder traveller exhorted his companion to make good speed and persevere in the path, discoursing so aptly that his arguments seemed rather to spring up in the bosom of his auditor than to be suggested by himself. As they went, he plucked a branch of maple to serve for a walking stick, and began to strip it of the twigs and little boughs, which were wet with evening dew. The moment his fingers touched them they became strangely withered and dried up as with a week's sunshine. Thus the pair proceeded, at a good free pace, until suddenly, in a gloomy hollow of the road, Goodman Brown sat himself down on the stump of a tree and refused to go any farther.

"Friend," he said, stubbornly, "my mind is made up. Not another step will I budge on this errand. What if a wretched old woman do choose to go to the devil when I thought she was going to heaven: is that any reason why I should quit my dear Faith and go after her?"

"You will think better of this by and by," said his acquaintance, composedly. "Sit here and rest yourself a while; and when you feel like moving again, there is my staff to help you along."

Without more words, he threw his companion the maple stick, and was as speedily out of sight as if he had vanished into the deepening gloom. The young man sat a few moments by the roadside, applauding himself greatly, and thinking with how clear a conscience he should meet the minister in his morning walk, nor shrink from the eye of good old Deacon Gookin. And what calm sleep would be his that very night, which was to have been spent so wickedly, but so purely and sweetly now, in the arms of Faith! Amidst these pleasant and praiseworthy meditations, Goodman Brown heard the tramp of horses along the road, and deemed it advisable to conceal himself within the verge of the forest, conscious of the guilty purpose that had brought him thither, though now so happily turned from it.

On came the hoof tramps and the voices of the riders, two grave old voices, conversing soberly as they drew near. These mingled sounds appeared to pass along the road, within a few yards of the young man's hiding-place; but, owing doubtless to the depth of the gloom at that particular spot, neither the travellers nor their steeds were visible. Though their figures brushed the small boughs by the wayside, it could not be seen that they intercepted, even for a moment, the faint gleam from the strip of bright sky athwart which they must have passed. Goodman Brown alternately crouched and stood on tiptoe, pulling aside the branches and thrusting forth his head as far as he durst without discerning so much as a shadow. It vexed him the more, because he could have sworn, were such a thing possible, that he recognized the voices of the minister and Deacon Gookin, jogging along quietly, as they were wont to do, when bound to some ordination or ecclesiastical council. While yet within hearing, one of the riders stopped to pluck a switch.

"Of the two, reverend sir," said the voice like the deacon's, "I had rather miss an ordination dinner than to-night's meeting. They tell me that some of our community are to be here from Falmouth and beyond, and others from Connecticut and Rhode Island, besides several of the Indian powwows, who, after their fashion, know almost as much deviltry as the best of us. Moreover, there is a goodly young woman to be taken into communion."

"Mighty well, Deacon Gookin!" replied the solemn old tones of the minister. "Spur up, or we shall be late. Nothing can be done, you know, until I get on the ground."

The hoofs clattered again; and the voices, talking so strangely in the empty air, passed on through the forest, where no church had ever been gathered or solitary Christian prayed. Whither, then, could these holy men be journeying so deep into the heathen wilderness? Young Goodman Brown caught hold of a tree for support, being ready to sink down on the ground, faint and overburdened with the heavy sickness of his heart. He looked up to the sky, doubting whether there really was a heaven above him. Yet there was the blue arch, and the stars brightening in it.

"With heaven above and Faith below, I will yet stand firm against the devil!" cried Goodman Brown.

While he still gazed upward into the deep arch of the firmament and had lifted his hands to pray, a cloud, though no wind was stirring, hurried across the zenith and hid the brightening stars. The blue sky was still visible, except directly overhead, where this black mass of cloud was sweeping swiftly northward. Aloft in the air, as if from the depths of the cloud, came a confused and doubtful sound of voices. Once the listener fancied that he could distinguish the accents of towns-people of his own, men and women, both pious and ungodly, many of whom he had met at the communion table, and had seen others rioting at the tavern. The next moment, so indistinct were the sounds, he doubted whether he had heard aught but the murmur of the old forest, whispering without a wind. Then came a stronger swell of those familiar tones, heard daily in the sunshine at Salem village, but never until now from a cloud of night. There was one voice, of a young woman, uttering lamentations, yet with an uncertain sorrow, and entreating for some favor, which, perhaps, it would grieve her to obtain; and all the unseen multitude, both saints and sinners, seemed to encourage her onward.

"Faith!" shouted Goodman Brown, in a voice of agony and desperation; and the echoes of the forest mocked him, crying, "Faith! Faith!" as if bewildered wretches were seeking her all through the wilderness.

The cry of grief, rage, and terror was yet piercing the night, when the unhappy husband held his breath for a response. There was a scream, drowned immediately in a louder murmur of voices, fading into far-off laughter, as the dark cloud swept away, leaving the clear and silent sky above Goodman Brown. But something fluttered lightly down through the air and caught on the branch of a tree. The young man seized it, and beheld a pink ribbon.

"My Faith is gone!" cried he after one stupefied moment. "There is no good on earth; and sin is but a name. Come, devil; for to thee is this world given."

And, maddened with despair, so that he laughed loud and long, did Goodman Brown grasp his staff and set forth again, at such a rate that he seemed to fly along the forest path rather than to walk or run. The road grew wilder and drearier and more faintly traced, and vanished at length, leaving him in the heart of the dark wilderness, still rushing onward with the instinct that guides mortal man to evil. The whole forest was peopled with frightful sounds — the creaking of the trees, the howling of wild beasts, and the yell of Indians; while sometimes the wind tolled like a distant church bell, and sometimes gave a broad roar around the traveller, as if all Nature were laughing him to scorn. But he was himself the chief horror of the scene, and shrank not from its other horrors.

"Ha! ha! ha!" roared Goodman Brown when the wind laughed at him. "Let us hear which will laugh loudest. Think not to frighten me with your deviltry. Come witch, come wizard, come Indian powwow, come devil himself, and here comes Goodman Brown. You may as well fear him as he fear you."

In truth, all through the haunted forest there could be nothing more frightful than the figure of Goodman Brown. On he flew among the black pines, brandishing his staff with frenzied gestures, now giving vent to an inspiration of horrid blasphemy, and now shouting forth such laughter as set all the echoes of the forest laughing like demons around him. The fiend in his own shape is less hideous than when he rages in the breast of man. Thus sped the demoniac on his course, until, quivering among the trees, he saw a red light before him, as when the felled trunks and branches of a clearing have been set on fire, and throw up their lurid blaze against the sky, at the hour of midnight. He paused, in a lull of the tempest that had driven him onward, and heard the swell of what seemed a hymn, rolling solemnly from a distance with the weight of many voices. He knew the tune; it was a familiar one in the choir of the village meeting-house. The verse died heavily away, and was lengthened by a chorus, not of human voices, but of all the sounds of the benighted wilderness pealing in awful harmony together. Goodman Brown cried out, and his cry was lost to his own ear by its unison with the cry of the desert.

In the interval of silence he stole forward until the light glared full upon his eyes. At one extremity of an open space, hemmed in by the dark wall of the forest, arose a rock, bearing some rude, natural resemblance either to an altar or a pulpit, and surrounded by four blazing pines, their tops aflame, their stems untouched, like candles at an evening meeting. The mass of foliage that had overgrown the summit of the rock was all on fire, blazing high into the night and fitfully illuminating the whole field. Each pendent twig and leafy festoon was in a blaze. As the red light arose and fell, a numerous congregation alternately shone forth, then disappeared in shadow, and again grew, as it were, out of the darkness, peopling the heart of the solitary woods at once.

"A grave and dark-clad company," quoth Goodman Brown.

In truth they were such. Among them, quivering to and fro between gloom and splendor, appeared faces that would be seen next day at the council board of the province, and others which, Sabbath after Sabbath, looked devoutly heavenward, and benignantly over the crowded pews, from the holiest pulpits in the land. Some affirm that the lady of the governor was there. At least there were high dames well known to her, and wives of honored husbands, and widows, a great multitude, and ancient maidens, all of excellent repute, and fair young girls, who trembled lest their mothers should espy them. Either the sudden gleams of light flashing over the obscure field bedazzled Goodman Brown, or he recognized a score of the church members of Salem village famous for their especial sanctity. Good old Deacon Gookin had arrived, and waited at the skirts of that venerable saint, his revered pastor. But, irreverently consorting with these grave, reputable, and pious people, these elders of the church, these chaste dames and dewy virgins, there were men of dissolute lives and women of spotted fame, wretches given over to all mean and filthy vice, and suspected even of horrid crimes. It was strange to see that the good shrank not from the wicked, nor were the sinners abashed by the saints. Scattered also among their pale-faced enemies were the Indian priests, or powwows, who had often scared their native forest with more hideous incantations than any known to English witchcraft.

"But where is Faith?" thought Goodman Brown; and, as hope came into his heart, he trembled.

Another verse of the hymn arose, a slow and mournful strain, such as the pious love, but joined to words which expressed all that our nature can conceive of sin, and darkly hinted at far more. Unfathomable to mere mortals is the lore of fiends. Verse after verse was sung; and still the chorus of the desert swelled between like the deepest tone of a mighty organ; and with the final peal of that dreadful anthem there came a sound, as if the roaring wind, the rushing streams, the howling beasts, and every other voice of the unconcerted wilderness were mingling and according with the voice of guilty man in homage to the prince of all. The four blazing pines threw up a loftier flame, and obscurely discovered shapes and visages of horror on the smoke wreaths above the impious assembly. At the same moment the fire on the rock shot redly forth and formed a flowing arch above its base, where now appeared a figure. With reverence be it spoken, the figure bore no slight similitude, both in garb and manner, to some grave divine of the New England churches.

"Bring forth the converts!" cried a voice that echoed through the field and rolled into the forest.

At the word, Goodman Brown stepped forth from the shadow of the trees and approached the congregation, with whom he felt a loathful brotherhood by the sympathy of all that was wicked in his heart. He could have well-nigh sworn that the shape of his own dead father beckoned him to advance, looking downward from a smoke wreath, while a woman, with dim features of despair, threw out her hand to warn him back. Was it his mother? But he had no power to retreat one step, nor to resist, even in thought, when the minister and good old Deacon Gookin seized his arms and led him to the blazing rock. Thither came also the slender form of a veiled female, led between Goody Cloyse, that pious teacher of the catechism, and Martha Carrier, who had received the devil's promise to be queen of hell. A rampant hag was she. And there stood the proselytes beneath the canopy of fire.

"Welcome, my children," said the dark figure, "to the communion of your race. Ye have found thus young your nature and your destiny. My children, look behind you!"

They turned; and flashing forth, as it were, in a sheet of flame, the fiend worshippers were seen; the smile of welcome gleamed darkly on every visage.

"There," resumed the sable form, "are all whom ye have reverenced from youth. Ye deemed them holier than yourselves and shrank from your own sin, contrasting it with their lives of righteousness and prayerful aspirations heavenward. Yet here are they all in my worshipping assembly. This night it shall be granted you to know their secret deeds: how hoary-bearded elders of the church have whispered wanton words to the young maids of their households; how many a woman, eager for widows' weeds, has given her husband a drink at bedtime and let him sleep his last sleep in her bosom; how beardless youths have made haste to inherit their fathers' wealth; and how fair damsels — blush not, sweet ones — have dug little graves in the garden, and bidden me, the sole guest, to an infant's funeral. By the sympathy of your human hearts for sin ye shall scent out all the places — whether in church, bedchamber, street, field, or forest — where crime has been committed, and shall exult to behold the whole earth one stain of guilt, one mighty blood spot. Far more than this. It shall be yours to penetrate, in every bosom, the deep mystery of sin, the fountain of all wicked arts, and which inexhaustibly supplies more evil impulses than human power — than my power at its utmost — can make manifest in deeds. And now, my children, look upon each other."

They did so; and, by the blaze of the hell-kindled torches, the wretched man beheld his Faith, and the wife her husband, trembling before that unhallowed altar.

"Lo, there ye stand, my children," said the figure, in a deep and solemn tone, almost sad with its despairing awfulness, as if his once angelic nature could yet mourn for our miserable race. "Depending upon one another's hearts, ye had still hoped that virtue were not all a dream. Now are ye undeceived. Evil is the nature of mankind. Evil must be your only happiness. Welcome again, my children, to the communion of your race."

"Welcome," repeated the fiend worshippers, in one cry of despair and triumph.

And there they stood, the only pair, as it seemed, who were yet hesitating on the verge of wickedness in this dark world. A basin was hallowed, naturally, in the rock. Did it contain water, reddened by the lurid light? or was it blood? or, perchance, a liquid flame? Herein did the shape of evil dip his hand and prepare to lay the mark of baptism upon their foreheads, that they might be partakers of the mystery of sin, more conscious of the secret guilt of others, both in deed and thought, than they could now be of their own. The husband cast one look at his pale wife, and Faith at him. What polluted wretches would the next glance show them to each other, shuddering alike at what they disclosed and what they saw!

"Faith! Faith!" cried the husband, "look up to heaven, and resist the wicked one."

Whether Faith obeyed he knew not. Hardly had he spoken when he found himself amid calm night and solitude, listening to a roar of the wind which died heavily away through the forest. He staggered against the rock, and felt it chill and damp; while a hanging twig, that had been all on fire, besprinkled his cheek with the coldest dew.

The next morning young Goodman Brown came slowly into the street of Salem village, staring around him like a bewildered man. The good old minister was taking a walk along the graveyard to get an appetite for breakfast and meditate his sermon, and bestowed a blessing, as he passed, on Goodman Brown. He shrank from the venerable saint as if to avoid an anathema. Old Deacon Gookin was at domestic worship, and the holy words of his prayer were heard through the open window. "What God doth the wizard pray to?" quoth Goodman Brown. Goody Cloyse, that excellent old Christian, stood in the early sunshine at her own lattice, catechizing a little girl who had brought her a pint of morning's milk. Goodman Brown snatched away the child as from the grasp of the fiend himself. Turning the corner by the meeting-house, he spied the head of Faith, with the pink ribbons, gazing anxiously forth, and bursting into such joy at sight of him that she skipped along the street and almost kissed her husband before the whole village. But Goodman Brown looked sternly and sadly into her face, and passed on without a greeting.

Had Goodman Brown fallen asleep in the forest and only dreamed a wild dream of a witch-meeting?

Be it so if you will; but, alas! it was a dream of evil omen for young Goodman Brown. A stern, a sad, a darkly meditative, a distrustful, if not a desperate man did he become from the night of that fearful dream. On the Sabbath day, when the congregation were singing a holy psalm, he could not listen because an anthem of sin rushed loudly upon his ear and drowned all the blessed strain. When the minister spoke from the pulpit with power and fervid eloquence, and, with his hand on the open Bible, of the sacred truths of our religion, and of saint-like lives and triumphant deaths, and of future bliss or misery unutterable, then did Goodman Brown turn pale, dreading lest the roof should thunder down upon the gray blasphemer and his hearers. Often, awaking suddenly at midnight, he shrank from the bosom of Faith; and at morning or eventide, when the family knelt down at prayer, he scowled and muttered to himself, and gazed sternly at his wife, and turned away. And when he had lived long, and was borne to his grave a hoary corpse, followed by Faith, an aged woman, and children and grandchildren, a goodly procession, besides neighbors not a few, they carved no hopeful verse upon his tombstone, for his dying hour was gloom.

Marjorie Kemper

....

God's Goodness

FIRST, LAST, AND FOREMOST, Ling Tan thought of herself as a Christian. So when Mrs. Sheriday said, "Tell me a little
something about yourself," Ling didn't even draw breath before
responding, "I am good Christian." And so saying, she sat up even
straighter in her chair, like a star pupil providing the correct answer to
a teacher.

But the employment counselor didn't smile. She didn't even look
up. She went on regarding the papers on her desk and said, "Well, yes,
I'm sure that you are. But what I meant was, tell me more about your
work experience. I see that you were enrolled in a practical-nursing
program at Long Beach Memorial Hospital but you didn't complete
the course of study."

Ling ducked her head.

"Why was that?"

Ling said nothing.

"Why, exactly, did you drop out?"

Ling smiled and shrugged.

The other woman waited.

The silence got too big for Ling. Twisting her hands, she said, "Had
late classes. Afraid to ride bus home at night."

"I see." Mrs. Sheriday looked back down at the papers. "Next time
try taking morning classes, because you need more credits." She
pointed her pen at Ling's thin résumé. "Your references are very good;
I can see you're good with patients. But our doctors and care manag-
ers like to see more academic training. You still have time to register
for some classes at Long Beach Community College."

Ling nodded.

"Even if you were just enrolled, I could list them."

"Next semester I enroll," Ling said, and smiled. Americans liked smiling, and Californians smiled all the time, so Ling made it a habit to smile constantly. She smiled when she was alone; she might even have smiled in her sleep.

As Ling got up to leave, Mrs. Sheriday said, "Check with me mid-week — I might have something then. I see you've worked with children. I have a pediatric oncologist who is looking for somebody to live in and provide custodial care for a patient who is terminal. You wouldn't have any expenses, and you could save your wages for next school term."

Ling nodded, and in acknowledgment of the seriousness of this new topic, the mortal illness of a child, attempted to stop smiling. But this was not quite possible.

Back in her furnished room, two hours later, Ling drank three glasses of water. She drank the first one because she was thirsty from sitting on the bus-stop bench in the hot sun for an hour; she drank the second and third to trick her stomach into thinking she had fed it breakfast and lunch. She sat in a chair she had placed at the uncurtained window of her second-story room. It was spring, and in a yard beyond a shabby garage two plum trees — unpruned for a generation — were struggling into bloom. Ling let her eyes rest on the white blossoms and took the time to thank God for the beauty he had created in every moment and in every place. Even now, even here. Wherever she looked she could see evidence of his goodness. And the flowering plums were beautiful — if Ling looked only at their canopies, if her eye didn't follow the scaling trunks down to the array of old paint cans and junk lumber nestled in the weeds beneath.

Ling took a deep breath and thanked God for his unceasing goodness to her — air in abundance, strong lungs to take it in, the flowering plums, even the water in her plastic glass. Ling sat in her chair and watched the plum trees until dusk fell and the blossoms melted into the darkness. Then, having no food and no money to buy it, she went to bed. In her neighborhood children played late; car alarms went on and off, seemingly at random; police cars and ambulances wailed on their way to St. Mary's Hospital, a block away. Even after she'd pulled the shades down, the orange streetlights cast a hellish glow on the ceiling. Ling shut her eyes and prayed. She was deep in a prayer of thanksgiving for her many blessings when she fell asleep.

*   *   *

Ling called Mrs. Sheriday on Wednesday from a pay phone on the corner of her street. "Ling, I'm glad you called. I got a call from the doctor about that boy. I made a tentative appointment for you to go out and meet his mother, Mrs. Tipton. The parents are divorced."

Ling smiled furiously into the phone.

Martha Tipton, the sick boy's mother, opened the door to Ling Tan. While still in the vestibule, Mrs. Tipton said, "Oh, dear, you don't look very strong — you're shorter than Mike."

"Oh, very strong," Ling said. "Not big, not tall, but very strong. Used to working with children."

"Mike's sixteen. He doesn't weigh what he should, of course, but he's tall for his age."

Ling smiled. "Very strong," she repeated.

Mrs. Tipton led the way into the living room. "Well, if you say so. Mrs. Sheriday said you'd be bringing references. May I see them?"

Ling opened her purse and proffered the letters, and Mrs. Tipton sat down on the edge of the sofa to read them. Ling remained standing. The living room was sparsely furnished — a sofa, a piano, a bare coffee table. All of Mrs. Tipton's domestic efforts appeared to have gone into her yard and her plants. From the sidewalk Ling had already noticed, with approval, Mrs. Tipton's well-kept garden. Now Ling's eyes went to a row of African violets on a low windowsill — pink ones, white ones, purple ones — all blooming! Mrs. Tipton was a good steward.

"These are remarkable," Mrs. Tipton said, handing the letters back to Ling. "Let's go back to Mike's room and see if he's awake." When they got there, Mrs. Tipton stuck her head inside. "He's sleeping," she whispered, closing the door quietly.

"Will I sleep close by, so can hear boy if he call?" Ling asked.

Mrs. Tipton nodded and opened the next door — into a small room containing a bureau, a sewing machine, an ironing board, and a single bed. "I've cleared out the bureau for your things," she said.

The room had French doors. Outside, healthy ferns and fuchsias cascaded from hanging baskets, and nasturtiums bordered the brick walk. God's goodness, as well as Mrs. Tipton's fine stewardship, was much in evidence.

Ling transported her belongings — a green-leatherette suitcase and a canvas satchel holding her Bible and her Bible-study books — on the bus later that afternoon. When she arrived, at six, Mike was asleep again, and Mrs. Tipton was preparing to leave for an appointment with her tax man.

"Mike's had his dinner," she said. "He usually eats at five-thirty. Just go in and introduce yourself when he wakes up. And when you do, give him the pills in this paper cup. I've told him about you, and he's expecting to meet you. If you should need me, the number is on the refrigerator, beside Doctor Mackenzie's."

After Mrs. Tipton had gone, Ling checked on Mike. She stood in the doorway to his room and studied her new charge for a long time. He was blond, pale, and tall, as his mother had said — or, more accurate in the circumstances, long. His bare arms were covered with a light blond down. Ling — who had been orphaned at eight and had survived typhus and thirty-two days in an open boat — could not accept the inevitability of the sleeping boy's death. Inevitability was a concept that ran contrary to her experience. That afternoon, while discussing Mike's illness with Mrs. Tipton, Ling had said that she would pray for a miracle for Mike. Mrs. Tipton's brow had furrowed, and she'd said that it was a little late in the day for that. Ling had quickly dropped the subject, but she could not drop the hope. To Ling, who regarded her own life as an unfolding miracle, miracles were a commonplace.

Later, when Ling heard Mike's dry little cough floating down the hall, she ran to his doorway and spoke quietly. "Mike, I Ling Tan. I here to help Mother take care of you until you get better." She smiled at the boy — who pushed himself higher on his pillows and studied her face. Ling went on, "Mother just go to see tax man. Back very soon."

"I don't know where you got your information, Ling Tan," Mike said severely, "but I'm not getting better. I'm in the process of getting worse."

"Naughty boy!" Ling exclaimed, laughing as she rushed forward into the room to tuck in a loose cover at the foot of his bed. "Now Ling here, you stop getting worse. Start getting better!"

"You could maybe benefit from a little chat with my oncologist," Mike said, taking a pillow from behind his back and pounding it into a new shape.

"I tell him thing or two. You hungry?"

"No."

"Mother make you little snack. Leave in refrigerator."

Ling went to the kitchen and came back with a bowl of sliced peaches. "Here," she said. "Look good. Eat peach. Give you energy to get better."

"Have you ever heard of white cells?"

"No."

"Lucky you."

Ling nodded. "Lucky all my life — but not luck really. *Grace*." She sat down at the foot of Mike's bed. "Grace better than luck. You pray for grace, Mike. Not look nice to pray for luck."

Mike ate a peach slice. "I'll remember that," he said, and he picked up the TV remote from his bedside table. As the TV sprang to life, a sitcom audience screamed with laughter; Mike muted the TV. "I'd like to know what's so damn funny," he said.

Ling said, "Nothing that funny, don't think. I read in magazine, studio bring crazy people to TV shows in buses, to laugh like pack of monkeys."

"Hyenas," Mike corrected. "The expression is 'pack of hyenas.'"

Ling nodded. "Hyenas," she repeated. "Bring them from crazy house."

"That explains a lot," Mike said. He flipped through the channels until he found a rerun of *M*A*S*H*.

"Oh, like this program," Ling said enthusiastically. "Good doctors on this program. Funny."

"Not very realistic, though," Mike said. "I've yet to meet a doctor with even a rudimentary sense of humor."

Ling nodded brightly.

"Aren't you supposed to bring me my meds?"

Ling looked away from the TV, where Klinger was dressed like a woman. "Oh, I forget! I get them right now."

She handed Mike a glass of water and watched while he transferred six pills from the paper cup to his mouth and swallowed them. She said, "So many!"

"Yes, and they accomplish so little."

"But good for you — make you better."

Mike turned the TV back up. Ling returned to the foot of his bed. She sat sideways and turned her head to watch. "Klinger wear same dress as my auntie," she told Mike, and giggled.

Mike snorted. "I hope it looked better on her."

"Didn't," Ling said with a laugh. "Auntie not look good, but Auntie good inside." Ling tapped her breast. "Here."

She gazed around Mike's room. It had a wall of bookshelves, and a desk and chair by the window. A picture of Mike's parents sat on the bureau, taken when they were much younger. They were holding hands. Ling turned away; photos made her nervous. They were always of things that were over with, gone — a moment, a smile, a person, sometimes a whole country. A poster of an old man with scraggly hair was on the back of Mike's door. The man was sticking his tongue out. Why did Mike have a picture of a crazy person on his door? "Who is that?" she asked cautiously, in case it was a relative.

"Einstein."

Ling smiled and nodded.

"He was a physicist," Mike said. "A genius," he added for Ling's benefit, because she still looked blank. "You've heard of E equals MC squared?"

Ling smiled and nodded. "Are you genius too? Have so many books!"

"I'm smart, but possibly not a genius."

"How come he make that face?"

"Why not?"

"I try go to college, learn more, but my English not very good," Ling confided. "I quit before bad grades get on permanent record." She had never told this to anyone before.

"Your English isn't so bad," Mike said. "Considering."

"Maybe you help me — tell me when I using wrong word."

"It would have to be a crash course. My mother must have told you I'm on my way out. We're talking months here, Ling Tan." Mike ran through the channels with the remote. "Two, maybe three." He clicked the set off. "Tops."

"Mother can't know everything. Doctors either. I wait and see."

"An empiricist in our midst," Mike said.

"A what?"

"An empiricist is someone who draws conclusions from the evidence."

"Not empiricist — Christian. Believe in God's goodness. In miracles."

"That's what it would take."

Ling nodded smartly. "Already praying. Start without you. You see. God is good. He bless us every day."

"You could have fooled me," Mike said.

★   ★   ★

Ling quickly fit herself into the routine of the Tipton household. Fitting in was what she did best; it was her special gift. She could be quiet, as she had been when her family had hidden from the soldiers in the forest. She could make herself small, as she had in the boat. If necessary, she could even push herself forward and talk fast and loud, as she had in the refugee camp. With Mike she was cheerful as a rule. Early on they developed a vaudeville routine of sorts, with Mike playing Baby Curmudgeon to her Cheerful Naif.

With Mrs. Tipton, Ling was careful to be quiet and pleasant. Mrs. Tipton's nerves were ragged, and she frequently burst into tears in the course of ordinary conversations. Not wanting Mike to see her cry, she spent a lot of time outside, working in her garden. She came into her son's room at frequent intervals, but rarely stayed long. Usually she rushed off, saying she needed to check on something — just seconds before bursting into tears.

When Mr. Tipton came over, Ling endeavored to make herself invisible. Though she suspected that Mr. Tipton was every bit as sad as his ex-wife, he seemed more angry than sad. He seemed to be angry all the time, at everything and everyone except Mike.

When Ling first met him, she recognized him right away from the photo in his son's room. Unlike poor Mrs. Tipton, Mr. Tipton looked the same as in Mike's photo. When Ling opened the door to him, she said, "Oh! Mike's father! He will be so happy to see you."

"Where's Martha?"

"Go to market. Back soon. I'm Ling Tan."

When she heard Mrs. Tipton's car in the driveway, Ling went out to help carry the groceries. "Mr. Tipton here with Mike," she said. Ling put away the groceries while Mrs. Tipton went back to Mike's room.

Shortly thereafter Mr. Tipton came out to the kitchen. He looked very angry. "Mike tells me you're praying for him."

Ling felt herself accused, and ducked her head. "Yes," she admitted.

"Well, naturally you're free to pray day and night, but I'd appreciate your not talking to Mike about it. Or about miracles. We've spent two years choking on hope around here; hope is ancient history. I appreciate your intentions, but the last thing we need is a latecomer peddling miracles."

Mr. Tipton had spoken quickly and softly, and though Ling had certainly gotten the sense of what he'd said, she'd missed some of the words. What, for instance, did "peddling" mean? Looking down at the floor, she said, "Just try to keep up boy's spirits."

Every morning, when she brought in Mike's breakfast and pills, she opened his drapes and delivered her line: "Look, Mikey! God make another beautiful day just for you. He expect you to *look* at it."

His line was "Close the damn drapes. It's too bright."

"Too bright for moles, maybe," Ling always responded. "You not mole. You boy."

One morning when Ling opened the drapes she saw Mike's mother kneeling in the garden. "Look, Mikey, Mother planting new flowers for you to see out window. Wave at her." Mike rolled his eyes, but he waved. His mother was kneeling in the dirt, transferring pansies from flats into a flower bed around the deodar tree in the side yard. Surprised, she smiled and waved back.

"Your mother best gardener I know," Ling observed. "She love her plants. They feel it and grow big for her."

"She loves me too, but this is as big as I'm getting."

"You plenty big already," Ling said. "Bigger than me."

"What *is* this?" Mike asked when Ling lifted the lid from a bowl on his breakfast tray.

"Oatmeal."

"I don't like oatmeal."

"Oatmeal good for you. You eat, then maybe I bring something you like."

"Whose bright idea is this?"

"My idea. I read in magazine when we at Doctor Mackenzie's office, oatmeal cleanse the blood."

"Jesus, Ling, get a clue."

"Won't hurt you to eat little bowl of oatmeal," Ling said.

Because Mrs. Tipton took pills and slept soundly, one of Ling's jobs was to listen for Mike during the night. If he needed her, he knocked on their shared wall. After helping him to the bathroom, or getting him something to drink or a pill or — on a bad night — a shot, or rubbing his foot when he had a cramp, Ling kept him company until he was able to sleep again. One night, curled up like a cat at the foot of Mike's bed, Ling asked, "You want to watch TV? Maybe *M*A*S*H* on." It usually was.

"Not really. Has my dad bawled you out about this miracle deal?"

"Not know 'bawled out.'"

"Did he yell at you?"

"Not yell," Ling said. "Father worried for you. Not want me upset you."

"I was afraid of that. I want you to know I didn't complain about you. I only mentioned it to him because I thought he'd get a kick out of it. I was a little off the mark there. Shows you how well I know dear old Dad. Anyway, I hope he didn't hurt your feelings."

"Not hurt my feelings. Don't need Father's permission to pray. Don't need permission for miracle either."

"I wouldn't think so."

"Father love you very much. Tell me getting special doctor for you." Mr. Tipton had informed Ling and Mrs. Tipton that he'd arranged for a psychiatrist who worked with terminally ill children and adolescents to visit Mike.

"You mean the shrink?"

Ling smiled and shook her head to indicate that she didn't know the word.

"S-H-R-I-N-K — that's another word for a head doctor. One of the high priests of humanism."

"Ah," Ling said. "Father's priest?"

Mike snorted. "Close enough. He's supposed to make me feel better about dying."

"He can do that?"

"We shall see." Mike closed his eyes.

"You want me read to you?"

"Sure."

"Same book Father read this afternoon?" Father and son were reading Hegel. Ling had no idea what it was about; all she knew was that it had more hard words than the Bible and no story at all.

"Not this time of night. You pick something."

Ling ran to her room and came back with her Bible. "I read to you from *my* book." Laughing, she held it up for Mike to see.

"Oh, Dad would love this!"

"He say not talk about miracle. Didn't say about *Bible*."

"True," Mike said. "I know — read the Book of Job. Let's get a standard of comparison."

"Oh, Job *sad* story."

"My favorite kind."

But about fifteen minutes into Job's travails Mike's pain pill took effect, and he fell asleep. Ling stopped reading. She sat very still until she was certain that the boy was sleeping soundly, and then she moved to the desk chair. Ling tried to go on reading (she'd left off where Job said, "Wearisome nights are appointed to me"), but the light from the little bedside lamp was too distant to read by, so she shut the book and put her head down on the desk. The miracle she'd been praying for since arriving at the Tiptons' was nowhere in sight, and even Ling, always optimistic, always on the lookout for a blessing, understood that they were running low on time. Mike kept getting thinner, despite the nice meals his mother prepared, meals that Ling spent hours coaxing the boy to eat. Fortunately, she'd been telling Mrs. Tipton the truth when she'd said that she was strong, because nowadays she more carried than walked Mike to the bathroom. They had stopped going downtown to the medical building to see his oncologist. Now Dr. Mackenzie came to the house, rushing in and staying only long enough to rationalize his big bill and to cast a pall over everyone's spirits. Mike's cough had grown worse. At last count nine pills were in the paper cup after dinner, and, most ominous, syringes of pain medicine were now kept in the refrigerator for the relief of Mike's severe headaches, which came on without warning. All in all, Ling had a lot to pray for and about; her head cradled in her thin arms, she was still praying when the sun came up.

The new doctor, Dr. Hanson, the shrink, came to the house three afternoons a week. On his first visit, every time Mike had said anything, Dr. Hanson had responded, "How does that make you feel, Mike?"

"Like death warmed over," Mike had said, trying to fluster him. Or "Makes me want to die," or "Scares me to death." Ling and Mike had exchanged conspiratorial glances, and Ling had laughed behind her hand.

But Dr. Hanson proved to be such a nice young man that teasing him wasn't much fun. In fact, after he'd been coming for a couple of weeks, Mike told Ling that he felt sorry for Dr. Hanson.

"Why sorry for him?" she snapped. "You the sick one."

"Yeah, but he's so damn hopeful, you know?"

"Bible say hope a virtue. Have to hope."

"For what?"

Ling shrugged. "Just hope." She had begun to resent this particular injunction.

"You're saying that this mandatory hope has no object?"

Ling thought for a minute and said, "Hope is to prop open door, so good things can come in. Maybe when you not looking."

"I see. Hope as a metaphysical doorstop. Good one, Ling. Well, anyway, at least Doctor Hanson *talks*. Doctor Mackenzie hasn't said two personal words to me in weeks."

"He lose interest in us, I think."

"I know. I shouldn't have played so hard to get. And probably I should have eaten more *oatmeal*. It's abundantly clear that I've no one to blame for all this but myself."

Ling looked at the floor. She'd thrown the box of oatmeal in the garbage a week before. "Maybe should invite some boys, Mikey, come talk to you. You have some nice friends own age?"

"Not really. Do you?"

"Not really," Ling admitted. "We each other's friend now, I think."

"Works for me."

As Mike grew worse, the room filled with sickroom apparatus — first a walker, then a commode, and finally, after a series of consecutive bad nights, a rollaway bed for Ling. While Mike slept, Ling went through the Book of Job, which had become a favorite of Mike's, with a fine-tooth comb, hoping to find some consolation. After God had let the Devil have his way with Job, after Job had brought credit on him, God took him back. The Bible even said that afterward God gave Job new sons and daughters, new cattle and sheep. And, Ling supposed, cattle were cattle, and one cow was as good as another, but children were not cattle. Children had souls. You could not replace one with another. So where was the comfort in all this?

But Mike read Job over and over. He memorized great hunks of it, and insisted on reading his favorite bits aloud to Ling. Sometimes he stopped mid-sentence and laughed.

"I'm in your debt for suggesting this, Ling."

"No problem," Ling said. "God's word count for something in this world, but I not go to college, and not a genius, so I not always sure what."

"Yes you are," Mike said.

Ling shook her head.

"You believe in God's goodness still, don't you?"

Ling turned her back on Mike and looked out the window.

"You do, don't you, Ling?"

"Have to believe in that when I look at God's big world," Ling said.

"There you go," Mike said. "The world is very, very big. It stands to reason that it's beyond our understanding, yes?"

"Yes," Ling whispered. "But used to understand."

"And now you don't. You see, you've learned something already."

"What I am learning?"

"That there's more to heaven and earth than oatmeal and a positive attitude. More than Ling Tan was born knowing. Humility — not to put too fine a point on it."

Humility was a hard lesson, worse than English grammar, and Ling missed her old, blithe assurance as keenly as she might have missed a beloved pet. But she believed what she had told Mikey about hope — that you could use it to prop open a door so that something good might come in. So she hoped. And waited. And prayed for something good to slip through their open door. Maybe at night, while they slept.

Dr. Hanson was an even bigger smiler than Ling — who these days had to remind herself to smile, and who thought that the young doctor overdid it.

"Doctor Hanson always so cheerful," Ling remarked one day, while she folded laundry on Mike's bed. She didn't mean it as a compliment.

"And why not?" Mike asked. "He's not the one who's dying. Though I don't know why he doesn't get right on it, since he sees it as such a gigantic opportunity for what he calls 'personal growth.'"

Ling giggled. "I think he already grow big *enough*." The doctor was a little on the plump side.

Mike laughed. "When he was here yesterday, I quoted some Job at him — 'Thine hands have made me and fashioned me together round about; yet thou dost destroy me.' I wanted his take on that."

"What did he say?"

"He said, 'Beautiful, beautiful!' With this huge, ecstatic smile plastered on that big round face of his."

"How did that make you feel?" Ling said, joking.

"Like I'd been dead three days," Mike shot back.

"Maybe Job beautiful if not about *you*," Ling said, smoothing a pillowcase. She almost wished she hadn't introduced Mikey to the Bible. She'd certainly had it with Job and his comforters — even Job's God, whom she'd just barely contrived to keep separate from her own. These days, when she had the time and the energy to read, she stuck strictly to the Psalms and the Gospels. But Mike liked Job almost as much as he liked Einstein. Certainly more than Mr. Tipton at this point in the proceedings liked Hegel. Mike had told his mother that Job was his favorite book — which caused Mrs. Tipton to run out of the room in tears, and which she wisely did not pass on to her ex-husband. When Ling brought in Mike's breakfast, he always quoted, in a rising falsetto, "Or is there *any* taste in the white of an egg?"

Folding towels, Ling said, "I think Doctor Hanson look better if he grow beard. Then his face not seem so wide."

"I'll tell him."

"No, Mikey! Then he know we notice his face fat." Piling the folded laundry back in the basket, Ling confessed, "Mikey, worried about miracle. Afraid prayers aren't getting through."

"Sure they are," Mike said. "It's the answers that seem to be snagged up."

"Same thing," Ling said.

"Not necessarily."

Ling nodded. "Study guide say God answer prayers, but his answer not always one we want. No, I say it wrong: it say, maybe not answer we *expect*."

"Ah, the element of surprise. One of his favorite devices. As we've learned."

Ling took a deep breath and tried to smile at Mike's little joke. "Not giving up, Mikey. I keep praying. Promise."

"Everyone should have a hobby," Mike said, "to quote the estimable Doctor Hanson." He flipped on the TV.

Dr. Hanson had asked Mike what his hobbies were, and Mike had said that just lately his hobby was dying.

Undeterred, Dr. Hanson had said, "That's more of a full-time job, isn't it? I'm talking recreation. Do you play chess?"

After that Dr. Hanson and Mike played chess. Mike consistently beat him. But instead of saying, "Checkmate," Mike would say, "How does that make you feel?"

"Beat," Dr. Hanson would reply. "Walloped."

"You don't think he's letting me win, do you?" Mike asked Ling later that week. He was having one of what he and Ling were calling his "bad days." He'd had a solid week of them. The smell of Dr. Hanson's after-shave still lingered in the room. Even his after-shave, Ling had protested to Mike, was cheerful.

"Doctor Hanson can't beat genius, Mikey."

"I may not be a genius, Ling. It's impossible at this point to tell for sure."

"Close. Maybe not like old Uncle." Ling pointed at the Einstein poster. "But you not old like him either. Smarter than Doctor Hanson for sure! What he thinking? *Smiling* every minute at boy supposed to be dying!"

"You should talk."

"I know. Used to smile like hyena."

"Monkey! No, monkeys *grin*, don't they? Hyenas laugh. *Lings* smile."

"Ling not so much smiling now. Only when something to smile about. You notice?"

"Actually, I've been meaning to talk to you about that. I think it's time to paste a big old smile on your face and leave it there, because we're definitely running out of reasons. Anyway, on you a smile has always looked good."

Ling smiled. It was an effort.

A month later Dr. Hanson stopped smiling. Mike was in a coma. Still Dr. Hanson came at his appointed times and sat beside Mike's bed and held the boy's hand — now studded like a clove orange with IVs. Dr. Mackenzie came every day, and a registered nurse came morning and evening. Mr. and Mrs. Tipton took turns sitting in Mike's room — Mrs. Tipton crying freely now, her hands clasped in her lap; Mr. Tipton staring at an open book, the pages of which he rarely turned. Ling sat out of the way, in Mike's desk chair, which she had pulled over to the window so that she could look out at Mrs. Tipton's garden.

On the night before he'd slipped into the coma, Ling and Mike had tried to watch *M*A*S*H*, but Mike had a terrible headache, and the light from the TV hurt his eyes. Ling had turned it off.

"We see that one already," she said briskly. By then they'd seen them all. "That one sad anyway. Even Hawkeye cry." Mike, eyes shut, nodded. Ling gave him his pain shot and rubbed his temples with a Chinese herbal lotion that her auntie had used for migraines.

"My God, what is this stuff?" Mike protested. "It smells like a bog!"

"All natural," Ling assured him. "Very good for headache. Cleanse the blood. Good for bad nerves."

"I can't *believe* you're still trying to cleanse this treacherous blood of mine! However," Mike conceded, "my nerves could not be worse."

"Auntie swear by it," Ling said. She smoothed his thin hair back, rubbing his forehead.

Mike looked up into her eyes. "You know where we made our mistake, don't you?"

Ling shook her head.

"Praying for grace instead of luck. We tipped our hand. We indicated we were willing to *settle*."

Ling bit her lower lip and didn't answer.

"Come on, Ling. 'How does that make you feel?'"

Ling giggled weakly. "Don't," she said. "Too tired to joke."

It was three in the morning. The only noise in the house was the refrigerator humming in the kitchen. Mike closed his eyes and quoted: "God thundereth marvelously with his voice; great things doeth he, which we cannot comprehend."

"That not God, that the refrigerator."

"Maybe, maybe not. You'll admit that the universe, or God — whatever you like to call it — *does* stuff we don't get. Hegel didn't get it. I'm not even sure Einstein got it."

"He get it. That's why he stick tongue out."

Mike snorted.

Ling took a long breath. She put the cap back on the bottle of Auntie's lotion and said, "Maybe God blessing us this moment, and we not knowing it."

"Thanks for trying, Ling, but that may be the single most depressing thing you've said to me."

"Not depressing, Mikey. I only mean he bless me with you and he bless you with me."

The morning after Mike died, after she'd packed and before she left Mrs. Tipton's house forever, Ling went into Mike's room. She had made up the empty bed the night before. Now she went to the window and pulled back the drapes.

"God make another beautiful day, Mikey," she said. Then, after blowing her nose and replacing the ragged Kleenex in the pocket of her sweater, she added, "But this one not for you."

Ling stood staring out Mike's window. The dew was still on the grass; though Mrs. Tipton lay sedated in her bed, her lawn shone brightly in the morning light. The little faces of her pansies were turned up to the sun. The beauty of the flowers, and the sunshine they sought, were, Ling still believed, firm and undeniable evidence of God's goodness. Even here and even now. But this knowledge no longer lifted her up. She placed the palm of her hand on Mikey's empty bed and briefly bowed her head.

When she turned to go, her gaze met Einstein's. She had noticed a month before that except for the rude face he was making, Mikey's old scientist looked a lot like the illustrations of God the Father in her Bible-study guide. She had shown Mikey, who had thought this a hilarious coincidence. Now, her hand on the doorknob, Ling looked into the old face that had looked down on them for months, silently regarding everything they had done and suffered.

"Good-bye, Mr. Genius," she said softly. Then, before she sailed out the door, and in recognition, or solidarity, or maybe just farewell, Ling stuck out her little pink tongue.

Hanif Kureishi

....

My Son the Fanatic

S URREPTITIOUSLY the father began going into his son's
bedroom. He would sit there for hours, rousing himself only to
seek clues. What bewildered him was that Ali was getting ti-
dier. Instead of the usual tangle of clothes, books, cricket bats, video
games, the room was becoming neat and ordered; spaces began appearing where before there had been only mess.

Initially Parvez had been pleased: his son was outgrowing his teen-
age attitudes. But one day, beside the dustbin, Parvez found a torn bag
which contained not only old toys, but computer discs, videotapes,
new books, and fashionable clothes the boy had bought a few months
before. Also without explanation, Ali had parted from the English girlfriend who used to come often to the house. His old friends stopped
ringing.

For reasons he didn't himself understand, Parvez wasn't able to
bring up the subject of Ali's unusual behavior. He was aware that he
had become slightly afraid of his son, who, alongside his silences, was
developing a sharp tongue. One remark Parvez did make, "You don't
play your guitar anymore," elicited the mysterious but conclusive reply, "There are more important things to be done."

Yet Parvez felt his son's eccentricity as an injustice. He had always
been aware of the pitfalls which other men's sons had fallen into in
England. And so, for Ali, he worked long hours and spent a lot of
money paying for his education as an accountant. He had bought him
good suits, all the books he required, and a computer. And now the
boy was throwing his possessions out!

The TV, video, and sound system followed the guitar. Soon the room was practically bare. Even the unhappy walls bore marks where Ali's pictures had been removed.

Parvez couldn't sleep; he went more to the whisky bottle, even when he was at work. He realized it was imperative to discuss the matter with someone sympathetic.

Parvez had been a taxi driver for twenty years. Half that time he'd worked for the same firm. Like him, most of the other drivers were Punjabis. They preferred to work at night, the roads were clearer and the money better. They slept during the day, avoiding their wives. Together they led almost a boy's life in the cabbies' office, playing cards and practical jokes, exchanging lewd stories, eating together, and discussing politics and their problems.

But Parvez had been unable to bring this subject up with his friends. He was too ashamed. And he was afraid, too, that they would blame him for the wrong turning his boy had taken, just as he had blamed other fathers whose sons had taken to running around with bad girls, truanting from school, and joining gangs.

For years Parvez had boasted to the other men about how Ali excelled at cricket, swimming, and football, and how attentive a scholar he was, getting straight A's in most subjects. Was it asking too much for Ali to get a good job now, marry the right girl, and start a family? Once this happened, Parvez would be happy. His dreams of doing well in England would have come true. Where had he gone wrong?

But one night, sitting in the taxi office on busted chairs with his two closest friends watching a Sylvester Stallone film, he broke his silence.

"I can't understand it!" he burst out. "Everything is going from his room. And I can't talk to him anymore. We were not father and son — we were brothers! Where has he gone? Why is he torturing me!"

And Parvez put his head in his hands.

Even as he poured out his account the men shook their heads and gave one another knowing glances. From their grave looks Parvez realized they understood the situation.

"Tell me what is happening!" he demanded.

The reply was almost triumphant. They had guessed something was going wrong. Now it was clear: Ali was taking drugs and selling his possessions to pay for them. That was why his bedroom was emptying.

"What must I do then?"

Parvez's friends instructed him to watch Ali scrupulously and then be severe with him, before the boy went mad, overdosed, or murdered someone.

Parvez staggered out into the early-morning air, terrified they were right. His boy — the drug addict killer!

To his relief he found Bettina sitting in his car.

Usually the last customers of the night were local "brasses" or prostitutes. The taxi drivers knew them well, often driving them to liaisons. At the end of the girls' night, the men would ferry them home, though sometimes the women would join them for a drinking session in the office. Occasionally the drivers would go with the girls. "A ride in exchange for a ride," it was called.

Bettina had known Parvez for three years. She lived outside the town and on the long drive home, where she sat not in the passenger seat but beside him, Parvez had talked to her about his life and hopes, just as she talked about hers. They saw each other most nights.

He could talk to her about things he'd never be able to discuss with his own wife. Bettina, in turn, always reported on her night's activities. He liked to know where she was and with whom. Once he had rescued her from a violent client, and since then they had come to care for one another.

Though Bettina had never met the boy, she heard about Ali continually. That late night, when he told Bettina that he suspected Ali was on drugs, she judged neither the boy nor his father, but became businesslike and told him what to watch for.

"It's all in the eyes," she said. They might be bloodshot; the pupils might be dilated; he might look tired. He could be liable to sweats, or sudden mood changes. "Okay?"

Parvez began his vigil gratefully. Now he knew what the problem might be, he felt better. And surely, he figured, things couldn't have gone too far? With Bettina's help he would soon sort it out.

He watched each mouthful the boy took. He sat beside him at every opportunity and looked into his eyes. When he could he took the boy's hand, checking his temperature. If the boy wasn't at home Parvez was active, looking under the carpet, in his drawers, behind the empty wardrobe, sniffing, inspecting, probing. He knew what to look for: Bettina had drawn pictures of capsules, syringes, pills, powders, rocks.

Every night she waited to hear news of what he'd witnessed.

After a few days of constant observation, Parvez was able to report that although the boy had given up sports, he seemed healthy, with clear eyes. He didn't, as his father expected, flinch guiltily from his gaze. In fact the boy's mood was alert and steady in this sense: as well as being sullen, he was very watchful. He returned his father's long looks with more than a hint of criticism, of reproach even, so much so that Parvez began to feel that it was he who was in the wrong, and not the boy!

"And there's nothing else physically different?" Bettina asked.

"No!" Parvez thought for a moment. "But he is growing a beard."

One night, after sitting with Bettina in an all-night coffee shop, Parvez came home particularly late. Reluctantly he and Bettina had abandoned their only explanation, the drug theory, for Parvez had found nothing resembling any drug in Ali's room. Besides, Ali wasn't selling his belongings. He threw them out, gave them away, or donated them to charity shops.

Standing in the hall, Parvez heard his boy's alarm clock go off. Parvez hurried into his bedroom where his wife was still awake, sewing in bed. He ordered her to sit down and keep quiet, though she had neither stood up nor said a word. From this post, and with her watching him curiously, he observed his son through the crack of the door.

The boy went into the bathroom to wash. When he returned to his room Parvez sprang across the hall and set his ear at Ali's door. A muttering sound came from within. Parvez was puzzled but relieved.

Once this clue had been established, Parvez watched him at other times. The boy was praying. Without fail, when he was at home, he prayed five times a day.

Parvez had grown up in Lahore where all the boys had been taught the Koran. To stop him falling asleep when he studied, the Moulvi had attached a piece of string to the ceiling and tied it to Parvez's hair, so that if his head fell forward, he would instantly awake. After this indignity Parvez had avoided all religions. Not that the other taxi drivers had more respect. In fact they made jokes about the local mullahs walking around with their caps and beards, thinking they could tell people how to live, while their eyes roved over the boys and girls in their care.

Parvez described to Bettina what he had discovered. He informed the men in the taxi office. The friends, who had been so curious before, now became oddly silent. They could hardly condemn the boy for his devotions.

Parvez decided to take a night off and go out with the boy. They could talk things over. He wanted to hear how things were going at college; he wanted to tell him stories about their family in Pakistan. More than anything he yearned to understand how Ali had discovered the "spiritual dimension," as Bettina described it.

To Parvez's surprise, the boy refused to accompany him. He claimed he had an appointment. Parvez had to insist that no appointment could be more important than that of a son with his father, and, reluctantly, Ali accompanied him.

The next day, Parvez went immediately to the street where Bettina stood in the rain wearing high heels, a short skirt, and a long mac on top, which she would hopefully open at passing cars.

"Get in, get in!" he said.

They drove out across the moors and parked at the spot where, on better days, with a view unimpeded for many miles by nothing but wild deer and horses, they'd lie back, with their eyes half-closed, saying, "This is the life." This time Parvez was trembling. Bettina put her arms around him.

"What's happened?"

"I've just had the worst experience of my life."

As Bettina rubbed his head Parvez told her that the previous evening, as he and his son studied the menu, the waiter, whom Parvez knew, brought him his usual whisky and water. Parvez was so nervous he had even prepared a question. He was going to ask Ali if he was worried about his imminent exams. But first, wanting to relax, he loosened his tie, crunched a popadom, and took a long drink.

Before Parvez could speak, Ali made a face.

"Don't you know it's wrong to drink alcohol?" he said.

"He spoke to me very harshly," Parvez said to Bettina. "I was about to castigate the boy for being insolent, but managed to control myself."

He had explained patiently that for years he had worked more than ten hours a day, had few enjoyments or hobbies, and never went on holiday. Surely it wasn't a crime to have a drink when he wanted one?

"But it is forbidden," the boy said.

Parvez shrugged. "I know."

"And so is gambling, isn't it?"

"Yes. But surely we are only human?"

Each time Parvez took a drink, the boy made, as an accompaniment, some kind of wince or fastidious face. This made Parvez drink more quickly. The waiter, wanting to please his friend, brought another glass of whisky. Parvez knew he was getting drunk, but he couldn't stop himself. Ali had a horrible look, full of disgust and censure. It was as if he hated his father.

Halfway through the meal Parvez suddenly lost his temper and threw a plate on the floor. He felt like ripping the cloth from the table, but the waiters and other customers were staring at him. Yet he wouldn't stand for his own son telling him the difference between right and wrong. He knew he wasn't a bad man. He had a conscience. There were a few things of which he was ashamed, but on the whole he had lived a decent life.

"When have I had time to be wicked?" he told Ali.

In a low monotonous voice the boy explained that Parvez had not, in fact, lived a good life. He had broken countless rules of the Koran.

"For instance?" Parvez demanded.

Ali didn't need to think. As if he had been waiting for this moment, he asked his father if he didn't relish pork pies.

"Well?"

Parvez couldn't deny that he loved crispy bacon smothered with mushrooms and mustard and sandwiched between slices of fried bread. In fact he ate this for breakfast every morning.

Ali then reminded him that Parvez had ordered his own wife to cook pork sausages, saying to her, "You're not in the village now, this is England. We have to fit in!"

Parvez was so annoyed and perplexed by this attack that he called for more drink.

"The problem is this," the boy said. He leaned across the table. For the first time that night his eyes were alive. "You are too implicated in Western civilization."

Parvez burped: he thought he was going to choke. "Implicated!" he said. "But we live here!"

"The Western materialists hate us," Ali said. "Papa, how can you love something which hates you?"

"What is the answer then?" Parvez said miserably. "According to you."

Ali didn't need to think. He addressed his father fluently, as if Parvez were a rowdy crowd that had to be quelled and convinced. The Law of Islam would rule the world; the skin of the infidel would burn off again and again; the Jews and Christers would be routed. The West was a sink of hypocrites, adulterers, homosexuals, drug-takers, and prostitutes.

As Ali talked, Parvez looked out of the window as if to check that they were still in London.

"My people have taken enough. If the persecution doesn't stop there will be jihad. I, and millions of others, will gladly give our lives for the cause."

"But why, why?" Parvez said.

"For us the reward will be in paradise."

"Paradise!"

Finally, as Parvez's eyes filled with tears, the boy urged him to mend his ways.

"How is that possible?" Parvez asked.

"Pray," said Ali. "Pray beside me."

Parvez called for the bill and ushered his boy out of there as soon as he was able. He couldn't take any more. Ali sounded as if he'd swallowed someone else's voice.

On the way home the boy sat in the back of the taxi as if he were a customer.

"What has made you like this?" Parvez asked him, afraid that somehow he was to blame for all this. "Is there a particular event which has influenced you?"

"Living in this country."

"But I love England," Parvez said, watching his boy in the mirror. "They let you do almost anything here."

"That is the problem," he replied.

For the first time in years Parvez couldn't see straight. He knocked the side of the car against a lorry, ripping off the wing mirror. They were lucky not to have been stopped by the police: Parvez would have lost his license and therefore his job.

Getting out of the car back at the house, Parvez stumbled and fell in the road, scraping his hands and ripping his trousers. He managed to haul himself up. The boy didn't even offer him his hand.

Parvez told Bettina he was willing to pray, if that was what the boy wanted, if it would dislodge the pitiless look from his eyes.

"But what I object to," he said, "is being told by my own son that I am going to hell!"

What finished Parvez off was that the boy had said he was giving up accountancy. When Parvez had asked why, Ali said sarcastically that it was obvious.

"Western education cultivates an anti-religious attitude."

And in the world of accountants it was usual to meet women, drink alcohol, and practice usury.

"But it's well-paid work," Parvez argued. "For years you've been preparing!"

Ali said he was going to begin to work in prisons, with poor Muslims who were struggling to maintain their purity in the face of corruption. Finally, at the end of the evening, as Ali went up to bed, he had asked his father why he didn't have a beard, or at least a mustache.

"I feel as if I've lost my son," Parvez told Bettina. "I can't bear to be looked at as if I'm a criminal. I've decided what to do."

"What is it?"

"I'm going to tell him to pick up his prayer mat and get out of my house. It will be the hardest thing I've ever done, but tonight I'm going to do it."

"But you mustn't give up on him," said Bettina. "Many young people fall into cults and superstitious groups. It doesn't mean they'll always feel the same way."

She said Parvez had to stick by his boy, giving him support, until he came through.

Parvez was persuaded that she was right, even though he didn't feel like giving his son more love when he had hardly been thanked for all he had already given.

Nevertheless, Parvez tried to endure his son's looks and reproaches. He attempted to make conversation about his beliefs. But if Parvez ventured any criticism, Ali always had a brusque reply. On one occasion Ali accused Parvez of "groveling" to the whites; in contrast, he explained, he was not "inferior": there was more to the world than the West, though the West always thought it was best.

"How is it you know that," Parvez said, "seeing as you've never left England?"

Ali replied with a look of contempt.

One night, having ensured there was no alcohol on his breath, Parvez sat down at the kitchen table with Ali. He hoped Ali would compliment him on the beard he was growing but Ali didn't appear to notice.

The previous day Parvez had been telling Bettina that he thought people in the West sometimes felt inwardly empty and that people needed a philosophy to live by.

"Yes," said Bettina. "That's the answer. You must tell him what your

philosophy of life is. Then he will understand that there are other beliefs."

After some fatiguing consideration, Parvez was ready to begin. The
boy watched him as if he expected nothing.

Haltingly Parvez said that people had to treat one another with respect, particularly children their parents. This did seem, for a moment,
to affect the boy. Heartened, Parvez continued. In his view this life was
all there was and when you died you rotted in the earth. "Grass and
flowers will grow out of me, but something of me will live on."

"How?"

"In other people. I will continue — in you." At this the boy appeared a little distressed. "And your grandchildren," Parvez added for
good measure. "But while I am here on earth I want to make the best
of it. And I want you to, as well!"

"What d'you mean by 'make the best of it'?" asked the boy.

"Well," said Parvez. "For a start . . . you should enjoy yourself. Yes.
Enjoy yourself without hurting others."

Ali said enjoyment was a "bottomless pit."

"But I don't mean enjoyment like that!" said Parvez. "I mean the
beauty of living!"

"All over the world our people are oppressed" was the boy's reply.

"I know," Parvez replied, not entirely sure who "our people" were,
"but still, life is for living!"

Ali said, "Real morality has existed for hundreds of years. Around
the world millions and millions of people share my beliefs. Are you
saying you are right and they are all wrong?"

And Ali looked at his father with such aggressive confidence that
Parvez could say no more.

One evening Bettina was sitting in Parvez's car, after visiting a client, when they passed a boy on the street.

"That's my son," Parvez said suddenly. They were on the other side
of town, in a poor district, where there were two mosques.

Parvez set his face hard.

Bettina turned to watch him. "Slow down then, slow down!" She
said. "He's good-looking. Reminds me of you. But with a more determined face. Please, can't we stop?"

"What for?"

"I'd like to talk to him."

Parvez turned the cab round and stopped beside the boy.

"Coming home?" Parvez asked. "It's quite a way."

The sullen boy shrugged and got into the back seat. Bettina sat in the front. Parvez became aware of Bettina's short skirt, gaudy rings, and ice-blue eye shadow. He became conscious that the smell of her perfume, which he loved, filled the cab. He opened the window.

While Parvez drove as fast as he could, Bettina said gently to Ali, "Where have you been?"

"The mosque," he said.

"And how are you getting on at college? Are you working hard?"

"Who are you to ask me these questions?" he said, looking out of the window. Then they hit bad traffic and the car came to a standstill.

By now Bettina had inadvertently laid her hand on Parvez's shoulder. She said, "Your father, who is a good man, is very worried about you. You know he loves you more than his own life."

"You say he loves me," the boy said.

"Yes!" said Bettina.

"Then why is he letting a woman like you touch him like that?"

If Bettina looked at the boy in anger, he looked back at her with twice as much cold fury.

She said, "What kind of woman am I that deserves to be spoken to like that?"

"You know," he said. "Now let me out."

"Never," Parvez replied.

"Don't worry, I'm getting out," Bettina said.

"No, don't!" said Parvez. But even as the car moved she opened the door, threw herself out, and ran away across the road. Parvez shouted after her, several times called after her, but she had gone.

Parvez took Ali back to the house, saying nothing more to him. Ali went straight to his room. Parvez was unable to read the paper, watch television, or even sit down. He kept pouring himself drinks.

At last he went upstairs and paced up and down outside Ali's room. When, finally, he opened the door, Ali was praying. The boy didn't even glance his way.

Parvez kicked him over. Then he dragged the boy up by his shirt and hit him. The boy fell back. Parvez hit him again. The boy's face was bloody. Parvez was panting, he knew the boy was unreachable, but he struck him nonetheless. The boy neither covered himself nor retaliated; there was no fear in his eyes. He only said, through his split lip, "So who's the fanatic now?"

John L'Heureux

....

The Comedian

CORINNE HASN'T PLANNED to have a baby. She is thirty-eight and happy and she wants to get on with it. She is a stand-up comedian with a husband, her second, and with no thought of a child, and what she wants out of life now is a lot of laughs. To give them, and especially to get them. And here she is, by accident, pregnant.

The doctor sees her chagrin and is surprised, because he thinks of her as a competent and sturdy woman. But that's how things are these days and so he suggests an abortion. Corinne says she'll let him know; she has to do some thinking. A baby.

"That's great," Russ says. "If you want it, I mean. I want it. I mean, I want it if you do. It's up to you, though. You know what I mean?"

And so they decide that, of course, they will have the baby, of course they want the baby, the baby is just exactly what they need.

In the bathroom mirror that night, Russ looks through his eyes into his cranium for a long time. Finally he sees his mind. As he watches, it knots like a fist. And he continues to watch, glad, as that fist beats the new baby flat and thin, a dead slick silverfish.

Mother. Mother and baby. A little baby. A big baby. Bouncing babies. At once Corinne sees twenty babies, twenty pink basketball babies, bouncing down the court and then up into the air and — whoosh — they swish neatly through the net. Babies.

Baby is its own excuse for being. Or is it? Well, Corinne was a Catholic right up until the end of her first marriage, so she thinks maybe it is. One thing is sure: the only subject you can't make a good joke about is abortion.

Yes, they will have the baby. Yes, she will be the mother. Yes.

But the next morning, while Russ is at work, Corinne turns off the television and sits on the edge of the couch. She squeezes her thighs together, tight; she contracts her stomach; she arches her back. This is no joke. This is the real thing. By an act of the will, she is going to expel this baby, this invader, this insidious little murderer. She pushes and pushes and nothing happens. She pushes again, hard. And once more she pushes. Finally she gives up and lies back against the sofa, resting.

After a while she puts her hand on her belly, and as she does so, she is astonished to hear singing.

It is the baby. It has a soft reedy voice and it sings slightly off-key. Corinne listens to the words: "Some of these days, you'll miss me, honey . . ."

Corinne faints then, and it is quite some time before she wakes up.

When she wakes, she opens her eyes only a slit and looks carefully from left to right. She sits on the couch, vigilant, listening, but she hears nothing. After a while she says three Hail Marys and an Act of Contrition, and then, confused and a little embarrassed, she does the laundry.

She does not tell Russ about this.

Well, it's a time of strain, Corinne tells herself, even though in California there isn't supposed to be any strain. Just surfing and tans and divorce and a lot of interfacing. No strain and no babies.

Corinne thinks for a second about interfacing babies, but forces the thought from her mind and goes back to thinking about her act. Sometimes she does a very funny set on interfacing, but only if the audience is middle-aged. The younger ones don't seem to know that interfacing is laughable. Come to think of it, *nobody* laughs much in California. Everybody smiles, but who laughs?

Laughs: that's something she can use. She does Garbo's laugh: "I am so hap-py." What was that movie? "I am so hap-py." She does the Garbo laugh again. Not bad. Who else laughs? Joe E. Brown. The Wicked Witch of the West. Who was she? Somebody Hamilton. Will anybody remember these people? Ruth Buzzi? Goldie Hawn? Yes, that great giggle. Of course, the best giggle is Burt Reynolds's. High and fey. Why does he do that? Is he sending up his own image?

Corinne is thinking of images, Burt Reynolds's and Tom Selleck's, when she hears singing: "Cal-i-for-nia, here I come, Right back where I started from . . ." Corinne stops pacing and stands in the doorway to the kitchen — as if I'm waiting for the earthquake, she thinks. But there is no earthquake; there is only the thin sweet voice, singing.

Corinne leans against the door frame and listens. She closes her eyes. At once it is Easter, and she is a child again at Sacred Heart Grammar School, and the thirty-five members of the children's choir, earnest and angelic, look out at her from where they stand, massed about the altar. They wear red cassocks and white surplices, starched, and they seem to have descended from heaven for this one occasion. Their voices are pure, high, untouched by adolescence or by pain; and, with a conviction born of absolute innocence, they sing to God and to Corinne, "Cal-i-for-nia, here I come."

Corinne leans against the door frame and listens truly now. Imagination aside, drama aside — she listens. It is a single voice she hears, thin and reedy. So, she did not imagine it the first time. It is true. The baby sings.

That night, when Russ comes home, he takes his shower, and they settle in with their first martini and everything is cozy.

Corinne asks him about his day, and he tells her. It was a lousy day. Russ started his own construction company a year ago just as the bottom fell out of the building business, and now there are no jobs to speak of. Just renovation stuff. Cleanup after fires. Sometimes Victorian restorations down in the gay district. But that's about it. So whatever comes his way is bound to be lousy. Corinne knows this, but she asks how his day was anyhow, and he tells her. This is Russ's second marriage, though, so he knows not to go too far with a lousy day. Who needs it?

"But I've got you, babe," he says, and pulls her toward him, and kisses her.

"We've got each other," Corinne says, and kisses him back. "And the baby," she says.

He holds her close then, so that she can't see his face. She makes big eyes like an actor in a bad comedy — she doesn't know why; she just always sees the absurd in everything. After a while they pull away, smiling, secret, and sip their martinis.

"Do you know something?" she says. "Can I tell you something?"

"What?" he says. "Tell me."

"You won't laugh?"

"No," he says, laughing. "I'm sorry. No, I won't laugh."

"Okay," she says. "Here goes."

There is a long silence, and then he says, "Well?"

"It sings."

"It sings?"

"The baby. The fetus. It sings."

Russ is stalled, but only for a second. Then he says, "Plain chant? Or rock-and-roll?" He begins to laugh, and he laughs so hard that he chokes and sloshes martini onto the couch. "You're wonderful," he says. "You're really a funny, funny girl. Woman." He laughs some more. "Is that for your act? I love it."

"I'm serious," she says. "I mean it."

"Well, it's great," he says. "They'll love it."

Corinne puts her hand on her stomach and thinks she has never been so alone in her life. She looks at Russ, with his big square jaw and all those white teeth and his green eyes so trusting and innocent, and she realizes for one second how corrupt she is, how lost, how deserving of a baby who sings; and then she pulls herself together because real life has to go on.

"Let's eat out," she says. "Spaghetti. It's cheap." She kisses him gently on his left eyelid, on his right. She gazes into his eyes and smiles, so that he will not guess she is thinking: Who is this man? Who am I?

Corinne has a job, Fridays and Saturdays for the next three weeks — at the Ironworks. It's not The Comedy Shop, but it's a legitimate gig, and the money is good. Moreover, it will give her something to think about besides whether or not she should go through with the abortion. She and Russ have put that on hold.

She is well into her third month, but she isn't showing yet, so she figures she can handle the three weekends easily. She wishes, in a way, that she were showing. As it is, she only looks . . . She searches for the word, but not for long. The word is *fat*. She looks fat.

She could do fat-girl jokes, but she hates jokes that put down women. And she hates jokes that are blue. Jokes that ridicule husbands. Jokes that ridicule the joker's looks. Jokes about nationalities. Jokes that play into audience prejudice. Jokes about the terrible small town you came from. Jokes about how poor you were, how ugly, how unpopular. Phyllis Diller jokes. Joan Rivers jokes. Jokes about small boobs, wrinkles, sexual inadequacy. Why is she in this business? she wonders. She hates jokes.

She thinks she hears herself praying: Please, please.

What should she do at the Ironworks? What should she do about the baby? What should she do?

The baby is the only one who's decided what to do. The baby sings.

Its voice is filling out nicely and it has enlarged its repertoire considerably. It sings a lot of classical melodies Corinne thinks she remembers from somewhere, churchy stuff, but it also favors golden oldies from the forties and fifties, with a few real old-timers thrown in when they seem appropriate. Once, right at the beginning, for instance, after Corinne and Russ had quarreled, Corinne locked herself in the bathroom to sulk and after a while was surprised, and then grateful, to hear the baby crooning, "Oh, my man, I love him so." It struck Corinne a day or so later that this could be a baby that would sell out for *any* one-liner . . . if indeed she decided to have the baby . . . and so she was relieved when the baby turned to more classical pieces.

The baby sings only now and then, and it sings better at some times than at others, but Corinne is convinced it sings best on weekend evenings when she is preparing for her gig. Before she leaves home, Corinne always has a long hot soak in the tub. She lies in the suds with her little orange bath pillow at her head and, as she runs through the night's possibilities, preparing ad-libs, heckler put-downs, segues, the baby sings to her.

There is some connection, she is sure, between her work and the baby's singing, but she can't guess what it is. It doesn't matter. She loves this: just she and the baby, together, in song.

Thank you, thank you, she prays.

The Ironworks gig goes extremely well. It is a young crowd, mostly, and so Corinne sticks to her young jokes: life in California, diets, dating, school. The audience laughs, and Russ says she is better than ever, but at the end of the three weeks the manager tells her, "You got it, honey. You got all the moves. You really make them laugh, you know? But they laugh from here only" — he taps his head — "not from the gut. You gotta get gut. You know? Like feeling."

So now the gig is over and Corinne lies in her tub trying to think of gut. She's gotta get gut, she's gotta get feeling. Has she ever *felt*? Well, she feels for Russ; she loves him. She felt for Alan, that bastard; well, maybe he wasn't so bad; maybe he just wasn't ready for marriage, any more than she was. Maybe it's California; maybe nobody *can* feel in California.

Enough about feeling, already. Deliberately, she puts feeling out of her mind, and calls up babies instead. A happy baby, she thinks, and at once the bathroom is crowded with laughing babies, each one roaring and carrying on like Ed McMahon. A fat baby, and she sees a Shelley Winters baby, an Elizabeth Taylor baby, an Orson Welles baby. An active baby: a mile of trampolines and babies doing quadruple somersaults, back flips, high dives. A healthy baby: babies lifting weights, swimming the Channel. Babies.

But abortion is the issue, not babies. Should she have it, or not?

At once she sees a bloody mess, a crushed-looking thing, half animal, half human. Its hands open and close. She gasps. "No," she says aloud, and shakes her head to get rid of the awful picture. "No," and she covers her face.

Gradually she realizes that she has been listening to humming, and now the humming turns to song — "It ain't necessarily so," sung in a good clear mezzo.

Her eyes hurt and she has a headache. In fact, her eyes hurt all the time.

Corinne has finally convinced Russ that she hears the baby singing. Actually, he is convinced that Corinne is halfway around the bend with worry, and he is surprised, when he thinks about it, to find that he loves her anyway, crazy or not. He tells her that as much as he hates the idea, maybe she ought to think about having an abortion.

"I've actually gotten to like the singing," she says.

"Corinne," he says.

"It's the things I see that scare me to death."

"What things? What do you see?"

At once she sees a little crimson baby. It has been squashed into a mason jar. The tiny eyes almost disappear into the puffed cheeks, the cheeks into the neck, the neck into the torso. It is a pickled baby, ancient, preserved.

"Tell me," he says.

"Nothing," she says. "It's just that my eyes hurt."

It's getting late for an abortion, the doctor says, but she can still have one safely.

He's known her for twenty years, all through the first marriage and now through this one, and he's puzzled that a funny and sensible girl like Corinne should be having such a tough time with pregnancy. He had recommended abortion right from the start, because she didn't seem to want the baby and because she was almost forty, but he hadn't really expected her to take him up on it. Looking at her now, though, it is clear to him that she'll never make it. She'll be wacko — if not during the pregnancy, then sure as hell afterward.

So what does she think? What does Russ think?

Well, first, she explains in her new, sort of wandering way, there's something else she wants to ask about; not really important, she supposes, but just something, well, kind of different she probably should mention. It's the old problem of the baby . . . well, um, singing.

"Singing?"

"Singing?" he asks again.

"And humming," Corinne says.

They sit in silence for a minute, the doctor trying to decide whether or not this is a joke. She's got this great poker face. She really is a good comic. So after a while he laughs, and then when she laughs, he knows he's done the right thing. But what a crazy sense of humor!

"You're terrific," he says. "Anything else? How's Russ? How was the Ironworks job?"

"My eyes hurt," she says. "I have headaches."

And so they discuss her vision for a while, and stand-up comedy, and she makes him laugh. And that's that.

At the door he says to her, "Have an abortion, Corinne. Now, before it's too late."

They have just made love and now Russ puts off the light and they lie together in the dark, his hand on her belly.

"Listen," he says. "I want to say something. I've been thinking about what the doctor said, about an abortion. I hate it, I hate the whole idea, but you know, we've got to think of you. And I think this baby is too much for you, I think maybe that's why you've been having those headaches and stuff. Don't you think?"

Corinne puts her hand on his hand and says nothing. After a long while Russ speaks again, into the darkness.

"I've been a lousy father. Two sons I never see. Beth took them back when they were, what, four and two, I guess. Back east. I never see them. The stepfather's good to them, though; he's a good father. I thought maybe I'd have another chance at it, do it right this time, like the marriage. Besides, the business isn't always going to be this bad, you know; I'll get jobs; I'll get money. We could afford it, you know? A son. A daughter. It would be nice. But what I mean is, we've got to take other things into consideration, we've got to consider your health. You're not strong enough, I guess. I always think of you as strong, because you do those gigs and you're funny and all, but, I mean, you're almost forty, and the doctor thinks that maybe an abortion is the way to go, and what do I know? I don't know. The singing. The headaches. I don't know."

Russ looks into the dark, seeing nothing.

"I worry about you, you want to know the truth? I do. Corinne?"

Corinne lies beside him, listening to him, refusing to listen to the baby, who all this time has been singing. Russ is as alone as she is, even more alone. She is dumbfounded. She is speechless with love. If he were a whirlpool, she thinks, she would fling herself into it. If he were . . . but he is who he is, and she loves only him, and she makes her decision.

"Corinne?" There is fear in his voice now.

"You think I'm losing my mind," she says.

Silence.

"Yes."

More silence.

"Well, I'm not. Headaches are a normal part of lots of pregnancies, the doctor said, and the singing doesn't mean anything at all. He explained what was really going on, why I thought I heard it sing. You see," Corinne says, improvising freely now, making it all up, for him, her gift to him, "you see, when you get somebody as high-strung as me and you add pregnancy right at the time I'm about to make it big as a stand-up, then the pressures get to be so much that sometimes the imagination can take over, the doctor said, and when you tune in to the normal sounds of your body, you hear them really loud, as if they were amplified by a three-thousand-watt PA system, and it can sound like singing. See?"

Russ says nothing.

"So you see, it all makes sense, really. You don't have to worry about me."

"Come on," Russ says. "Do you mean to tell me you never heard the baby singing?"

"Well, I heard it, sort of. You know? It was really all in my mind. I mean, the *sound* was in my body physiologically, but my hearing it as *singing* was just . . ."

"Just your imagination."

Corinne does not answer.

"Well?"

"Right," she says, making the total gift. "It was just my imagination."

And the baby — who has not stopped singing all this time, love songs mostly — stops singing now, and does not sing again until the day scheduled for the abortion.

The baby has not sung in three weeks. It is Corinne's fifth month now, and at last they have been able to do an amniocentesis. The news is bad. One of the baby's chromosomes does not match up to anything in hers, anything in Russ's. What this means, they tell her, is that the baby is not normal. It will be deformed in some way; in what way, they have no idea.

Corinne and Russ decide on abortion.

They talk very little about their decision now that they have made it. In fact, they talk very little about anything. Corinne's face grows daily more haggard, and Corinne avoids Russ's eyes. She is silent much of the time, thinking. The baby is silent all the time.

The abortion will be by hypertonic saline injection, a simple procedure, complicated only by the fact that Corinne has waited so long. She has been given a booklet to read and she has listened to a tape, and so she knows about the injection of the saline solution, she knows about the contractions that will begin slowly and then get more and more frequent, and she knows about the dangers of infection and excessive bleeding.

She knows moreover that it will be a formed fetus she will expel.

Russ has come with her to the hospital and is outside in the waiting room. Corinne thinks of him, of how she loves him, of how their lives will be better, safer, without this baby who sings. This deformed baby. Who sings. If only she could hear the singing once more, just once.

Corinne lies on the table with her legs in the thigh rests, and one of the nurses drapes the examining sheet over and around her. The other nurse, or someone — Corinne is getting confused; her eyesight seems fuzzy — takes her pulse and her blood pressure. She feels someone washing her, the careful hands, the warm fluid. So, it is beginning.

Corinne closes her eyes and tries to make her mind a blank. Dark, she thinks. Dark. She squeezes her eyes tight against the light, she wants to remain in this cool darkness forever, she wants to cease being. And then, amazingly, the dark does close in on her. Though she opens her eyes, she sees nothing. She can remain this way forever if she wills it. The dark is cool to the touch, and it is comforting somehow; it invites her in. She can lean into it, give herself up to it, and be safe, alone, forever.

She tries to sit up. She will enter this dark. She will do it. Please, please, she hears herself say. And then all at once she thinks of Russ and the baby, and instead of surrendering to the dark, she pushes it away.

With one sweep of her hand she pushes the sheet from her and flings it to the floor. She pulls her legs from the thigh rests and manages to sit up, blinded still, but fighting.

"Here now," a nurse says, caught off-guard, unsure what to do. "Hold on now. It's all right. It's fine."

"Easy now. Easy," the doctor says, thinking Yes, here it is, what else is new.

Together the nurses and the doctor make an effort to stop her, but they are too late, because by this time Corinne has fought free of any restraints. She is off the examining couch and, naked, huddles in the corner of the small room.

"No," she shouts. "I want the baby. I want the baby." And later, when she has stopped shouting, when she has stopped crying, still she clutches her knees to her chest and whispers over and over, "I want the baby."

So there is no abortion after all.

By the time she is discharged, Corinne's vision has returned, dimly. Moreover, though she tells nobody, she has heard humming, and once or twice a whole line of music. The baby has begun to sing again.

Corinne has more offers than she wants: The Hungry I, The Purple Onion, The Comedy Shop. Suddenly everybody decides it's time to take a look at her, but she is in no shape to be looked at, so she signs for two weeks at My Uncle's Bureau and lets it go at that.

She is only marginally pretty now, she is six months pregnant, and she is carrying a deformed child. Furthermore, she can see very little, and what she does see, she often sees double.

Her humor, therefore, is spare and grim, but audiences love it. She begins slow: "When I was a girl, I always wanted to look like Elizabeth Taylor," she says, and glances down at her swollen belly. Two beats. "And now I do." They laugh with her, and applaud. Now she can quicken the pace, sharpen the humor. They follow her; they are completely captivated.

She has found some new way of holding her body — tipping her head, thrusting out her belly — and instead of putting off her audience, or embarrassing them, it charms them. The laughter is *with* her, the applause *for* her. She could do anything out there and get away with it. And she knows it. They simply love her.

In her dressing room after the show she tells herself that somehow, magically, she's learned to work from the heart instead of just from the head. She's got gut. She's got feeling. But she knows it's something more than that.

By the end of the two weeks she is convinced that the successful new element in her act is the baby. This deformed baby, this abnormal baby she has tried to kill. And what interests her most is that she no longer cares about success as a stand-up.

Corinne falls asleep that night to the sound of the baby's crooning. She is trying to pray, Please, please, but with Russ's snoring and the baby's lullaby, they all get mixed up together in her mind — God, Russ, the baby — and she forgets to whom she is praying or why. She sleeps.

The baby sings all the time now. It starts first thing in the morning with a nice soft piece by Telemann or Brahms; there are assorted lullabies at bedtime; and throughout the day it is bop, opera, ragtime, blues, a little rock-and-roll, big-band stuff — the baby never tires.

Corinne tells no one about this, not even Russ.

She and Russ talk about almost everything now: their love for each other, their hopes for the baby, their plans. They have lots of plans. Russ has assured Corinne that whatever happens, he's ready for it.

Corinne is his whole life, and no matter how badly the baby is deformed, they'll manage. They'll do the right thing. They'll survive.

They talk about almost everything, but they do not talk about the baby's singing.

For Corinne the singing is secret, mysterious. It contains some revelation, of course, but she does not want to know what that revelation might be.

The singing is somehow tied up with her work; but more than that, with her life. It is part of her fate. It is inescapable. And she is perfectly content to wait.

Corinne has been in labor for three hours, and the baby has been singing the whole time. The doctor has administered a mild anesthetic and a nurse remains at bedside, but the birth does not seem imminent, and so for Corinne it is a period of pain and waiting. And for the baby, singing.

"These lights are so strong," Corinne says, or thinks she says. "The lights are blinding."

The nurse looks at her for a moment and then goes back to the letter she is writing.

"Please," Corinne says, "thank you."

She is unconscious, she supposes; she is imagining the lights. Or perhaps the lights are indeed bright and she sees them as they really are *because* she is unconscious. Or perhaps her sight has come back, as strong as it used to be. Whatever the case, she doesn't want to think about it now. Besides, for some reason or other, even though the lights are blinding, they are not blinding her. They do not even bother her. It is as if light is her natural element.

"Thank you," she says. To someone.

The singing is wonderful, a cappella things Corinne recognizes as Brahms, Mozart, Bach. The baby's voice can assume any dimension it wants now, swelling from a single thin note to choir volume; it can take on the tone and resonance of musical instruments, violin, viola, flute; it can become all sounds; it enchants.

The contractions are more frequent; even unconscious, Corinne can tell that. Good. Soon the waiting will be over and she will have her wonderful baby, her perfect baby. But at once she realizes hers will not be a perfect baby; it will be deformed. "Please," she says, "please," as if prayer can keep Russ from being told — as he will be soon after the birth — that his baby has been born dumb. Russ, who has never understood comedians.

But now the singing has begun to swell in volume. It is as if the baby has become a full choir, with many voices, with great strength.

The baby will be fine, however it is, she thinks. She thinks of Russ, worried half to death. She is no longer worried. She accepts what will be.

The contractions are very frequent now and the light is much brighter. She knows the doctor has come into the room, because she hears his voice. There is another nurse too. And soon there will be the baby.

The light is so bright that she can see none of them. She can see into the light, it is true; she can see the soft fleecy nimbus flowing beyond the light, but she can see nothing in the room.

The singing. The singing and the light. It is Palestrina she hears, in polyphony, each voice lambent. The light envelops her, catches her up from this table where the doctor bends over her and where already can be seen the shimmering yellow hair of the baby. The light lifts her, and the singing lifts her, and she says, "Yes," she says, "thank you."

She accepts what will be. She accepts what is.

The room is filled with singing and with light, and the singing is transformed into light, more light, more lucency, and still she says, "Yes," until she cannot bear it, and she reaches up and tears the light aside. And sees.

James A. Michener

....

Voyage Four: 1661

FOR SOME TIME NOW the community had been suspicious of him. His master had confided to the governor that "Edward Paxmore, whose indenture I purchased seven years ago, has taken to wandering about the colony without my permission, robbing me of labor justly mine." As a result, spies watched his movements, reporting any unusual behavior to the committee of ministers, and the family from which he hoped to buy a piece of land for his carpentry shop when his indenture ended refused to sell.

Informers told the governor, "He has traveled from Salisbury to Rowly to Ipswich and has been contentious in arguing with passersby about the works of God." Therefore, when Paxmore returned to Boston and reappeared at the house of his master, the sheriff was waiting to haul him off to court.

At the hearing, his master whined, "Edward is a good carpenter who builds well. But in this final year with me he has taken to arguing about the works of God. He has cheated me of his labors and I am sorely done."

"What remedy?"

"Please, your honor, extend his indenture for another ten months. It's only fair."

The governor, a thin, arduous man, was little concerned with financial restitution to masters; such cases were common and could be handled by ordinary judges. But this ominous phrase, "arguing about the works of God," disturbed him mightily, for it was clearly blasphemous and smacked of Quakerism. Within recent years the governor had ordered the hanging of three Quakers and had personally attended their executions. He had no intention of allowing this pernicious heresy to gain a foothold in Massachusetts, for it was an abomination.

The governor had a firm mind in all things, but he was perplexed by the man who stood before him, this tall, thin workman in homespun jacket too short at the wrists, in pants too skimpy at the ankles. He was awkward-looking, yet all had testified that he was an excellent carpenter. It was the Adam's apple and the eyes that troubled: the former jumped about like those in witches; the latter carried that intense fire which marked those who believe they have seen God. Such men were dangerous, yet this carpenter had such a gentle manner, was so deferential to the court and so respectful of his master that he could not be a common criminal. Deep matters were involved, and they must be gone into.

"Edward Paxmore, I fear you may have fallen into evil ways. I hand you back to the sheriff for presentation in court on Monday next for proper interrogation." Having said this, he stared balefully at Paxmore and stalked from the room.

The trial should have been of little consequence, for Paxmore, thirty-two years old and with an excellent reputation for hard work, would normally have been rebuked for wandering and depriving his rightful master of his labor. The judge would add an additional six months to the indenture — never as many as the master claimed — and when these had been discharged, the carpenter would become a free man and a valued addition to the citizenry of Massachusetts.

But Paxmore's trial was to be different, for when the court convened on Monday morning Judge Goddard, a tall, heavy man who spoke in ponderous sentences, had the grim but satisfying task of putting final touches to the case of Thomas Kenworthy, confessed Quaker and recusant. On three occasions Judge Goddard had ordered Kenworthy to be whipped and banished from Massachusetts, and thrice the Quaker had crept back into the colony.

Paxmore and his master were already seated in court when the sheriff brought Kenworthy in. The Quaker was a man of forty, thin, dark of face, with deep-set eyes and the manner of a fanatic who looked piercingly at people. His hands were bound and he seemed reluctant to step before the judge; the sheriff had to push him along, but when at last he was in place he stared defiantly at the judge and asked in a strong voice, "Wherefore does thee judge me?"

And Goddard thundered, "We have a law."

"It is thy law and not God's."

"Silence that man!"

"I will not be silenced, for God has ordered me to speak."

"Stifle that blasphemy!" the judge roared, and the sheriff clapped his hand over the prisoner's mouth.

When silence once more prevailed in the small white room Judge Goddard resumed control of the case, placing his large hands on the table and looking with contempt at Kenworthy. "Three times I have ordered you whipped, and three times you have continued your heresy. Do you learn nothing?"

"I have learned that God does not need governors or judges or ministers to speak to His people."

"Sheriff, remove that man's shirt."

The sheriff, a tall, lean man who betrayed a sense of satisfaction with his job, untied the prisoner's hands and ripped away the woolen shirt. Paxmore gasped. The man's back was a network of small round scars, but not like any he had seen before. These formed little cups across the man's back and Paxmore would never forget the strange remark of the man at his elbow: "You could hide a pea in each of them."

Judge Goddard said, "Are you aware, Thomas Kenworthy, of how your back looks?"

"I feel it each night before I go to sleep. It is the badge of my devotion to God."

"Apparently you are of such a contumacious character that ordinary whippings have no effect on you. My order that you quit this colony has been ignored, three times. You have not only persisted in your Quaker heresy, but you have made so bold as to preach to others, infecting them, and there is no humility in you."

"There is love of God in me," Kenworthy said.

"Nor respect, neither," the judge continued. "In your three other trials you refused, did you not, to remove your hat in the presence of the governor and his court?"

"I did, and if I could have my hat now, I would wear it, for Jesus Christ so commanded." His eyes fell on the hat Paxmore had worn into court, and in a sudden breakaway from the sheriff he seized the hat and placed it defiantly on his head. The sheriff started to fight for possession of the hat, but Judge Goddard rebuked him, "Let the criminal wear his hat, if it will help him hear my sentence," then lowered his voice and said, more slowly, "Thomas Kenworthy, it is my duty to pass sentence upon you."

"God has already done so, and thy words are nothing."

"You speak falsehood," the judge thundered, allowing his voice to rise.

"I speak the instructions of God, and they are never false."

"Do you then nominate yourself a minister, that you comprehend the teachings of God?"

"Each man is minister, yes, and each woman too." Kenworthy turned to face the spectators, and because he stood nearest Edward Paxmore he pointed a long finger at him and said, "This prisoner haled before the court is also a minister. He speaks directly to God, and God speaks to him."

"Silence him again," the judge shouted, and once more Kenworthy's hands were tied and his mouth covered.

Paxmore, trembling from the effect of having been twice involved in this trial, watched with fascination as the judge painstakingly arranged the papers on his table, obviously seeking to compose himself lest anger make him appear foolish. Taking a deep breath, he leaned forward to address the Quaker in measured phrases.

"The Colony of Massachusetts has been most lenient with you, Thomas Kenworthy. It has received your heresy and done its best to make you see the falsity of your ways. Three times it has allowed you to wander about our towns and villages, spewing your blasphemy. And you have shown no contrition. Therefore, the sentence of this court is that you shall be lashed to a great cannon and whipped thirty times, after which you shall be taken to the public square and hanged."

The cruel sentence had no effect on Thomas Kenworthy, for he was already living in a kind of ecstasy in which whippings and gibbets were no longer of much concern, but it had a devastating effect on Edward Paxmore, who leaped to his feet and shouted at the judge, "If you're going to hang him, why whip him first?"

The question was so explosive, and so obviously germane, that Judge Goddard imprudently allowed himself to be trapped into answering. "To punish him," he said spontaneously.

"Is not death punishment?" Paxmore cried.

"Not enough," the judge responded. And then, realizing what he had done — that he had spoken like a fool — he bellowed, "Lock that man up." And he stormed from the small white room.

The sheriff took his two prisoners to the jail, a dank room below the level of the public streets, and there directed the blacksmith to apply one set of leg irons to the two men. When this difficult and untidy job was completed, and the two men were lashed together as one, the smith and the sheriff departed, leaving the condemned Quaker and the carpenter in semi-darkness.

Then began the dialogue of salvation. Thomas Kenworthy, one of the first Quaker preachers in America, a graduate of Oxford and a man versed in both Greek and Latin, interpreted the simple revolution in theology that had taken place in England less than twenty years before: "George Fox is not a holy man, not a priest in any sense of that word, no different from thee and me."

"Why do you use *thee*?"

"It was the way Jesus spoke to His friends." Kenworthy explained how Fox, this unpretentious Englishman, had come to see that many of the manifestations of religion were vain trappings and that the ritual was unnecessary: "Thee does not require priests or blessings. Or ministers' sermons or benedictions or the laying on of hands. God speaks directly to the human heart, and the blessings of Jesus Christ are available to every man and woman."

Paxmore noticed that Kenworthy never said man in the religious sense without adding *woman*, and the Quaker told him, "When I was whipped in Virginia, one woman hung beside me at the tail of the cart, and she was braver than I could ever be. The cords hurt me, but they tore the woman apart, and she refused to whimper."

"Does it hurt, the lashings?"

"In Virginia, I wept and cursed, but in Ipswich, God came to me and asked, 'If my Son could bear His crucifixion, cannot thee endure a mere whipping?'"

Paxmore asked if he could touch the scars, and Kenworthy said no. "It would make them too important. The dignity of my back lies in my heart, where I have forgiven the whipmen of Virginia and Massachusetts. They were like the Roman soldiers, doing their duty."

He was describing to Paxmore the other tenets of the Quakers — equality of women, refusal to bear arms, tithing, no hymns or outward manifestations in worship, no priests, no ministers, and, above all, the direct relationship of God and man — when the carpenter exclaimed, "Thomas, I left Boston and wandered through the country-side because I was searching. Is this the revelation I was seeking?"

"It is no revelation, no mystery, and thee did not have to leave Boston to entertain it. It is the simple discovery that each man is his own pathway to God."

Long after nightfall a jailer brought food to the prisoners, but neither could eat. Leg bound to leg, they wanted to talk about the spiritual revolution of which Quakerism was only a minor manifestation. "There will be many others like me," Kenworthy predicted. "There will have to be, because God approaches people in different ways."

"Is the governor right in his religion?"

"Of course he is. For him, what he says and what he believes in are altogether right."

"Then why does he condemn — What was the word he used?"

"Quakers," the Oxford man said. "Our enemies accuse us of quaking in the presence of God, and we do."

"Why does he condemn you to death?"

"Because he is afraid."

"Is that why the judge ordered you to be whipped . . . and hanged?"

"It is. When he saw my scarred back in court, scars he put there, and realized how little effect they had had upon me — Edward, the last time in Roxbury, I did not even feel the cords . . ." In a sweep of spiritual insight he lost his line of thought, and his awareness of jail, and any sense of pressure from the leg irons. He tried to rise, then tried to kneel in prayer. Defeated in each effort, he sat on the bench and folded his hands over his heart, saying, "If thee had not told me that thee had left Boston to go a-searching, I would not presume to tell thee what I am about to say, for I am putting a heavy burden on thee, Edward. But God has summoned thee."

"I believe He has," Paxmore said, and the two men talked through the night.

On Friday morning the blacksmith came in to cut the leg clamps, separating them, and while doing so, advised Kenworthy that he was to hang this day. From his leg the clamp was removed entirely, but on Paxmore's the iron cuff was allowed to remain and a seven-foot chain was attached to it. "All prisoners must watch the hanging," the smith explained, "and with this chain the sheriff can hold you so you don't run away."

When the two prisoners were left alone in their cell Paxmore supposed that Kenworthy would want to pray, but the Oxford man was in such a state of exaltation that he did not need prayer to prepare him for the death that waited: "We are children of God, and reunion with Him can never be painful. I go with additional peace in my heart because I know that thee has taken up the burden I leave behind."

"Could we pray?" Paxmore asked.

"If you feel the need."

"I have not the understanding you have —" He corrected himself, and for the first time used the Quaker expression: "The understanding thee has."

"Thee has, Edward. That is, the capacity for it. All men and women do. What is required is the unfolding of truth. And that will come."

They knelt and Paxmore began a tortured prayer, but Kenworthy placed his hand on the carpenter's arm and said, "The words are not necessary. God hears thee," and the two men prayed in silence.

They were in this position when the jailers came. They were stocky men with powerful arms and seemed to enjoy their work, for they attacked it with a kind of easy joviality. "Time's come," the heavier of the two men announced, taking Kenworthy by the upper arm. The other grabbed Paxmore's chain and told him, "The sheriff's handling you special." The two Quakers were separated for the last time, but not before Paxmore had a chance to cry, "I will be on the scaffold with thee, Thomas," to which Kenworthy replied, "All Boston will be."

Paxmore and three other prisoners — two men and a woman who had questioned some small detail of Puritanism — were led to the hanging ground, where a large crowd of watchers waited with varying kinds of delight. Some were fascinated by the gibbet from which a man would soon hang, others by the monstrous cannon to whose wheel the heretic would be lashed. Eight men of the town had already volunteered to pull the cannon and were busy attaching ropes to the carriage. But all experienced a heightened sense of existence, because their church was about to cleanse itself.

Paxmore, standing with the other prisoners, who were constantly jeered at by the townspeople, looked in vain for Kenworthy; he was being held back until the colony officials put in their appearance, and now from the white church, where they had been praying, came the governor and Judge Goddard, dressed in black, followed by the town fathers, grim-lipped and ready.

"Bring forth the prisoner!" the governor shouted. It was clear that he intended to supervise personally the death of this obnoxious dissenter. When Kenworthy was produced, the governor went to him, thrust his face forward, and demanded, "Are you satisfied now that we have the power to silence you?"

"My voice will be stronger tomorrow than it ever was," Kenworthy replied.

"To the cannon!" the governor cried, and the sheriff dropped the chain that held Paxmore and summoned three helpers, who came forward to grab the Oxford man and lash him, legs and arms far separated, to the iron wheel of the cannon, face inward.

"Jailer," the governor commanded, "thirty lashes, well laid on."

The heavier of the two jailers stepped forward, and the town clerk handed him a length of wood to which had been fastened nine heavy cords of the kind used for guiding light sail. Into each had been tied three stout knots, and as the jailer approached the cannon he snapped the whip expertly, close to the ear of the prostrate prisoner.

"That one don't count," he said, and the crowd laughed.

"One!" the clerk intoned impassively, and the nine cords cut into the scarred back of the Quaker.

"Two!" the clerk counted, then "Three!" and "Four!"

"Make him cry out," a woman in the crowd shouted, but Kenworthy uttered no sound.

"Seven" and "Eight" passed with still no sound from the wheel, so the governor said, "Pull the cannon forward," and the men on the ropes strained until the wheel moved into a new position, exposing different parts of Kenworthy's body to the lash.

"Lay on, lay on!" the governor cried, and when the next strokes still failed to elicit any cry of pain from the prisoner, the governor stepped forward angrily and took the lash from the hands of the first jailer, handing it to the second. "Lay on! Destroy that man!"

The second jailer, eager for an opportunity to display the kind of service he was ready to give his colony and his church, raised on his toes and brought the lashes down with savage force, causing Kenworthy's whole body to shudder. At the fifteenth stroke the body went limp, and as the enthusiastic jailer was about to apply the lash again, Edward Paxmore shouted, "He's fainted. Stop! Stop!"

"Who cried out?" the governor demanded, and Judge Goddard, who had been watching Paxmore, replied, "That one," and the governor stopped to mark the culprit. "We'll take care of him later," he said.

Then he cried, "Men, move the cannon," and the great wheel revolved.

By the twenty-fifth lash Thomas Kenworthy was nearly dead, but now the governor directed that the whip be turned over to a new aspirant eager to show how well he could strike, and pieces of flesh flicked off the bloody mass.

"Give it to him!" a woman called as the clerk finished his litany: "Twenty-nine, thirty, and done."

"Water in his face," the sheriff ordered, and after this was done, the limp body was cut down.

"To the gibbet," the governor said, and he led the way to the hanging spot.

The water and the walk revived the prisoner, and after he was dragged aloft to the platform from which he would be dropped, he said in a voice which could be heard some distance, "Thee will be ashamed of this day's work."

A minister who had watched the whipping ran to the scaffold and cried in fierce, condemnatory accents, "Heretic, separatist! God has shown us the true religion and you traduce it. You have a right to die."

"Hangman, to your task," the governor said, and a black bag was placed over Kenworthy's head. As the radiant face disappeared, Paxmore whispered, "Oh, God! He is not as old as I."

The rope was lowered over the black mask, and the knot was located at the base of the neck. "Let him die!" cried the woman who had shouted before, and the trapdoor was sprung.

Yukio Mishima

....

The Priest and His Love

TRANSLATED BY IVAN MORRIS

Translator's note: The interview behind the blind toward the end of the story may require a few words of explanation. As readers of *The Tale of Genji* will recall, it was customary in the Heian period for noblewomen to be hidden by a ceremonial screen or blind when receiving male visitors. To invite a man behind the screen normally meant that a woman was prepared to accept his advances.

ACCORDING TO Eshin's "Essentials of Salvation," the Ten Pleasures are but a drop in the ocean when compared to the joys of the Pure Land. In that land the earth is made of emerald and the roads that lead across it are lined by cordons of gold rope. The surface is endlessly level and there are no boundaries. Within each of the sacred precincts are fifty thousand million halls and towers wrought of gold, silver, lapis lazuli, crystal, coral, agate, and pearls; and wondrous garments are spread out on all the jeweled daises. Within the halls and above the towers a multitude of angels are forever playing sacred music and singing paeans of praise to the Tathagata Buddha. In the gardens that surround the halls and the towers and the cloisters are great gold and emerald ponds where the faithful may perform their ablutions; the gold ponds are lined with silver sand, and the emerald ponds are lined with crystal sand. The ponds are covered with lotus plants which sparkle in variegated colors and, as the breeze wafts over the surface of the water, magnificent lights crisscross in all directions. Both day and night the air is filled with the songs of cranes, geese, mandarin ducks, peacocks, parrots, and sweet-voiced Kalavinkas, who have the faces of beautiful women. All these and the myriad other hundred-jeweled birds are raising their melodious voices in praise of the Buddha. (However sweet their voices may sound, so immense a collection of birds must be extremely noisy.)

The borders of the ponds and the banks of the rivers are lined with groves of sacred treasure trees. These trees have golden stems and silver branches and coral blossoms, and their beauty is mirrored in the waters. The air is full of jeweled cords, and from these cords hang the myriad treasure bells which forever ring out the Supreme Law of Buddha; and strange musical instruments, which play by themselves without ever being touched, also stretch far into the pellucid sky.

If one feels like having something to eat, there automatically appears before one's eyes a seven-jeweled table on whose shining surface rest seven-jeweled bowls heaped high with the choicest delicacies. But there is no need to pick up these viands and put them in one's mouth. All that is necessary is to look at their inviting colors and to enjoy their aroma; thereby the stomach is filled and the body nourished, while one remains oneself spiritually and physically pure. When one has thus finished one's meal without any eating, the bowls and the table are instantly wafted off.

Likewise, one's body is automatically arrayed in clothes, without any need for sewing, laundering, dyeing, or repairing. Lamps, too, are unnecessary, for the sky is illumined by an omnipresent light. Furthermore, the Pure Land enjoys a moderate temperature all year round, so that neither heating nor cooling is required. A hundred thousand subtle scents perfume the air, and lotus petals rain down constantly.

In the chapter on the Inspection Gate we are told that, since uninitiated sightseers cannot hope to penetrate deep into the Pure Land, they must concentrate, first, on awakening their powers of "external imagination" and, thereafter, on steadily expanding these powers. Imaginative power can provide a shortcut for escaping from the trammels of our mundane life and for seeing the Buddha. If we are endowed with a rich, turbulent imagination, we can focus our attention on a single lotus flower and from there can spread out to infinite horizons.

By means of microscopic observation and astronomical projection the lotus flower can become the foundation for an entire theory of the universe and an agent whereby we may perceive Truth. And first we must know that each of the petals has eighty-four thousand veins and that each vein gives off eighty-four thousand lights. Furthermore, the smallest of these flowers has a diameter of two hundred and fifty yojana. Thus, assuming that the yojana of which we read in the Holy Writings correspond to seventy-five miles each, we may conclude that a lotus flower with a diameter of nineteen thousand miles is on the small side.

Now such a flower has eighty-four thousand petals and between each of the petals there are one million jewels, each emitting one thousand lights. Above the beautifully adorned calyx of the flower rise four bejeweled pillars and each of these pillars is one hundred billion times as great as Mount Sumeru, which towers in the center of the Buddhist universe. From the pillars hang great draperies and each drapery is adorned with fifty thousand million jewels, and each jewel emits eighty-four thousand lights, and each light is composed of eighty-four thousand different golden colors, and each of those golden colors in its turn is variously transmogrified.

To concentrate on such images is known as "thinking of the Lotus Seat on which Lord Buddha sits"; and the conceptual world that hovers in the background of our story is a world imagined on such a scale.

The Great Priest of Shiga Temple was a man of the most eminent virtue. His eyebrows were white, and it was as much as he could do to move his old bones along as he hobbled on his stick from one part of the temple to another.

In the eyes of this learned ascetic, the world was a mere pile of rubbish. He had lived away from it for many a long year, and the little pine sapling that he had planted with his own hands on moving into his present cell had grown into a great tree whose branches swelled in the wind. A monk who had succeeded in abandoning the Floating World for so long a time must feel secure about his afterlife.

When the Great Priest saw the rich and the noble, he smiled with compassion and wondered how it was that these people did not recognize their pleasures for the empty dreams that they were. When he noticed beautiful women, his only reaction was to be moved with pity for men who still inhabited the world of delusion and who were tossed about on the waves of carnal pleasure.

From the moment that a man no longer responds in the slightest to the motives that regulate the material world, that world appears to be at complete repose. In the eyes of the Great Priest the world showed only repose; it had become a mere picture drawn on a piece of paper, a map of some foreign land. When one has attained a state of mind from which the evil passions of the present world have been so utterly winnowed, fear too is forgotten. Thus it was that the priest no longer could understand why Hell should exist. He knew beyond all peradventure that the present world no longer had any power left over him; but, as he was completely devoid of conceit, it did not occur to him that this was the effect of his own eminent virtue.

So far as his body was concerned, one might say that the priest had well nigh been deserted by his own flesh. On such occasions as he observed it — when taking a bath, for instance — he would rejoice to see how his protruding bones were precariously covered by his withered skin. Now that his body had reached this stage, he felt that he could come to terms with it, as if it belonged to someone else. Such a body, it seemed, was already more suited for the nourishment of the Pure Land than for terrestrial food and drink.

In his dreams he lived nightly in the Pure Land, and when he awoke he knew that to subsist in the present world was to be tied to a sad and evanescent dream.

In the flower-viewing season large numbers of people came from the Capital to visit the village of Shiga. This did not trouble the priest in the slightest, for he had long since transcended that state in which the clamors of the world can irritate the mind. One spring evening he left his cell, leaning on his stick, and walked down to the lake. It was the hour when dusky shadows slowly begin to thrust their way into the bright light of the afternoon. There was not the slightest ripple to disturb the surface of the water. The priest stood by himself at the edge of the lake and began to perform the holy rite of Water Contemplation.

At that moment an ox-drawn carriage, clearly belonging to a person of high rank, came round the lake and stopped close to where the priest was standing. The owner was a court lady from the Kyōgoku district of the Capital who held the exalted title of Great Imperial Concubine. This lady had come to view the springtime scenery in Shiga and now on her return she stopped the carriage and raised the blind in order to have a final look at the lake.

Unwittingly the Great Priest glanced in her direction and at once he was overwhelmed by her beauty. His eyes met hers and, as he did nothing to avert his gaze, she did not take it upon herself to turn away. It was not that her liberality of spirit was such as to allow men to gaze on her with brazen looks; but the motives of this austere old ascetic could hardly, she felt, be those of ordinary men.

After a few moments the lady pulled down the blind. Her carriage started to move and, having gone through the Shiga Pass, rolled slowly down the road that led to the Capital. Night fell and the carriage made its way toward the city along the Road of the Silver Temple. Until the carriage had become a pinprick that disappeared between the distant trees, the Great Priest stood rooted to the spot.

In the twinkling of an eye the present world had wreaked its revenge on the priest with terrible force. What he had imagined to be completely safe had collapsed in ruins.

He returned to the temple, faced the main image of Buddha, and invoked the Sacred Name. But impure thoughts now cast their opaque shadows about him. A woman's beauty, he told himself, was but a fleeting apparition, a temporary phenomenon composed of flesh — of flesh that was soon to be destroyed. Yet, try as he might to ward it off, the ineffable beauty which had overpowered him at that instant by the lake now pressed on his heart with the force of something that has come from an infinite distance. The Great Priest was not young enough, either spiritually or physically, to believe that this new feeling was simply a trick that his flesh had played on him. A man's flesh, he knew full well, could not alter so rapidly. Rather, he seemed to have been immersed in some swift, subtle poison which had abruptly transmuted his spirit.

The Great Priest had never broken his vow of chastity. The inner fight that he had waged in his youth against the demands of the flesh had made him think of women as mere carnal beings. The only real flesh was the flesh that existed in his imagination. Since, therefore, he regarded the flesh as an ideal abstraction, rather than as a physical fact, he had relied on his spiritual strength to subjugate it. In this effort the priest had achieved success — success, indeed, that no one who knew him could possibly doubt.

Yet the face of the woman who had raised the carriage blind and gazed across the lake was too harmonious, too refulgent, to be designated as a mere object of flesh, and the priest did not know what name to give it. He could only think that, in order to bring about that wondrous moment, something which had for a long time lurked deceptively within him had finally revealed itself. That thing was nothing other than the present world, which until then had been in repose, but which had now suddenly lifted itself out of the darkness and begun to stir.

It was as if he had been standing by the highway that led to the Capital, with his hands firmly covering both ears, and had watched two great ox carts rumble past each other. All of a sudden he had removed his hands and the noise from outside had surged all about him.

To perceive the ebb and flow of passing phenomena, to have their noise roaring in one's ears, was to enter into the circle of the present world. For a man like the Great Priest, who had severed his relations with all outside things, it was to place himself once again into a state of relationship.

Even as he read the sutras, he would time after time hear himself heaving great sighs of anguish. Perhaps nature, he thought, might serve to distract his spirit, and he gazed out the window of his cell at the mountains that towered in the distance under the evening sky. Yet his thoughts, instead of concentrating on the beauty, broke up like tufts of cloud and drifted away. He fixed his gaze on the moon, but his thoughts continued to wander as before; and when once again he went and stood before the main image in a desperate effort to regain his purity of mind, the countenance of the Buddha was transformed and looked like the face of the lady in the carriage. His universe had been imprisoned within the confines of a small circle: at one point was the Great Priest and opposite was the Great Imperial Concubine.

The Great Imperial Concubine of Kyōgoku had soon forgotten about the old priest whom she had noticed gazing so intently at her by the lake at Shiga. After some time, however, a rumor came to her ears and she was reminded of the incident. One of the villagers happened to have caught sight of the Great Priest as he had stood watching the lady's carriage disappear into the distance. He had mentioned the matter to a court gentleman who had come to Shiga for flower viewing, and had added that since that day the priest had behaved like one crazed.

The Imperial Concubine pretended to disbelieve the rumor. The virtue of this particular priest, however, was noted throughout the Capital, and the incident was bound to feed the lady's vanity.

For she was utterly weary of the love that she received from the men of this world. The Imperial Concubine was fully aware of her own beauty, and she tended to be attracted by any force, such as religion, that treated her beauty and her high rank as things of no value. Being exceedingly bored with the present world, she believed in the Pure Land. It was inevitable that Jōdo Buddhism, which rejected all the beauty and brilliance of the visual world as being mere filth and defilement, should have a particular appeal for someone like the Imperial Concubine, who was thoroughly disillusioned with the superficial elegance of court life — an elegance that seemed unmistakably to bespeak the Latter Days of the Law and their degeneracy.

Among those whose special interest was love, the Great Imperial Concubine was held in honor as the very personification of courtly refinement. The fact that she was known never to have given her love to any man added to this reputation. Though she performed her duties toward the Emperor with the most perfect decorum, no one for a moment believed that she loved him from her heart. The Great Imperial Concubine dreamed of a passion that lay on the boundary of the impossible.

The Great Priest of Shiga Temple was famous for his virtue, and everyone in the Capital knew how this aged prelate had totally abandoned the present world. All the more startling, then, was the rumor that he had been dazzled by the charms of the Imperial Concubine and that for her sake he had sacrificed the future world. To give up the joys of the Pure Land which were so close at hand — there could be no greater sacrifice than this, no greater gift.

The Great Imperial Concubine was utterly indifferent to the charms of the young rakes who flocked about the court and of the handsome noblemen who came her way. The physical attributes of men no longer meant anything to her. Her only concern was to find a man who could give her the strongest and deepest possible love. A woman with such aspirations is a truly terrifying creature. If she is a mere courtesan, she will no doubt be satisfied with worldly wealth. The Great Imperial Concubine, however, already enjoyed all those things that the wealth of the world can provide. The man whom she awaited must offer her the wealth of the future world.

The rumors of the Great Priest's infatuation spread throughout the court. In the end the story was even told half jokingly to the Emperor himself. The Great Concubine took no pleasure in this bantering gossip and preserved a cool, indifferent mien. As she was well aware, there were two reasons that the people of the court could joke freely about a matter which would normally have been forbidden: first, by referring to the Great Priest's love they were paying a compliment to the beauty of the woman who could inspire even an ecclesiastic of such great virtue to forsake his meditations; second, everyone fully realized that the old man's love for the noblewoman could never possibly be requited.

The Great Imperial Concubine called to mind the face of the old priest whom she had seen through her carriage window. It did not bear the remotest resemblance to the face of any of the men who had loved her until then. Strange it was that love should spring up in the heart of a man who did not have the slightest qualification for being loved. The lady recalled such phrases as "my love forlorn and without hope" that were widely used by poetasters in the palace when they wished to awaken some sympathy in the hearts of their indifferent paramours. Compared to the hopeless situation in which the Great Priest now found himself, the state of the least fortunate of these elegant lovers was almost enviable, and their poetic tags struck her now as mere trappings of worldly dalliance, inspired by vanity and utterly devoid of pathos.

At this point it will be clear to the reader that the Great Imperial Concubine was not, as was so widely believed, the personification of courtly elegance, but rather a person who found the real relish of life in the knowledge of being loved. Despite her high rank, she was first of all a woman; and all the power and authority in the world seemed to her empty things if they were bereft of this knowledge. The men about her might devote themselves to struggles for political power; but she dreamed of subduing the world by different means, by purely feminine means. Many of the women whom she had known had taken the tonsure and retired from the world. Such women struck her as laughable. For, whatever a woman may say about abandoning the world, it is almost impossible for her to give up the things that she possesses. Only men are really capable of giving up what they possess.

That old priest by the lake had at a certain stage in his life given up the Floating World and all its pleasures. In the eyes of the Imperial Concubine he was far more of a man than all the nobles whom she knew at court. And, just as he had once abandoned this present Floating World, so now on her behalf he was about to give up the future world as well.

The Imperial Concubine recalled the notion of the sacred lotus flower, which her own deep faith had vividly imprinted upon her mind. She thought of the huge lotus with its width of two hundred and fifty yojana. That preposterous plant was far more fitted to her tastes than those puny lotus flowers which floated on the ponds of the Capital. At night when she listened to the wind soughing through the trees in her garden, the sound seemed to her extremely insipid when compared to the delicate music in the Pure Land when the wind blew through the sacred treasure trees. When she thought of the strange instruments that hung in the sky and that played by themselves without ever being touched, the sound of the harp that echoed through the palace halls seemed to her a paltry imitation.

The Great Priest of Shiga Temple was fighting. In the fight that he had waged against the flesh in his youth he had always been buoyed up by the hope of inheriting the future world. But this desperate fight of his old age was linked with a sense of irreparable loss.

The impossibility of consummating his love for the Great Imperial Concubine was as clear to him as the sun in the sky. At the same time he was fully aware of the impossibility of advancing toward the Pure Land so long as he remained in thrall to this love. The Great Priest, who had lived in an incomparably free state of mind, had in a twinkling been enclosed in darkness, and the future was totally obscure. It may have been that the courage which had seen him through his youthful struggles had grown out of self-confidence and pride in the fact that he was voluntarily depriving himself of pleasure that could have been his for the asking.

The Great Priest once more possessed himself of fear. Until that noble carriage had approached the side of Lake Shiga, he had believed that what lay in wait for him, close at hand, was nothing less than the final release of Nirvana. But now he had awakened into the darkness of the present world, where it is impossible to see what lurks a single step ahead.

The various forms of religious meditation were all in vain. He tried the Contemplation of the Chrysanthemum, the Contemplation of the Total Aspect, and the Contemplation of the Parts; but each time he started to concentrate, the beautiful visage of the concubine appeared before his eyes. Water Contemplation, too, was useless, for invariably her lovely face would float up shimmering from beneath the ripples of the lake.

This, no doubt, was a natural consequence of his infatuation. Concentration, the priest soon realized, did more harm than good, and next he tried to dull his spirit by dispersal. It astonished him that spiritual concentration should have the paradoxical effect of leading him still deeper into his delusions; but he soon realized that to try the contrary method by dispersing his thoughts meant that he was, in effect, admitting these very delusions. As his spirit began to yield under the weight, the priest decided that, rather than pursue a futile struggle, it were better to escape from the effort of escaping by deliberately concentrating his thoughts on the figure of the Great Imperial Concubine.

The Great Priest found a new pleasure in adorning his vision of the lady in various ways, just as though he were adorning a Buddhist statue with diadems and baldachins. In so doing, he turned the object of his love into an increasingly resplendent, distant, impossible being; and this afforded him particular joy. But why? Surely it would be more natural for him to envisage the Great Imperial Concubine as an ordinary female, close at hand and possessing normal human frailties. Thus he could better turn her to advantage, at least in his imagination.

As he pondered this question, the truth dawned on him. What he was depicting in the Great Imperial Concubine was not a creature of flesh, nor was it a mere vision; rather, it was a symbol of reality, a symbol of the essence of things. It was strange, indeed, to pursue that essence in the figure of a woman. Yet the reason was not far to seek. Even when falling in love, the Great Priest of Shiga had not discarded the habit, to which he had trained himself during his long years of contemplation, of striving to approach the essence of things by means of constant abstraction. The Great Imperial Concubine of Kyōgoku had now become uniform with his vision of the immense lotus of two hundred and fifty yojana. As she reclined on the water supported by all the lotus flowers, she had become vaster than Mount Sumeru, vaster than an entire realm.

The more the Great Priest turned his love into something impossible, the more deeply was he betraying the Buddha. For the impossibility of this love had become bound up with the impossibility of attaining enlightenment. The more he thought of his love as hopeless, the firmer grew the fantasy that supported it and the deeper-rooted became his impure thoughts. So long as he regarded his love as being even remotely feasible, it was paradoxically possible for him to resign himself; but now that the Great Concubine had grown into a fabulous and utterly unattainable creature, the priest's love became motionless like a great, stagnant lake which firmly, obdurately covers the earth's surface.

He hoped that somehow he might see the lady's face once more, yet he feared that when he met her, that figure, which had now become like a giant lotus, would crumble away without a trace. If that were to happen, he would without doubt be saved. Yes, this time he was bound to attain enlightenment. And the very prospect filled the Great Priest with fear and awe.

The priest's lonely love had begun to devise strange, self-deceiving guiles, and when at length he reached the decision to go and see the lady, he was under the delusion that he had almost recovered from the illness that was searing his body. The bemused priest even mistook the joy that accompanied his decision for relief at having finally escaped from the trammels of his love.

None of the Great Concubine's people found anything especially strange in the sight of an old priest standing silently in the corner of the garden, leaning on a stick and gazing somberly at the residence. Ascetics and beggars frequently stood outside the great houses of the Capital and waited for alms. One of the ladies in attendance mentioned the matter to her mistress. The Great Imperial Concubine casually glanced through the blind that separated her from the garden. There in the shadow of the fresh green foliage stood a withered old priest with faded black robes and bowed head. For some time the lady looked at him. When she realized that this was without any question the priest whom she had seen by the lake at Shiga, her pale face turned paler still.

After a few moments of indecision, she gave orders that the priest's presence in her garden should be ignored. Her attendants bowed and withdrew.

Now for the first time the lady fell prey to uneasiness. In her lifetime she had seen many people who had abandoned the world, but never before had she laid eyes on someone who had abandoned the future world. The sight was ominous and inexpressibly fearful. All the pleasure that her imagination had conjured up from the idea of the priest's love disappeared in a flash. Much as he might have surrendered the future world on her behalf, that world, she now realized, would never pass into her own hands.

The Great Imperial Concubine looked down at her elegant clothes and at her beautiful hands, and then she looked across the garden at the uncomely features of the old priest and at his shabby robes. There was a horrible fascination in the fact that a connection should exist between them.

How different it all was from the splendid vision! The Great Priest seemed now like a person who had hobbled out of Hell itself. Nothing remained of that man of virtuous presence who had trailed the brightness of the Pure Land behind him. The brilliance which had resided within him and which had called to mind the glory of the Pure Land had vanished utterly. Though this was certainly the man who had stood by Shiga Lake, it was at the same time a totally different person.

Like most people of the court, the Great Imperial Concubine tended to be on her guard against her own emotions, especially when she was confronted with something that could be expected to affect her deeply. Now on seeing this evidence of the Great Priest's love, she felt disheartened at the thought that the consummate passion of which she had dreamed during all these years should assume so colorless a form.

When the priest had finally limped into the Capital leaning on his stick, he had almost forgotten his exhaustion. Secretly he made his way into the grounds of the Great Imperial Concubine's residence at Kyōgoku and looked across the garden. Behind those blinds, he thought, was sitting none other than the lady whom he loved.

Now that his adoration had assumed an immaculate form, the future world once again began to exert its charm on the Great Priest. Never before had he envisaged the Pure Land in so immaculate, so poignant an aspect. His yearning for it became almost sensual. Nothing remained for him but the formality of meeting the Great Concubine, of declaring his love, and of thus ridding himself once and for all of the impure thoughts that tied him to this world and prevented him from attaining the Pure Land. That was all that remained to be done.

It was painful for him to stand there supporting his old body on his stick. The bright rays of the May sun poured through the leaves and beat down on his shaven head. Time after time he felt himself losing consciousness, and without his stick he would certainly have collapsed. If only the lady would realize the situation and invite him into her presence, so that the formality might be over with! The Great

Priest waited. He waited and supported his ever-growing weariness on his stick. At length the sun was covered with the evening clouds. Dusk gathered. Yet still no word came from the Great Imperial Concubine.

She, of course, had no way of knowing that the priest was looking through her, beyond her, into the Pure Land. Time after time she glanced out through the blinds. He was standing there immobile. The evening light thrust its way into the garden. Still he continued standing there.

The Great Imperial Concubine became frightened. She felt that what she saw in the garden was an incarnation of that "deep-rooted delusion" of which she had read in the sutras. She was overcome by the fear of tumbling into Hell. Now that she had led astray a priest of such high virtue, it was not the Pure Land to which she could look forward, but Hell itself, whose terrors she and those about her knew in such detail. The supreme love of which she had dreamed had already been shattered. To be loved as she was — that in itself represented damnation. Whereas the Great Priest looked beyond her into the Pure Land, she now looked beyond the priest into the horrid realms of Hell.

Yet this haughty noblewoman of Kyōgoku was too proud to succumb to her fears without a fight, and she now summoned forth all the resources of her inbred ruthlessness. The Great Priest, she told herself, was bound to collapse sooner or later. She looked through the blind, thinking that by now he must be lying on the ground. To her annoyance, the silent figure stood there motionless.

Night fell and in the moonlight the figure of the priest looked like a pile of chalk-white bones.

The lady could not sleep for fear. She no longer looked through the blind and she turned her back to the garden. Yet all the time she seemed to feel the piercing gaze of the Great Priest on her back.

This, she knew, was no commonplace love. From fear of being loved, from fear of falling into Hell, the Great Imperial Concubine prayed more earnestly than ever for the Pure Land. It was for her own private Pure Land that she prayed — a Pure Land which she tried to preserve invulnerable within her heart. This was a different Pure Land from the priest's and it had no connection with his love. She felt sure that if she were ever to mention it to him, it would instantly disintegrate.

The priest's love, she told herself, had nothing to do with her. It was a one-sided affair, in which her own feelings had no part, and there was no reason that it should disqualify her from being received into her Pure Land. Even if the Great Priest were to collapse and die, she would remain unscathed. Yet, as the night advanced and the air became colder, this confidence began to desert her.

The priest remained standing in the garden. When the moon was hidden by the clouds, he looked like a strange, gnarled old tree.

"That form out there has nothing to do with me," thought the lady, almost beside herself with anguish, and the words seemed to boom within her heart. "Why in Heaven's name should this have happened?"

At that moment, strangely, the Great Imperial Concubine completely forgot her own beauty. Or perhaps it would be more correct to say that she had made herself forget it.

Finally, faint traces of white began to break through the dark sky and the priest's figure emerged in the dawn twilight. He was still standing. The Great Imperial Concubine had been defeated. She summoned a maid and told her to invite the priest to come in from the garden and to kneel outside her blind.

The Great Priest was at the very boundary of oblivion, when the flesh is on the verge of crumbling away. He no longer knew whether it was for the Great Imperial Concubine that he was waiting or for the future world. Though he saw the figure of the maid approaching from the residence into the dusky garden, it did not occur to him that what he had been awaiting was finally at hand.

The maid delivered her mistress's message. When she had finished, the priest uttered a dreadful, almost inhuman cry. The maid tried to lead him by the hand, but he pulled away and walked by himself toward the house with fantastically swift, firm steps.

It was dark on the other side of the blind and from outside it was impossible to see the lady's form. The priest knelt down and, covering his face with his hands, he wept. For a long time he stayed there without a word and his body shook convulsively.

Then in the dawn darkness a white hand gently emerged from behind the lowered blind. The priest of the Shiga Temple took it in his own hands and pressed it to his forehead and cheek.

The Great Imperial Concubine of Kyōgoku felt a strange, cold hand touching her hand. At the same time she was aware of a warm moisture. Her hand was being bedewed by someone else's tears. Yet when the pallid shafts of morning light began to reach her through the blind, the lady's fervent faith imbued her with a wonderful inspiration: she became convinced that the unknown hand which touched hers belonged to none other than the Buddha.

Then the great vision sprang up anew in the lady's heart: the emerald earth of the Pure Land, the millions of seven-jeweled towers, the angels playing music, the golden ponds strewn with silver sand, the resplendent lotus, and the sweet voices of the Kalavinkas — all this was born afresh. If this was the Pure Land that she was to inherit — and so she now believed — why should she not accept the Great Priest's love?

She waited for the man with the hands of Buddha to ask her to raise the blind that separated her from him. Presently he would ask her; and then she would remove the barrier and her incomparably beautiful body would appear before him as it had on that day by the edge of the lake at Shiga; and she would invite him to come in.

The Great Imperial Concubine waited.

But the priest of Shiga Temple did not utter a word. He asked her for nothing. After a while his old hands relaxed their grip and the lady's snow-white hand was left alone in the dawn light. The priest departed. The heart of the Great Imperial Concubine turned cold.

A few days later a rumor reached the court that the Great Priest's spirit had achieved its final liberation in his cell at Shiga. At this news the lady of Kyōgoku set to copying the sutras in roll after roll of beautiful writing.

Joyce Carol Oates

....

At the Seminary

M R. DOWNEY LEFT the expressway at the right exit, but ten minutes later he was lost. His wife was sitting in the back seat of the car, her round serious face made unfamiliar by the sunglasses she wore, and when he glanced at her in the rearview mirror she did not seem to acknowledge him. His daughter, a big girl in a yellow sleeveless dress, was bent over the map and tracing something with her finger. "Just what I thought, that turn back there," she said. "That one to the left, by the hot dog stand. I thought that was the turn."

His stomach was too upset; he could not argue. He did not argue with his daughter or his wife or his son Peter, though he could remember a time when he had argued with someone — his father, perhaps. His daughter, Sally, sat confidently beside him with her fingernail still poised against a tiny line on the map, as if she feared moving it would precipitate them into the wilderness. "Turn around, Daddy, for heaven's sake," she said. "You keep on driving way out of the way."

"Well, I didn't notice any sign," his wife said suddenly.

His daughter turned slowly. She too wore sunglasses, white plastic glasses with ornate frames and dark curved lenses. He could see her eyes close. "You weren't watching, then. I'm the one with the map anyway. I was pretty sure that was the turn, back there, but he went by too fast. I had to look it up on the map."

"Why didn't you say anything before?"

"I don't know." Sally shrugged her shoulders.

"Well, I didn't see any sign back there."

They had argued for the last hundred miles, off and on. Mr. Downey tried to shut out their voices, not looking at them, concentrating now on finding a place to turn the car around before his daughter complained again. They were on a narrow blacktop road in the country, with untended fields on either side. Mr. Downey slowed. "There's a big ditch out there," Sally said. She tapped at the window with her nails. "Be careful, Daddy."

"How much room does he have?"

"He's got — oh — some room yet — Keep on going, Daddy. Keep on — Wait. No, Daddy, wait."

He braked the car. He could tell by his daughter's stiff, alert back that they had nearly gone into the ditch. "Okay, Daddy, great. Now pull ahead." Sally began waving her hand toward him, her pink fingernails glistening roguishly. "Pull ahead, Daddy, that's it. That's it."

He had managed to turn around. Now the sun was slanted before them again; they had been driving into it all day. "How far back was that road?" he said.

"Oh, a few miles, Daddy. No trouble."

They arrived at the crossroads. "See, there's the sign. There it is," Sally said. She was quite excited. Though she had been overweight by twenty or twenty-five pounds for years, she often bounced about to demonstrate her childish pleasure; she did so now. "See, what did I tell you? Mom? There it is, there's the sign. U.S. 274, going east, and there's the hot dog stand."

"It's closed."

"Yes, it's closed, I can see that, it's boarded up but it's there," Sally said. She had turned slightly to face her mother, the pink flesh creasing along her neck, her eyes again shut in patient exasperation.

They drove east on 274. "It's only thirty more miles," Sally said. "Can I turn on the radio now?" Immediately she snapped it on. In a moment they heard a voice accompanied by guitars and drums. The music made Mr. Downey's stomach cringe. He drove on, his eyes searching the top of the next ridge, as if he expected to see the handsome buildings of the seminary beckoning to him, assuring him. His wife threw down a magazine in the back seat. "Sally, please turn that off. That's too loud. You know you're only pretending to like it and it's giving your father a headache."

"Is it?" Sally said in his ear.

"It's too loud. Turn it off," his wife said.

"Daddy, is it?"

He began to shake his head, began to nod it, said he didn't know. "This business about Pete," he said apologetically.

Sally paused. Then she snapped off the radio briskly. She seemed to throw herself back against the seat, her arms folded so tightly that the thick flesh of her upper arm began to drain white. They drove for a while in silence. "Well, all right, turn it on," Mr. Downey said. He glanced at Sally, who refused to move. She was twenty-three, not what anyone would call fat, yet noticeably plump, her cheeks rounded and generous. Behind the dark glasses her eyes were glittering, threatened by stubborn tears. She wore a bright yellow cotton dress that strained about her, the color made fierce by the sun, as if it would be hot to the touch. "You can turn it on, Sally," Mr. Downey said. "I don't care."

"It gives you a headache," his wife said. She had thrown down the magazine again. "Why do you always give in to her?"

Sally snorted.

"She doesn't care about Peter!" his wife cried. Her anguish was sudden and unfeigned; both Mr. Downey and Sally stiffened. They looked ahead at the signs — advertisements for hotels, motels, service stations, restaurants. "Got to find a motel for tonight," Sally muttered.

"She doesn't care, neither of you cares," Mr. Downey's wife went on. "The burden always falls on me. He wrote the letter to me, I was the one who had to open it —"

"Daddy got a letter too. He got one right after," Sally said sullenly.

"But Peter wrote to me first. He understood."

"He always was a mommy's boy!"

"I don't want to hear that. I never want to hear that."

"Nevertheless," said Sally.

"I said I don't want to hear that again. Ever."

"Okay, you won't. Don't get excited."

Mr. Downey pulled off the road suddenly. He stopped the car and sat with his head bowed; other automobiles rushed past. "I won't be able to go on," he said. "Not if you keep this up."

Embarrassed, wife and daughter said nothing. They stared at nothing. Sally, after a moment, rubbed her nose with her fist. She felt her jaw clench as it did sometimes at night, while she slept, as if she were biting down hard upon something ugly but could not let go. Outside, in a wild field, was a gigantic billboard advertising a motel. From a great height a woman in a red bathing suit was diving into a bright aqua swimming pool. Mrs. Downey, taking her rosary out of her purse, stared out at this sign also, felt her daughter staring at it, thought what her daughter thought. In the awkward silence they felt closer to each other than either did to Mr. Downey. They said nothing, proudly. After a while, getting no answer, Mr. Downey started the car again and drove on.

The drive up to the seminary was made of blacktop, very smart and precise, turning gently about the hill, back and forth amid cascades of evergreens and nameless trees with rich foliage. It was early September, warm and muggy. The seminary buildings looked sleek and cool. Mr. Downey had the feeling that he could not possibly be going to see anyone he knew or had known, that this trip was a mystery, that the young man who awaited him, related obscurely to him by ties of blood and name, was a mystery that exhausted rather than interested him. Mr. Downey had been no more worried by his wife's hopes that Peter would become a priest than he had by her hopes that Sally would enter a convent; he had supposed both possibilities equally absurd. Yet, now that Peter had made his decision, now that Mr. Downey had grown accustomed to thinking of him in the way one thinks of a child who is somehow maimed and disqualified for life and therefore deserving of love, he felt as disturbed as his wife by Peter's letters. His son's "problem" could not be named, evidently; Peter himself did not understand it, could not explain it: he spoke of "wearing out," of "losing control," of seeing no one in the mirror when he went to look at himself. He complained of grit in his room, of hairs in food, of ballpoint ink he could not wash off his hands. Nothing that made sense. He spoke of not being able to remember his *name,* and this had disturbed Mr. Downey most of all; the hairs reported in his food had disturbed Mrs. Downey most of all. Nowhere had the boy said anything of quitting, however, and they thought that puzzling. If he had spoken in his incoherent letters of wanting to quit, of going to college, of traveling about the country to observe "life," of doing nothing at all, Mr. Downey would not have felt so frightened. He could not parrot, as his wife did, the words of the novice master who had telephoned them that week: Peter was suffering a "spiritual crisis." It was the fact that Peter had suggested no alternatives to his condition that alarmed his father. It might almost have been — and Mr. Downey had not mentioned this to his wife — that the alternative to the religious life had come to Peter to be no less than death.

God knew, Mr. Downey thought, he had wanted something else for Peter. He had wanted something else for them all, but he could not recall what it was. He blamed Peter's condition on his wife; at least Sally had escaped her mother's influence, there was nothing wrong with her. She was a healthy girl, loud and sure of herself, always her father's favorite. But perhaps behind her quick robust laugh there was the same sniveling sensitivity that had ruined Peter's young life for him. Sally had played boisterously with other girls and boys in the neighborhood, a leader in their games, running heavily about the house and through the bushes, while Peter had withdrawn to his solitary occupations, arranging and rearranging dead birds and butterflies in the backyard; but in the end, going up to bed, their slippers scuffing on the floor and their shoulders set as if resigned to the familiar terrors of the night, they had always seemed to Mr. Downey to be truly sister and brother, and related in no way to himself and his wife.

The seminary buildings were only three years old. Magnificently modern, aqua and beige, with great flights of glass and beds of complex plants on both the outside and the inside, huddling together against glass partitions so that the eye, dazed, could not tell where the outside stopped and the inside began: Mr. Downey felt uncertain and overwhelmed. He had not thought convincing the rector's speech, given on the day they had brought Peter up here, about the middle-class temperament that would relegate all religious matters to older forms, forms safely out-of-date. The rector had spoken passionately of the beauty of contemporary art and its stark contrast with the forms of nature, something Mr. Downey had not understood; nor had he understood what religion had to do with beauty or with art; nor had he understood how the buildings could have cost five million dollars. "Boy, is this place something," Sally said resentfully. "He's nuts if he wants to leave it and come back *home.*" "He never said anything about leaving it," her mother said sharply.

They were met by Father Greer, with whom they had talked on the telephone earlier that week and who, standing alone on the evergreen-edged flagstone walk, seemed by his excessive calmness to be obscuring from them the fact of Peter's not being there. He was dark and smiling, taller than Mr. Downey and many years younger. "So very glad to see you," he said. "I hope you had an enjoyable ride? Peter is expected down at any moment." Very enjoyable, they assured him. Sally stood behind her father, as if suddenly shy. Mrs. Downey was touching her hair and nodding anxiously at Father Greer's words. In an awkward group they headed toward the entrance. Mr. Downey was smiling but as the young priest spoke, pointing out buildings and interesting sights, his eyes jumped about as if seeking out his son, expecting him to emerge around the corner of a building, out of an evergreen shrub. "The dormitory," Father Greer said, pointing. A building constructed into a hill, its first story disappearing into a riot of shrubs, much gleaming glass and metal. Beside it was the chapel, with a great brilliant cross that caught the sunlight and reflected it viciously. The light from the buildings, reflected and refracted by their thick glass, blinded Mr. Downey to whatever lay behind them — hills and forests and remote horizons. "No, we don't regret for an instant our having built out here," Father Greer was saying. They were in the lobby now. Mr. Downey looked around for Peter but saw no one. "They told us in the city that we'd go mad out here, but that was just jealousy. This is the ideal location for a college like ours. Absolutely ideal." They agreed. Mr. Downey could not recall just when he had noticed that some priests were younger than he, but he remembered a time when all priests were older, were truly "fathers" to him. "Please sit down here," Father Greer said. "This is a very comfortable spot." He too was looking about. Mr. Downey believed he could see, beyond the priest's cautious diplomatic charm, an expression of irritation. They were in an area blocked off from the rest of the lobby by thick plates of aqua-tinted glass. Great potted plants stood about in stone vases, the floor was tiled in a design of deep maroon and gray, the long low sofa on which they sat curved about a round marble coffee table of a most coldly beautiful, veined, fleshly color. Father Greer did not sit, but stood with his hands slightly extended and raised, as if he were blessing them against his will. "Will you all take martinis?" he said. They smiled self-consciously; Mrs. Downey said that Sally did not drink. "I'll take a martini," Sally said without looking up. Father Greer smiled.

Someone approached them, but it was not Peter. A boy Peter's age, dressed in a novice's outfit but wearing a white apron over it, came shyly to take their orders from Father Greer. "Peter will be down in a minute," Father Greer said. "Then we can all relax and talk and see what has developed. And we'll be having dinner precisely at six-thirty, I hope, in a very pleasant room at the back of this building — a kind of fireside room we use for special banquets and meetings. You didn't see it the last time you were here because it's just been completed this summer. If anyone would like to wash up —" He indicated graciously restrooms at the far end of the area, GENTLEMEN, LADIES. Mrs. Downey stood, fingering her purse; Sally said crudely, "I'm all right." She had not taken off her sunglasses. Mrs. Downey left; they could smell the faint pleasant odor of her cologne. "He said he would be down promptly," Father Greer said in a slightly different voice, a confidential voice directed toward Mr. Downey, "but he may have forgotten. That's one of the — you know — one of the problems he has been having — he tends to forget things unless he writes them down. We discussed it Tuesday evening." "Yes, yes," Mr. Downey said, reddening. "He was never like that — at home —" "His mind seems somewhere else. He seems lost in contemplation — in another world," Father Greer said, not unkindly. "Sometimes this is a magnificent thing, you know, sometimes it develops into a higher, keener consciousness of one's vocation . . . Sometimes it's greatly to be desired." He made Peter sound mysterious and talented, in a way, so that Sally found herself looking forward to meeting him. "If you'll excuse me for just a minute," Father Greer said, "I think I'll run over to his room and see how he is. Please excuse me —"

Sally and her father, left alone, had nothing to say to each other. Sally peered over the rims of her glasses at the lobby, but did not take the glasses off. She felt hot, heavy, vaguely sick, a little frightened; but at the thought of being frightened of something so trivial as seeing Peter again her mouth twisted into a smirk. She knew him too well. She knew him better than anyone knew him, and therefore resented the gravity with which he was always discussed, while her "problems" (whatever they were; she knew she was supposed to have some) were discussed by her mother and aunts as if they were immortal, immutable, impersonal problems like death and poverty, unfortunate conditions no one could change, and not very interesting.

Her mother returned, her shoulders bent forward anxiously as if she were straining ahead. "Where did he go?" she said, gazing from Mr. Downey to Sally. "Nothing happened, did it?" "He'll be right back," Sally said. "Sit down. Stop worrying." Her mother sat slowly; Sally could see the little white knobs of vertebrae at the top of her neck, curiously fragile. When the novice returned he was carrying a tray of cocktails. Another boy in an identical outfit appeared with a tray of shrimp and sauce and tiny golden crackers, which he set down on the marble table. Both young men were modest and shy, like magicians appearing and disappearing. "Suppose we better wait," Mr. Downey said regretfully, looking at the drinks.

But when Peter did arrive, with Father Greer just behind him, they were disappointed. He looked the same: a little pale, perhaps thinner, but his complexion seemed blemished in approximately the same way it had been for years, his shoulders were inclined forward, just like his mother's, so that he looked anxious and hungry, like a chicken searching in the dirt. There were agreeable murmurs of surprise and welcome. Peter shook hands with his father, allowed his mother to hug him, and nodded to Sally with the self-conscious look he always directed toward her. He was a tall, eager boy with a rather narrow, bony face, given to blinking excessively but also to smiling very easily and agreeably, so that most people liked him at once though they did not feel quite at ease with him. In his novice's dress he took the light angularly and harshly, as if he were in strident mourning. And what could be the matter with him, Sally thought enviously, what secrets did he have, what problems that would endear him all the more to their parents? "Here, do have some of this. This looks delicious," Father Greer said, passing the tray of shrimp and crackers around. Sally's mouth watered violently, in spite of herself; she indicated with an abrupt wave of her hand that she did not want any. "Here, Peter, you always loved shrimp, every Friday we had to have shrimp," Mrs. Downey said in a trembling voice. She held the tray out to Peter, who had sat beside her. He hesitated, staring at the shrimp. "The sauce smells so good —" Mrs. Downey said coaxingly. At last Peter's arm moved. He picked up a toothpick and impaled a shrimp upon it; as they all watched, he dipped it into the sauce. Everyone sighed slightly. They settled back and crossed their legs.

They began to talk. Of the weather, first, and of the drive. The good and bad points of the expressway. Of all expressways, of encroaching civilization and the destruction of nature, yet at the same time the brilliant steps forward in the conquering of malignant nature. Peter chewed at the shrimp, Sally saw, but did not seem to have swallowed it. Talk fluttered about his head; now and then he glanced up, smiled, and replied. Sally, finding no one watching her, began to eat shrimp and could not stop. The more she ate, the more angry she felt at the people before her and at the boys who had served the drinks and food and at the seminary itself. She could feel her face freezing into that expression of disdain she hated in her mother but could not help in herself: so she faced everything she disapproved of, flighty vain girls no older than she in fur coats and glittering jewelry, young men in expensive sports cars, gossiping old ladies, old men who drank, young mothers who were obviously so proud and pleased with their lives they would just as soon spit in your eye when you passed them on the sidewalk, pushing baby buggies along as if that were a noble task! Sally did not approve of people talking in church or looking around, craning their bony old necks, nor did she approve of children — any children — who were noisy and restless and were apt to ask you why you were so fat, in front of everyone; she did not approve of people photographed on society pages or on magazine covers, or houses that were not made of brick or stone but were in poor neighborhoods with scrawny front lawns, but also she did not approve of lower-class white people who hated Negroes, as if they were any better themselves. She did not approve of high school boys and girls who swung along the sidewalks with their arms around each other, laughing vulgarly, and she did not approve of college students who did the same thing. While at college she had been so isolated by the sternness of her disapproval that no roommate had suited her and she had finally moved to a single room, where she had stayed for four years, studying angrily so that she could get good grades (which she did) and eating cookies and cakes and pies her mother sent her every week. She had loved her mother then and knew her mother loved her, since they never saw each other, but now that she was home and waiting for the placement bureau to send her notice of a decent job, something they evidently were not capable of doing, she and her mother hardly spoke and could feel each other's presence in the house as one feels or suspects the presence of an insect nearby. Her mother had wanted her to be pretty, she thought, and deliberately she was not pretty. (And Peter, there, still chewing, was homely too, she had never really noticed that before.) Sometimes she went to bed without washing her face. Certainly she did not wash her hair more than once a week, no matter what was coming up; and she had pretended severely not to care when her mother appropriated for herself the expensive lavender dress she had worn to the important functions at college when she had been twenty or thirty pounds lighter. She wore no makeup except lipstick, a girlish pink, and her shoes were always scuffed and marked by water lines, and she often deliberately bought dresses too large so the shoulders hung down sloppily. Everything angered her: the vanities of the world, the pettiness of most people, the banal luxuries she saw through at once — like this seminary, and the cocktails, when their own priest back home had new missions every week or new approaches to the Bishop's Relief Fund. She picked up the martini and sipped at it; its bitterness angered her. She put it down. She would not drink it and collaborate in this vanity. Even the graceful gleaming glass, finely shaped like a work of art, annoyed her, for beside it her own stumpy fingers and uneven nails looked ugly. What place was there in the real world for such things? She felt the real world to be elsewhere — she did not know where — in the little town they had passed through on the way up to the seminary, perhaps, where the ugly storefronts faced each other across a cobbled main street fifty years old, and where country people dawdled about in new shoes and new clothes, dressed for Saturday, looking on everything with admiration and pleasure. But what were these people talking about? She hunched forward in an exaggerated attitude of listening. Baseball. She was ashamed of her father, who spoke of baseball players familiarly, slowly, choosing his words as if each were important, so making a fool of himself. Father Greer, debonair and charming, was bored of course but would not show it. Mrs. Downey looked puzzled, as if she could not quite keep up with the conversation; the martini had made her dizzy. Peter, beside her, his awkward hands crossed on his knees, stared at something in the air. He was waiting, as they were all waiting, Sally supposed, for this conversation to veer suddenly around to him, confront him in his odd transfixed fear and demand from him some explanation of himself. Sally sipped at the cocktail and felt its bitterness expand to take in all of the scene before her. If Peter glanced at her she would look away; she would not help him. She needed no one herself, and wanted no one to need her. Yet she wondered why he did not look at her — why he sat so stiff, as if frozen, while about him chatter shot this way and that to ricochet harmlessly off surfaces.

The subject had been changed. "Peter made some particularly perceptive remarks on the *Antigone* of Sophocles this summer," Father Greer was saying. He had finished his martini and rolled the glass slowly between his palms, the delicate stem turning and glinting against his tanned skin. "We study a number of Greek tragedies in the original Greek. The boys find them strangely intriguing. Puzzles." Mr.

and Mrs. Downey were both sitting forward a little, listening. "The worldview of the Greeks," Father Greer said severely, "is so astonishingly different from our own." Sally drew in her breath suddenly. "I wouldn't say that, precisely," she remarked. Father Greer smiled at her. "Of course there are many aspects of our civilizations that are similar," he said. "What strikes us as most barbaric, however, is their utter denial of the freedom of man's will." He thought her no antagonist, obviously; he spoke with a faintly condescending smile Sally detested because she believed she had been seeing it all her life. "But that might not be so strange, after all," she drawled. Her mother was frowning, picking at something imaginary on the rim of her cocktail glass. Her father was watching her as if she were performing a foolish and dangerous trick, like standing on her head. But Peter, sitting across from her with his long fingers clasped together on his knees, his back not touching the sofa, was staring at her and through her with a queer theatrical look of recognition, as if he had not really noticed her before. "And their violence," Sally said. "The violence of their lives — that might not be so strange to us either." "There is no violence in Greek drama," Father Greer said. Sally felt her face close up, suddenly. Her eyes began to narrow; her lips pursed themselves in a prim little book of defiance; the very contours of her generous face began to hunch themselves inward.

An awkward minute passed. "You still on that diet?" Peter said.

Sally's eyes opened. Peter was looking at her with a little smile. Her face burned. "What? Me? I —"

"Why, Peter," their mother said. "What do you mean?"

Peter's gaze plummeted. He examined his fingers. Sally, more stunned than angry, watched him as if he had become suddenly an antagonist, an open enemy; she saw that his hands were streaked with something — it looked like red ink or blood, something scrubbed into his skin.

"Sorry," Peter muttered.

In this crisis Father Greer seemed to fall back; his spine might have failed him unaccountably. The very light turned harsh and queer; churned about gently in the air-conditioned lounge, it seemed not to be illuminating them but to be pushing them away from each other, emphasizing certain details that were not to be cherished: Peter's acne, Mrs. Downey's tiny double chin and the network of fine wrinkles that seemed to hold together her expression, Mr. Downey's sluggish mouth, drooping as if under the impact of a sudden invisible blow, even the surface gloss of Father Greer's professional charm dented by a dull embarrassed gleam at the tip of his nose. And Sally was glad of being fat and unattractive, with a greasy nose, coarse skin, a dress stained with perspiration, glad she could delight no one's eyes, fulfill no one's expectations of her —

"I don't believe you've seen our chapel," Father Greer said. He made a tentative movement that was not really tentative but commanding; Sally saw how Peter's shoulders and arms jerked up, mimicking the priest, before he himself had decided to stand. They all stood, smoothing their clothing, smiling down at the martini glasses and what was left of the shrimp and crackers, as if bidding good-bye to acquaintances newly made. "It's very beautiful, we commissioned the Polish architect Radomski to design it for us — the same Radomski who did the campus at St. Aquinas University — you might remember the pictures in *Life?*"

They agreed vaguely, moving along. Father Greer seemed to be herding them. Sally, at the rear, caught a glimpse of the young priest's face, as he turned, and was startled by the blunt, naked intensity of his concern — an instant's expression of annoyance, alarm, helplessness that immediately faded — and what an attractive man he was, in spite of his deep-set eyes, she thought, what a pity — a pity — But she did not know what the pity was for. Out of spite she kept her martini glass in hand; it was still half full. She wandered at the back of the small group, looking around, squinting through her dark glasses. Several young priests passed them, nodding hello. They walked on. The building smelled like nothing, absolutely nothing. It did not even have the bitter antiseptic smell of soap. Nothing had an odor, nothing was out of place, nothing disturbed the range of the eye: the building and its people might not yet have been born, might be awaiting birth and baptism, immersion in smells and disorder. On the broad flagstone walk to the chapel Sally walked with the martini glass extended as if it were a symbol of some kind, an offering she carried to the chapel under the secret gazes of all those secret boys, cloistered there in that faceless building.

In the chapel they fell silent. Sally frowned. She was going to take off her sunglasses, but stopped. The chapel was gigantic: a ceiling dull and remote as the sky itself, finely lined, veined as if with the chill of distance or time, luring the eye up and forward, relentlessly forward, to the great statue of the crucified Christ behind the altar. There it was. The walls of the buildings might have fallen away, the veneer of words themselves might have been peeled back, to reveal this agonized body nailed to the cross: the contours of the statue so glib, so perfect, that they seemed to Sally to be but the mocking surfaces of another statue, a fossilized creature caught forever within that crust — the human model for it, suffocated and buried. Father Greer chatted excitedly about something: about that sleek white Christ, a perfect immaculate white, the veins of his feet and throat throbbing a frozen immaculate white. About his head drops of white blood had coagulated over the centuries; a hard white crown of thorns pierced his skin lovingly, rendered by art into something fragile and fine. The chapel was empty. No, not empty; at the very front a figure knelt, praying. The air was cold and stagnant. Nothing swirled here; time itself had run out, run down. Sally felt perspiration on her forehead and under her arms. She had begun to ache strangely, her head and her body; she could not locate the dull throbbing pain. Her head craning stupidly, she stared up at the gigantic statue. Yes, yes, she would agree to Father Greer's questioning glance: was it not magnificent? Yes, but what was it that was magnificent? What did they know? What were they looking at? How did they know — and she thought of this for no reason, absolutely no reason — what their names were, their stupid names? How did they know anything? Her glance fell in confusion to her parents' nervous smiles and she felt she did not recognize them. And to Peter's awkward profile, so self-pitying; was it to tell them he could no longer believe in Christ that he had brought them to the seminary? But she understood, staring at her brother's rigid face, that he could no more not believe in Christ than she could: that the great milky statue itself could more easily twitch into life than they could disbelieve the ghostly contours that lay behind that form, lost in history — and that they were doomed, brother and sister, doomed in some obscure inexplicable vexing way neither could understand, and their parents and this priest, whispering rather loudly about "seating capacity," could never understand. The three adults walked toward the front of the chapel, down the side aisle. Peter stumbled as if a rock had rolled suddenly before his feet; Sally could not move. She stared up at the statue with the martini glass in her hand. She and Peter might have been awaiting a vision, patiently as always. Yet it will only end, she thought savagely, in steak for dinner — a delicate tossed salad — wine — And as her body flinched in outrage at this vision (so powerful as to have evoked in her a rush of hunger, in spite of herself) she felt a sudden release of pressure, a gentle aching relaxation she did not at first recognize. A minute flow of blood. She did not move, paralyzed, her mouth slowly opening in an expression of awe that might have been religious, so total and commanding was it. Her entire life, her being, her very soul might have been conjured up and superimposed upon that rigid white statue, so intensely did she stare at it, her horror transformed into a prayer of utter silence, utter wordlessness, as she felt the unmistakable relentless flow of blood begin in her loins. Then her face went slack. She looked at the martini glass, brought it to her mouth, finished the drink. She smirked. She had known this would happen, had thought of it the day before, then had forgotten. She had forgotten. She could not have forgotten but she did, and it was for this reason she grinned at the smudged glass in her hand. Now Peter turned and followed the others; she followed him. Bleeding warmly and secretly. Her gaze was hot upon the backs of her parents, her mother especially, cleanly odored well-dressed woman: what a surprise! What a surprise she had for her! "I'm afraid this is cloistered," Father Greer whispered. He looked sorry. They headed in another direction, through a broad passageway, then out, out and into a spacious foyer; now they could breathe.

"What beauty! Immeasurable beauty!" Father Greer said aloud. His eyes were brittle with awe, an awe perhaps forced from him; he looked quite moved. Yet what was he moved at, Sally thought angrily, what had they been looking at, what did they *know?* Peter wiped at his nose, surreptitiously, but of course everyone saw him. What did they know? What had they seen? What might they ever trust again in a world of closed surfaces, of panels just sliding shut? She was shaken, and only after a moment did she notice her mother glaring at her, at the cocktail glass and the sunglasses. Her mother's face was white and handsome with the splendor of her hatred. Sally smirked. She felt the faithful blood inside her seeping, easing downward. Father Greer pointed out something further — someone agreed — she felt the hot blood on her legs. She was paralyzed, charmed. The others walked on but she did not move. Her mother glanced around. "Sally?" she said. Sally took a step, precariously. Nothing. Perhaps she would be safe. She caught her mother's gaze and held it, as if seeking help, hoping for her mother to draw her safely to her by the sheer force of her impatience. Then, for no reason, she took a hard, brutal step forward, bringing her flat heel down hard on the floor. Then again. She strode forward, brusquely, as if trying to dent the marble floor. The others were waiting for her, not especially watching her. She slammed down her heel so that it stung, and the blood jerked free. It ran instantly down the inside of her leg to her foot. She was breathing hard, excited and terrified and somehow pleased, waiting for her mother to notice. Why didn't she notice? Sally glanced down, was startled to see how big her stomach was, billowing out in the babyish yellow dress she had worn here out of spite, and saw the delicate trickle of blood there — on her calf, her ankle (which was not too clean), inside her scuffed shoe and so out of sight! At the door the others waited: the slim priest in black, who could see everything and nothing, politely, omnipotently; her father and mother, strangers also, who would see and suffer their vision as it swelled deafeningly upon them, their absolute disbelief at what they saw; her brother Peter, who was staring down at the floor just before her robust feet as if he had seen something that had turned him to stone.

Sally smiled angrily. She faced her mother, her father. Nothing. They looked away, they did not look at each other. Father Greer was holding the door open. No one spoke. Sally wanted to say, "That sure must have cost a lot!" but she could not speak. She saw Father Greer's legs hold themselves in stride, she could nearly see his muscles resist the desperate ache they felt to carry him somewhere — the end of this corridor, through one of the mysterious doors, or back to the cloistered sanctuary behind them. "And these, these," he said, "these are tiny chapels — all along here — Down there the main sacristy —" His words fell upon them from a distance, entirely without emotion. He showed nothing. Sally stomped on the floor as if killing insects, yet he did not look around. She felt blood trickling down her legs, a sensation she thought somehow quite pleasant, and in her shoes her toes wriggled in anticipation of the shame soon to befall them. On they walked. At each of Father Greer's words they leaned forward, anxious not to be denied, anxious to catch his eye, force upon him the knowledge that they saw nothing, knew nothing, heard only what he told them. Sally began to giggle. She wanted to ask Father Greer something, but the rigidity of her hysteria was too inflexible; she found she could not open her mouth. Her jaws seemed locked together. But this isn't my fault, she cried mockingly to their incredulous accusing backs, I never asked for it, I never asked God to make me a woman! She could not stop grinning. What beauty! What immeasurable beauty! It was that she grinned at, nothing else. That immeasurable beauty. Each heavy step, each ponderous straining of her thick thighs, centuries old, each sigh that swelled up into her chest and throat, each shy glance from her brother, all these faded into a sensation of over-whelming light or sound, something dazzling and roaring at once, that seemed to her to make her existence suddenly beautiful: com-plete: ended.

Then Peter was upon her. He grabbed for her throat. His face was anguished, she was able to see that much, and as she screamed and lunged back against the wall her parents and the priest turned, whirled back, seemed for an instant to be attacking her as well. "Damn you! Damn you!" Peter cried. His voice rose to a scream, a girl's scream. He managed to break away from Father Greer's arms and struck her, his fists pounding, a child's battle Sally seemed to be watching from across the corridor, through a door, across a span of years — "Damn you! Now I can't leave! I can't leave!" he cried. They pulled him back. He had gone limp. He hid his face and sobbed; she remembered him sobbing that way, often. Of course. His habitual sob, sheer helpless-ness before her strength, her superior age, weight, complacency. She gasped, her body still shuddering in alarm, ready to fight, to kill, her strong competent legs spread apart to give her balance. Her heart pounded like a magnificent angel demanding to be released, to be set upon her enemies. Peter turned away, into the priest's embrace, still sobbing. He showed nothing of his face but a patch by his jaw, a splotched patch of adolescent skin.

Mr. Downey entered the expressway without slackening speed. It was late, nearly midnight. He had far to go. Fortified by alcohol, dizzily confident, he seemed to be driving into a wild darkness made familiar by concrete, signs, maps, and his own skillful driving. Beside him his daughter sat with the map in hand again, but they would not need it. He knew where he was driving them. The expressway was deserted, held no challenge to him, the sheer depthless dark beyond the range of his headlights could not touch him, fortified as he was by the knowledge of precisely where he was going. Signs, illuminated by his headlights, flashed up clearly and were gone, they were unmistakable, they would not betray him, just as visions of that evening flashed up to him, without terror, and were gone. They knew what to do. None of this surprised them. Nothing surprised them. (He thought of the confessional; that explained it.) A few weeks of rest, nothing more, the boy would be safe, there was nothing to worry about. And he felt, numbly, that there really was nothing to worry about any longer, that everything had been somehow decided, that it had happened in his presence but he had not quite seen it. The priests were right: Father Greer and the older priest, a very kindly Irishman Mr. Downey had trusted at once. Something had been decided, delivered over. It was all right. In the back seat his wife sat impassive and mindless, watching the road that led inexorably back home. Beside him his daughter sat heavily, her arms folded. She yawned. Then she reached out casually to turn on the radio. "Please, Sally," her mother said at once, as if stirred to life. The radio clicked on. Static, a man's voice. Music. "Sally," her mother said. Sally's plump arm waited, her fingers still on the knob. "It bothers your father," Mrs. Downey said, "you know it gives him a headache." "I'll turn it down real low," Sally said. Out of the corner of Mr. Downey's eye her face loomed blank and milky, like a threatening moon he dared not look upon.

Edna O'Brien

....

Sister Imelda

SISTER IMELDA did not take classes on her first day back in the convent but we spotted her in the grounds after the evening rosary. Excitement and curiosity impelled us to follow her and try to see what she looked like, but she thwarted us by walking with head bent and eyelids down. All we could be certain of was that she was tall and limber and that she prayed while she walked. No looking at nature for her, or no curiosity about seventy boarders in gabardine coats and black shoes and stockings. We might just as well have been crows, so impervious was she to our stares and to abortive attempts at trying to say, "Hello, Sister."

We had returned from our long summer holiday and we were all wretched. The convent, with its high stone wall and green iron gates enfolding us again, seemed more of a prison than ever — for after our spell in the outside world we all felt very much older and more sophisticated, and my friend Baba and I were dreaming of our final escape, which would be in a year. And so, on that damp autumn evening when I saw the chrysanthemums and saw the new nun intent on prayer I pitied her and thought how alone she must be, cut off from her friends and conversation, with only God as her intangible spouse.

The next day she came into our classroom to take geometry. Her pale, slightly long face I saw as formidable, but her eyes were different, being blue-black and full of verve. Her lips were very purple, as if she had put puce pencil on them. They were the lips of a woman who might sing in a cabaret, and unconsciously she had formed the habit of turning them inward, as if she, too, was aware of their provocativeness. She had spent the last four years — the same span that Baba and

I had spent in the convent — at the university in Dublin, where she studied languages. We couldn't understand how she had resisted the temptations of the hectic world and willingly come back to this. Her spell in the outside world made her different from the other nuns; there was more bounce in her walk, more excitement in the way she tackled teaching, reminding us that it was the most important thing in the world as she uttered the phrase "Praise be the Incarnate World." She began each day's class by reading from Cardinal Newman, who was a favorite of hers. She read how God dwelt in light unapproachable, and how with Him there was neither change nor shadow of alteration. It was amazing how her looks changed. Some days, when her eyes were flashing, she looked almost profane and made me wonder what events inside the precincts of the convent caused her to be suddenly so excited. She might have been a girl going to a dance, except for her habit.

"Hasn't she wonderful eyes," I said to Baba. That particular day they were like blackberries, large and soft and shiny.

"Something wrong in her upstairs department," Baba said, and added that with makeup Imelda would be a cinch.

"Still, she has a vocation!" I said, and even aired the idiotic view that I might have one. At certain moments it did seem enticing to become a nun, to lead a life unspotted by sin, never to have to have babies, and to wear a ring that singled one out as the Bride of Christ. But there was the other side to it, the silence, the gravity of it, having to get up two or three times a night to pray and, above all, never having the opportunity of leaving the confines of the place except for the funeral of one's parents. For us boarders it was torture, but for the nuns it was nothing short of doom. Also, we could complain to each other, and we did, food being the source of the greatest grumbles. Lunch was either bacon and cabbage or a peculiar stringy meat followed by tapioca pudding; tea consisted of bread dolloped with lard and occasionally, as a treat, fairly green rhubarb jam, which did not have enough sugar. Through the long curtainless windows we saw the conifer trees and a sky that was scarcely ever without the promise of rain or a downpour.

She was a right lunatic, then, Baba said, having gone to university for four years and willingly come back to incarceration, to poverty, chastity, and obedience. We concocted scenes of agony in some Dublin hostel, while a boy, or even a young man, stood beneath her bed-

room window throwing up chunks of clay or whistles or a supplica-
tion. In our version of it he was slightly older than her, and possibly a
medical student, since medical students had a knack with women, because of studying diagrams and skeletons. His advances, like those of
a sudden storm, would intermittently rise and overwhelm her, and the
memory of these sudden flaying advances of his would haunt her until she died, and if ever she contracted fever, these secrets would out. It
was also rumored that she possessed a fierce temper and that, while a
postulant, she had hit a girl so badly with her leather strap that the girl
had to be put to bed because of wounds. Yet another black mark
against Sister Imelda was that her brother Ambrose had been sued by
a nurse for breach of promise.

That first morning when she came into our classroom and modestly
introduced herself, I had no idea how terribly she would infiltrate my
life, how in time she would be not just one of those teachers or nuns
but rather a special one, almost like a ghost who passed the boundaries of common exchange and who crept inside one, devouring so
much of one's thoughts, so much of one's passion, invading the place
that was called one's heart. She talked in a low voice, as if she did not
want her words to go beyond the bounds of the wall, and constantly
she stressed the value of work both to enlarge the mind and to discipline the thought. One of her eyelids was red and swollen, as if she
was getting a sty. I reckoned that she overmortified herself by not eating at all. I saw in her some terrible premonition of sacrifice which I
would have to emulate. Then, in direct contrast, she absently held the
stick of chalk between her first and second fingers, the very same as if
it were a cigarette, and Baba whispered to me that she might have
been a smoker when in Dublin. Sister Imelda looked down sharply at
me and said what was the secret and would I like to share it, since it
seemed so comical. I said, "Nothing, Sister, nothing," and her dark
eyes exuded such vehemence that I prayed she would never have occasion to punish me.

November came and the tiled walls of the recreation hall oozed
moisture and gloom. Most girls had sore throats and were told to suffer this inconvenience to mortify themselves in order to lend a glorious hand in that communion of spirit that linked the living with the
dead. It was the month of the Suffering Souls in Purgatory, and as we
heard of their twofold agony, the yearning for Christ and the ferocity

of the leaping flames that burned and charred their poor limbs, we were asked to make acts of mortification. Some girls gave up jam or sweets and some gave up talking, and so in recreation time they were like dummies making signs with thumb and finger to merely say, "How are you?" Baba said that saner people were locked in the lunatic asylum, which was only a mile away. We saw them in the grounds, pacing back and forth, with their mouths agape and dribble coming out of them, like melting icicles. Among our many fears was that one of those lunatics would break out and head straight for the convent and assault some of the girls.

Yet in the thick of all these dreads I found myself becoming dreadfully happy. I had met Sister Imelda outside of class a few times and I felt that there was an attachment between us. Once it was in the grounds, when she did a reckless thing. She broke off a chrysanthemum and offered it to me to smell. It had no smell, or at least only something faint that suggested autumn, and feeling this to be the case herself, she said it was not a gardenia, was it? Another time we met in the chapel porch, and as she drew her shawl more tightly around her body, I felt how human she was, and prey to the cold.

In the classroom things were not so congenial between us. Geometry was my worst subject, indeed, a total mystery to me. She had not taught more than four classes when she realized this and threw a duster at me in a rage. A few girls gasped as she asked me to stand up and make a spectacle of myself. Her face had reddened, and presently she took out her handkerchief and patted the eye which was red and swollen. I not only felt a fool but felt in imminent danger of sneezing as I inhaled the smell of chalk that had fallen onto my gym frock. Suddenly she fled from the room, leaving us ten minutes free until the next class. Some girls said it was a disgrace, said I should write home and say I had been assaulted. Others welcomed the few minutes in which to gabble. All I wanted was to run after her and say that I was sorry to have caused her such distemper, because I knew dimly that it was as much to do with liking as it was with dislike. In me then there came a sort of speechless tenderness for her, and I might have known that I was stirred.

"We could get her defrocked," Baba said, and elbowed me in God's name to sit down.

That evening at Benediction I had the most overwhelming surprise. It was a particularly happy evening, with the choir nuns in full soaring form and the rows of candles like so many little ladders to the golden chalice that glittered all the more because of the beams of fitful flame. I was full of tears when I discovered a new holy picture had been put in my prayer book, and before I dared look on the back to see who had given it to me, I felt and guessed that this was no ordinary picture from an ordinary girlfriend, that this was a talisman and a peace offering from Sister Imelda. It was a pale-blue picture, so pale that it was almost gray, like the down of a pigeon, and it showed a mother looking down on the infant child. On the back, in her beautiful ornate handwriting, she had written a verse:

> Trust Him when dark doubts assail thee,
> Trust Him when thy faith is small,
> Trust Him when to simply trust Him
> Seems the hardest thing of all.

This was her atonement. To think that she had located the compartment in the chapel where I kept my prayer book and to think that she had been so naked as to write in it and give me a chance to boast about it and to show it to other girls. When I thanked her next day, she bowed but did not speak. Mostly the nuns were on silence and only permitted to talk during class.

In no time I had received another present, a little miniature prayer book with a leather cover and gold edging. The prayers were in French and the lettering so minute it was as if a tiny insect had fashioned them. Soon I was publicly known as her pet. I opened the doors for her, raised the blackboard two pegs higher (she was taller than other nuns), and handed out the exercise books which she had corrected. Now in the margins of my geometry propositions I would find "Good" or "Excellent," when in the past she used to splash "Disgraceful." Baba said it was foul to be a nun's pet and that any girl who sucked up to a nun could not be trusted.

About a month later Sister Imelda asked me to carry her books up four flights of stairs to the cookery kitchen. She taught cookery to a junior class. As she walked ahead of me, I thought how supple she was and how thoroughbred, and when she paused on the landing to look out through the long curtainless window, I too paused. Down below, two women in suede boots were chatting and smoking as they moved along the street with shopping baskets. Nearby a lay nun was on her knees scrubbing the granite steps, and the cold air was full of the raw smell of Jeyes Fluid. There was a potted plant on the landing, and Sister Imelda put her fingers in the earth and went, "Tch tch tch," saying it needed water. I said I would water it later on. I was happy in my prison then, happy to be near her, happy to walk behind her as she twirled her beads and bowed to the servile nun. I no longer cried for my mother, no longer counted the days on a pocket calendar until the Christmas holidays.

"Come back at five," she said as she stood on the threshold of the cookery kitchen door. The girls, all in white overalls, were arranged around the long wooden table waiting for her. It was as if every girl was in love with her. Because, as she entered, their faces broke into smiles, and in different tones of audacity they said her name. She must have liked cookery class, because she beamed and called to someone, anyone, to get up a blazing fire. Then she went across to the cast-iron stove and spat on it to test its temperature. It was hot, because her spit rose up and sizzled.

When I got back later, she was sitting on the edge of the table swaying her legs. There was something reckless about her pose, something defiant. It seemed as if any minute she would take out a cigarette case, snap it open, and then archly offer me one. The wonderful smell of baking made me realize how hungry I was, but far more so, it brought back to me my own home, my mother testing orange cakes with a knitting needle and letting me lick the line of half-baked dough down the length of the needle. I wondered if she had supplanted my mother, and I hoped not, because I had aimed to outstep my original world and take my place in a new and hallowed one.

"I bet you have a sweet tooth," she said, and then she got up, crossed the kitchen, and from under a wonderful shining silver cloche she produced two jam tarts with a crisscross design on them where the pastry was latticed over the dark jam. They were still warm.

"What will I do with them?" I asked.

"Eat them, you goose," she said, and she watched me eat as if she herself derived some peculiar pleasure from it, whereas I was embarrassed about the pastry crumbling and the bits of blackberry jam staining my lips. She was amused. It was one of the most awkward yet thrilling moments I had lived, and inherent in the pleasure was the terrible sense of danger. Had we been caught, she, no doubt, would have had to make massive sacrifice. I looked at her and thought how peerless and how brave, and I wondered if she felt hungry. She had a white overall over her black habit and this made her warmer and freer, and caused me to think of the happiness that would be ours, the laissez-faire if we were away from the convent in an ordinary kitchen doing something easy and customary. But we weren't. It was clear to me then that my version of pleasure was inextricable from pain, that they existed side by side and were interdependent, like the two forces of an electric current.

"Had you a friend when you were in Dublin at university?" I asked daringly.

"I shared a desk with a sister from Howth and stayed in the same hostel," she said.

But what about boys? I thought, and what of your life now and do you long to go out into the world? But could not say it.

We knew something about the nuns' routine. It was rumored that they wore itchy wool underwear, ate dry bread for breakfast, rarely had meat, cakes, or dainties, kept certain hours of strict silence with each other, as well as constant vigil on their thoughts; so that if their minds wandered to the subject of food or pleasure, they would quickly revert to thoughts of God and their eternal souls. They slept on hard beds with no sheets and hairy blankets. At four o'clock in the morning while we slept, each nun got out of bed, in her habit — which was also her death habit — and chanting, they all flocked down the wooden stairs like ravens, to fling themselves on the tiled floor of the chapel. Each nun — even the Mother Superior — flung herself in total submission, saying prayers in Latin and offering up the moment to God. Then silently back to their cells for one more hour of rest. It was not difficult to imagine Sister Imelda face downward, arms outstretched, prostrate on the tiled floor. I often heard their chanting when I wakened suddenly from a nightmare, because, although we slept in a different building, both adjoined, and if one wakened one often heard that monotonous Latin chanting, long before the birds began, long before our own bell summoned us to rise at six.

"Do you eat nice food?" I asked.

"Of course," she said, and smiled. She sometimes broke into an eager smile, which she did much to conceal.

"Have you ever thought of what you will be?" she asked.

I shook my head. My design changed from day to day.

She looked at her man's silver pocket watch, closed the damper of

the range, and prepared to leave. She checked that all the wall cupboards were locked by running her hand over them.

"Sister," I called, gathering enough courage at last — we must have
some secret, something to join us together — "what color hair have
you?"

We never saw the nuns' hair, or their eyebrows, or ears, as all that
part was covered by a stiff white wimple.

"You shouldn't ask such a thing," she said, getting pink in the face,
and then she turned back and whispered, "I'll tell you on your last day
here, provided your geometry has improved."

She had scarcely gone when Baba, who had been lurking behind
some pillar, stuck her head in the door and said, "Christsake, save me a
bit." She finished the second pastry, then went around looking in
kitchen drawers. Because of everything being locked, she found only
some castor sugar in a china shaker. She ate a little and threw the re-
mainder into the dying fire, so that it flared up for a minute with a yellow spluttering flame. Baba showed her jealousy by putting it around
the school that I was in the cookery kitchen every evening, gorging
cakes with Sister Imelda and telling tales.

I did not speak to Sister Imelda again in private until the evening of
our Christmas theatricals. She came to help us put on makeup and get
into our stage clothes and fancy headgear. These clothes were kept in
a trunk from one year to the next, and though sumptuous and strewn
with braiding and gold, they smelled of camphor. Yet as we donned
them we felt different, and as we sponged pancake makeup onto our
faces, we became saucy and emphasized these new guises by adding
dark pencil to the eyes and making the lips bright carmine. There was
only one tube of lipstick and each girl clamored for it. The evening's
entertainment was to comprise scenes from Shakespeare and laughing
sketches. I had been chosen to recite Mark Antony's lament over
Caesar's body, and for this I was to wear a purple toga, white knee-
length socks, and patent buckle shoes. The shoes were too big and I
moved in them as if in clogs. She said to take them off, to go barefoot.
I realized that I was getting nervous and that in an effort to memorize
my speech, the words were getting all askew and flying about in my
head, like the separate pieces of a jigsaw puzzle. She sensed my panic
and very slowly put her hand on my face and enjoined me to look at
her. I looked into her eyes, which seemed fathomless, and saw that she

was willing me to be calm and obliging me to be master of my fears, and I little knew that one day she would have to do the same as regards the swoop of my feelings for her. As we continued to stare I felt myself becoming calm and the words were restored to me in their right and fluent order. The lights were being lowered out in the recreation hall, and we knew now that all the nuns had arrived, had settled themselves down, and were eagerly awaiting this annual hotchpotch of amateur entertainment. There was that fearsome hush as the hall went dark and the few spotlights were turned on. She kissed her crucifix and I realized that she was saying a prayer for me. Then she raised her arm as if depicting the stance of a Greek goddess; walking onto the stage, I was fired by her ardor.

Baba could say that I bawled like a bloody bull, but Sister Imelda, who stood in the wings, said that temporarily she had felt the streets of Rome, had seen the corpse of Caesar, as I delivered those poignant, distempered lines. When I came offstage she put her arms around me and I was encased in a shower of silent kisses. After we had taken down the decorations and put the fancy clothes back in the trunk, I gave her two half-pound boxes of chocolates — bought for me illicitly by one of the day girls — and she gave me a casket made from the insides of match boxes and covered over with gilt paint and gold dust. It was like holding moths and finding their powder adhering to the fingers.

"What will you do on Christmas Day, Sister?" I said.

"I'll pray for you," she said.

It was useless to say, "Will you have turkey?" or, "Will you have plum pudding?" or, "Will you loll in bed?" because I believed that Christmas Day would be as bleak and deprived as any other day in her life. Yet she was radiant as if such austerity was joyful. Maybe she was basking in some secret realization involving her and me.

On the cold snowy afternoon three weeks later when we returned from our holidays, Sister Imelda came up to the dormitory to welcome me back. All the other girls had gone down to the recreation hall to do barn dances and I could hear someone banging on the piano. I did not want to go down and clump around with sixty other girls, having nothing to look forward to, only tea and the rosary and early bed. The beds were damp after our stay at home, and when I put my hand between the sheets, it was like feeling dew but did not have the freshness of outdoors. What depressed me further was that I had seen a mouse in one of the cupboards, seen its tail curl with terror as it slipped away into a crevice. If there was one mouse, there were God knows how many, and the cakes we hid in secret would not be safe. I was still unpacking as she came down the narrow passage between the rows of iron beds and I saw in her walk such agitation.

"Tut, tut, tut, you've curled your hair," she said, offended.

Yes, the world outside was somehow declared in this perm, and for a second I remembered the scalding pain as the trickles of ammonia dribbled down my forehead and then the joy as the hairdresser said that she would make me look like Movita, a Mexican star. Now suddenly that world and those aspirations seemed trite and I wanted to take a brush and straighten my hair and revert to the dark gawky somber girl that I had been. I offered her iced queen cakes that my mother had made, but she refused them and said she could only stay a second. She lent me a notebook of hers, which she had had as a pupil, and into which she had copied favorite quotations, some religious, some not. I read at random:

> Twice or thrice had I loved thee,
> Before I knew thy face or name.
> So in a voice, so in a shapeless flame,
> Angels affect us oft . . .

"Are you well?" I asked.

She looked pale. It may have been the day, which was wretched and gray with sleet, or it may have been the white bedspreads, but she appeared to be ailing.

"I missed you," she said.

"Me too," I said.

At home, gorging, eating trifle at all hours, even for breakfast, having little ratafias to dip in cups of tea, fitting on new shoes and silk stockings, I wished that she could be with us, enjoying the fire and the freedom.

"You know it is not proper for us to be so friendly."

"It's not wrong," I said.

I dreaded that she might decide to turn away from me, that she might stamp on our love and might suddenly draw a curtain over it, a black crepe curtain that would denote its death. I dreaded it and knew it was going to happen.

"We must not become attached," she said, and I could not say we already were, no more than I could remind her of the day of the revels and the intimacy between us. Convents were dungeons and no doubt about it.

From then on she treated me as less of a favorite. She said my name sharply in class, and once she said if I must cough, could I wait until class had finished. Baba was delighted, as were the other girls, because they were glad to see me receding in her eyes. Yet I knew that the crispness was part of her love, because no matter how callously she looked at me, she would occasionally soften. Reading her notebook helped me, and I copied out her quotations into my own book, trying as accurately as possible to imitate her handwriting.

But some little time later when she came to supervise our study one evening, I got a smile from her as she sat on the rostrum looking down at us all. I continued to look up at her and by slight frowning indicated that I had a problem with my geometry. She beckoned to me lightly and I went up, bringing my copybook and the pen. Standing close to her, and also because her wimple was crooked, I saw one of her eyebrows for the first time. She saw that I noticed it and said did that satisfy my curiosity. I said not really. She said what else did I want to see, her swan's neck perhaps, and I went scarlet. I was amazed that she would say such a thing in the hearing of other girls, and then she said a worse thing, she said that G. K. Chesterton was very forgetful and had once put on his trousers backward. She expected me to laugh. I was so close to her that a rumble in her stomach seemed to be taking place in my own, and about this she also laughed. It occurred to me for one terrible moment that maybe she had decided to leave the convent, to jump over the wall. Having done the theorem for me, she marked it "100 out of 100" and then asked if I had any other problems. My eyes filled with tears, I wanted her to realize that her recent coolness had wrought havoc with my nerves and my peace of mind.

"What is it?" she said.

I could cry, or I could tremble to try to convey the emotion, but I could not tell her. As if on cue, the Mother Superior came in and saw this glaring intimacy and frowned as she approached the rostrum.

"Would you please go back to your desk," she said, "and in future kindly allow Sister Imelda to get on with her duties."

I tiptoed back and sat with head down, bursting with fear and shame. Then she looked at a tray on which the milk cups were laid, and finding one cup of milk untouched, she asked which girl had not drunk her milk.

"Me, Sister," I said, and I was called up to drink it and stand under the clock as a punishment. The milk was tepid and dusty, and I thought of cows on the fairs days at home and the farmers hitting them as they slid and slithered over the muddy streets.

For weeks I tried to see my nun in private; I even lurked outside doors where I knew she was due, only to be rebuffed again and again. I suspected the Mother Superior had warned her against making a favorite of me. But I still clung to a belief that a bond existed between us and that her coldness and even some glares which I had received were a charade, a mask. I would wonder how she felt alone in bed and what way she slept and if she thought of me, or refusing to think of me, if she dreamed of me as I did of her. She certainly got thinner, because her nun's silver ring slipped easily and sometimes unavoidably off her marriage finger. It occurred to me that she was having a nervous breakdown.

One day in March the sun came out, the radiators were turned off, and though there was a lashing wind, we were told that officially spring had arrived and that we could play games. We all trooped up to the games field and, to our surprise, saw that Sister Imelda was officiating that day. The daffodils in the field tossed and turned; they were a very bright shocking yellow, but they were not as fetching as the little timid snowdrops that trembled in the wind. We played rounders, and when my turn came to hit the ball with the long wooden pound, I crumbled and missed, fearing that the ball would hit me.

"Champ . . . ," said Baba, jeering.

After three such failures Sister Imelda said that if I liked I could sit and watch, and when I was sitting in the greenhouse swallowing my shame, she came in and said that I must not give way to tears, because humiliation was the greatest test of Christ's love, or indeed *any* love.

"When you are a nun you will know that," she said, and instantly I made up my mind that I would be a nun and that though we might never be free to express our feelings, we would be under the same roof, in the same cloister, in mental and spiritual conjunction all our lives.

"Is it very hard at first?" I said.

"It's awful," she said, and she slipped a little medal into my gym-frock pocket. It was warm from being in her pocket, and as I held it, I knew that once again we were near and that in fact we had never severed. Walking down from the playing field to our Sunday lunch of mutton and cabbage, everyone chattered to Sister Imelda. The girls milled around her, linking her, trying to hold her hand, counting the various keys on her bunch of keys, and asking impudent questions.

"Sister, did you ever ride a motorbicycle?"

"Sister, did you ever wear seamless stockings?"

"Sister, who's your favorite film star — male?"

"Sister, what's your favorite food?"

"Sister, if you had a wish, what would it be?"

"Sister, what do you do when you want to scratch your head?"

Yes, she had ridden a motorcycle, and she had worn silk stockings, but they were seamed. She liked bananas best, and if she had a wish, it would be to go home for a few hours to see her parents and her brother.

That afternoon as we walked through the town, the sight of closed shops with porter barrels outside and mongrel dogs did not dispel my refound ecstasy. The medal was in my pocket, and every other second I would touch it for confirmation. Baba saw a Swiss roll in a confectioner's window laid on a doily and dusted with castor sugar, and it made her cry out with hunger and rail against being in a bloody reformatory, surrounded by drips and mopes. On impulse she took her nail file out of her pocket and dashed across to the window to see if she could cut the glass. The prefect rushed up from the back of the line and asked Baba if she wanted to be locked up.

"I am anyhow," Baba said, and sawed at one of her nails, to maintain her independence and vent her spleen. Baba was the only girl who could stand up to a prefect. When she felt like it, she dropped out of a walk, sat on a stone wall, and waited until we all came back. She said that if there was one thing more boring than studying it was walking. She used to roll down her stockings and examine her calves and say that she could see varicose veins coming from this bloody daily walk. Her legs, like all our legs, were black from the dye of the stockings; we were forbidden to bathe, because baths were immoral. We washed each night in an enamel basin beside our beds. When girls splashed

cold water onto their chests, they let out cries, though this was forbidden.

After the walk we wrote home. We were allowed to write home
once a week; our letters were always censored. I told my mother that I
had made up my mind to be a nun, and asked if she could send me bananas when a batch arrived at our local grocery shop. That evening,
perhaps as I wrote to my mother on the ruled white paper, a telegram
arrived which said that Sister Imelda's brother had been killed in a van
while on his way home from a hurling match. The Mother Superior
announced it, and asked us to pray for his soul and write letters of
sympathy to Sister Imelda's parents. We all wrote identical letters, because in our first year at school we had been given specimen letters for
various occasions, and we all referred back to our specimen letter of
sympathy.

Next day the town hire-car drove up to the convent, and Sister
Imelda, accompanied by another nun, went home for the funeral. She
looked as white as a sheet, with eyes swollen, and she wore a heavy
knitted shawl over her shoulders. Although she came back that night (I
stayed awake to hear the car), we did not see her for a whole week, except to catch a glimpse of her back, in the chapel. When she resumed
class, she was peaky and distant, making no reference at all to her recent tragedy.

The day the bananas came I waited outside the door and gave her a
bunch wrapped in tissue paper. Some were still a little green, and she
said that Mother Superior would put them in the glasshouse to ripen. I
felt that Sister Imelda would never taste them; they would be kept for
a visiting priest or bishop.

"Oh, Sister, I'm sorry about your brother," I said in a burst.

"It will come to us all, sooner or later," Sister Imelda said dolefully.

I dared to touch her wrist to communicate my sadness. She went
quickly, probably for fear of breaking down. At times she grew irrita-
ble and had a boil on her cheek. She missed some classes and was replaced in the cookery kitchen by a younger nun. She asked me to pray
for her brother's soul and to avoid seeing her alone. Each time as she
came down a corridor toward me, I was obliged to turn the other way.
Now Baba or some other girl moved the blackboard two pegs higher
and spread her shawl, when wet, over the radiator to dry.

I got flu and was put to bed. Sickness took the same bleak course, a
cup of hot senna delivered in person by the head nun, who stood

there while I drank it, tea at lunchtime with thin slices of brown bread (because it was just after the war, food was still rationed, so the butter was mixed with lard and had white streaks running through it and a faintly rancid smell), hours of just lying there surveying the empty dormitory, the empty iron beds with white counterpanes on each one, and metal crucifixes laid on each white, frilled pillow slip. I knew that she would miss me and hoped that Baba would tell her where I was. I counted the number of tiles from the ceiling to the head of my bed, thought of my mother at home on the farm mixing hen food, thought of my father, losing his temper perhaps and stamping on the kitchen floor with nailed boots, and I recalled the money owing for my school fees and hoped that Sister Imelda would never get to hear of it. During the Christmas holiday I had seen a bill sent by the head nun to my father which said, "Please remit this week without fail." I hated being in bed causing extra trouble and therefore reminding the head nun of the unpaid liability. We had no clock in the dormitory, so there was no way of guessing the time, but the hours dragged.

Marigold, one of the maids, came to take off the counterpanes at five and brought with her two gifts from Sister Imelda — an orange and a pencil sharpener. I kept the orange peel in my hand, smelling it, and planning how I would thank her. Thinking of her I fell into a feverish sleep and was wakened when the girls came to bed at ten and switched on the various ceiling lights.

At Easter Sister Imelda warned me not to give her chocolates, so I got her a flashlamp instead and spare batteries. Pleased with such a useful gift (perhaps she read her letters in bed), she put her arms around me and allowed one cheek to adhere but not to make the sound of a kiss. It made up for the seven weeks of withdrawal, and as I drove down the convent drive with Baba, she waved to me, as she had promised, from the window of her cell.

In the last term at school, studying was intensive because of the examinations which loomed at the end of June. Like all the other nuns, Sister Imelda thought only of these examinations. She crammed us with knowledge, lost her temper every other day, and gritted her teeth whenever the blackboard was too greasy to take the imprint of the chalk. If ever I met her in the corridor, she asked if I knew such and such a thing, and coming down from Sunday games, she went over various questions with us. The fateful examination day arrived and we sat at single desks supervised by some strange woman from Dublin. Opening a locked trunk, she took out the pink examination papers and distributed them around. Geometry was on the fourth day. When we came out from it, Sister Imelda was in the hall with all the answers, so that we could compare our answers with hers. Then she called me aside and we went up toward the cookery kitchen and sat on the stairs while she went over the paper with me, question for question. I knew that I had three right and two wrong, but did not tell her so.

"It is black," she said then, rather suddenly. I thought she meant the dark light where we were sitting.

"It's cool, though," I said.

Summer had come; our white skins baked under the heavy uniform, and dark violet pansies bloomed in the convent grounds. She looked well again, and her pale skin was once more unblemished.

"My hair," she whispered, "is black." And she told me how she had spent her last night before entering the convent. She had gone cycling with a boy and ridden for miles, and they'd lost their way up a mountain, and she became afraid she would be so late home that she would sleep it out the next morning. It was understood between us that I was going to enter the convent in September and that I could have a last fling too.

Two days later we prepared to go home. There were farewells and outlandish promises, and autograph books signed, and girls trudging up the recreation hall, their cases bursting open with clothes and books. Baba scattered biscuit crumbs in the dormitory for the mice and stuffed all her prayer books under a mattress. Her father promised to collect us at four. I had arranged with Sister Imelda secretly that I would meet her in one of the summerhouses around the walks, where we would spend our last half-hour together. I expected that she would tell me something of what my life as a postulant would be like. But Baba's father came an hour early. He had something urgent to do later and came at three instead. All I could do was ask Marigold to take a note to Sister Imelda.

> Remembrance is all I ask,
> But if remembrance should prove a task,
> Forget me.

I hated Baba, hated her busy father, hated the thought of my mother standing in the doorway in her good dress, welcoming me home at last. I would have become a nun that minute if I could.

I wrote to my nun that night and again the next day and then every week for a month. Her letters were censored, so I tried to convey my feelings indirectly. In one of her letters to me (they were allowed one letter a month) she said that she looked forward to seeing me in September. But by September Baba and I had left for the university in Dublin. I stopped writing to Sister Imelda then, reluctant to tell her that I no longer wished to be a nun.

In Dublin we enrolled at the college where she had surpassed herself. I saw her maiden name on a list, for having graduated with special honors, and for days was again sad and remorseful. I rushed out and bought batteries for the flashlamp I'd given her, and posted them without any note enclosed. No mention of my missing vocation, no mention of why I had stopped writing.

One Sunday about two years later, Baba and I were going out to Howth on a bus. Baba had met some businessmen who played golf there and she had done a lot of scheming to get us invited out. The bus was packed, mostly mothers with babies and children on their way to Dollymount Strand. We drove along the coast road and saw the sea, bright green and glinting in the sun, and because of the way the water was carved up into millions of little wavelets, its surface seemed like an endless heap of dark-green broken bottles. Near the shore the sand looked warm and was biscuit-colored. We never swam or sunbathed, we never did anything that was good for us. Life was geared to work and to meeting men, and yet one knew that mating could only lead to one's being a mother and hawking obstreperous children out to the seaside on Sunday. "They know not what they do" could surely be said of us.

We were very made up; even the conductor seemed to disapprove and snapped at having to give change of ten shillings. For no reason at all I thought of our makeup rituals before the school play and how innocent it was in comparison, because now our skins were smothered beneath layers of it and we never took it off at night. Thinking of the convent, I suddenly thought of Sister Imelda, and then, as if prey to a dream, I heard the rustle of serge, smelled the Jeyes Fluid and the boiled cabbage, and saw her pale shocked face in the months after her brother died. Then I looked around and saw her in earnest, and at first thought I was imagining things. But no, she had got on accompanied by another nun and they were settling themselves in the back seat nearest the door. She looked older, but she had the same aloof quality and the same eyes, and my heart began to race with a mixture of excitement and dread. At first it raced with a prodigal strength, and then it began to falter and I thought it was going to give out. My fear of her and my love came back in one fell realization. I would have gone through the window except that it was not wide enough. The thing was how to escape her. Baba gurgled with delight, stood up, and in the most flagrant way looked around to make sure that it was Imelda. She recognized the other nun as one with the nickname of Johnny who taught piano lessons. Baba's first thought was revenge, as she enumerated the punishments they had meted out to us and said how nice it would be to go back and shock them and say, "Mud in your eye, Sisters," or, "Get lost," or something worse. Baba could not understand why I was quaking, no more than she could understand why I began to wipe off the lipstick. Above all, I knew that I could not confront them.

"You're going to have to," Baba said.

"I can't," I said.

It was not just my attire; it was the fact of my never having written and of my broken promise. Baba kept looking back and said they weren't saying a word and that children were gawking at them. It wasn't often that nuns traveled in buses, and we speculated as to where they might be going.

"They might be off to meet two fellows," Baba said, and visualized them in the golf club getting blotto and hoisting up their skirts. For me it was no laughing matter. She came up with a strategy: it was that as we approached our stop and the bus was still moving, I was to jump up and go down the aisle and pass them without even looking. She said most likely they would not notice us, as their eyes were lowered and they seemed to be praying.

"I can't run down the bus," I said. There was a matter of shaking limbs and already a terrible vertigo.

"You're going to," Baba said, and though insisting that I couldn't, I had already begun to rehearse an apology. While doing this, I kept blessing myself over and over again, and Baba kept reminding me that there was only one more stop before ours. When the dreadful moment came, I jumped up and put on my face what can only be called an apology of a smile. I followed Baba to the rear of the bus. But already they had gone. I saw the back of their two sable, identical figures with their veils being blown wildly about in the wind. They looked so cold and lost as they hurried along the pavement and I wanted to run after them. In some way I felt worse than if I had confronted them. I cannot be certain what I would have said. I knew that there is something sad and faintly distasteful about love's ending, particularly love that has never been fully realized. I might have hinted at that, but I doubt it. In our deepest moments we say the most inadequate things.

Katherine Anne Porter

....

The Jilting of
Granny Weatherall

S HE FLICKED her wrist neatly out of Doctor Harry's pudgy careful fingers and pulled the sheet up to her chin. The brat ought to be in knee breeches. Doctoring around the country with spectacles on his nose! "Get along now, take your schoolbooks and go. There's nothing wrong with me."

Doctor Harry spread a warm paw like a cushion on her forehead where the forked green vein danced and made her eyelids twitch. "Now, now, be a good girl, and we'll have you up in no time."

"That's no way to speak to a woman nearly eighty years old just because she's down. I'd have you respect your elders, young man."

"Well, Missy, excuse me." Doctor Harry patted her cheek. "But I've got to warn you, haven't I? You're a marvel, but you must be careful or you're going to be good and sorry."

"Don't tell me what I'm going to be. I'm on my feet now, morally speaking. It's Cornelia. I had to go to bed to get rid of her."

Her bones felt loose, and floated around in her skin, and Doctor Harry floated like a balloon around the foot of the bed. He floated and pulled down his waistcoat and swung his glasses on a cord. "Well, stay where you are, it certainly can't hurt you."

"Get along and doctor your sick," said Granny Weatherall. "Leave a well woman alone. I'll call for you when I want you . . . Where were you forty years ago when I pulled through milk leg and double pneumonia? You weren't even born. Don't let Cornelia lead you on," she shouted, because Doctor Harry appeared to float up to the ceiling and out. "I pay my own bills, and I don't throw my money away on nonsense!"

She meant to wave good-bye, but it was too much trouble. Her eyes closed of themselves, it was like a dark curtain drawn around the bed. The pillow rose and floated under her, pleasant as a hammock in a light wind. She listened to the leaves rustling outside the window. No, somebody was swishing newspapers: no, Cornelia and Doctor Harry were whispering together. She leaped broad awake, thinking they whispered in her ear.

"She was never like this, *never* like this!" "Well, what can we expect?" "Yes, eighty years old . . ."

Well, and what if she was? She still had ears. It was like Cornelia to whisper around doors. She always kept things secret in such a public way. She was always being tactful and kind. Cornelia was dutiful; that was the trouble with her. Dutiful and good: "So good and dutiful," said Granny, "that I'd like to spank her." She saw herself spanking Cornelia and making a fine job of it.

"What'd you say, Mother?"

Granny felt her face tying up in hard knots.

"Can't a body think, I'd like to know?"

"I thought you might want something."

"I do. I want a lot of things. First off, go away and don't whisper."

She lay and drowsed, hoping in her sleep that the children would keep out and let her rest a minute. It had been a long day. Not that she was tired. It was always pleasant to snatch a minute now and then. There was always so much to be done, let me see: tomorrow.

Tomorrow was far away and there was nothing to trouble about. Things were finished somehow when the time came; thank God there was always a little margin over for peace: then a person could spread out the plan of life and tuck in the edges orderly. It was good to have everything clean and folded away, with the hairbrushes and tonic bottles sitting straight on the white embroidered linen: the day started without fuss and the pantry shelves laid out with rows of jelly glasses and brown jugs and white stone-china jars with blue whirligigs and words painted on them: coffee, tea, sugar, ginger, cinnamon, allspice: and the bronze clock with the lion on top nicely dusted off. The dust that lion could collect in twenty-four hours! The box in the attic with all those letters tied up, well, she'd have to go through that tomorrow. All those letters — George's letters and John's letters and her letters to them both — lying around for the children to find afterwards made her uneasy. Yes, that would be tomorrow's business. No use to let them know how silly she had been once.

While she was rummaging around she found death in her mind and it felt clammy and unfamiliar. She had spent so much time preparing for death there was no need for bringing it up again. Let it take care of itself now. When she was sixty she had felt very old, finished, and went around making farewell trips to see her children and grandchildren, with a secret in her mind: This is the very last of your mother, children! Then she made her will and came down with a long fever. That was all just a notion like a lot of other things, but it was lucky too, for she had once for all got over the idea of dying for a long time. Now she couldn't be worried. She hoped she had better sense now. Her father had lived to be one hundred and two years old and had drunk a noggin of strong hot toddy on his last birthday. He told the reporters it was his daily habit, and he owed his long life to that. He had made quite a scandal and was very pleased about it. She believed she'd just plague Cornelia a little.

"Cornelia! Cornelia!" No footsteps, but a sudden hand on her cheek. "Bless you, where have you been?"

"Here, Mother."

"Well, Cornelia, I want a noggin of hot toddy."

"Are you cold, darling?"

"I'm chilly, Cornelia. Lying in bed stops the circulation. I must have told you that a thousand times."

Well, she could just hear Cornelia telling her husband that Mother was getting a little childish and they'd have to humor her. The thing that most annoyed her was that Cornelia thought she was deaf, dumb, and blind. Little hasty glances and tiny gestures tossed around her and over her head saying, "Don't cross her, let her have her way, she's eighty years old," and she sitting there as if she lived in a thin glass cage. Sometimes Granny almost made up her mind to pack up and move back to her own house, where nobody could remind her every minute that she was old. Wait, wait, Cornelia, till your own children whisper behind your back!

In her day she had kept a better house and had got more work done. She wasn't too old yet for Lydia to be driving eighty miles for advice when one of the children jumped the track, and Jimmy still dropped in and talked things over: "Now, Mammy, you've a good business head, I want to know what you think of this . . ." Old. Cornelia couldn't change the furniture around without asking. Little things, little things! They had been so sweet when they were little. Granny wished the old days were back again with the children young and everything to be done over. It had been a hard pull, but not too much for her. When she thought of all the food she had cooked, and all the clothes she had cut and sewed, and all the gardens she had made — well, the children showed it. There they were, made out of her, and they couldn't get away from that. Sometimes she wanted to see John again and point to them and say, Well, I didn't do so badly, did I? But that would have to wait. That was for tomorrow. She used to think of him as a man, but now all the children were older than their father, and he would be a child beside her if she saw him now. It seemed strange and there was something wrong in the idea. Why, he couldn't possibly recognize her. She had fenced in a hundred acres once, digging the post holes herself and clamping the wires with just a Negro boy to help. That changed a woman. John would be looking for a young woman with the peaked Spanish comb in her hair and the painted fan. Digging post holes changed a woman. Riding country roads in the winter when women had their babies was another thing: sitting up nights with sick horses and sick Negroes and sick children and hardly ever losing one. John, I hardly ever lost one of them! John would see that in a minute, that would be something he could understand, she wouldn't have to explain anything!

It made her feel like rolling up her sleeves and putting the whole place to rights again. No matter if Cornelia was determined to be everywhere at once, there were a great many things left undone on this place. She would start tomorrow and do them. It was good to be strong enough for everything, even if all you made melted and changed and slipped under your hands, so that by the time you finished you almost forgot what you were working for. What was it I set out to do? she asked herself intently, but she could not remember. A fog rose over the valley, she saw it marching across the creek swallowing the trees and moving up the hill like an army of ghosts. Soon it would be at the near edge of the orchard, and then it was time to go in and light the lamps. Come in, children, don't stay out in the night air.

Lighting the lamps had been beautiful. The children huddled up to her and breathed like little calves waiting at the bars in the twilight. Their eyes followed the match and watched the flame rise and settle in a blue curve, then they moved away from her. The lamp was lit, they didn't have to be scared and hang on to Mother anymore. Never,

never, never more. God, for all my life I thank Thee. Without Thee, my God, I could never have done it. Hail Mary, full of grace.

I want you to pick all the fruit this year and see that nothing is wasted. There's always someone who can use it. Don't let good things rot for want of using. You waste life when you waste good food. Don't let things get lost. It's bitter to lose things. Now, don't let me get to thinking, not when I am tired and taking a little nap before supper . . .

The pillow rose about her shoulders and pressed against her heart and the memory was being squeezed out of it: oh, push down the pillow, somebody: it would smother her if she tried to hold it. Such a fresh breeze blowing and such a green day with no threats in it. But he had not come, just the same. What does a woman do when she has put on the white veil and set out the white cake for a man and he doesn't come? She tried to remember. No, I swear he never harmed me but in that. He never harmed me but in that . . . and what if he did? There was the day, the day, but a whirl of dark smoke rose and covered it, crept up and over into the bright field where everything was planted so carefully in orderly rows. That was hell, she knew hell when she saw it. For sixty years she had prayed against remembering him and against losing her soul in the deep pit of hell, and now the two things were mingled in one and the thought of him was a smoky cloud from hell that moved and crept in her head when she had just got rid of Doctor Harry and was trying to rest a minute. Wounded vanity, Ellen, said a sharp voice in the top of her mind. Don't let your wounded vanity get the upper hand of you. Plenty of girls get jilted. You were jilted, weren't you? Then stand up to it. Her eyelids wavered and let in streamers of blue-gray light like tissue paper over her eyes. She must get up and pull the shades down or she'd never sleep. She was in bed again and the shades were not down. How could that happen? Better turn over, hide from the light, sleeping in the light gave you nightmares. "Mother, how do you feel now?" and a stinging wetness on her forehead. But I don't like having my face washed in cold water!

Hapsy? George? Lydia? Jimmy? No, Cornelia, and her features were swollen and full of little puddles. "They're coming, darling, they'll all be here soon." Go wash your face, child, you look funny.

Instead of obeying, Cornelia knelt down and put her head on the pillow. She seemed to be talking but there was no sound. "Well, are you tongue-tied? Whose birthday is it? Are you going to give a party?"

Cornelia's mouth moved urgently in strange shapes. "Don't do that, you bother me, daughter."

"Oh, no, Mother. Oh, no . . ."

Nonsense. It was strange about children. They disputed your every word. "No what, Cornelia?"

"Here's Doctor Harry."

"I won't see that boy again. He just left five minutes ago."

"That was this morning, Mother. It's night now. Here's the nurse."

"This is Doctor Harry, Mrs. Weatherall. I never saw you look so young and happy!"

"Ah, I'll never be young again — but I'd be happy if they'd let me lie in peace and get rested."

She thought she spoke up loudly, but no one answered. A warm weight on her forehead, a warm bracelet on her wrist, and a breeze went on whispering, trying to tell her something. A shuffle of leaves in the everlasting hand of God, He blew on them and they danced and rattled. "Mother, don't mind, we're going to give you a little hypodermic." "Look here, daughter, how do ants get in this bed? I saw sugar ants yesterday." Did you send for Hapsy too?

It was Hapsy she really wanted. She had to go a long way back through a great many rooms to find Hapsy standing with a baby on her arm. She seemed to herself to be Hapsy also, and the baby on Hapsy's arm was Hapsy and himself and herself, all at once, and there was no surprise in the meeting. Then Hapsy melted from within and turned flimsy as gray gauze and the baby was a gauzy shadow, and Hapsy came up close and said, "I thought you'd never come," and looked at her very searchingly and said, "You haven't changed a bit!" They leaned forward to kiss, when Cornelia began whispering from a long way off, "Oh, is there anything you want to tell me? Is there anything I can do for you?"

Yes, she had changed her mind after sixty years and she would like to see George. I want you to find George. Find him and be sure to tell him I forgot him. I want him to know I had my husband just the same and my children and my house like any other woman. A good house too and a good husband that I loved and fine children out of him. Better than I hoped for even. Tell him I was given back everything he took away and more. Oh, no, oh, God, no, there was something else besides the house and the man and the children. Oh, surely they were not all? What was it? Something not given back . . . Her breath crowded down under her ribs and grew into a monstrous frightening shape with cutting edges; it bored up into her head, and the agony was unbelievable: Yes, John, get the Doctor now, no more talk, my time has come.

When this one was born it should be the last. The last. It should have been born first, for it was the one she had truly wanted. Everything came in good time. Nothing left out, left over. She was strong, in three days she would be as well as ever. Better. A woman needed milk in her to have her full health.

"Mother, do you hear me?"

"I've been telling you —"

"Mother, Father Connolly's here."

"I went to Holy Communion only last week. Tell him I'm not so sinful as all that."

"Father just wants to speak to you."

He could speak as much as he pleased. It was like him to drop in and inquire about her soul as if it were a teething baby, and then stay on for a cup of tea and a round of cards and gossip. He always had a funny story of some sort, usually about an Irishman who made his little mistakes and confessed them, and the point lay in some absurd thing he would blurt out in the confessional showing his struggles between native piety and original sin. Granny felt easy about her soul. Cornelia, where are your manners? Give Father Connolly a chair. She had her secret comfortable understanding with a few favorite saints who cleared a straight road to God for her. All as surely signed and sealed as the papers for the new Forty Acres. Forever . . . heirs and assigns forever. Since the day the wedding cake was not cut, but thrown out and wasted. The whole bottom dropped out of the world, and there she was blind and sweating with nothing under her feet and the walls falling away. His hand had caught her under the breast, she had not fallen, there was the freshly polished floor with the green rug on it, just as before. He had cursed like a sailor's parrot and said, "I'll kill him for you." Don't lay a hand on him, for my sake leave something to God. "Now, Ellen, you must believe what I tell you . . ."

So there was nothing, nothing to worry about anymore, except sometimes in the night one of the children screamed in a nightmare, and they both hustled out shaking and hunting for the matches and calling, "There, wait a minute, here we are!" John, get the doctor now, Hapsy's time has come. But there was Hapsy standing by the bed in a white cap. "Cornelia, tell Hapsy to take off her cap. I can't see her plain."

Her eyes opened very wide and the room stood out like a picture she had seen somewhere. Dark colors with the shadows rising towards the ceiling in long angles. The tall black dresser gleamed with nothing on it but John's picture, enlarged from a little one, with John's eyes very black when they should have been blue. You never saw him, so how do you know how he looked? But the man insisted the copy was perfect, it was very rich and handsome. For a picture, yes, but it's not my husband. The table by the bed had a linen cover and a candle and a crucifix. The light was blue from Cornelia's silk lampshades. No sort of light at all, just frippery. You had to live forty years with kerosene lamps to appreciate honest electricity. She felt very strong and she saw Doctor Harry with a rosy nimbus around him.

"You look like a saint, Doctor Harry, and I vow that's as near as you'll ever come to it."

"She's saying something."

"I heard you, Cornelia. What's all this carrying on?"

"Father Connolly's saying —"

Cornelia's voice staggered and bumped like a cart in a bad road. It rounded corners and turned back again and arrived nowhere. Granny stepped up in the cart very lightly and reached for the reins, but a man sat beside her and she knew him by his hands, driving the cart. She did not look in his face, for she knew without seeing, but looked instead down the road where the trees leaned over and bowed to each other and a thousand birds were singing a mass. She felt like singing too, but she put her hand in the bosom of her dress and pulled out a rosary, and Father Connolly murmured Latin in a very solemn voice and tickled her feet. My God, will you stop that nonsense? I'm a married woman. What if he did run away and leave me to face the priest by myself? I found another a whole world better. I wouldn't have exchanged my husband for anybody except Saint Michael himself, and you may tell him that for me with a thank-you in the bargain.

Light flashed on her closed eyelids, and a deep roaring shook her. Cornelia, is that lightning? I hear thunder. There's going to be a storm. Close all the windows. Call the children in . . . "Mother, here we are, all of us." "Is that you, Hapsy?" "Oh, no, I'm Lydia. We drove as fast as we could." Their faces drifted above her, drifted away. The rosary fell out of her hands and Lydia put it back. Jimmy tried to help, their hands fumbled together, and Granny closed two fingers around Jimmy's thumb. Beads wouldn't do, it must be something alive. She was so amazed her thoughts ran round and round. So, my dear Lord, this is my death and I wasn't even thinking about it. My children have come to see me die. But I can't, it's not time. Oh, I always hated surprises. I wanted to give Cornelia the amethyst set — Cornelia, you're to have the amethyst set, but Hapsy's to wear it when she wants, and, Doctor Harry, do shut up. Nobody sent for you. Oh, my dear Lord, do wait a minute. I meant to do something about the Forty Acres, Jimmy doesn't need it and Lydia will later on, with that worthless husband of hers. I meant to finish the altar cloth and send six bottles of wine to Sister Borgia for her dyspepsia. I want to send six bottles of wine to Sister Borgia, Father Connolly, now don't let me forget.

Cornelia's voice made short turns and tilted over and crashed. "Oh, Mother, oh, Mother, oh, Mother . . ."

"I'm not going, Cornelia. I'm taken by surprise. I can't go."

You'll see Hapsy again. What about her? "I thought you'd never come." Granny made a long journey outward, looking for Hapsy. What if I don't find her? What then? Her heart sank down and down, there was no bottom to death, she couldn't come to the end of it. The blue light from Cornelia's lampshade drew into a tiny point in the center of her brain, it flickered and winked like an eye, quietly it fluttered and dwindled. Granny lay curled down within herself, amazed and watchful, staring at the point of light that was herself; her body was now only a deeper mass of shadow in an endless darkness and this darkness would curl around the light and swallow it up. God, give a sign!

For the second time there was no sign. Again no bridegroom and the priest in the house. She could not remember any other sorrow because this grief wiped them all away. Oh, no, there's nothing more cruel than this — I'll never forgive it. She stretched herself with a deep breath and blew out the light.

Reynolds Price

....

Full Day

EARLY AFTERNOON in the midst of fall; but the sun was behind him, raw-egg streaks of speedy light from a ball-sized furnace in a white sky. Buck even skewed his rearview mirror to dodge the hot glare that would only be natural three hours from now. *Am I nodding off?* He thought he should maybe pull to the shoulder and rest for ten minutes. No, he'd yet to eat; his breakfast biscuit was thinning out. One more call; then he'd push on home, be there by dark. But he took the next sharp bend in the road; and damn, the light was still pouring at him, redder now.

Buck shrugged in his mind and thought of a favorite fact of his boyhood — how he'd searched old papers and books of his father's for any word on the great Krakatoa volcanic eruption in 1883. He'd heard about it years later in school — how an entire island went up that August in the grandest blast yet known to man. The sea for miles was coated with powdered rock so thick that ships couldn't move. And for more than a year, sunsets everywhere on earth were reddened by millions of tons of airborne dust. Buck's mother would tell him, each time he asked, that the night before her wedding in 1884, the sunset scared her worse than his father did.

Like boys in general, he'd consumed disasters of all shapes and sizes but only from books and the silent movies of his childhood. Otherwise he often thought of himself as an average tame fish, safe in his tank. He'd missed the First War by only a month and was several years too old at Pearl Harbor; so even now, at fifty-three, he'd never witnessed anything worse than a simple crossroads collision, one death with very little blood. He suddenly saw how the light this afternoon was similar to that, though hadn't he watched the wreck in spring-time? Early April maybe — surely dogwood was blooming.

Buck had sat at the Stop sign in what felt like a globe of silence and watched, slow-motion, as an old man plowed his toy Model A broad-side into a gasoline truck, which failed to explode. Buck had got out and joined the young truck driver in trying to ease the trapped old man (a country doctor, named Burton Vass, crushed by the steer-ing wheel). Awful looking as he was, pinned into the seat, Dr. Vass wouldn't hear of their trying to move him till an ambulance came. But a good ten minutes before it appeared, the doctor actually grinned at their eyes. Then he said, "I'm leaving," and left for good. So yes, Buck was maybe a fish in a tank. *Whose tank?* he wondered. But since he mostly thought about God in his prayers at night, he dropped the question now. God knew, he spent his life in a tank, this Chrysler gun-boat, working to bring electric ease to country wives — stoves, steam irons, washers, freezers, fans.

He turned the mirror down again and tried the sun. It was now even stranger; and the leaves, that had only begun to die, were individ-ually pelted by light till they shivered and flashed. Buck slowed and pulled to the narrow shoulder by a tall pine woods. He'd pushed too far but, on the back seat, he had a wedge of rat cheese, a few saltines, and a hot bottled drink. That would calm his head.

The next thing he knew a voice was speaking from a great distance, toward his left ear. *It's nothing but your name. You're dreaming; dream on.* But the voice was only saying *Sir?* Eventually a second voice, young and hectic, echoed the word — *Sir? Please wake up.* Something in the pitch of the *please* helped him rouse. But he didn't reflect that the tone of the voice was much like the younger of his two sons at home.

It was almost night; he thought that first. But then he realized his eyes had cleared. It was dimmer, yes; the sun was tamer. He glanced at the clock — a quarter past four.

Then from as far off as in his sleep, the older voice came at him again, "Are you all right?"

He looked to his left and was startled to see a woman and a child. Young woman, boy child — maybe thirty and ten. They were two steps back from his side of the car; but at once their faces made him want them closer, though both were tense with doubt and fear. He lowered the window. "Good afternoon."

The woman was the one who retreated a step.

Fearless, the boy came on to the car.

Buck could have touched him. But he settled for touching the brim of his hat, a worn World War II bomber's cap. "Was I snoring too loud?"

The boy said, "I'm Gid Abernathy. No sir, I just thought you were dead."

It struck Buck cold. He actually put a hand out before him and flexed his fingers; then he worked them quickly one by one as if at a keyboard, running scales. He smiled at the boy. "Thanks, Gid, but not yet."

Gid's worry wasn't spent. "The school bus sets me down right here. Ten minutes ago, when I got out, I saw you slumped at the wheel and all; so I knocked on your glass and you didn't budge. I even tried to open your door —"

Buck noticed that oddly he'd locked it on stopping, a first time surely. It didn't strike him as brave or risky that a child tried to help so trustingly. This time and place — 1953 in the coastal plain of North Carolina — were slow and safe; everybody knew it and moved accordingly. Gid was curious and very likely kind, not heroic. Still Buck thanked him and started explaining how tired he'd got from skipping lunch. He should have known not to mention hunger in a woman's presence, not in those times. Maybe in fact he did know it and, half-aware, brought down the rest of the day on himself.

The woman was wearing a clean housedress with short sleeves that showed her strong, but not plump, arms. Her face was an open country face; surely she also had never met with harm or deceit. While Buck thought that, she stepped up slowly through his thoughts and rested a long hand on Gid's bony shoulder. "I'm Gid's mother, Nell Abernathy. He always eats an after-school sandwich. I'll fix you and him one together, if you like." It seemed as natural, and she seemed as ready, as if they were in a cool kitchen now and she were slicing homemade bread and spreading butter that her own hands had churned.

Buck fixed on the best of her homely features. She had an amazing abundance of hair, not the new rust-red you saw so often now since the war but the deep auburn you imagine on women in daguerreotypes, the hair that looks as if each strand bears a vein that pipes blood through it. He'd never seen the like in his time; and he wanted to say so but thought it would sound too forward, too fast. He felt he was smiling anyhow and that now was the moment to say his own name, open the door, and stand up at least. But while his eyes had cleared in the nap, he suddenly wondered if his legs would obey. They felt long gone, not asleep exactly but not all there. He tried it though.

A half-hour later he'd drunk buttermilk, eaten a thick tomato sandwich on store-bought bread, and said what he thought would be good-bye to Gid. Gid said he was due at a touch-football game a mile due north in the woods from here. As he shook Buck's hand, the boy made his plan sound natural as any town child's game. Only when his thin short gallant frame had shut the porch door and run down the steps did Buck recall his own country boyhood. *Whoever played football in the woods?* But he quickly imagined a clearing big enough for two pygmy teams. And for the first time, he thought of a father, *Who's the man around here? Is he dead, run off, or still at work?* But it didn't seem urgent to ask for him yet.

So he looked to Gid's mother, here at the sink four steps away. Her back was to him, and he knew on sight that now she'd literally forgot he was here. Plain as she was, she was that good to see, that empty of wishes for him to perform. All his life he'd tried to show women the boundless thanks he felt for their being. From his long-dead mother on the day he was born, to Lib his wife just yesterday morning, Buck tried to tell each woman who helped him the strongest fact he knew in life, *You're reason enough to stay on here.* He honestly felt it and toward most women. To be sure, he knew there were bad women somewhere; he'd never met one. So he always meant the praise he gave them, mostly selfless praise with no hopes of any dramatic answer. And here past fifty, still he fell in love several times a month, with a face in a diner or crossing the street ahead of his bumper or dark on his back in a hot hotel room, staring at nothing better to see than a ceiling fan and old piss stains from the room above. He knew, and still could cherish, the fact of love-on-sight whenever his mind saw a winning girl; it would gently lie back on itself and tell him, *Buck, rest here for good.*

Not that he had. When he was twenty-seven he married Lib and had touched no other woman since, not with a purpose warmer than courtesy. That never stopped the joy or his ceaseless thanks. Hell, women had not only made him but named him — *Will* from his mother, *Buckeye* in childhood from his favorite sister. Now he fished out his pocket watch — quarter to five, Lib would be starting supper. He'd be half an hour late, no major crime. He folded the paper napkin with a care due Irish linen, and he said, "I'm going to be late for supper." But his legs didn't move to stand and leave.

Buck's guess had been right; Nell jerked at the sudden sound of his voice and looked around, wild-eyed for an instant. But calm again, she said, "You sure?"

"Of what?" Now his legs were trying to stand.

"That you can make it home?"

"Do I look that bad?"

She took the question seriously enough to move a step toward him and study his face. "You look all right. I just mean, you being dizzy on the road and sleeping so deep in the car when Gid found you —"

He was upright now but his head was light. "I could drive this last stretch, bound and blindfolded."

She looked again and said, "You may have to."

Buck meant for his grin to force one from Nell. But no, it didn't work; she was solemn as church, though better to see. Could he look that bad? He tried to remember where his car was parked. Had he driven on here from where he pulled off? Had he left it there and walked here with them? And where was here? He looked all round him — a normal kitchen in a well-worn house, maybe sixty years old, a high dim ceiling, heart-pine floor, white walls smoked to an even gray. He said, "Did we leave my car by the road?"

Nell seemed to nod.

So he looked to the door that Gid had walked through and aimed for that. At first he thought he crossed half the distance, but the final half then doubled on him and kept on multiplying the space till each further step was harder to take; and he thought his feet were sinking through the floor, then his calves and knees, his waist and chest, till even his mouth had sunk and was mute before he could call on Nell or God or the air itself for strength or rescue.

It felt like a healing year of nights, endless dark with heart-easing dreams. But when his eyes opened, it looked to Buck no darker than when he had tried to leave the woman's kitchen. He heard a clock tick, it was near his face, it said five-forty — a black Big Ben, with the bone-rattling bell that he used to wake up early to beat. His mother solemnly gave him one, the day he left home for his first real job. But surely he'd told Lib to chuck it, years back. Or was he doing the thing he'd done so often lately — dreaming he was young, in his first big boarding house, strong as a boy, with the body to prove it in daylight and dark?

He was lying on his stomach on some kind of bed, under light cover. With both dry hands, he felt down his length from the top of his butt to nearly the knees. All that skin was bare; and upward, the sides of his chest and shoulders were warm but naked too. And when he felt beneath himself, his dick and balls were warm and soft. Still what surprised Buck was the calm soul in him — no fear, no regret in a mind as fearful as any not locked in a state institution. He shut both eyes and gradually searched the sheet beneath him, as far as he could reach. His right hand soon met a block that was big but soft. His fingers stopped against it.

A woman's voice said, "You know you're safe."

Buck's eyes were still shut. In the hope of knowing whether this was a dream, he thought *In three seconds I'll open my eyes, I'll look straight ahead, then shut them again.* He counted to three, looked, saw the same clock — five-forty-two — and shut them again. It proved he was alive, awake and sane, though apparently stripped in a woman's bed. *Nell,* he finally thought of the name; then the memory of her face. He firmly believed he still hadn't touched her. *Two things may have happened. I fainted, somehow Nell got me in here, but why am I stripped? Or I've been here days, maybe years, and am sick.*

He had not been prone to wild thoughts, not in his life till now at least; and he halfway liked it. He suspected he smiled. *But Gid — oh Christ. Is Gid on hand?* Buck tried to see if his hand could lift off the pillow — yes. He held it up and listened to the house. No sounds at all, not even from Nell. He settled back, brought his right hand to his face, and felt for beard — the normal stubble of late afternoon. So he told her, "It feels very safe. Thanks, Nell. But did I collapse? Am I someway sick?"

She had seemed to sit on the edge of the bed, facing out from him toward the door — Buck saw the open door and a blank hall beyond it. And now she gave no sign of moving, surely not toward him. She said, "You had a little sinking spell. You may have blanked out, but you didn't fall hard. I helped you in here. You slept half an hour."

"With you here beside me?"

"I just got back," she said.

"From where?"

"The phone. I called your wife."

"How do you know her?"

Her voice was smiling. "You'll have to excuse me, but I searched your pocket and found her number. I didn't know what —"

Buck said, "Don't worry. But what did you say?"

"That you stopped by here, just feeling weak. That I thought you'd be back on the road soon, but did she know anything I ought to know?"

Buck almost laughed. "Such as, am I a killer?"

Her voice stayed pleasant. "Such as, do you have seizures? Are you diabetic?"

"What did Lib say?"

"Is Lib your wife? She said you were normal, far as she knew, just maybe exhausted."

Buck smiled but, on its own, his mind thought *Exactly. Nobody but Lib's allowed to be sick.* Lib was having what she herself called "the longest menopause on human record." Goodhearted as she was till five years ago, in the midst of that winter — with no word of warning — she suddenly balled up tight as wax till, for weeks on end, Buck could hardly see her, much less touch and warm her. Next she seemed to grow in-turned eyes, set all down her body, to watch herself — her own long stock of pains and self-pity, when he'd been the famous complainer so long.

By now they could sometimes laugh about it; and everywhere else in her life with others — their sons, her friends — Lib seemed to be waking from a long hard dream. She'd yet to welcome him truly back. And even if she did, the harm was done now and might never heal. She'd turned from his care and need so often that Buck was permanently lonesome in ways he hadn't felt since boyhood, roaming the deep woods north of his house and pressing his lips to dry tree bark, just for something to lean his body against, some living thing to know that young Buck was clean and warm and could be touched with pleasure.

His right hand had stayed where it found Nell's hip. Three layers of cover kept them apart; he'd never probed or tried to stroke her, and she'd never pressed back into his fingers. As he went on waking, he began to like their balked contact. It gave him a trace of the friendly

warmth of his sister Lulie, who was less than one year older than he
and with whom he'd slept till his sixth birthday — pups in a box,
warm and moving like a single heart.

He thought the next question and asked it clearly, "Whose room is
this?" Before Nell could speak, he thought of the several answers he
dreaded — her husband's and hers, even young Gid's. Not that he
feared their linen and blankets, he just hoped to be in an open space,
one he could rest in from here on out. He felt that happy and it sprang
up through him in a peaceful flow.

Nell said, "My father built this bed, oh, sixty years ago. He and
Mother used it, all their life together. She died and he came here to live
with me, brought nothing much but his clothes and this bed. He
helped us a lot till he went, last winter."

"He died?"

"Pneumonia."

"No, it's you and the boy, on your own now?"

"Seems like," she said. She gave a little chuckle as if she sat alone on
the moon and watched her distant amazing life.

"How do you live?"

She laughed out brightly. "Like squirrels in the trees! No, I sew
for people. Gid works in the summer, on the next farm over. My dad
left us a small piece of money. We do all right, nothing grand but
enough."

Then the lack of a husband and father was sure. *I'll ask to stay.* Buck
understood that the thought should have shocked him. It didn't. The
calm poured on through his chest, and for several minutes he napped
again. When he came to, his right hand was back by his side; and he
spoke without looking, "Why am I naked?"

She said, "Remember? It was your idea. You had a little accident,
when you blacked out."

"Oh God, I'm sorry."

Nell said, "Forget it. It was just in the front, a spot the size of a
baby's head."

"Did I wet my shirt too?"

"Not a bit," she said. "That was your idea; I tried to stop you."

Then I have to stay.

She said, "I've got you some clean clothes out."

"You're a lightning seamstress." But then he thought *Her husband's
clothes.*

"My dad's," she said. "You're his same size."

"I couldn't accept them."

"Oh, he'd be thrilled. He couldn't bear to waste a half-inch of string. And Gid'll be way too tall when he's grown."

"You good at predicting the future?" Buck said.

She laughed again. "Height runs in his family, most of the men —"

Buck rushed to stop her before she clouded the good air between them with a useless name. "I'll be much obliged then, for one pair of pants."

Nell said, "They're laid out here on the chair, khakis as clean as cloth ever gets and a clean pair of step-ins. I'm bound to go now and start our supper. You think you feel like trying to stand?" She seemed unhurried but as bent on leaving as if a walk to the dark heart of Africa faced her now.

Never, no ma'am, I'll lie right here. But he tried to move both legs and they worked. And his eyes were clear. All that refused was his mind, *Stay here. You're actually needed here. Not so, she and Gid are doing all right. Ask her though; just see what she says.* Buck heard his voice say the reckless thing. "Nell, what if I said, 'Please let me stay'?"

He expected she'd wait to think that through. And at once she rose from the edge of the bed and took three steps on the bare wood floor. Then she said, "We had this time, here now. Your own supper's cooking, up the road, this minute."

As her low voice moved, Buck knew she was right. She seemed to know much more than he remembered; whatever had happened, if anything new, it hadn't changed the tone of her voice. So at least he could trust that he hadn't been cruel or made a promise that he couldn't keep. Then he saw his course clearly. The decent thing was to try standing up, getting dressed, saying thank you, and heading on home. So he turned to his side and threw off the cover. He saw his bare body; then said, *"I'm sorry,"* and reached again for the sheet at least, to hide his lap. For the first time, that he remembered here, he looked toward Nell.

She stood by a tall mahogany wardrobe and was half turned away, lifting a bathrobe from the high-backed chair. She was naked as he and had been naked all that time she was near him. Before she could cover herself, Buck rushed to print her body deep in his mind. She was still young everywhere, with firm pale skin and no visible scars. (Lib's side was pocked by the cavernous scar of a ruptured appendix.) And the hair of her crotch was the same high color of life and health that she showed the world on her striking head. Then she was hid in the faded robe; and with no further look or word, she brushed on past him and left the room.

Buck went to the same chair, found his pants in a clean ragged towel, his shirt on a hanger — Nell had managed to iron it — a pair of blue boxer shorts and the khakis she mentioned. He put on his socks first, the shirt, then the pants. They were stiff with starch and two inches short. He thought of his mother's old comic greeting for out-grown pants, "Son, I see you're expecting high water." (They lived twenty miles from the Roanoke River, a famous flooder.)

Was this time-out, here under this roof, some high-water mark in all his life? With the tender mind and heart he got from his mother at birth, Buck had wanted an unadventurous life. And except for Lib's three awful labors (two live boys and one dead girl), he'd virtually got it. His chief adventures had come in his head. Alone on the road, he sometimes lived through active nights with imaginary women. But mostly he still enacted each possible threat to life and limb, anytime his family stepped out of sight. And his own body, strong till now, had always seemed a rickety bridge over too deep a gorge for a confident life in someplace hard as the present world.

So sure, whatever had happened here — if nothing but what Nell owned up to, a fainting spell and a half-hour rest — was like a splendid volunteer, the giant flower that suddenly blooms at the edge of the yard, where you least expect, from a secret hybrid in last year's seed that has bided its time. When he'd tied his shoes, he stepped to the dark old mirror and smoothed his tangled hair. *Nothing visibly changed, not to my eyes — and who knows me better? Well, Lib, but she won't see this time, whatever happened here. And if anything did, it was gentle and finished.* He could hear Nell drawing water in the kitchen. In less than an hour, if fate agreed, he'd be in his own house, among his first duties. He bent again to the peeling mirror and awarded his face a final grin. Then he went out to thank Nell Abernathy for one happy day.

In four months Buck will die from a growth that reached decisive weight in his body this full afternoon and threw him down.

His elder son has made this unreal gift for his father on the eighty-ninth passing of Buck's birthday, though he died these thirty-five years ago. ✝

Tova Reich

....

The Third Generation

T HIS WAS NOT the first time that the father-and-son team
Maurice and Norman Messer, respectively chairman of the
board and president of Holocaust Connections, Inc., had traveled home from Poland, but it was definitely the saddest. In all their
business dealings for clients they had always come through with flying
colors, which was how they had built their enviable reputation and
their legendary success. But this time, in a most painful personal matter involving an exceedingly close member of their immediate family, indeed, the very future of their line, they had failed completely.
Nechama, only child of an only son, had absolutely refused to see her
father or her grandfather, either one-on-one or in any constellation. In
any case, as they were categorically informed, she had taken a vow of
silence. This was communicated to the two men by a matronly nun in
sunglasses, who came to meet them outside the gate of the Carmelite
convent — the new convent, that is, a little farther back from the pe-
rimeter of the Auschwitz death camp, to which the nuns had moved
after all that fuss. "Sister Consolatia asks that you respect her right to
choose," the nun told them with finality, in English, though Maurice
of course knew Polish. Hearing the signature phrasing, the Messers,
father and son, could not deceive themselves that this was anything
other than a direct quotation from their apostate offspring, their lost
Nechama, now reborn as Sister Consolatia.

Nevertheless, despite their unquestionably genuine and heartbreak-
ing disappointment, they made themselves comfortable, as usual, in
their ample seats in the first-class compartment of the LOT airplane.
They always flew Polish, as a matter of policy, to maintain healthy

relations with the government with which they had so many dealings; and they always flew first class, because to do otherwise would be unseemly for men like themselves, steeped as they were in such nearly mythic tragic history, a history that set them apart from ordinary people and therefore required that they be seated apart. And from a practical, business point of view, to go economy would look bad, as if their enterprise were falling on hard times. Everything in their line of work, naturally, hung on image. "Look," as Norman formulated it, with the pauses and swallows that usually heralded the delivery of one of his aphorisms, "we already did cattle cars. From now on it's first class all the way." Clients expected a premium operation from the Messers, and were billed accordingly. This trip, for example, had been paid for by an anti-fur organization that was eager to firm up its honorary Holocaust status, and Norman had managed, even in the midst of his private anguish, to do a little work for them, still in its early stages, admittedly, involving the creative use of the mountains of hair in the Auschwitz museum, shorn from the gassed victims — a ghoulish idea on the face of it, which he was now massaging and dignifying in order to establish the relevant ethical connection that would ennoble the agenda of the fur account and give it that moral stamp of the Holocaust.

By now, of course, father and son knew all the flight attendants on the airline. Maurice persisted in referring to them, politically incorrectly, as "hoistesses," a teasing liberty for which he took the precaution of propitiating them, just in case, with little offerings from the luxury hotels of Warsaw and Kraków — miniature shampoos or scented soaps from the bathrooms, chocolate hearts wrapped in gold foil plucked off the pillows. He squeezed and harassed their vivid blondeness and springy buxomness hello and good-bye and thank you, muttering, "Don't worry, girls, don't worry, I'm safe."

"And he gets away with it too," Norman painstakingly and unnecessarily explained to his wife, Arlene, "because he's this cute little tubby old bald Jewish guy with pudgy hands and a funny accent, and the dumb chicks from Czestochowa, they think he's harmless — big mistake, ladies! — so it turns into a stereotypical Polish joke."

They boarded the plane ahead of the common passengers, wearing to the very last minute their trademark trench coats — the sexy semiotics, as Maurice and Norman interpreted it, of international mystery and intrigue. Then one of the attendants, Magda or Wanda or

someone, without even inquiring, her brain imprinted with their pref-
erences as if the storage of such information were her reason for existence, glided forward with a welcoming smile such as had long vanished from their wives' repertoires, bearing in front of her two living
and breathing breasts a tray with their usual — for Maurice, a glass of
Bordeaux ("I'm a red-wine male," he liked to confide urbanely at official functions), for Norman, rum with Coca-Cola, two containers of
chocolate milk, and a dozen bags of honey-roasted peanuts.

For a long time they sat side by side in silence, each with his own
thoughts, perfectly at ease with the other, apart yet joined, Norman
tearing open with his teeth pack after pack of the peanuts, pouring
them out into the ladle of his palm, jiggling them around like dice,
and then, with his head tilted slightly back, dumping them into his
mouth with a smack. He went on doing this automatically, mechani-
cally. Dispatching the nuts this way was okay when he traveled alongside his father. The old man didn't mind, most likely didn't even notice; like most survivor parents, he probably just registered gratefully
that at least his son was eating, and for Norman, it was a stolen pleasure, because this was not a snacking style in which he could ever
have indulged had he been with his wife or daughter. That robotic,
cranelike up-and-down motion of his arm drove the two of them
crazy; they could feel its vibration even if they weren't looking directly at him. Maybe that's why Nechama went into the convent, Norman speculated — because of his annoying habits.
    As for Arlene, well, he was just not going to think about his upcom-
ing meeting with her while he was masticating. He simply refused
even to begin to plan how he would manage her on the Nechama
problem when he got home, how he would confirm that, unfortunately, it looked, at least for the time being, as if this nun thing was a
done deal. They could do nothing about it for the moment except, of
course, to use Arlene's idiom, go on being supportive, love their
daughter unconditionally, always be there for her, but, at the same
time, they needed to allow time to grieve — figuratively grieve, that is,
not actually go into mourning by sitting shiva for seven days, like
those ultra-Orthodox fanatics when one of their kids converted —
and then, of course, they'd need closure, they'd need to move on with
their own lives, to let go of all this bad stuff, put it behind them, give
the healing process a chance to work, blah blah.

"Look at it this way," he could say to Arlene. "The bad news is, it's a fact: she's a nun, so that makes her a Christian, I guess, a goy, a shiksa, even worse, a Catholic. We just have to face it. And also it's a problem, I suppose, that she had to go and pick that Carmelite convent right by Auschwitz, of all places, for her nun phase, where three-quarters of our family were incinerated. Know what I mean? On the other hand" — and here he would slow down and suck in air for greater effect — "the good news is, she's safe, she has a guaranteed roof over her head and food to eat every day, guys can't bother her anymore, and, from a parent's point of view, we will now always know exactly where she is at all times."

Hey, he loved the girl as much as Arlene did, Norman thought resentfully. Why was he always the one on the defensive? Did he really need this added grief? Nechama was his daughter too, for God's sake. This whole mess was no less an embarrassment for him than it was for Arlene. Jesus, this could even impact their business, their lifestyle — you hear that, Mrs. Messer, hel-lo? How was it going to look, he demanded of his wife in his head: "Holocaust Heiress Dumps Jews"? It was an emergency damage-control situation requiring a rapid response. He had to figure out some way to market this negative to their advantage, to turn it around — something like, you know, the ongoing trauma of the Holocaust, the continuing threat to our survival, the Holocaust is not yet over, et cetera et cetera.

No problem; he was prepared to deal with it. But there was one thing he wanted to know, just one thing — why was he always the one who had to be, as Arlene would put it, supportive, like some Goddamn jockstrap? Why couldn't she be supportive of him once in a while for a change? Had it penetrated her ozone layer yet that everywhere her poor schlump of a husband went, he was a big man, he was greeted like a hero? Was she cognizant of that fact? In Warsaw the women adored him, especially since he had lost all that weight; but the fact is, over there they had always loved him, they loved him in any shape or form, they loved him for himself. They came up to his hotel room carrying bouquets of flowers and bottles of champagne, with beautifully made-up faces and beautifully sprayed hair, in shiny high-heeled shoes and gorgeous real-leather mini-dresses with exposed industrial-strength steel zippers running from neck to hem — not that he carped the diem, needless to say. In the States they worshiped him, idolized him for his aura of suffering, like a saint, like a holy man out of Dostoevski. They revered him for never letting up on this miserable Holocaust business, for immersing himself in it every minute, for schlepping the Shoah around on his back day and night, for sacrificing his happiness to keep the flame going — not for his own health, obviously, but for the moral and ethical health of humankind. The anguish in his eyes, the melancholy in the set of his mouth, the manifest depression in the way he blow-dried his hair, the sorrowful awareness of man's inhumanity to man in the way he belted his trench coat — it turned them on, yes, it turned them on.

So big deal, his wife didn't appreciate him. So what else was new? She was happiest when he was away from home, that was obvious; she was delighted that his job required so much traveling. Fine, he could live with that too, as long as somebody appreciated him, as long as someone somewhere was glad to see him once in a while and showed him a little respect. But it was another thing entirely to blame him for the whole fiasco. C'mon, was he the one who put the kid in the nunnery? Please! And why was he going home now, of his own free will, to listen to all that garbage? He must be meshugga. It was masochism, pure and simple, a sick craving for punishment — he should see a shrink. Did he have any doubts whatsoever about what Arlene was going to dump on him, with her squeegee social worker's brain and her prepackaged psychological explanations? Oh, it was an old song; he had heard it a thousand times already. She would start in again with the whole bloody litany — how it was all his fault, everything that had happened was his fault. Right from the start. First of all, what kind of sick idea was it to insist on naming a baby Nechama? A poor, innocent baby, to give her a name like Comfort, as in "Comfort ye, comfort ye, oh my people," like some sort of replacement Jew, like some sort of post-catastrophe consolation prize, as if they were all depending on her to make things right again after the disaster. Such a heavy load, such an impossible burden to saddle a kid with — no wonder the poor girl took herself out of this world. Did he think names don't matter? There was a whole literature on the subject, on the effect of names on development and identity and self-image. What kind of father would do such a thing to his own flesh and blood? It was criminal, unforgivable. Why couldn't she have been given a normal name, some sort of hopeful, pursuit-of-happiness American name that people could at least pronounce, like Stacy, or Tracy?

And then this whole second-generation business that he had gotten himself involved with, dragging Nechama along like some sort of archetypal sacrificial lamb, like Jephthah's daughter, like Iphigenia. As a matter of fact, Norman knew very well that most mental-health types just loved the second-generation concept. They ate it up. But Arlene — surprise, surprise — didn't believe in it at all. Why? It was completely predictable: because it served Norman's agenda, that's why, because it legitimized and explained his obsession, and gave it status. There was nothing in it for Arlene. As far as Arlene was concerned, second-generation was a made-up category, an indulgence for a bunch of whiners and self-pitiers with a terminal case of arrested development. The so-called survivors were the first generation; they were the ones who had been there, had experienced it all firsthand, and after them came their children, this bogus second generation, the survivor proxies, these Holocaust hangers-on, Norman and company, throwing a tantrum for a piece of Shoah action. So all those tough, shrewd, paranoid refugees who came out of the war — you don't even want to begin to think about how they made it through — suddenly they get turned into sacred, saintly survivors with unutterable knowledge, and then the second generation, born and reared in Brooklyn or somewhere, far, far from the gas chambers and the crematoria, gets crowned as honorary survivors. Suddenly these lightweight descendants are endowed with gravitas, with importance, with all the seriousness and rewards that come from sucking up to suffering. What could be neater? All the benefits of Auschwitz without having to actually live through that nastiness.

And what did they do to deserve this honor, this second generation? What exactly are their suffering bona fides? Well, they had it rough, poor babies — they are victims too, you can't take it away from them. They suffered the psychic wounds of being raised by traumatized, overprotective parents with impossible expectations. They bore the weight of having to transmit the torch of memory, that kitschy memorial candle, from past to future. They endured a devastating blow to their self-esteem in consequence of the knowledge that their lives were a paltry sideshow compared with their parents' epic stories. It was sick, sick, pathetic — "Holocaust envy," a new term in the profession, coming your way soon in the updated, revised edition of *DSM-IV*. And to think that he would expose his own child to such a pathological situation — to think he'd go ahead now and render this acute condition chronic by prolonging the agony, by trying to pass the whole load on to Nechama like a life sentence, like indentured servitude, like guilt unto the tenth generation. Was it an accident, then, that she abandoned the Jews for the ultimate martyr religion, complete with vicarious suffering as its main value and a tortured skinny guy on a cross as its main icon? Was it an accident that she found her way back to the gates of Auschwitz? Had it never dawned on him where this morbid Holocaust fixation would lead?

"Maybe we should've come with one of those deprogramming fellas," Maurice was now saying. "Maybe we should've climbed the wall from the convent like that crazy rabbi — what's his name? — when it used to be in the other building where they used to keep the gas in the war. Maybe we should've kidnapped her from the *schwesters.*"

Norman shook his head. "Bad idea, Pop." He swallowed portentously before elaborating. "It would have been disastrous for Polish-Jewish relations, a nightmare for Catholic-Jewish relations, not to mention curtains for business relations."

"Nu. Anyway, you have to be a younger man for that kind of monkey business, climbing walls. You know what I mean? And you're not so young anymore, Normie, ha ha, and I'm not in such good shape — like your mama says, svelte. I'm not so svelte like I used to be when I was a leader from the partisans and fought against the Nazis in the woods."

Norman had to catch his breath and squeeze the bridge of his nose to stem the keen rush of longing for his daughter that swept over him at that moment, as Maurice recited the familiar refrain in exactly those words about having been a partisan leader who fought the Nazis in the woods. It was a private joke between Norman and Nechama. They would mouth those exact words every time Maurice uttered them, flawlessly imitating his grimaces and gestures, mouth them behind the old man's back at gatherings with friends and family or even at the public speeches that he regularly gave in synagogues, community centers, and schools about his career as a resistance fighter, which he always began with the sentence "I'm here to debunk the myth that the Jews went like sheep to the shlaughter." Norman and Nechama would mouth this sentence too, in fits of choking, mute hilarity. It was a harmless father-daughter ritual that had started when she was about eighteen or nineteen years old, after Maurice had given his standard talk, at Nechama's invitation, in her college's Jewish students' center, opening, as usual, with that sentence about the sheep-to-the-slaughter myth, and ending, as usual, by snapping smartly to attention when they played the Partisans' Hymn, "Never Say That You Have Reached the Final Road."

In a moment alone with Nechama during the reception following Maurice's talk, the two of them facing each other with their clear-plastic wineglasses filled with sparkling cider, as if playing a couple just introduced at a social gathering, Norman casually mentioned — in another context entirely, he forgot what — that of course nobody really knew exactly what Maurice Messer had done during the Holocaust except that he had hidden in the woods all day and stolen chickens at night. No shame in that, of course, under the circumstances. "You just gotta face it, kiddo," Norman went on, in the grip of something beyond his control, "he never shot in the woods — he shat in the woods!"

"You mean Grandpa wasn't really a partisan leader who fought the Nazis?" The child seemed genuinely shocked.

Norman raised an eyebrow. His daughter was not being ironic. Maybe he had gone too far this time. Maybe she really was an innocent; maybe she was just too fragile for this kind of realpolitik. Incredibly, it looked as if she truly hadn't fathomed until that moment that her grandfather's story was just an innocuous piece of self-promoting fiction. But when, after a long pause to absorb the new information, she mischievously blurted out, "Okay, Dad, I won't be the one to tell the Holocaust deniers that it's all made up," he breathed again with relief, impressed by how quickly she had caught on, how alert she was to where her interests lay and her loyalties belonged, how sophisticated she was in accepting human weakness as another amusing fact of life.

"Look," Norman intoned, "it's not as if he didn't really suffer. You think it's easy being considered a victim all the time, having people feel sorry for you — especially if you're a macho type like Grandpa? Who's going to be hurt by an old man's little screenplay starring himself as the big hero? Tell me that, please." He slowed down emphatically now to make way for the flourish. "The Holocaust market is not about to collapse due to one old man's inflations, trust me. Those loonies who say the whole thing never happened should not take comfort."

Should not take comfort, he had said — not take *nechama*. Anyway, it was from that time on, as he recalled it, that they engaged in their tradition of delicious mockery, all in affectionate fun, whenever Maurice warmed up and delivered his partisan spiel. It had evolved into their own personal father-daughter thing. And it was the memory of this innocent conspiratorial bonding with his child that took possession of him now and overcame him.

"Nu, Normie," Maurice was saying. "Yes or no? Why you not talkin'? You remember that hoo-hah with the *schwesters* at the convent with that crazy rabbi, like your mama calls him?"

Maurice, whenever possible, liked to quote his wife, to whom he gallantly conceded a superior mastery of English idiom and pronunciation, and whom he regarded as a nearly oracular source of common sense. For example, whenever the subject came up of that rabbi who had caused an international incident with his protest against the presence of a Catholic convent at Auschwitz, where a million Jews had been gassed — the very same convent in which, in a more acceptable location ordained by the Pope himself, their granddaughter Nechama was now a nun praying for the salvation of the souls of the Jewish dead — Blanche would open her eyes wide and exclaim, "But, darling, he's crazy!" In consequence, Maurice never failed, when referring to that event at the old Carmelite convent, to include the epithet "that crazy rabbi" — as if the rabbi's mental state were a genuine clinical diagnosis, because Blanche, with her peerless common sense, had declared it to be so. Common sense, in Maurice's opinion, was an exceedingly desirable quality in a woman, and there was a time when he had advised Norman to put it at the top of his list of qualities in choosing a mate. To which Blanche would always remark coyly, "When they tell you a girl has common sense, that's a code for not so ay-yay-yay — in other words, not so pretty." "Common sense together with pretty," Maurice would then chime in with alacrity, "just like mine Blanchie."

They discussed everything, he and Blanche, even the subjects they did not discuss. They discussed but did not discuss, for instance, their shared sense of the limitations of their Norman's capabilities. It was not an understanding that they cared to seal in words. But around the time they sold their ladies' undergarments company, Messers' Foundations, from which they had made a more than comfortable living, the Holocaust had become fashionable, more fashionable even than padded brassieres and spandex girdles. At first the two of them had booked up their retirement by becoming leaders in the survivor community and popular lecturers on the oral-testimony circuit. The Holocaust was hot, no question about it. Blanche then urged Maurice to start the consulting business, Holocaust Connections, Inc., and to take Norman in as an equal partner. "Make Your Cause a Holocaust," as their smart-aleck Norman packaged it; he was just too much. It would be first and second generation working and playing together, an ideal setup, a perfect outlet for their Norman, the original futzer and putzer, as they lovingly called him, whose jobs until then, they agreed, had been totally beneath him, totally unsatisfactory and unchallenging. Now Norman could hang around all day long, talking creatively with clients on the telephone, holding forth with all his brilliant opinions, cracking his wicked jokes, writing an article now and then for a Jewish newspaper, traveling and schmoozing in diplomatic channels and the corridors of power with all the other politicians and insiders — the best possible use of his considerable gifts and talents. Unspoken was their shared sense that Norman needed their help, that fundamentally he was a weak person, that he could never manage on his own. Never mind that he had gone to Princeton University — Princeton, Shminceton! — where he had even taken part in a sit-in in the president's office for three days and nights, though his mother had marched right into the middle of that nonstop orgy to personally hand him his allergy medicine. Never mind that he had a law degree from Rutgers, where they trained poor schlemiels to become a bunch of creepers and crawlers. Never mind that he was an adult, to all appearances a grown man, with a social-worker wife and a beautiful but moody daughter. They knew in their hearts that if the war broke out tomorrow, their Norman would never make it. Without saying it out loud, they recognized that, unlike themselves, Norman would not have survived.

Survival — that was the bottom line. You couldn't argue with it. It was the fact on the ground that separated the living from the dead. That was the lesson they had struggled to drum into their Norman: first you survive, then you worry about such niceties as morality and feelings. When someone tells you he's going to kill you, you pay attention, you take him seriously, you believe him. You wake up earlier the next morning and you kill him. If you survive, you win. If you don't survive, you lose. If you lose, you're nothing. What is Rule No. 1 for survival? Never trust anyone. Suspect everyone. Take it as a given that the other guy is out to destroy you, and eat him alive before he gets the chance. Why had they survived? Luck, they always said. It was luck. But they didn't believe it for a minute. It was the accepted thing to say, so as not to insult the memory of the ones who hadn't survived, the ones who were now piles of gray ash and crushed bone that people stepped on. The real truth, they knew, was that they had survived because they were stronger, better — fitter. Look at the survivors today, the ones who had staggered out of the camps like the living dead. They were your classic greenhorns, eternal immigrants, afraid to offend by harping on the Holocaust — why make a federal case of it? — a bunch of nobodies until they had their consciousness raised by the survivor elite, by Blanche and Maurice's circle, the ones who survived with style, the fearless ones. "Me? I'm never afraid!" Maurice always said. It was his motto. Now, thanks to them, the Holocaust was a household word. They built monuments and museums. They were millionaires, big shots, movers and shakers. They ran the country. Survival of the fittest. Blanche had once read in a magazine that cancer cells were the fittest form of life, because they ate everything else up, they spread, they reproduced, they survived, they won. Maybe this wasn't such a wonderful example; maybe this didn't reflect so nicely on her and Maurice and the rest — to be compared to cancer. Cancer was bad, but in this world if you survive, you win, and if you win, you're good.

They were a formidable team, Blanche and Maurice Messer, a fierce couple, and proud of it. For their fortieth wedding anniversary Norman and Arlene had given them a plaque engraved with the words "Don't Mess with the Messers," which they hung in "Holocaust Central," their den off the living room, right above the composition that Nechama had written when she was eight years old, in third grade. The topic was "My Hero"; Nechama had chosen Maurice.

> Grandpa had a gun in World War II. He killed bad Germans with the gun. He was a Germ killer. He saved the Jewish people. He loved the gun. He kissed the gun goodnight every night. He slept with the gun. After the war they gave Grandpa a ride on a tank. He was holding the gun. Then they took the gun away. Grandpa was sad. He cried because he missed his gun. So he married Grandma.

The teacher gave her only a "Fair" for this effort, but Blanche said, "What does she know? It's not by accident that she's a teacher," and she hung the composition, expensively framed, on the wall. "I'm the gun," she asserted defiantly. Maurice also didn't care much for this composition. "What for is she telling the *ganze velt* this partisan story? It's private, just for family." "What are you worrying about, Maurie?" Blanche said. "Every survivor is a partisan. Survival is resistance." "Don't be so paranoid, Pop," Norman said. "It's safe to come out of the closet now." Then, swallowing deliberately and pausing pregnantly, he added, "Ziggy and Manny and Feivel and Yankel, and everyone else who was with you in the woods in those days, they're all dead by now, may they rest in peace — and quiet."

Again, it was a question of survival, this time the survival of the Jewish people in an age of assimilation and intermarriage and the mixed-blessing decline of anti-Semitism in America — another Holocaust, frankly, even more dangerous in its way because it was insidious, underground. Blanche and Maurice would do anything to ensure Jewish survival. No effort or sacrifice was too great, and, as they knew very well, nothing could compare to the Holocaust for bagging a straying Jew; it was the best-seller, it was the top of the line, it got the customer every time. Why did God give us the Holocaust? For one reason only: to drive home the lesson that once a Jew, always a Jew. You could try to blend in and fade out, you could try to mix and match, but it was all useless, hopeless. There was no place to hide, no way to run. Hitler would find you wherever you were and flush you out like a cockroach.

And what could be more effective in sending this message loud and clear than a partisan leader and his wife — herself a survivor of three death camps, maybe four, depending on how you counted — telling their story over and over again until they were blue in the face, pounding in nonstop, day and night, the lessons of the Holocaust. Whatever it took to beat in the message, even if it meant pushing themselves into the limelight in crude ways that ran thoroughly counter to their refined nature, even if it meant giving the misleading impression that they were exploiting the dead, they would do it, not for personal fame and glory, God forbid, but for the cause, because this was their mission. This was why they had been chosen. This was the reason they had survived. They were the first generation, the eyewitnesses. Norman was the connecting link. Nechama was continuity.

Yes, continuity. She was their designated kaddish, their living memorial candle, the third generation. And now she was a Christian. This was tragic — tragic! How could it have happened? Who could ever have foreseen such an outcome? It was beyond human imagining.

They had thrown everything they had into that girl. She had always been the ideal apprentice and protégée. She was, as Maurice used to say in his speeches, the spitting image of his mother, Shprintza Chaya Messer the guerrilla fighter, shot down by the Nazis during the roundup in Wieliczka while she screamed at the top of her lungs, "Fight, Yidalech, fight!"

To this day people still talked about Nechama's bat-mitzvah speech — how she had turned to address the ghost of the Vilna girl with whom she had insisted on being twinned with the words "Rosa, my sister, you were cruelly cut down by the Nazis during the Holocaust. You never had a bat mitzvah. Today I give back to you what was so wrongfully taken away — because today I am you." Arlene, with her naive American Oh-say-can-you-see attitude, had called this gruesome, morbid, a form of child abuse, and had walked out of the sanctuary, but everyone else felt spiritually uplifted and morally renewed by Nechama's words, and wept contentedly. And who could forget the Holocaust assemblies that Nechama had organized in high school, at which either Maurice or Blanche gave testimony? Once even Norman, as the ambassador of the second generation, addressed the teenagers, with their yellow paper stars for Jews pinned to their Nine Inch Nails T-shirts, their pink triangles for homosexuals, black triangles for Gypsies. Especially, who could forget Nechama's original dance composition, presented each year, "Requiem for the Absent," with the flowing, twisting scarves and the arms reaching poignantly toward the heavens? She had always been so proud of her family, those Holocaust relics who would have mortified your average adolescent, and had even invited her grandparents and her father to accompany her to Poland for the March of the Living, with thousands of other Jewish girls and boys from all over the world — but she was in a class apart. She was a Holocaust princess. And she wasn't ashamed of the VIP treatment that she received because of her family's position in the Holocaust hierarchy, and she wasn't embarrassed to walk at a slower pace alongside the old folks for the three-kilometer march from Auschwitz to the actual killing center in Birkenau, with its remains of gas chambers and crematoria, and ash and powdered bone underfoot. She had turned to them and said — they would never forget it — "I see them, I hear them, I feel them. The dead are walking beside us." And then, in her essay for her college application, she had written, "The one thing about me that you may or may not have learned so far from this application is that I am, in the most positive and constructive sense, a Holo-

caust nut. What this means is that I am totally obsessed by the Holocaust, the murder of six million of my people, and am determined to
do everything in my power to make sure that these dead shall not have
died in vain." "Beautiful, beautiful," Maurice had declared, "like the
Star-Spangled Banana!" She was rejected by Princeton, even though
she was legacy, because deep down they were, as Maurice put it, "a
bunch of anti-Semitten and shtinkers." So she went to Brown.

With such Holocaust credentials, who would ever have predicted
that she would turn her back on her people and become, of all things,
a nun? Convent and continuity — these were two concepts that
definitely did not go together. They did not mix well. They were not a
natural couple. The idea of a nun was very foreign to Jewish thinking.
Among Jews every girl got married one way or another, every girl had
children, and if one didn't — well, that just never happened. Who ever
heard of such a thing? Ever since she was a little girl, she had talked so
movingly about how she would have at least twelve children to help
make up for the millions who had been murdered — hurled alive into
flaming pits, shot, gassed, their heads bashed against stone walls. She
was going to be a baby machine for Jewish continuity. She was a pretty
girl, everyone remarked — a little full, maybe. "Zaftig," Maurice said.
"Baby fat," Blanche said. Her favorite food, according to family lore,
was marzipan, and even that preference was regarded as a sign of her
superiority. It was so European, so Old World — what ordinary American Mars Bars kid knows from marzipan? The boys who were attracted to her were usually considerably older, usually foreigners. One
of the family's favorite stories was about how she had stayed out very
late one night, and when she finally came home, at five in the morning, her excuse to her worried parents was that this Salvadoran guy
named Salvador had asked her out, and she didn't want to hurt his
feelings, so she had to explain to him that she could never date a non-
Jew because of the Holocaust — it was nothing personal, but her duty
was to replace the six million. And then, of course, she had to tell him
the whole history of the Holocaust, so that he'd understand where
she was coming from — starting with Hitler's rise to power, in 1933,
and continuing to the end of World War II, in 1945, which took a long
time. Which was why she was so late. She hoped they weren't mad.
"So what did Salvador say?" Norman had asked, obviously not mad at
all, obviously gratified. "Oh, he said, 'I only asked you out for a cup of
coffee. I didn't ask you to marry me.' But that's not the point."

And she never did date a non-Jew, so far as they knew. In any case, soon after she entered college, her romantic life became a mystery to them, off-limits as a subject. She did, it is true, bring home a number of gentile boys, but this was "purely platonic," as she put it — "We're just friends." She knew them in connection with her activities to end the persecution of Christians throughout the world. "A Christian Holocaust is going on as we speak," she declared at dinner in the presence of one of these guests, "and as a Jew who could have been turned into a lampshade, I cannot in good conscience remain a silent bystander." She brought home a Chinese graduate student who described how he had been beaten and tortured because of his membership in an underground church. She brought home a Sudanese lab technician whose family members had been burned or sold into slavery for practicing their faith. As they narrated their stories at the table, she listened raptly, her eyes moist, her mouth slightly open, even though she had surely heard them before. "Any guy who wants her will have to show torture marks," Arlene said. "What for is she foolin' with the Christians?" Maurice complained to Norman. "Where you think Hitler got all his big ideas from about the Jews, tell me that. And the Pope, you should excuse me, His Holiness, where was he during the war — playing pinochle?" "They're trying to hijack the Holocaust," Norman wailed. "Christians are not — I repeat, not! — acceptable Holocaust material. This is where we draw the line."

They tried to wean her from this new fixation by offering her a partnership in their business — complete control of the Women's Holocaust portfolio: abortion, sexual harassment, female genital mutilation, rape, the whole gamut — but she wasn't buying. "The Christians are the new Jews," she said. "Christians have a right to a Holocaust too. Since when do Jews have a monopoly? That's the problem with Jews. They never share." So they broke down after all and offered to take on the Christian Holocaust as part of their business, however alien and distasteful it was to them — to have her create and head up, in fact, a new department devoted entirely to this area. "Forget it," she said. "You guys are too compromised and politicized for me. You'd sell out the victims for the first embassy dinner invitation."

The last time any member of the family had seen her was a few days after she called to say that she would be entering the Carmelite convent near Auschwitz as a postulant, and because it was a contemplative, enclosed, "hermit" order, she would not be available much afterward for visitors. She insisted that though she would soon become a novice and then eventually take vows, she would always consider herself to be a Jewish nun. They should keep that in mind. They were not losing her. They should not despair. The family decided that Arlene would go alone to see her. She accepted the mission despite her frequently voiced resolve never to set foot in that "huge cemetery called Poland — it's no place for a live Jew; this back-to-the-shtetl nostalgia is obscene; these grand tours of the death camps are grotesque." The day after Nechama called, Arlene flew to Warsaw.

When Nechama had converted to Catholicism, she had told them that it was a necessary step toward the fulfillment of her "vocation" but they should know and understand that, like the first Christians, she remained also a Jew. "What you mean?" Maurice had demanded. "Are you with us or against us? Are you a goy or a Jew? You can't have it both ways. You can't have your kishke and eat it also!" Norman wanted to know if this was some kind of Jews-for-Jesus deal, but no, she said, it was in the best tradition of the early church fathers. Norman then made the hopeful point to the family that nowadays maybe you could be both a Christian and a Jew, just as you could, as everyone knew, be both a Buddhist and a Jew — "a Jew-Bude" it was called, something pareve, nothing to get excited about, neither milk nor meat.

Even so, her conversion was a devastating blow, though not entirely unexpected, given her increasing immersion in the Christian Holocaust. After college she had worked full-time for the cause at its Washington headquarters, and then had set out on what she called her "pilgrimage," her "crusade," to bear witness to the persecution firsthand at the actual sites throughout the world, and to offer comfort and strength to the oppressed. She had been kicked out of Pakistan for agitation and promoting disorder. In Ethiopia she had been arrested, and major string-pulling had been required to spring her, which, fortunately, her family was able to manage discreetly, thanks to its position in the world and its fancy connections in high places ("A little schmear here, a little kvetch there," as Maurice recounted with satisfaction). As it became clearer and clearer to them that she was heading toward conversion, Norman had tried to make the case to her that she was far more useful to the Christian Holocaust as a Jew, that her Jewishness was an extremely effective media hook. It piqued people's curiosity — what was a nice Jewish girl like her doing in a place like this? It made her far more interesting and, let's face it, bizarre, especially as she was so Jewishly identified, with her family so prominent in Holocaust circles, bringing even greater attention and visibility to the cause. "Besides," Norman added deliberately, "you don't have to be Christian to love the Christian Holocaust. When I do the Whale Holocaust, do I become a whale? Think about it, Nechama'le. Think again, baby."

From contacts in Poland they knew almost immediately when Nechama had arrived there. She began a slow circuit of the main extermination camps, stopping for a few days at each one to fast and pray — first Treblinka, then Chelmno, Sobibór, Majdanek, Belzec, until she came, finally, to Auschwitz-Birkenau. She called home to say that she had lit a memorial candle in front of the Carmelite convent for a "blessed Jewish nun," Saint Edith Stein ("Sister Teresa Benedicta of the Cross," Nechama called her), who was martyred in the gas chambers there. "Oy vey," Maurice had said. "She's talkin' about that convert Edit' Shtein? I'm not feelin' so good!" In another telephone conversation she had made the comment that traditional Judaism provides no real outlet for a woman's spirituality. "I mean, suppose a Jewish woman wants to dedicate her whole heart and soul and all of her strength to loving God and to prayer. Where is there a Jewish convent for that? Does Judaism even acknowledge the existence of a woman's spirituality in any context other than home and family?" She took a room in Oświęcim to be near the nuns. "They're such holy, holy women, it's humbling and uplifting, both at once. How could anyone ever accuse them of trying to Christianize Auschwitz? It's just ridiculous. Everything they do they do out of love."

Nechama arranged to have Arlene meet her at the large cross near the now-abandoned old convent, the building in which, during the Holocaust, the canisters of Zyklon B gas with which the Jews were asphyxiated had been stored, just at the edge of the death camp. She was already there, praying on her knees, when Arlene's car drove up. Arlene asked the driver to wait for her; she had no intention whatsoever of visiting the camp. After she finished with Nechama, she would go directly back to Kraków. She would be in Warsaw by evening. She would be on a plane flying out of this cursed country the next morning. As she approached the cross with her daughter kneeling before it, she could see two nuns in full habit posted in the distance. Nechama herself was wearing an unfamiliar sort of rough garment — probably some sort of nun's training outfit, Arlene thought.

Nechama heard Arlene approaching, and with her back still turned

she signaled with her thumb and index finger rounded into a circle —
a gesture she had picked up during a teen trip to Israel — for her
mother to wait a few seconds more as she finished her devotions.
Then, after placing her lips directly on the wood of the cross and kissing it passionately, she rose to her feet. "Mommy," she cried, and she
ran to embrace her mother. Arlene shocked herself by breaking down
in racking sobs that swept over her like a flash storm. Her mascara
streaked down her cheeks.

"I'm sorry, I'm sorry," she kept on repeating.

"What are you sorry about? Go on, cry. Crying is good for you — it
cleanses the spirit. There's nothing to be ashamed of."

"I'm sorry for letting them screw you up," Arlene sputtered into the
coarse cloth of Nechama's garment. She had not planned to begin this
way, but she could not stop herself now. "I'm sorry for not fighting
harder to keep them from poisoning you with their Holocaust crazi-
ness. I should have fought them like a lioness protecting her cub. They
crippled you, crippled you, they destroyed any chance you might have
had to lead a normal life — and I did nothing to prevent it."

"Mom?" Nechama pushed Arlene to arm's length. "Two things,
Mom. Number one, I'm not screwed up, and number two, the Holocaust, believe it or not, is the best thing that has ever happened to me.
It has made me what I am today. I'm proud of what I am. I'm doing vi-
tal, redemptive work. I'm bringing healing to the world. Do you understand? I don't want you to pathologize me — okay, Mom? I'm not
a sicko."

Wiping her eyes with a tissue that she held clutched in her fist,
Arlene now took the time to look closely at her daughter. Nechama's
face, framed by a kerchief that concealed all of her thick, curly hair,
her best feature, was exposed and clear — no makeup, and no sign either of the acne that had distressed her well into her twenties. So convents are good for the complexion, Arlene concluded bitterly. Instead
of contact lenses she was wearing glasses with translucent pale-pink
plastic frames. The expression in her eyes was serene and benevolent
— too placid, Arlene thought; she looked drugged, brainwashed, dead
to life. A faint mustache lay over her top lip; in her new life of poverty, chastity, and obedience, in her tight schedule between Lauds
and Compline, there was no place for the facial bleaching that Arlene
had taught her as part of the beauty regimen of every dark-haired
woman. Around her neck was a daunting cross made from some base

metal. The womanly fullness of her barren hips bore down earthward against her skirts, pulled down inevitably by gravity whether they fulfilled their biological function or not, Arlene could see. She had put on a little weight — not that it mattered anymore. At least she was getting enough to eat.

Nechama quickly sensed her mother's appraising eye, and for a moment she was seized by a familiar irritation that she recognized from those times in the past when her mother had rated her appearance down to the last fraction of an ounce and had registered mute disappointment. By an act of will Nechama shook off this feeling, which she considered unworthy and a vanity.

"You look nice," Arlene finally said. She avoided Nechama's eyes, gazing up instead at the twenty-six-foot wooden cross looming behind them. "So this is the famous cross that the Jews and the Poles are beating up on each other about."

"Yes — isn't it silly?" Nechama said. "I guess I'll just never understand what Jews have against a cross."

The Crusades. The Inquisition. Pogroms. Blood libels. The Holocaust. If she can't figure out what we have against the cross, Arlene thought, especially when it is planted right in this spot, where a million Jews were gassed and burned, then she has strayed a long, long way from home. She has gone very far indeed. She is lost to us.

"I mean," Nechama went on, "what everyone has to realize now, if we're ever going to get beyond this, is that each Jew who was murdered in the Holocaust is another Christ crucified on the cross. When I pray to Him, I pray to each one of them. I pray every day to each of the six million Christs."

Suffering and salvation. Martyrdom and redemption. This was not a language that Arlene recognized. The cross cast its long dark shadow over them and onto the blood-soaked ground beyond. The afternoon was passing. Arlene adjusted the strap of the stylish black-leather bag on her shoulder and glanced toward the waiting car. More than anything else in the world now, she wanted to get away from here, from this madness that bred more madness, from this alien sacred imagery that justified unspeakable atrocities. She wanted ordinariness, dailiness, routine — plans, schedules, menus, lists, programs, things, material goods. "Do you need anything, Nechama?" Arlene asked. "I mean, before I go — like underwear, vitamins, toiletries? Tell me what you need, and I'll see that you get it."

"Oh, I don't need anything anymore. I'm finished with needing things," Nechama said, breaking her mother's heart. "We live very simply here. Other people have needs. They send us long lists of what they need, and we pray for them. That's what we do. I can pray for you, too, Mommy. Tell me what you need."

What did she need? She needed to think and see clearly. She needed to remember everything she had forgotten — or she would soon lose faith that she had ever existed at all. "I need to have you back with me," Arlene said quietly, in the voice she would use when she lay down in bed beside her daughter at night, to ease the child into sleep.

Nechama smiled rapturously. "We'll pray for you," she said, and her glance moved from her mother and the cross above them to encompass her whole world, the two nuns motionless in the distance, and the million dead inside the camp who never rested.

Rémy Rougeau

....

Cello

DOM JACQUES BOUVRAY, the abbot, informed the entire community that very soon they would receive four Buddhist monks as visitors. Brother Antoine sat with the assembled Cistercian monks and scrutinized their expressions as the abbot spoke. Forty-six of his brothers were seated on benches opposite one another along the chapter-room walls, while the abbot sat on a raised throne at the end, under a crucifix.

"As you know," Dom Jacques said in French, "Benedictine and Cistercian monks and nuns have been given a Vatican mandate to establish dialogue with monks of other religions. This is why we have invited the Buddhists. I am certain that if we are open-minded and hospitable, this exchange will be a singular learning experience for us."

Old Fathers Cyprien and Marie-Nizier were asleep, their heads shamelessly bowed to their chests. Antoine smiled as he observed how the other monks looked toward the abbot with open mouths and raised eyebrows. Excellent, he thought. The Buddhists will be good for them.

"We need a volunteer," the abbot said, "to look after details of the visit," and he peered out over his reading glasses. Antoine saw no hands. After an awkward moment the abbot spoke again.

"We need someone friendly and open-minded, someone interested in world religions."

Still no hands. Antoine felt uncomfortable and nervously scratched at a spot on his scalp, behind the left ear.

"Thank you, Brother Antoine," the abbot said. "You're just the person for the job. I appoint you our official East-West Dialogue Contact Person."

Antoine was caught by surprise, but in the days following, his job grew on him. At first it sounded ridiculous. How many Buddhist monks lived in Manitoba? East and West were a very long way from each other in some parts of the world. From where would these monks come? A Buddhist monastery in Asia?

Antoine read the stack of material given him by Dom Jacques and discovered that Dharmsala, India, was exactly where the visitors were coming from. Several Roman Catholic monasteries had combined efforts and shared expenses to bring Tibetan Buddhist monks to North America. Antoine also learned, from bulky correspondence, that several abbesses took issue with the arrangements. These women carefully explained that although in theory they were not opposed in any way to the visiting Tibetans, they could not put them up in their monasteries, because the visitors were men, and men were strictly excluded from the papal enclosure of women. Benedictine and Cistercian abbots responded by reminding the nuns that women were likewise forbidden from entering most areas of men's abbeys — but such details, they said, should not inhibit hospitality. And in light of the fact that the Vatican had called for a cordial exchange, the nuns ought to find adequate sleeping quarters for the Tibetans outside the cloister, perhaps with friends. As long as the cloistered areas were respected, they said, with men remaining on one side and women on the other, the exchange could take place. In the end, the nuns withdrew from the arrangements. Nevertheless, six Canadian abbeys remained on the tour, and Brother Antoine's was fourth on the list. The Tibetans would arrive from Quebec and travel on, after Winnipeg, to an abbey in Saskatchewan and another in British Columbia.

Many details of the tour had not yet been arranged, however, and Antoine wrote and received several letters, and even spoke on the telephone when necessary. At first he was shy, but quickly he became more forward, even officious, receiving calls from Quebec and India with the full approval of the abbot. He often had to leave work in the dairy barn to handle this or that pressing detail, making long-distance arrangements with monks he did not know.

Antoine became enthusiastic and soon found himself studying. Because he knew next to nothing about Buddhism, Dom Jacques allowed him to read any Buddhist-related book he could get his hands on. He ordered exotic tomes through interlibrary loan, and Brother François picked these up when he went to Winnipeg for supplies. Antoine read about Zen monks in Japan who spent whole days in a folded position like the Buddha, impervious to disturbances. He was edified, and wondered why his Cistercian brothers could not do likewise. He noticed that they could not sit still for a moment, fussing and passing gas in choir during the most sacred moments of the liturgy. Antoine read of Tibetan monks who ate nothing for weeks at a time. This seemed inhuman. But surely, he thought, the intense discipline they practiced led to high levels of spiritual enlightenment. Otherwise, why would they bother? Cistercian monks grumbled if they were made to give up desserts for Lent. The more Antoine studied Buddhism, the less edified he was by his own brothers, and subconsciously he began to long for a better place to live. He imagined rows of motionless figures seated on the floor, solid and stonelike, their lips moving in a salubrious whisper of words. He wanted to be with *real* monks, who ate tiny portions of cooked rice and pickled vegetables, who slept on the floor, who remained for hours at a time in stationary meditation, unperturbed by one another, hardly noticing the world in their contemplation.

As Contact Person, Antoine learned that one of the Tibetan monks could speak both French and English. This was exciting news, and Antoine prepared himself to discuss religious matters by reading *The Tibetan Book of the Dead,* none of which he understood. He repeatedly attempted to gain some insight, some small bearing on the subject of Buddhism, in a washing ambiance of words, as he read books aloud in the pig barn. He tried several times to sit in the lotus position, but each time he forced his legs into a knitted arrangement in front of him, his feet went to sleep and he found walking difficult afterward. Nevertheless, Antoine eagerly kept after his preparation for the Tibetans, even though Contact Persons were advised to "be themselves" and to present the Buddhist monks with living Western monastic traditions.

Antoine asked himself, *What living Western monastic traditions?* After reading books about the great feats of Buddhist monks, he felt embarrassed by Western monasticism. He saw nothing extraordinary about his own abbey, and without realizing it he became even more anxious because of this low assessment. He corseted himself with Buddhist meditation practices as described in books by Western writers. He painted himself with a hodgepodge of Eastern attitudes that he lifted from footnotes. Antoine wanted to present a version of himself that he thought the Tibetans would admire, and in the meantime, his scorn for all things Western grew.

"Dear Brother," Dom Jacques said to him one day, after he saw Antoine building a Tibetan prayer wheel, "the Buddhists are coming here to see Western monks. Take pride in yourself and in your own monastic heritage. Why be embarrassed by your abbey's peculiarities? We will receive the Tibetans into our home under our terms."

"But you don't understand, *mon père abbé*," Antoine answered. "I don't want the Buddhists to think we are ignorant of their ways."

Secretly Antoine cut back on food. He hoped to become accustomed to less, so that if the Tibetans by chance noticed him in the refectory, they would be impressed by his nibbling on a piece of dry toast while his brothers shoveled oatmeal into their mouths. All Buddhists ate rice, he assumed, and rice was occasionally served at the abbey, though it was prepared in a slimy, gruel-like soup. Antoine took portions of this and passed on the cheese. Very often he had only a slice of bread. After a few weeks of his new diet he became anemic. He fainted in choir one day, and when he opened his eyes, Dom Jacques was slapping him on the cheek.

"Brother Antoine," he said, "why are you not eating properly?"

He told the abbot he had a delicate stomach. The abbot ordered the kitchen to serve Antoine whole milk at every meal, and from his place at table he watched Antoine swallow it all down.

Anemia was not what bothered Antoine. He was hardly aware of its symptoms, except for vague aches and pains when he worked among the dairy cows in the barn. His mind was preoccupied with psychological discomfort, for the more he studied Buddhist monasticism, the more he felt he had been tricked. After all, he had been with the Cistercians for four whole years, and to very little effect. He had thought that these austere-looking monks, shaved and scrubbed, would draw him up a ladder of monastic discipline that would lead to perfection. Antoine wanted to be flawless. He wanted to be a saint: as clean as a piece of carved ivory, as pure-smelling as beeswax. And why had it not happened? Why was he so unaccomplished in the spiritual life, bored with the everyday sameness of it all? Why had he made so little progress in four years?

Only one answer was possible. Surely, Antoine thought, he did not live with real monks. Real monks did not scratch in odd places when they assembled to hear their abbot speak. Real monks did not belch in choir. Real monks did not eat so hurriedly in the refectory. Real monks had manners.

One evening during supper Brother Antoine was called to the telephone to speak to a Cistercian monk from Quebec, a Father Léon Gaide-Chevronnay, who wanted to pass along information about the Tibetans' itinerary. He said he would be traveling with the Buddhists to ensure that they made the proper connections.

"I will be in complete charge of their tour in Canada," he said in French. "I have been to Japan, you see, and I am quite familiar with Buddhism. You need not concern yourself about anything, Brother, except for transportation to and from the airport and, of course, our lodgings."

The hair on Antoine's neck bristled. "I am the official East-West Dialogue Contact Person for our abbey," he said. "I will not relinquish my responsibility for their visit. And I know my fair share about Buddhism myself, thank you."

Father Léon apologized. He only wanted to be helpful, he explained, and he thought his being with the Tibetans would relieve others of a burden. Antoine detected trouble, however, and did not look forward to fighting with Léon over these monks.

Further complications arose. Brother Norbert Gignoux, who was assigned to work in the forge but in fact could never be found there, took Antoine by the sleeve one day and hauled him into the scriptorium.

"Brother Antoine, I have a question for you," he said. His bushy white eyebrows twitched. Antoine was already late for the afternoon milking.

"We're not allowed to speak in here," he reminded Norbert.

"When you get to be seventy-four," Norbert answered, "you can do exactly as you like. Now, Brother, I want to know if these monks coming, are they Catholic?"

"As in Roman Catholic?"

"Yes," Norbert said. "I want to know if these Buddhist people are Catholic."

Antoine had to close his eyes for a moment. "No," he said. "They are Buddhists, Norbert. There is no such thing as a Tibetan Buddhist Roman Catholic monk."

Norbert's eyebrows continued to twitch, and he snorted. "Well," he said, "we ought to pray for their salvation. Perhaps we could baptize them while they're here."

This was exactly the kind of nonsense Antoine had feared. He had no doubt that the Tibetans were monks of spiritual depth, far beyond anything Brother Norbert could imagine, and Antoine did not want someone of Norbert's ilk offering prayers for the Christian conversion of the Buddhist visitors even as they were listening. He asked the abbot to silence Norbert, to prevent his offering public prayers, but the abbot refused.

"Norbert means well," Dom Jacques said. "The Tibetans will understand."

The Buddhists arrived on a weekend in September. The air was cool, but ice had not yet formed on pools of water along the road. Leaves had turned into cascading colors of lemon, orange, and raspberry, and a vague smell of ripe apples hung in the air. Brother François and Brother Antoine met the Buddhists at the airport. Among the first passengers to disembark was Father Léon. He wore civilian clothes in public, just as François and Antoine did. Moments later three Tibetan monks appeared, clothed in identical oxblood robes. The first was Geshe Damchoe Gyaltsen, professor of dialectics. He was supported by two younger monks. Léon explained that Geshe Damchoe was not feeling well, having caught a severe cold in Montreal. He was supported on his left by the eighteen-year-old Venerable Sering Wangchuk, the geshe's English and French interpreter. On his right was the Venerable Tenzin Dechen, who also spoke some English. He was fifteen. He looked more like twelve. Father Léon introduced everyone and asked the Canadians to return the goodwill gestures of the Tibetans. They folded their hands and bowed. The Tibetans then put white scarves over their hosts' necks as a sign of best wishes. An awkward moment of silence followed, and just when Antoine was about to ask about the fourth monk, a shriveled peanut of a person appeared with the last of the passengers from the airplane. He wore the same oxblood robe. He smiled broadly and without benefit of a full set of teeth. This was the Venerable Ngawang Chonzin.

The heads of all the Tibetans were shaved. Sering and Tenzin both had smooth walnut-colored scalps. Their luminous eyes made them seem happy even when they were not smiling. The geshe had several weeks' worth of stubble on his overly large head. He looked sick and puffy in the face. Patches of yellow skin framed his eyes. On the tiny one — the old monk who got off the plane last — the lack of hair revealed a bumpy, gourdlike skull, discolored in places as if he had slept in dirt. He smiled incessantly.

Because of the sickly geshe, no time was wasted returning to the abbey. Father Léon proved to be pushy and difficult about all the arrangements, just as Antoine had feared. He demanded changes of schedule and accommodation, along with certain dietary adjustments.

"No meat," Léon said. "And, of course, they want no milk."

The Tibetans were given rooms inside the cloister grounds, in what was called the old seminary house, a big white clapboard building sheltered by trees near the river. The geshe went to bed at once, while the peanut Ngawang, who never left off smiling, put a pillow on the floor in the hallway and sat on it to say his beads.

"Mantras," Sering explained. "We're obliged to recite one thousand mantras a day, but Cello says ten thousand or more. The beads help keep track of the number."

"Cello?"

"Yes," Sering answered. "It's a nickname. You may use it if you like."

Because Antoine found the name Ngawang unpronounceable, "Cello" was a good alternative, and the little man did seem a brown, worn-out old instrument.

The abbot came to speak with Father Léon, and while they were thus occupied, the young monks asked Antoine to give them a tour. He took them to the wine cellar, where Father Cyprien made wine from Australian raisins; to the bakery, where Brother Jules made heavy whole-wheat and honey loaves each day; and to the scullery, where Father Casimir sliced cheese and laid out portions for the nightly collation. He also took them to the bee yard, where Father Anselme examined hives without benefit of a veil; to the forge, where Brother Emery repaired brake shoes and tractor gears; and to the barn, where Brother Gennade milked sixty Holstein cows by machine. As soon as the Tibetans saw the cows, they began to speak rapidly to each other in their own tongue; the flow and contour of their voices sounded like a gentle agitation of smooth stones in a brook. Tenzin became very shy and covered his face. Sering spoke to Brother Antoine in English, asking if they might have a drink of fresh, unpasteurized milk. Antoine hesitated for a moment, remembering Father Léon's orders, but then he went to fetch cups.

"We like," Tenzin said after he drank the foamy liquid. "We very much miss yak milk."

"Yes, yak milk," Sering said, looking at Antoine with large, shiny eyes. "It tastes very much like yak milk." Tenzin held a hand in front of his mouth to hide the mustache that had formed there. "Hot yak milk with tea and butter and salt. This is our very best favorite drink."

The information surprised Brother Antoine, and it made him question books. It also caused him to wonder how precise was Father Léon's knowledge of Tibetan monasticism. Perhaps Buddhist dietary laws in Japan differed from those in India.

Meanwhile, Father Léon had come in search of the young monks. He had gone through the abbey, and when he could not find them there, he looked around on the farm. He found Sering and Tenzin in the chicken coop with Antoine.

A bantam rooster had been holding the attention of the Tibetans; they were amused by his crowing and by the way he strutted before hens twice his size. When a hen fell down on her breast before the little rooster, he proved too small to climb on her back. Sering and Tenzin whooped and laughed over the little cock.

Father Léon cleared his throat with a sharp cough. "The Tibetans have their own schedule for meditation," he said. "We mustn't be keeping them."

Antoine glared at the priest. He was about to voice a complaint about how some people can ruin a good deal of fun, but Sering and Tenzin had already dropped their interest in the rooster, and they waved good-bye to Antoine, smiling politely. They walked away with Father Léon.

Chickens had never been so interesting, Antoine thought, and he was delighted with his new young friends, amazed by how lively monks could be. He decided that he enjoyed them even more than he had anticipated. But he was also confused, because they seemed such ordinary people. Antoine reminded himself that they were really only teenagers. He wondered if he would have shown as much understanding if he had seen Father Norbert laugh at a bantam rooster.

The Tibetans had their first formal encounter with the entire Cistercian community on the following day, in the chapter room. The abbot asked Father Léon to introduce the guests. The priest did so. Antoine closed his eyes and frowned: he considered Léon's words unctuous and condescending. Besides, Antoine had not been called upon to facilitate the meeting in any way.

The geshe was asked to speak first. He held seniority among the group, because of his learning: *geshe* meant "doctor" in their language. Although his face was sallow, he stood for the entire address. He did not flag at all. He spoke in a monotone that sounded almost like chant, and went on and on, sentence by sentence, for an hour and twenty minutes. Sering translated with confidence, as though he knew the geshe's words by heart. It was all about bad thoughts. When someone raised a hand, it was ignored. Later Antoine learned from Tenzin that Buddhists considered it bad manners to question a geshe before he was finished speaking.

Fathers Cyprien and Marie-Nizier were the first to nod off during the homily on bad thoughts. Nizier snored loudly, but this did not seem to affect the geshe's concentration in the least. Others began to drop their heads and breathe heavily. The geshe continued in his trancelike tone, moving his mouth in a steady, monosyllabic pace, without any hint of excitement in his eyes. All the while Antoine kept his eye on Cello, who paid no attention whatever to the geshe's delivery. He smiled broadly while reciting mantras on the rosary. His murmuring lips produced the sound of a baby chick calling in distress.

"Bad thoughts lead to bad actions," the geshe explained. Bad actions create more bad thoughts. A vicious cycle results, and produces unhappiness. "There is much unrest in the world," Sering translated. "People are not happy, because of their bad thoughts. And they take their bad karma with them into the next life. Over and over people struggle with bad thoughts and bad actions, while souls are reincarnated as worms or angry, howling ghosts. We must put away bad thoughts and keep our minds at peace." This was the substance of the geshe's vast speech.

When at last he bowed, all rose from their benches and left the chapter room for common prayer. Lunch followed in the refectory. Boiled potatoes and green beans were served, along with a noodle soup and thick slices of buttered bread. To Antoine's dismay, the geshe ate as heartily as anyone, taking potatoes into his mouth quickly and with evident relish. Though Antoine nursed only a small cup of broth, no one seemed to notice. Dom Jacques pulled him aside after the meal.

"The Tibetans look uncomfortable to me," he said. "They look cold. Perhaps you could find some coats and shoes." Robes and woven sandals were the extent of their dress, Antoine had noticed, and he was perturbed that Father Léon had not thought of their comfort in Quebec. He went to fetch coats and sweaters, thick socks and shoes, from the wardrobe in the attic, and took them over to the old seminary house in a wheelbarrow. When Sering and Tenzin saw the pile, they poked through it, examining each article, pulling at it and trying it on while laughing at each other. Tenzin went inside with a thick coat and threw it over Cello. Sering selected a coat, a sweater, woolen stockings, and shoes for the geshe. Then the teenagers chose colorful clothing for themselves, articles that seemed to blend well with their oxblood robes and saffron undergarments.

The next day the Cistercians were allowed to question the geshe. He sat alone under the crucifix, on the abbot's throne, while Sering translated the questions. Someone asked how old he was. Another asked at what age he had become a monk. A third asked if Buddhists believed in a heaven, and Brother Norbert wanted to know if Cello was saying the same rosary that Catholics said. To all these questions the geshe responded with the same answer: Bad thoughts must be banished from the mind.

While this was going on, Antoine nervously pulled at his ear. He began to realize that as long as the geshe was present, the other monks would remain silent, except of course for the necessary translation, and for Cello's incessant whispers. He made plans to get rid of the geshe.

That evening he tapped lightly on Father Léon's door. A moment passed, and he heard footsteps.

"Yes?" the priest asked. Only one eye and a nose were visible behind a crack in the doorway.

"Excuse me, Father, but I noticed today at the conference that the geshe is definitely not looking well. In fact, I see that his color has become worse since he arrived."

"Really?" Léon said, opening the door wider. "I thought he was perking up." He held a book in his hand, a finger stuck between the pages. He wore odd half-moon spectacles on his nose. Antoine continued in an evenly paced whisper, the most authoritative voice he could muster.

"Did you have a doctor look at him in Quebec?"

"Why, no," Léon said, rubbing the book against his nose. "We didn't have time, what with our schedule. Besides, it's just a case of the grippe, don't you suppose? I feel rather bad about hauling him all over the country this way, but we do have a schedule to keep."

Antoine lifted a hand to his mouth and paused for what he hoped would seem a grave moment of consideration.

"Well, now, Father," he said, "imagine the consequences if the geshe were to have serious complications. How would anyone know until it was too late? What if he had walking pneumonia, for instance? Or a bacterial infection of the lung? Who are we to say? The geshe could become dangerously weakened. And what would happen then? Your tour might be held up. You'd have to explain to everyone how seeing a doctor had never occurred to you. And if the geshe should die . . . Well, Father, you must understand how I want to save you embarrassment."

By four o'clock the next afternoon Father Léon and Geshe Damchoe were at the Victoria Hospital, in Winnipeg. While they were away, Antoine went to the abbot and told him that the remaining Tibetans wanted to speak to the community. Then he told the Tibetans that the community wanted to ask them questions. A conference was quickly arranged.

They gathered in the chapter room. This time Cello was given the abbot's throne. He crawled up into it and sat on a cushion with his feet dangling over. Thus seated, he smiled and muttered his prayers. Sering and Tenzin sat on either side of him. Cello took questions, answering them without hesitation. Sering translated.

"How many vows do you take?" someone asked.

"Tibetan monks take a vow to abandon each of the two hundred and fifty-three downfalls," Cello said. "Nuns vow to avoid only the eighteen root downfalls."

"Why do women take less?"

Cello rubbed his nose. "Because vows must be received from the novice by a living monk or nun, and the tantric tradition died out among Tibetan nuns."

"When did you enter the monastery?"

Cello laughed. "I was given to the monastery as a child," he said. "Most monks and nuns begin their monastic lives this way. In fact, the best monks and nuns are those who spend early formative years memorizing all the necessary scriptures and living a monastic life while they are most impressionable. Adults may enter the monastery, of course, but they never make very good monks or nuns, because they haven't memorized the necessary scriptures."

"How old are you?"

Cello had no idea. No record existed. He explained that he had been given to a monastery in Tibet, and when the Chinese occupied the country, his monastery was destroyed with all its records. The Chinese put an end to religious freedom, and Cello fled to India with thirty companions. Only three of them survived the trip through the mountains.

Brother Norbert raised his hand. Antoine felt the blood rush to his head. He thought Norbert would ask if Cello believed in the Virgin Mary, if the Tibetans would consider giving up the error of their ways and being baptized as Roman Catholics. Antoine feared that Norbert would offer a prayer on the spot for the conversion of the heathen and the liberation of the world from the dark fog of Buddhism. Antoine thought for sure Norbert would inform Cello how stupid it was to believe in reincarnation, to believe in howling ghosts or prayer wheels. But Norbert did none of these things.

"What does the name 'Cello' mean?" he asked.

Sering translated the question. Cello raised his eyebrows and then spoke briefly in the bubbling language they used. The whole room waited for a translation, but Sering hesitated. Cello waved a hand to encourage him.

"*Cheh'leh*," he said, "is the word for 'nun.' You see, Cello is a woman. She is the abbess of the famous Geden Choling nunnery, in India."

Mouths dropped open, and Antoine heard gasps. No one said a word. The Cistercians needed time to absorb the fact that the short, wrinkled person on the abbot's throne was not a monk. The cloister had been invaded. A woman had taken the abbot's throne.

Everyone turned to the abbot. He was seated on a bench like the others, portly and overheated. At first Antoine thought Dom Jacques's face was red with anger, but then he noticed that the abbot's shoulders were moving up and down. For a whole minute Antoine heard only the thick sound of his own pulse in his ears, while he wondered whether the abbot was laughing or weeping. Then he noticed the abbot's eyes, how they sparkled. Dom Jacques's mouth fell open, and he let out a short hoot that began the rumble of his laugh, and this set off a chain reaction with everyone in the room.

Cello smiled broadly, showing her four little teeth. Even with laughter coming from all around her, she took up her beads and continued her mantras.

The tension in the room dissipated. The laughter died down, but no one knew what to do next. Tenzin covered his mouth. Sering's cheeks were rosy with embarrassment, and he cleared his throat.

"We didn't want to tell you," he said, "because it seemed to us a discourtesy. We had no idea, in India, that you wanted only monks. We didn't know how very important it is for you to exclude women from your monasteries. After we brought Cello all this way across the ocean for our tour of North America, we thought it ungrateful for us to disappoint you, so we said nothing. After all, what were we to do with Cello? She is, after all, the abbess of the Geden Choling nunnery, and the founder of five other nunneries. Besides, who would know that she is a woman? Our heads are shaved. We wear the same clothing. She may as well be a monk. In our world, because we remain celibate, we are equal. We are more alike than different. And even without such considerations, each of us has been a man or a woman in a past life, and each of us will be a man or a woman again, unless we are reborn as higher spirits. So, you see, it makes no difference."

The abbot rose and adjourned the meeting. He immediately summoned Brother Antoine to his office. Antoine worried. As official East-West Dialogue Contact Person, he thought he would be blamed for having staged a debacle. Inside Dom Jacques's office he looked at the floor while sitting in a chair facing the abbot's wide oak desk.

"Brother Antoine, I thought it best to inform you about things as they are," Dom Jacques said. Antoine's palms began to sweat. "You know," the abbot continued, "that Father Léon insisted upon taking Geshe Damchoe Gyaltsen to the hospital. It was a very wise decision. The geshe has a bad cold, of course, but the doctors have discovered an aortic insufficiency near the lower left chamber of his heart. This condition may be life-threatening, and he has been persuaded to give up his tour. Father Léon will accompany him to a Tibetan monastery in Colorado, where he will be looked after by American doctors. Meanwhile, Sering, Tenzin, and Cello will continue on to Saskatchewan."

"I will notify the other abbeys that Cello is a nun," the abbot said. "She will be respected as an abbess, of course, but the cloister must be observed. I was startled and amused by this revelation of identity, but I must uphold the rules about cloister."

Antoine nodded and smiled. He kept silent, but he was fuming that Father Léon had been given credit for the hospital visit. Who cared about Cello, he thought. She was old. It didn't matter anymore if she was a man or a woman.

"A magnificent human being," the abbot said, "this woman who has suffered grave injustice, in the mountains watched her companions die, been in exile all these years — yet she is so cheerful. So humble."

Antoine nodded. But he said to himself, *She has no teeth. How can anyone with no teeth be "magnificent"?*

"She's not what I expected," he said to the abbot. "I mean, even beyond the surprise, her being a woman, she's too odd to be an abbess. I had hoped for someone more dignified."

The abbot opened his mouth to say something but tapped his fingers lightly against his lips instead.

"Brother Antoine," he said after a moment of silence, "I want to thank you for your assistance as Contact Person. The Tibetans are scheduled to continue their tour tomorrow. It has been a rare opportunity, this exchange of cultures. Perhaps you have some private questions for Cello? I give you my permission to speak with her."

Antoine rubbed his chin. "Oh, I don't know," he said. "I don't think I need to talk to her. I want someone more interested in meditation. She just says those mantras over and over. I find that boring."

The abbot leaned back in his chair. "You're missing a golden opportunity."

The only opportunity Antoine wanted was to take rightful credit for having saved the life of Geshe Damchoe Gyaltsen, something Father Léon did not deserve. Then an idea flashed into his head. He could explain to Cello, Sering, and Tenzin that *he*, Antoine, had saved the geshe. If he could tell them how it happened, how he had gone to Léon and begged the priest to take the geshe to a doctor, they would realize Antoine's virtue and how much they owed him.

"Yes!" Antoine said to Dom Jacques. "On second thought, there might be something I could discuss with Cello."

He went off to the old seminary house. He found Sering and Tenzin outside, pushing the wheelbarrow. Cello was seated in it, like a small Oriental dignitary. All her earthly belongings were in a little felt bag. She was speaking softly to her carriers, in a confident and reassuring tone, without the usual rosary in hand. Antoine made them stop.

"What are you doing?" he asked. "Where are you taking her?"

Cello stopped speaking. Sering smiled and said that they had been told to move the abbess out of the cloistered grounds to the gatehouse, where Brother Henri would give her a room.

"Oh, yes," Antoine said. "Such a bother." He stood in the path of the wheelbarrow. All three Tibetans smiled at him, but he did not move.

"I've come to set something straight," Antoine continued. "The geshe's being in the hospital — that was my idea. I'm the one who told Father Léon to take him there."

Sering looked at Tenzin, and they spoke briefly in their native tongue. Sering looked back at Antoine.

"This hospital is not a good idea?" he asked. "The geshe is in a bad place?"

"No," Antoine said. "You misunderstand. *I* am the one who saved Geshe Damchoe Gyaltsen's life. That was not Father Léon's idea."

"That's fine," Sering said. "We are not unhappy."

Before Antoine could explain further, the wheelbarrow was taken up, and he had to move out of the way. Cello continued speaking in a thin but expressive tone, much like a Chinese grandmother telling a bedtime story. Antoine followed alongside. The little procession moved down the road and past an orchard where red, nutlike crab apples hung in profusion on branches.

"What is she saying?" Antoine asked.

"She is giving us a teaching," Sering explained. "Her subject is Gelugpa, or the Yellow Hats, one of the principal sects of Tibetan Buddhism, to which His Holiness the Dalai Lama belongs."

Cello's cheerful, rocking words seemed somehow connected to the movement of the wheelbarrow, and Antoine had difficulty believing that she was talking about anything serious.

"Can you tell me what she is saying?" he asked.

"It's very complicated," Sering answered. "In general, she explains that the real ground of Gelugpa is knowledge of suffering. Only when a person is fully convinced of the immensity of suffering can enlightenment follow."

"Oh," Antoine said.

"This suffering," Sering continued, "must be recognized as a universal condition, and the monk or nun must want deliverance for *all* beings from this suffering. Only then can enlightenment, or *sunyata*, be experienced."

"Really," Antoine said.

They had reached a picket fence, and Antoine opened the gate for the wheelbarrow. After they had passed through, he turned back to check the latch, just above a yellow sign that read MONASTIC ENCLOSURE in black letters. Cello had finished speaking, and she pulled from her felt bag the old, discolored rosary. The road ran ahead of them into cool shadows of elm and ash trees, and just beyond that was the gatehouse. When they arrived there, Brother Henri was waiting for them on the screened porch. Rubbing his purple-veined nose, he offered no words, not even to the abbess, who seemed to be a man even yet, the same person as when she had arrived, bald and stooped with years. Henri came down the steps to collect her little bag, and the two of them disappeared into the gatehouse.

"Is she upset?" Antoine asked.

"Upset?"

"At being moved," Antoine said. "Is Cello upset inside?"

"Oh, no," Sering answered. "She is perfectly healthy."

"I mean, is she angry, about being put out?"

Sering laughed and said something in Tibetan to Tenzin. The blush on Sering's face was of unmistakable innocence. "Cello would sleep on the sidewalk without hesitation," he said.

Brother Henri appeared on the porch with a rubber ball. "Eh?" he said to the Tibetans, and before he got an answer, he threw it out at Tenzin. The boy was delighted, and the ball was soon going back and forth in a wide arc between Sering and Tenzin. The teenagers whooped and laughed, and Henri, without so much as a grin, turned and re-entered the gatehouse. *Just as I expected,* he seemed to be thinking. *Boys are the same everywhere.*

Antoine caught the ball once, but then waved himself out of the game. The Tibetans ran down the road on which they had come, looking spry in the late-afternoon light. Antoine followed them as far as the crab-apple orchard. He felt sad that they would leave tomorrow, to travel on to Saskatchewan. He wished that he were taking Father Léon's place, but he had to admit that he knew next to nothing about airports — probably less than the Tibetans — and besides, Brother Gennade depended on his help in the barn.

With the Tibetans gone, Antoine knew, he would no longer be official East-West Dialogue Contact Person. Life would sink to the ordinary again.

He opened the gate in the picket fence and went inside the monastic enclosure to the orchard. Sitting beneath an apple tree, he asked himself what he had learned from his contact with Buddhists. The first thing that came into his head was how little he had learned from books. "People are far more complicated than books!" he said aloud.

The short, twisted trees in the orchard offered their tiny crab apples. The fruit was plentiful even as the branches were losing their leaves. From where he sat he could see the white seminary house, flanked by several yellow elms. The air was cool and thick with the odor of pumpkins that grew just over a hedge and down by the river.

Antoine felt on the cusp of grasping something important about monasticism, some common thread between East and West that he could identify and present to the abbot, who would be suitably impressed with his insight. And then perhaps Antoine would discuss it with the Tibetans before they left in the morning. Yes, but he could not quite name it, the lofty idea he was after, and he decided that what he needed was a bit of meditation to shake the thought loose.

Though he sat for some time under the tree, no profound thoughts occurred to him. The sun was not visible behind the abbey, to the west, but the evening sky was bathed with its scarlet influence. Birds sang across the fields up and down the river, their chorus resonating sweetly.

He pulled out his rosary and made the sign of the cross. Antoine said his prayers in a whisper. Wrapping his feet beneath him, he attempted to be very solemn. He wanted to banish all bad thoughts and put his mind perfectly at peace.

His prayer went well. He imagined that he looked like the Buddha himself, under a flowering lotus tree, serene in meditation. He imagined himself to be Saint Benedict or Saint Bernard, caught up in tender and undisturbed prayer.

On a nearby tree a flock of cedar waxwings pecked at the shiny crab apples. They exhibited identical rose plumage, with tiny crests of feathers. Suddenly they all flew at the same instant.

A gentle breeze played at Antoine's ears. He closed his eyes to the birds. His mind was nearly empty of distractions when he heard something peculiar: a dull repeated noise. It would not go away. Antoine whispered his rosary louder, but the noise continued. It sounded like heavy apples falling on the ground, one by one, methodically. He struggled to put the noise out of his mind, but he could not, and the more he tried, the more exasperated he became.

The rhythmic thuds persisted. Antoine ground his teeth. Sweat rolled down his forehead. He simply had to know the cause of the noise.

He opened his eyes. Slowly he got to his feet and began to walk toward the sound, hunched and stalking. Over the short grass, a few trees away, he saw the small, bent figure of Cello in her oxblood robes. With her bare feet she was stomping on fallen crab apples, one after another, breaking them open, beating them with her heel into a pulp. This done, she would bend low and pick at them, putting bits of apple paste into her mouth.

From a distance she looked like an abandoned and hungry child. Antoine was transfixed. He had never seen anything so peculiar: there she was, the Venerable Cello, spiritual mother to six thousand nuns, eating crab apples from the grass.

As sunlight drew away from the orchard, it came to him: the thread that bound their lives together. Cello was abandoned by society. She was marginal. Antoine realized that the abbess was as defenseless and as irrelevant to the world as an orphan. And being a monk, so was he.

The experience of many days clicked into a clear order in his head. Antoine saw before him a Cello who had survived immense suffering in the Himalayas to offer a living witness to anyone interested: nothing less than the reversal of world order. Weak as she was — weak as all human beings are — she had found freedom from pain, which was the same as freedom from the desire for fame and fortune.

Cello seemed unaware of Antoine's flabbergasted stare. She straightened her rounded back. She looked at the crab-apple tree. Then, brushing her knotted fingers back and forth over its trunk, she appeared to thank a perfect living creature for its fruit. And when the wind died and the birds stopped singing, Cello walked back toward the gatehouse, making her way to bed.

Salman Rushdie

....

The Prophet's Hair

EARLY IN THE YEAR 19—, when Srinagar was under the spell of a winter so fierce it could crack men's bones as if they were glass, a young man upon whose cold-pinked skin there lay, like a frost, the unmistakable sheen of wealth was to be seen entering the most wretched and disreputable part of the city, where the houses of wood and corrugated iron seemed perpetually on the verge of losing their balance, and asking in low, grave tones where he might go to engage the services of a dependably professional burglar. The young man's name was Atta, and the rogues in that part of town directed him gleefully into ever darker and less public alleys, until in a yard wet with the blood of a slaughtered chicken he was set upon by two men whose faces he never saw, robbed of the substantial bankroll which he had insanely brought on his solitary excursion, and beaten within an inch of his life.

Night fell. His body was carried by anonymous hands to the edge of the lake, whence it was transported by shikara across the water and deposited, torn and bleeding, on the deserted embankment of the canal which led to the gardens of Shalimar. At dawn the next morning a flower vendor was rowing his boat through water to which the cold of the night had given the cloudy consistency of wild honey when he saw the prone form of young Atta, who was just beginning to stir and moan, and on whose now deathly pale skin the sheen of wealth could still be made out dimly beneath an actual layer of frost.

The flower vendor moored his craft and by stooping over the mouth of the injured man was able to learn the poor fellow's address, which was mumbled through lips that could scarcely move; whereupon, hoping for a large tip, the hawker rowed Atta home to a large house on the shores of the lake, where a beautiful but inexplicably bruised young woman and her distraught, but equally handsome mother, neither of whom, it was clear from their eyes, had slept a wink from worrying, screamed at the sight of their Atta — who was the elder brother of the beautiful young woman — lying motionless amidst the funereally stunted winter blooms of the hopeful florist.

The flower vendor was indeed paid off handsomely, not least to ensure his silence, and plays no further part in our story. Atta himself, suffering terribly from exposure as well as a broken skull, entered a coma which caused the city's finest doctors to shrug helplessly. It was therefore all the more remarkable that on the very next evening the most wretched and disreputable part of the city received a second unexpected visitor. This was Huma, the sister of the unfortunate young man, and her question was the same as her brother's, and asked in the same low, grave tones:

"Where may I hire a thief?"

The story of the rich idiot who had come looking for a burglar was already common knowledge in those insalubrious gullies, but this time the young woman added: "I should say that I am carrying no money, nor am I wearing any jewelry items. My father has disowned me and will pay no ransom if I am kidnapped; and a letter has been lodged with the Deputy Commissioner of Police, my uncle, to be opened in the event of my not being safe at home by morning. In that letter he will find full details of my journey here, and he will move heaven and earth to punish my assailants."

Her exceptional beauty, which was visible even through the enormous welts and bruises disfiguring her arms and forehead, coupled with the oddity of her inquiries, had attracted a sizable group of curious onlookers, and because her little speech seemed to them to cover just about everything, no one attempted to injure her in any way, although there were some raucous comments to the effect that it was pretty peculiar for someone who was trying to hire a crook to invoke the protection of a high-up policeman uncle.

She was directed into ever darker and less public alleys until finally in a gully as dark as ink an old woman with eyes which stared so piercingly that Huma instantly understood she was blind motioned her through a doorway from which darkness seemed to be pouring like smoke. Clenching her fists, angrily ordering her heart to behave normally, Huma followed the old woman into the gloom-wrapped house.

The faintest conceivable rivulet of candlelight trickled through the darkness; following this unreliable yellow thread (because she could no longer see the old lady), Huma received a sudden sharp blow to the shins and cried out involuntarily, after which she at once bit her lip, angry at having revealed her mounting terror to whoever or whatever waited before her, shrouded in blackness.

She had, in fact, collided with a low table on which a single candle burned and beyond which a mountainous figure could be made out, sitting cross-legged on the floor. "Sit, sit," said a man's calm, deep voice, and her legs, needing no more flowery invitation, buckled beneath her at the terse command. Clutching her left hand in her right, she forced her voice to respond evenly:

"And you, sir, will be the thief I have been requesting?"

Shifting its weight very slightly, the shadow-mountain informed Huma that all criminal activity originating in this zone was well organized and also centrally controlled, so that all requests for what might be termed freelance work had to be channeled through this room.

He demanded comprehensive details of the crime to be committed, including a precise inventory of items to be acquired, also a clear statement of all financial inducements being offered with no gratuities excluded, plus, for filing purposes only, a summary of the motives for the application.

At this, Huma, as though remembering something, stiffened both in body and resolve and replied loudly that her motives were entirely a matter for herself; that she would discuss details with no one but the thief himself; but that the rewards she proposed could only be described as "lavish."

"All I am willing to disclose to you, sir, since it appears that I am on the premises of some sort of employment agency, is that in return for such lavish rewards I must have the most desperate criminal at your disposal, a man for whom life holds no terrors, not even the fear of God.

"The worst of fellows, I tell you — nothing less will do!"

    * * *

At this a paraffin storm lantern was lighted, and Huma saw facing her a gray-haired giant down whose left cheek ran the most sinister of scars, a cicatrice in the shape of the letter *sin* in the Nastaliq script. She was gripped by the insupportably nostalgic notion that the bogeyman of her childhood nursery had risen up to confront her, because her ayah had always forestalled any incipient acts of disobedience by threatening Huma and Atta: "You don't watch out and I'll send that one to steal you away — that Sheikh Sín, the Thief of Thieves!"

Here, gray-haired but unquestionably scarred, was the notorious criminal himself — and was she out of her mind, were her ears playing tricks, or had he truly just announced that, given the stated circumstances, he himself was the only man for the job?

Struggling hard against the newborn goblins of nostalgia, Huma warned the fearsome volunteer that only a matter of extreme urgency and peril would have brought her unescorted into these ferocious streets.

"Because we can afford no last-minute backings-out," she continued, "I am determined to tell you everything, keeping back no secrets whatsoever. If, after hearing me out, you are still prepared to proceed, then we shall do everything in our power to assist you, and to make you rich."

The old thief shrugged, nodded, spat. Huma began her story.

Six days ago, everything in the household of her father, the wealthy moneylender Hashim, had been as it always was. At breakfast her mother had spooned khichri lovingly onto the moneylender's plate; the conversation had been filled with those expressions of courtesy and solicitude on which the family prided itself.

Hashim was fond of pointing out that while he was not a godly man he set great store by "living honorably in the world." In that spacious lakeside residence, all outsiders were greeted with the same formality and respect, even those unfortunates who came to negotiate for small fragments of Hashim's large fortune, and of whom he naturally asked an interest rate of over seventy percent, partly, as he told his khichri-spooning wife, "to teach these people the value of money; let them only learn that, and they will be cured of this fever of borrowing borrowing all the time — so you see that if my plans succeed, I shall put myself out of business!"

In their children, Atta and Huma, the moneylender and his wife had successfully sought to inculcate the virtues of thrift, plain dealing, and a healthy independence of spirit. On this, too, Hashim was fond of congratulating himself.

Breakfast ended; the family members wished one another a fulfilling day. Within a few hours, however, the glassy contentment of that household, of that life of porcelain delicacy and alabaster sensibilities, was to be shattered beyond all hope of repair.

The moneylender summoned his personal shikara and was on the point of stepping into it when, attracted by a glint of silver, he noticed a small vial floating between the boat and his private quay. On an impulse, he scooped it out of the glutinous water.

It was a cylinder of tinted glass cased in exquisitely wrought silver, and Hashim saw within its walls a silver pendant bearing a single strand of human hair.

Closing his fist around this unique discovery, he muttered to the boatman that he'd changed his plans, and hurried to his sanctum, where, behind closed doors, he feasted his eyes on his find.

There can be no doubt that Hashim the moneylender knew from the first that he was in possession of the famous relic of the Prophet Muhammad, that revered hair whose theft from its shrine at Hazratbal mosque the previous morning had created an unprecedented hue and cry in the valley.

The thieves — no doubt alarmed by the pandemonium, by the procession through the streets of endless ululating crocodiles of lamentation, by the riots, the political ramifications and by the massive police search which was commanded and carried out by men whose entire careers now hung upon the finding of this lost hair — had evidently panicked and hurled the vial into the gelatine bosom of the lake.

Having found it by a stroke of great good fortune, Hashim's duty as a citizen was clear: the hair must be restored to its shrine, and the state to equanimity and peace.

But the moneylender had a different notion.

All around him in his study was the evidence of his collector's mania. There were enormous glass cases full of impaled butterflies from Gulmarg, three dozen scale models in various metals of the legendary cannon Zamzama, innumerable swords, a Naga spear, ninety-four terracotta camels of the sort sold on railway station platforms, many samovars, and a whole zoology of tiny sandalwood animals, which had originally been carved to serve as children's bath-time toys.

"And after all," Hashim told himself, "the Prophet would have disapproved mightily of this relic worship. He abhorred the idea of being deified! So, by keeping this hair from its distracted devotees, I perform — do I not? — a finer service than I would by returning it! Naturally, I don't want it for its religious value . . . I'm a man of the world, of this world. I see it purely as a secular object of great rarity and blinding beauty. In short, it's the silver vial I desire, more than the hair.

"They say there are American millionaires who purchase stolen art masterpieces and hide them away — they would know how I feel. I must, must have it!"

Every collector must share his treasures with one other human being, and Hashim summoned — and told — his only son Atta, who was deeply perturbed but, having been sworn to secrecy, only spilled the beans when the troubles became too terrible to bear.

The youth excused himself and left his father alone in the crowded solitude of his collections. Hashim was sitting erect in a hard, straight-backed chair, gazing intently at the beautiful vial.

It was well known that the moneylender never ate lunch, so it was not until evening that a servant entered the sanctum to summon his master to the dining table. He found Hashim as Atta had left him. The same, and not the same — for now the moneylender looked swollen, distended. His eyes bulged even more than they always had, they were red-rimmed, and his knuckles were white.

He seemed to be on the point of bursting! As though, under the influence of the misappropriated relic, he had filled up with some spectral fluid which might at any moment ooze uncontrollably from his every bodily opening.

He had to be helped to the table, and then the explosion did indeed take place.

Seemingly careless of the effect of his words on the carefully constructed and fragile constitution of the family's life, Hashim began to gush, to spume long streams of awful truths. In horrified silence, his children heard their father turn upon his wife, and reveal to her that for many years their marriage had been the worst of his afflictions. "An end to politeness!" he thundered. "An end to hypocrisy!"

Next, and in the same spirit, he revealed to his family the existence of a mistress; he informed them also of his regular visits to paid women. He told his wife that, far from being the principal beneficiary of his will, she would receive no more than the eighth portion which was her due under Islamic law. Then he turned upon his children, screaming at Atta for his lack of academic ability — "A dope! I have been cursed with a dope!" — and accusing his daughter of lasciviousness, because she went around the city barefaced, which was unseemly for any good Muslim girl to do. She should, he commanded, enter purdah forthwith.

Hashim left the table without having eaten and fell into the deep sleep of a man who has got many things off his chest, leaving his children stunned, in tears, and the dinner going cold on the sideboard under the gaze of an anticipatory bearer.

At five o'clock the next morning the moneylender forced his family to rise, wash, and say their prayers. From then on, he began to pray five times daily for the first time in his life, and his wife and children were obliged to do likewise.

Before breakfast, Huma saw the servants, under her father's direction, constructing a great heap of books in the garden and setting fire to it. The only volume left untouched was the Qur'an, which Hashim wrapped in a silken cloth and placed on a table in the hall. He ordered each member of his family to read passages from this book for at least two hours per day. Visits to the cinema were forbidden. And if Atta invited male friends to the house, Huma was to retire to her room.

By now, the family had entered a state of shock and dismay; but there was worse to come.

That afternoon, a trembling debtor arrived at the house to confess his inability to pay the latest installment of interest owed, and made the mistake of reminding Hashim, in somewhat blustering fashion, of the Qur'an's strictures against usury. The moneylender flew into a rage and attacked the fellow with one of his large collection of bullwhips.

By mischance, later the same day a second defaulter came to plead for time, and was seen fleeing Hashim's study with a great gash in his arm, because Huma's father had called him a thief of other men's money and had tried to cut off the wretch's right hand with one of the thirty-eight kukri knives hanging on the study walls.

These breaches of the family's unwritten laws of decorum alarmed Atta and Huma, and when, that evening, their mother attempted to calm Hashim down, he struck her on the face with an open hand. Atta leapt to his mother's defense and he, too, was sent flying.

"From now on," Hashim bellowed, "there's going to be some discipline around here!"

The moneylender's wife began a fit of hysterics which continued throughout that night and the following day, and which so provoked her husband that he threatened her with divorce, at which she fled to her room, locked the door, and subsided into a raga of sniffling. Huma now lost her composure, challenged her father openly, and announced (with that same independence of spirit which he had encouraged in her) that she would wear no cloth over her face; apart from anything else, it was bad for the eyes.

On hearing this, her father disowned her on the spot and gave her one week in which to pack her bags and go.

By the fourth day, the fear in the air of the house had become so thick that it was difficult to walk around. Atta told his shock-numbed sister: "We are descending to gutter level — but I know what must be done."

That afternoon, Hashim left home accompanied by two hired thugs to extract the unpaid dues from his two insolvent clients. Atta went immediately to his father's study. Being the son and heir, he possessed his own key to the moneylender's safe. This he now used, and removing the little vial from its hiding-place, he slipped it into his trouser pocket and relocked the safe door.

Now he told Huma the secret of what his father had fished out of Lake Dal, and exclaimed: "Maybe I'm crazy — maybe the awful things that are happening have made me cracked — but I am convinced there will be no peace in our house until this hair is out of it."

His sister at once agreed that the hair must be returned, and Atta set off in a hired shikara to Hazratbal mosque. Only when the boat had delivered him into the throng of the distraught faithful which was swirling around the desecrated shrine did Atta discover that the relic was no longer in his pocket. There was only a hole, which his mother, usually so attentive to household matters, must have overlooked under the stress of recent events.

Atta's initial surge of chagrin was quickly replaced by a feeling of profound relief.

"Suppose," he imagined, "that I had already announced to the mullahs that the hair was on my person! They would never have believed me now — and this mob would have lynched me! At any rate, it has gone, and that's a load off my mind." Feeling more contented than he had for days, the young man returned home.

Here he found his sister bruised and weeping in the hall; upstairs, in her bedroom, his mother wailed like a brand-new widow. He begged Huma to tell him what had happened, and when she replied that their father, returning from his brutal business trip, had once again noticed a glint of silver between boat and quay, had once again scooped up the errant relic, and was consequently in a rage to end all rages, having beaten the truth out of her — then Atta buried his face in his hands and sobbed out his opinion, which was that the hair was persecuting them, and had come back to finish the job.

It was Huma's turn to think of a way out of their troubles.

While her arms turned black and blue and great stains spread across her forehead, she hugged her brother and whispered to him that she was determined to get rid of the hair *at all costs* — she repeated this last phrase several times.

"The hair," she then declared, "was stolen from the mosque; so it can be stolen from this house. But it must be a genuine robbery, carried out by a bona fide thief, not by one of us who are under the hair's thrall — by a thief so desperate that he fears neither capture nor curses."

Unfortunately, she added, the theft would be ten times harder to pull off now that their father, knowing that there had already been one attempt on the relic, was certainly on his guard.

"Can you do it?"

Huma, in a room lit by candle and storm lantern, ended her account with one further question: "What assurances can you give that the job holds no terrors for you still?"

The criminal, spitting, stated that he was not in the habit of providing references, as a cook might, or a gardener, but he was not alarmed so easily, certainly not by any children's djinni of a curse. Huma had to be content with this boast, and proceeded to describe the details of the proposed burglary.

"Since my brother's failure to return the hair to the mosque, my father has taken to sleeping with his precious treasure under his pillow. However, he sleeps alone, and very energetically; only enter his room without waking him, and he will certainly have tossed and turned quite enough to make the theft a simple matter. When you have the vial, come to my room," and here she handed Sheikh Sín a plan of her home, "and I will hand over all the jewelry owned by my mother and myself. You will find . . . it is worth . . . that is, you will be able to get a fortune for it . . ."

It was evident that her self-control was weakening and that she was on the point of physical collapse.

"Tonight," she burst out finally. "You must come tonight!"

No sooner had she left the room than the old criminal's body was convulsed by a fit of coughing: he spat blood into an old vanaspati can. The great Sheikh, the Thief of Thieves, had become a sick man, and every day the time drew nearer when some young pretender to his power would stick a dagger in his stomach. A lifelong addiction to gambling had left him almost as poor as he had been when, decades ago, he had started out in this line of work as a mere pickpocket's apprentice; so in the extraordinary commission he had accepted from the moneylender's daughter he saw his opportunity of amassing enough wealth at a stroke to leave the valley forever, and acquire the luxury of a respectable death which would leave his stomach intact.

As for the Prophet's hair, well, neither he nor his blind wife had ever had much to say for prophets — that was one thing they had in common with the moneylender's thunderstruck clan.

It would not do, however, to reveal the nature of this, his last crime, to his four sons. To his consternation, they had all grown up to be hopelessly devout men, who even spoke of making the pilgrimage to Mecca some day. "Absurd!" their father would laugh at them. "Just tell me how you will go." For, with a parent's absolutist love, he had made sure they were all provided with a lifelong source of high income by crippling them at birth, so that, as they dragged themselves around the city, they earned excellent money in the begging business.

The children, then, could look after themselves.

He and his wife would be off soon with the jewel boxes of the moneylender's women. It was a timely chance indeed that had brought the beautiful bruised girl into his corner of the town.

That night, the large house on the shore of the lake lay blindly waiting, with silence lapping at its walls. A burglar's night: clouds in the sky and mists on the winter water. Hashim the moneylender was asleep, the only member of his family to whom sleep had come that night. In another room, his son Atta lay deep in the coils of his coma with a blood clot forming on his brain, watched over by a mother who had let down her long graying hair to show her grief, a mother who placed warm compresses on his head with gestures redolent of impotence. In a third bedroom Huma waited, fully dressed, amidst the jewel-heavy caskets of her desperation.

At last a bulbul sang softly from the garden below her window and, creeping downstairs, she opened a door to the bird, on whose face there was a scar in the shape of the Nastaliq letter *sin*.

Noiselessly, the bird flew up the stairs behind her. At the head of the staircase they parted, moving in opposite directions along the corridor of their conspiracy without a glance at one another.

Entering the moneylender's room with professional ease, the burglar, Sín, discovered that Huma's predictions had been wholly accurate. Hashim lay sprawled diagonally across his bed, the pillow untenanted by his head, the prize easily accessible. Step by padded step, Sín moved towards the goal.

It was at this point that, in the bedroom next door, young Atta sat bolt upright in his bed, giving his mother a great fright, and without any warning — prompted by goodness knows what pressure of the blood clot upon his brain — began screaming at the top of his voice:

"*Thief! Thief! Thief!*"

It seems probable that his poor mind had been dwelling, in these last moments, upon his own father; but it is impossible to be certain, because having uttered these three emphatic words the young man fell back upon his pillow and died.

At once his mother set up a screeching and a wailing and a keening and a howling so earsplittingly intense that they completed the work which Atta's cry had begun — that is, her laments penetrated the walls of her husband's bedroom and brought Hashim wide awake.

Sheikh Sín was just deciding whether to dive beneath the bed or brain the moneylender good and proper when Hashim grabbed the tiger-striped swordstick which always stood propped up in a corner beside his bed, and rushed from the room without so much as noticing the burglar who stood on the opposite side of the bed in the darkness. Sín stooped quickly and removed the vial containing the Prophet's hair from its hiding place.

Meanwhile Hashim had erupted into the corridor, having un-sheathed the sword inside his cane. In his right hand he held the weapon and was waving it about dementedly. His left hand was shaking the stick. A shadow came rushing towards him through the midnight darkness of the passageway and, in his somnolent anger, the moneylender thrust his sword fatally through its heart. Turning up the light, he found that he had murdered his daughter, and under the dire influence of this accident he was so overwhelmed by remorse that he turned the sword upon himself, fell upon it, and so extinguished his life. His wife, the sole surviving member of the family, was driven mad by the general carnage and had to be committed to an asylum for the insane by her brother, the city's Deputy Commissioner of Police.

Sheikh Sín had quickly understood that the plan had gone awry.

Abandoning the dream of the jewel boxes when he was but a few yards from its fulfillment, he climbed out of Hashim's window and made his escape during the appalling events described above. Reaching home before dawn, he woke his wife and confessed his failure. It would be necessary, he whispered, for him to vanish for a while. Her blind eyes never opened until he had gone.

The noise in the Hashim household had roused their servants and even managed to awaken the night watchman, who had been fast asleep as usual on his charpoy by the street gate. They alerted the police, and the Deputy Commissioner himself was informed. When he heard of Huma's death, the mournful officer opened and read the sealed letter which his niece had given him, and instantly led a large detachment of armed men into the light-repellent gullies of the most wretched and disreputable part of the city.

The tongue of a malicious cat burglar named Huma's fellow conspirator; the finger of an ambitious bank robber pointed at the house in which he lay concealed; and although Sín managed to crawl through a hatch in the attic and attempt a rooftop escape, a bullet from the Deputy Commissioner's own rifle penetrated his stomach and brought him crashing messily to the ground at the feet of Huma's enraged uncle.

From the dead thief's pocket rolled a vial of tinted glass, cased in filigree silver.

The recovery of the Prophet's hair was announced at once on All-India Radio. One month later, the valley's holiest men assembled at the Hazratbal mosque and formally authenticated the relic. It sits to this day in a closely guarded vault by the shores of the loveliest of lakes in the heart of the valley which was once closer than any other place on earth to Paradise.

But before our story can properly be concluded, it is necessary to record that when the four sons of the dead Sheikh awoke on the morning of his death, having unwittingly spent a few minutes under the same roof as the famous hair, they found that a miracle had occurred, that they were all sound of limb and strong of wind, as whole as they might have been if their father had not thought to smash their legs in the first hours of their lives. They were, all four of them, very properly furious, because the miracle had reduced their earning powers by 75 percent, at the most conservative estimate; so they were ruined men.

Only the Sheikh's widow had some reason for feeling grateful, because although her husband was dead she had regained her sight, so that it was possible for her to spend her last days gazing once more upon the beauties of the valley of Kashmir.

William Saroyan

....

Resurrection of a Life

EVERYTHING BEGINS with inhale and exhale, and never
ends, moment after moment, yourself inhaling, and exhaling,
seeing, hearing, smelling, touching, tasting, moving, sleeping,
waking, day after day and year after year, until it is now, this moment,
the moment of your being, the last moment, which is saddest and
most glorious. It is because we remember, and I remember myself
having lived among dead moments, now deathless because of my remembrance, among people now dead, having been a part of the flux
which is now only a remembrance, of myself and this earth, a street I
was crossing and the people I saw walking in the opposite direction,
automobiles going away from me. Saxons, Dorts, Maxwells, and the
streetcars and trains, the horses and wagons, and myself, a small boy,
crossing a street, alive somehow, going somewhere.

First he sold newspapers. It was because he wanted to do something, he himself, standing in the city, shouting about what was happening in the world. He used to shout so loud, and he used to need to
shout so much, that he would forget he was supposed to be selling papers; he would get the idea that he was only supposed to shout, to
make people understand what was going on. He used to go through
the city like an alley cat, prowling all over the place, into saloons, upstairs into whorehouses, into gambling joints, to see: their faces, the
faces of those who were alive with him on the earth, and the expressions of their faces, and their forms, the faces of old whores, and the
way they talked, and the smell of all the ugly places, and the drabness
of all the old and rotting buildings, all of it, of his time and his life, a
part of him. He prowled through the city, seeing and smelling, talk-

ing, shouting about the big news, inhaling and exhaling, blood moving to the rhythm of the sea, coming and going, to the shore of self and back again to selflessness, inhale and newness, exhale and new death, and the boy in the city, walking through it like an alley cat, shouting headlines.

It was all ugly, but his being there was splendid and not an ugliness. His hands would be black with the filth of the city and his face would be black with it, but it was splendid, himself alive and walking, of the events of the earth, from day to day, new headlines every day, new things happening.

In the summer it would be very hot and his body would thirst for the sweet fluids of melons, and he would long for the shade of thick leaves and the coolness of a quiet stream, but always he would be in the city, shouting. It was his place and he was the guy, and he wanted the city to be the way it was, if that was the way. He would figure it out somehow. He used to stare at the rich people sitting at tables in hightone restaurants eating dishes of ice cream, electric fans making breezes for them, and he used to watch them ignoring the city, not going out to it and being of it, and it used to make him mad. Pigs, he used to say, having everything you want, having everything. What do you know of this place? What do you know of me, seeing this place with a clean eye, any of you? And he used to go, in the summer, to the Crystal Bar, and there he would study the fat man who slept in a chair all summer, a mountain of somebody, a man with a face and substance that lived, who slept all day every summer day, dreaming what? This fat man, three hundred pounds? What did he dream, sitting in the saloon, in the corner, not playing poker or pinochle like the other men, only sleeping and sometimes brushing the flies from his fat face? What was there for him to dream, anyway, with a body like that, and what was hidden beneath the fat of that body, what grace or gracelessness? He used to go into the saloon and spit on the floor like the men did and secretly watch the fat man sleeping, trying to figure it out. Him alive too? he used to ask. That great big sleeping thing alive? Like myself?

In the winter he wouldn't see the fat man. It would be only in the summer. The fat man was like the hot sun, very near everything, of everything, sleeping, flies on his big nose. In the winter it would be cold and there would be much rain. The rain would fall over him and his clothes would be wet, but he would never get out of the rain, and he would go on prowling around in the city, looking for whatever it was that was there and that nobody else was trying to see, and he would go in and out of all the ugly places to see how it was with the faces of the people when it rained, how the rain changed the expressions of their faces. His body would be wet with the rain, but he would go from one place to another, shouting headlines, telling the city about the things that were going on in the world.

I was this boy and he is dead now, but he will be prowling through the city when my body no longer makes a shadow upon the pavement, and if it is not this boy it will be another, myself again, another boy alive on earth, seeking the essential truth of the scene, seeking the static and precise beneath that which is in motion and which is imprecise.

The theater stood in the city like another universe, and he entered its darkness, seeking there in the falsity of pictures of man in motion the truth of his own city, and of himself, and the truth of all living. He saw their eyes: *While London Sleeps*. He saw the thin emaciated hand of theft twitching toward crime: *Jean Valjean*. In the darkness the false universe unfolded itself before him and he saw the phantoms of man going and coming, making quiet horrifying shadows: *The Cabinet of Dr. Caligari*. He saw the endless sea, smashing against rocks, birds flying, the great prairie and herds of horses, New York and greater mobs of men, monstrous trains, rolling ships, men marching to war, and a line of infantry charging another line of infantry: *The Birth of a Nation*. And sitting in the secrecy of the theater he entered the houses of the rich, saw them, the male and the female, the high ceilings, the huge marble pillars, the fancy furniture, great bathrooms, tables loaded with food, rich people laughing and eating and drinking, and then secrecy again and a male seeking a female, and himself watching carefully to understand, one pursuing and the other fleeing, and he felt the lust of man mounting in him, desire for the loveliest of them, the universal lady of the firm white shoulders and the thick round thighs, desire for her, he himself, ten years old, in the darkness.

He is dead and deathless, staring at the magnification of the kiss, straining at the mad embrace of male and female, walking alone from the theater, insane with the passion to live. And at school he could not bear them. Their shallowness was too much. Don't try to teach me. That was his attitude. Teach the idiots. Don't try to tell me anything. I am getting it direct, straight from the pit, the ugliness with the loveliness. Two times two is many million people all over the earth, lonely and shivering, groaning one at a time, trying to figure it out. Don't try to teach me. I'll figure it out for myself.

Daniel Boone? he said. Don't tell me. I knew him. Walking through Kentucky. He killed a bear. Lincoln? A big fellow walking alone, looking at things as if he pitied them, a face like the face of man. The whole countryside full of dead men, men he loved, and he himself alive. Don't ask me to memorize his speech. I know all about it, the way he stood, the way the words came from his being.

He used to get up before daybreak and walk to the San Joaquin Baking Company. It was good, the smell of freshly baked bread, and it was good to see the machine wrapping the loaves in wax paper. *Chicken bread,* he used to say, and the important man in the fine suit of clothes used to smile at him. The important man used to say, What kind of chickens you got at your house, kid? And the man would smile nicely so that there would be no insult, and he would never have to tell the man that he himself and his brother and sisters were eating the chicken bread. He would just stand by the bin, not saying anything, not asking for the best loaves, and the important man would understand, and he would pick out the best of the loaves and drop them into the sack the boy held open. If the man happened to drop a bad loaf into the sack the boy would say nothing, and a moment later the man would pick out the bad loaf and throw it back into the bin. Those chickens, he would say, they might not like that loaf. And the boy would say nothing. He would just smile. It was good bread, not too stale and sometimes very fresh, sometimes still warm, only it was bread that had fallen from the wrapping machine and couldn't be sold to rich people. It was made of the same dough, in the same ovens, only after the loaves fell they were called chicken bread and a whole sack full cost only a quarter. The important man never insulted. Maybe he himself had known hunger once, maybe as a boy he had known how it felt to be hungry for bread. He was very funny, always asking about the chickens. He knew there were no chickens, and he always picked out the best loaves.

Bread to eat, so that he could move through the city and shout. Bread to make him solid, to nourish his anger, to fill his substance with vigor that shouted at the earth. Bread to carry him to death and back again to life, inhaling, exhaling, keeping the inward flame alive. Chicken bread, he used to say, not feeling ashamed. We eat it. Sure,

sure. It isn't good enough for the rich. There are many at our house. We eat every bit of it, all the crumbs. We do not mind a little dirt on the crust. We put all of it inside. A sack of chicken bread. We know we're poor. When the wind comes up our house shakes, but we don't tremble. We can eat the bread that isn't good enough for the rich. Throw in the loaves. It is too good for chickens. It is our life. Sure we eat it. We're not ashamed. We're living on the money we earn selling newspapers. The roof of our house leaks and we catch the water in pans, but we are all there, all of us alive, and the floor of our house sags when we walk over it, and it is full of crickets and spiders, but we are in the house, living there. We eat this bread that isn't good enough for the rich, this bread that you call chicken bread.

Walking, this boy vanished, and now it is myself, another, no longer the boy, and the moment is now this moment, of my remembrance. The fig tree he loved: of all graceful things it was the most graceful, and in the winter it stood leafless, dancing, sculptural whiteness dancing. In the spring the new leaves appeared on the fig tree and the hard green figs. The sun came closer and closer and the heat increased, and he climbed the tree, eating the soft fat figs, the flowering of the lovely white woman, his lips kissing.

But always he returned to the city, back again to the place of man, the street, the structure, the door and window, the hall, the roof and floor, back again to the corners of dark secrecy, where they were dribbling out their lives, back again to the movement of mobs, to beds and chairs and stoves, away from the tree, away from the meadow and the brook. The tree was of the other earth, the older and lovelier earth, solid and quiet and of godly grace, of earth and water and sky, and of the time that was before, ancient places, quietly in the sun, Rome and Athens and Cairo, the white fig tree dancing. He talked to the tree, his mouth clenched, pulling himself over its smooth sensuous limbs, to be of you, he said, to be of your time, to be there, in the old world, and to be here as well, to eat your fruit, to feel your strength, to move with you as you dance, myself, alone in the world, with you only, my tree, that in myself which is of thee.

Dead, dead, the tree and the boy, and yet everlastingly alive, the white tree moving slowly in dance, and the boy talking to it in unspoken, unspeakable language: you, loveliness of the earth, the street waits for me, the moment of my time calls me back, and there he was suddenly, running through the streets, shouting that ten thousand huns had been destroyed. Huns? he asked. What do you mean, huns? They are men, aren't they? And he saw the people of the city smiling and talking with pleasure about the good news. He himself appreciated the goodness of the news because it helped him sell his papers, but after the shouting was over and he was himself again, he used to think of ten thousand men smashed from life to violent death, one man at a time, each man himself as he, the boy, was himself, bleeding, screaming, weeping, remembering life as dying men remember it, wanting it, gasping for breath, to go on inhaling and exhaling, living and dying, but always living somehow, stunned, horrified, ten thousand faces suddenly amazed at the monstrousness of the war, the beastliness of man, who could be so godly.

There were no words with which to articulate his rage. All that he could do was shout: but even now I cannot see the war as historians see it. Succeeding moments have carried the germ of myself to this face and form, the one of this moment, now, my being in this small room, alone, as always, remembering the boy, resurrecting him, and I cannot see the war as historians see it. Those clever fellows study all the facts and they see the war as a large thing, one of the biggest events in the legend of man, something general, involving multitudes. I see it as a large thing too, only I break it into small units of one man at a time, and I see it as a large and monstrous thing for each man involved. I see the war as death in one form or another for men dressed as soldiers, and all the men who survived the war, including myself, I see as men who died with their brothers, dressed as soldiers.

There is no such thing as a soldier. I see death as a private event, the destruction of the universe in the brain and in the senses of one man, and I cannot see any man's death as a contributing factor in the success or failure of a military campaign. The boy had to shout what had happened. Whatever happened, he had to shout it, making the city know. *Ten thousand huns killed, ten thousand,* one at a time, one, two, three, four, inestimably many, ten thousand, alive, and then dead, killed, shot, mangled, ten thousand huns, ten thousand men. I blame the historians for the distortion. I remember the coming of the gas mask to the face of man, the proper grimace of horror for the nightmare we were performing, artfully expressing the monstrousness of the inward face of man, the most pertinent truth that emerged from the whole affair. To the boy who is dead this war was the international epilepsy in the body and soul of man which brought about the systematic destruction of one man at a time until millions of men were destroyed.

There he is suddenly in the street, running, and it is 1917, shouting the most recent crime of man, extra, extra, ten thousand huns killed, himself alive, inhaling, exhaling, *ten thousand, ten thousand,* all the ugly buildings solid, all the streets solid, the city unmoved by the crime, *ten thousand,* windows opening, doors opening, and the people of the city smiling about it, good, good, ten thousand, ten thousand of them killed, good, good. Johnny, get your gun, and another trainload of boys in uniforms, going away, torn from home, from the roots of life, their tragic smiling, and the broken hearts, all things in the world broken. And the fat man, sleeping in a corner of the Crystal Bar, what of him? Sleeping there, somehow alive in spite of the lewd death in him, but never budging. Pig, he said, ten thousand huns killed, ten thousand men with solid bodies mangled to death. Does it mean nothing to you? Does it not disturb your fat dream? Boys with loves, men with wives and children. What have you, sleeping? They are all dead, all of them dead. Do you think you are alive? Do you dream you are alive? The fly on your nose is more alive than you.

Sunday would come, *O day of rest and gladness, O day of joy and light, O balm of care and sadness, Most beautiful, most bright,* and he would put on his best shirt and his best trousers, and he would try to comb his hair down, to be neat and clean, meeting God, and he would go to the small church and sit in the shadow of religion: in the beginning, the boy David felling the giant Goliath, beautiful Rebecca, mad Saul, Daniel among lions, Jesus talking quietly to the men, and in the boat shouting at them because they feared, angry at them because they had fear, calm yourselves, boys, calm yourselves, let the storm rage, let the boat sink, do you fear going to God? Ah that was lovely, that love of death was lovely, Jesus loving it: calm yourselves, boys, God damn you, calm yourselves, why are you afraid? *Still, still with thee, when purple morning breaketh, abide, abide, with me, fast falls the eventide,* ah lovely. He sat in the basement of the church, among his fellows, singing at the top of his voice. I do not believe, he said. I cannot believe. There cannot be a God. *Savior, breathe an evening blessing, sun of my soul, begin, my tongue, some heavenly theme, begin, my tongue, begin, begin.* Lovely, lovely, but I cannot believe. The poor and the rich, those who deserve life and those who deserve death, and the ugliness everywhere. Where is God? Big ships sinking at sea, submarines, men in the water, cannon booming, machine guns, men dying, ten thousand, where? But our singing, *Joy to the world, the Lord is come. Let earth receive her King. Silent Night, holy night. What grace, O Lord, my dear redeemer. Ride on, ride on, in majesty. Angels, roll the rock away; death, yield up thy mighty prey.*

No, he could not believe. He had seen for himself. It was there, in the city, all the godlessness, the eyes of the whores, the men at cards, the sleeping fat man, and the mad headlines, it was all there, unbelief, ungodliness, everywhere, all the world forgetting. How could he believe? But the music, so good and clean, so much of the best in man: *Lift up, lift up your voices now. Lo, he comes with clouds descending once for favored sinners slain. Arise, my soul, arise, shake off thy guilty fears, O for a thousand tongues to sing. Like a river glorious, holy Bible, book divine, precious treasure, thou art mine.* And spat, right on the floor of the Crystal Bar. And into Collette's Rooms, over the Rex Drug Store, the men buttoning their clothes, ten thousand huns killed, madam. *Break thou the bread of life, dear Lord, to me, as thou didst break the loaves, beside the sea.* And spat, on the floor, watching the fat man snoring. Another ship sunk. The Marne. Ypres. Russia. Poland. Spat. *Art thou weary, art thou languid, art thou sore distressed?* Zeppelin over Paris. The fat man sleeping. *Haste, traveler, haste, the night comes on.* Spat. *The storm is gathering in the west.* Cannon. Hutt! two three, four! Hutt! two three, four, how many men marching, how many? Onward, onward, un-Christian soldiers. *I was a wandering sheep.* Spat. *I did not love my home.* Your deal, Jim. Spat. *Take me, O my father, take me.* Collette, I adore you, ugly whore. Spat. *This holy bread, this holy wine. My God, is an hour so sweet?* Submarine plunging. Spat. *Take my life and let it be consecrated, Lord, to thee.* Spat.

He sat in the basement of the little church, deep in the shadow of faith, and of no faith: I cannot believe, it is too monstrous: where is the God of whom they speak, where? *Your harps, ye trembling saints, down from the willows take.* Where? Cannon. *Lead, oh lead, lead kindly light, amid the encircling gloom.* Spat. *Jesus, Savior, pilot me.* Airplane: spat: smash. *Guide me, O thou great Jehovah. Bread of heaven, bread of heaven, feed me till I want no more.* The universal lady of the dark theater: thy lips, beloved, thy shoulders and thighs, thy sea-surging blood. The tree, black figs in sunlight. Spat. *Rock of ages, cleft for me, let me hide myself in thee.* Spat. *Let the water and the blood, from thy riven side which flowed, be of sin the double cure.* Lady your arm, your arm: spat. The mountain of flesh sleeping through the summer. Ten thousand huns killed.

Sunday would come, turning him from the outward world to the inward, to the secrecy of the past, endless as the future, back to Jesus, to God; *when the weary, seeking rest, to thy goodness flee;* back to the earliest quiet: *He leadeth me, O blessed thought.* But he did not believe. He could not believe. Jesus was a remarkable fellow: you couldn't figure him out. He had a sort of pious love of death. An heroic fellow. And as for God. Well, he could not believe.

But the songs he loved and he sang them with all his might: *Hold thou my hand, O blessed nothingness, I walk with thee. Awake, my soul, stretch every nerve, and press with vigor on. Work, for the night is coming, work, for the day is done.* Spat. Right on the floor of the Crystal Bar. It is Sunday again: O blessed nothingness, we worship thee. Spat. And suddenly the sleeping fat man sneezes. Hallelujah. Amen. Spat. Sleep on, beloved sleep, and take thy rest. (Pig, he said.) *Lay down thy head upon thy Savior's breast.* We love thee well, but Jesus loves thee best. Jesus loves thee. For the Bible tells you so. Amen. The fat man sneezes. He could not believe and he could not disbelieve. Sense? There was none. But glory. There was an abundance of it. Everywhere. Madly everywhere. Those crazy birds vomiting song. Those vast trees, solid and quiet. And clouds. And sun. And night. And day. *It is not death to die,* he sang: *to leave this weary road, to be at home with God.* God? The same. Nothingness. Nowhere. Everywhere. The crazy glory, everywhere: Madam Collette's Rooms, all modern conveniences, including beds. Spat. *I know not, Oh I know not, what joys await us there.* Where? Heaven? No. Madam Collette's: in the church, the house of God, with such thoughts: the boy singing, remembering the city's lust.

Boom: Sunday morning: and the war still booming: after the singing he would go to the newspaper office and get his SPECIAL SUNDAY EXTRAS and run through the city with them, his hair combed for God, and he would shout the news: amen, *I gave my life for Jesus.* Oh yeah? Ten thousand huns killed, and I am the guy, inhaling, exhaling, running through the town, I, myself, seeing, hearing, touching, shouting, smelling, singing, wanting, I, the guy, the latest of the whole lot, alive by the grace of God: ten thousand, two times ten million, by the grace of God dead, by His grace smashed, amen, extra, extra: five cents a copy, extra, ten thousand killed.

I was this boy who is now lost and buried in the succeeding forms of myself, and I am now of this last moment, of this small room, and the night hush, time going, time coming, and gone, and gone, and again coming, and myself here, breathing, this last moment, inhale, exhale, the boy dead and alive. All that I have learned is that we breathe, from moment to moment, now, always now, and then we remember, and we see the boy moving through a city that has become lost, among people who have become dead, alive among dead moments, crossing a street, the scene thus, or standing by the bread bin in the bakery, a sack of chicken bread please so that we can live and shout about it, and it begins nowhere and it ends nowhere, and all that I know is that we are somehow alive, all of us in the light, making shadows, the sun overhead, space all around us, inhaling, exhaling, the face and form of man everywhere, pleasure and pain, sanity and madness, over and over again, war and no war, and peace and no peace, the earth solid and unaware of us, unaware of our cities, our dreams, unaware of this love I have for life, the love that was the boy's, unaware of all things, my going, my coming, the earth everlastingly itself, not of me, everlastingly precise, and the sea sullen with movement like my breathing, waves pounding the shore of myself, coming and going, and all that I know is that I am alive and glad to be, glad to be of this ugliness and this glory, somehow glad that I can remember, somehow remember the boy climbing the fig tree, unpraying but religious with joy, somehow of the earth, of the time of earth, somehow everlastingly of life, nothingness, blessed or unblessed, somehow deathless like myself, timeless, glad, insanely glad to be here, and so it is true, there is no death, somehow there is no death, and can never be.

Isaac Bashevis Singer

....

A Night in the Poorhouse

TRANSLATED BY JOSEPH SINGER

I

AT NINE in the evening the poorhouse attendant extinguished the kerosene lamp. He left burning a single tallow candle, which soon began to flicker. Outside, the frost glistened, but inside the poorhouse it was warm. The gravely ill lay in beds. The others slept on straw pallets on the floor.

Next to the oven lay Zeinvel the thief, whom peasants had crippled when they caught him stealing a horse, and Mottke the beadle, who for a long time had served as beadle to a bogus rabbi named Yontche, a cobbler who donned a Hasidic rabbi's attire and traveled through the Polish towns allegedly performing miracles. They had gone as far as Lithuania together. Yontche was subsequently caught in the act with a servant girl and fled to America. Mottke, too, tried to escape to America, but he was detained on Ellis Island and then deported because of trachoma. Later he became half blind. Both Mottke the beadle and Zeinvel the thief had lived in the poorhouse for years, although in separate rooms most of the time.

Zeinvel was tall, and as black as a gypsy, with slanted eyes, a head of black hair, and a mouth full of white teeth. Besides being lame, he suffered from consumption. As a young man he had had the reputation of being a dandy. He managed to trim his beard even in the poorhouse. Mottke was small, round like a barrel, with tufts of flax-blond hair around his scabby skull and with a yellow beard that grew on one cheek only. His eyes were always swollen and half closed. He was something of a scholar, and it was said that he and Yontche used to switch roles. One month Yontche would be the rabbi and Mottke the beadle; the next month it was the other way around.

After a while the tallow candle went out. A full moon was shining outside and its light reflected up from the snow upon the poorhouse walls. Zeinvel and Mottke never went to sleep before midnight. They chatted and told stories.

Mottke was saying, "Cold outside, eh? It's going to get even colder. Here in Poland the cold is still bearable, but when a frost comes up in Lithuania oaks burst in the forests. One thing is good there — wood is cheap. The villages are tiny, but almost all the men are learned. You meet a carpenter or a blacksmith — by day he planes a board or pounds his hammer on the anvil, but after the evening services he reads a chapter of the Mishnah to a group in the study house. They don't set much store by Hasidic rabbis. You can travel half of Lithuania without seeing a Hasid. The men avoided us, but the women used to come to us on the sly, and brought whatever they could — a chicken, a dozen eggs, a measure of buckwheat, even a garland of garlic. There's no lack of sickness anywhere, and we gave them all kinds of remedies — cow's eggs with duck milk, as well as various amulets and talismans we both invented. When we were in Lithuania, a thing happened that turned a village topsy-turvy."

"What happened?" Zeinvel asked.

"Something with a dybbuk."

"A dybbuk in Lithuania?"

"Yes, in Lithuania. I had been told that the Litvaks didn't believe in dybbuks. The Vilna Gaon didn't believe in such things, and from the Vilna Gaon to God is but one step. But what the eyes see can't be denied. The name of the village was Zabrynka. When Yontche and I got there, the ritual slaughterer invited us for the Sabbath repast. In Lithuania a Sabbath guest doesn't sleep in the poorhouse. A bed is made up for him at his host's house. The slaughterer's name was Bunem Leib, and his wife's Hiene — a name not heard in our parts. They had only one daughter, Freidke, a short girl with red hair and freckles. She was already engaged to a youth who was studying slaughtering under her father. His name was Chlavna. In Lithuania they have the queerest names. He was a handsome young man — tall, dark, well dressed. In Lithuania no one wears a satin robe on the Sabbath, unless maybe a rabbi. Nor are their earlocks as long as here in Poland. Everything with them is different. We put sugar into gefilte fish, they put pepper.

"Yontche was a glutton. The moment he entered a house, he took right to the food. I like to look around. I noticed that Freidke was madly in love with Chlavna. She never took her eyes off him. Her eyes were blue, sharp, and kind of melancholy. Why? It's in my nature that I notice things whether they concern me or not. A healthy young fellow should have an appetite, but it struck me that Chlavna hardly ate a thing. Whatever was served him, he left over — the Sabbath loaf, the soup, the meat, even the carrot stew. When Hiene served him a glass of tea, his hand trembled so that he spilled it on the tablecloth. Eh, I thought, a slaughterer's hand shouldn't tremble. That won't do.

"Yontche and I celebrated the Sabbath there, and after the Sabbath we went our way. We didn't know it then, but that winter was our last together. We hadn't had much luck in Lithuania, and Yontche acted more like a coachman than like a rabbi. Usually when I left a town I soon forgot everyone there, but I sat in the sleigh thinking about Freidke and Chlavna and I knew somehow that I'd be coming back to Zabrynka. But why? What did these strangers mean to me?

"We came to another town and there I really quarreled with Yontche, and told him that he was an outcast and that he should go to blazes. I felt so downhearted I went to a tavern. I sat down, took a shot of vodka, and someone came up to me — a little shipping agent — and said, 'You don't recognize me, but we met in Zabrynka. You are the beadle.'

"'What's happening in Zabrynka?' I asked, and he said, 'You haven't heard the news? A dybbuk has entered the slaughterer's daughter.'

"'A dybbuk?' I said. 'In Freidke?'

"And he told me this story: That Sabbath night, soon after we had left town, the butchers brought to Bunem Leib a large black bull with spiral horns, a tough beast. Since Freidke's fiancé, Chlavna, had learned the craft, with all its laws, and had already slaughtered several calves, Bunem Leib decided to let him slaughter it. When a bull is slaughtered, the butchers tie him with ropes, throw him to the ground, and hold him until he bleeds to death. But when Chlavna made the benediction and slashed the bull's throat the animal tore loose, lunged to its feet, and began to run round with such fury that he nearly brought down the slaughterhouse. He went racing across the marketplace and cracked a lamppost and overturned a wagon. All this time, the blood gushed from him as if from a tap. After a long chase, the butchers caught him and dragged him back to the slaughterhouse, already a carcass. Only then did they discover that Chlavna had vanished. Someone said that he was seen leaning over the well. Others saw him running toward the river. They searched with poles, but he wasn't found. The rabbi examined the knife Chlavna used and he found the blade jagged. The bull was declared unkosher. The butchers fell into such a rage against Bunem Leib for turning the job over to Chlavna that they shattered his windowpanes.

"That night was to Bunem Leib and to his household one long turmoil. At dawn, when he and his wife had finally dozed off, they were roused by a strange wail — not human but animal. Freidke stood naked in the center of the room bellowing like an ox. She was shaking, jerking, and lowing, as if she were the very bull her fiancé had botched. Then a terrible human voice tore itself out from her mouth. All Zabrynka came running, and it became clear that a dybbuk had entered Freidke. The dybbuk cried that he had been a man in life — an evildoer, a drunk, a lecher. When he died, his soul hadn't been allowed into Heaven but had been sentenced to be reincarnated as a bull. The Angel of Death told him that when this bull was slaughtered according to the ritual law and pious Jews ate his flesh after reciting the right benediction, he, the sinner, would be redeemed. Now that Chlavna had rendered the meat impure, the sinner's forsaken soul had entered Freidke.

"I was so taken aback by what the shipping agent told me that I left Yontche bag and baggage, grabbed my bundle, and headed back to Zabrynka. A deep snow had fallen and a bitter frost had settled in. I couldn't get a sleigh and I had to walk halfway there. The wind nearly blew me away. I was sure that my end had come and I began to say my confession."

"You fell in love with that Freidke, eh?"

"In love? You talk nonsense."

"What happened next?" Zeinvel asked.

"I came to Zabrynka in the middle of the night. The shutters were locked everywhere, but Bunem Leib's house was lit up and there were people inside. They seemed to have stayed to listen to the dybbuk instead of going to sleep. No one took notice of me when I entered. I learned later that Freidke's mother had become ill from grief and had been taken to some relative. I barely recognized Bunem Leib. He had become emaciated, yellow, and drained in the few days since I was there. Freidke stood there barefoot, half naked, with straggly red hair over her shoulders, her face as white as that of a corpse and her eyes bulging. She screamed with a voice I could never have believed could come out of a girl's tender throat. This was not a human voice but that of an ox. I heard her bellow, 'Slaughter me, Bunem Leib, slaughter me! I am the bull you caused to be *tref* and so doomed to eternal torment. You don't see them, but hordes of demons, hobgoblins, and devils are lurking right here waiting to tear me to pieces and carry me away to the wastelands behind the Dark Mountains. Neither your mezuzah nor the talismans and amulets you hung in all the corners of the house can help me. Look, if you are not completely blind: monsters with noses to their navels, with snakes instead of hair, with snouts of boars, as black as pitch, as red as fire, as green as gall! They dance and howl like the mad. Is it my fault, Bunem Leib, that you have chosen for your son-in-law a schlemiel, a mollycoddle who cannot wield a knife? He could as much be a slaughterer as you could be a wet nurse. His hands were shaking like those of a man of ninety. He was such a weakling that when he saw a drop of blood on the white of an egg he was ready to faint. A slaughterer cannot be afraid of blood. A real man doesn't run away from his bride-to-be when things go wrong. You picked a mama's boy for your daughter, a pampered little brat, a eunuch. He was more afraid of me, the bull, than I was of his knife! Slaughter me, Bunem Leib, and save me from all these vicious spirits. If not, I will catch you on my horns and gore you and carry you away to swamps from which there can never be any rescue.'

"'My daughter, what are you talking about? You are my child,' Bunem Leib said to her. 'Let this evil fiend only free you, and if Chlavna is not your destined one, I will find another spouse for you, God willing, and we will lead you to the wedding canopy. Merciful God, help me! I can't take any more of this anguish.'

"Bunem Leib was crying. But Freidke answered, 'I'm not your daughter but the bull you have given into the hands of a bungler. Take out your knife and slaughter me! Shed my blood! You, Bunem Leib, are a male, not a neuter. No ox, no cow, no sheep or rooster ever ran away from your knife. Kill me, Bunem Leib, kill me!'"

"You heard all this?" Zeinvel asked.

"May I hear the Messiah's ram's horn as clearly."

"Go on."

"It is impossible to tell it all. Toward dawn Bunem Leib became so tired and haggard that he had to go to sleep, but the town's rowdies took over the show. For them it was fun. Imagine, an only daughter, a quiet little dove, stands in the middle of the night, her breasts uncovered, her red hair wild as a witch's, and she confesses sins that make your head swim. I heard her say, 'While alive, I did everything to spite God. I shaved my beard, I ate pork on Yom Kippur, I fornicated with Gentile wenches and Jewish whores. I denied God, and I thought I would live to be a hundred and indulge in all my abominations. But suddenly I got sick with pox and saw that I was done for. Still, to my last breath I blasphemed God and served the idols. When I finally expired, the Burial Society wouldn't cleanse my body and they buried me without shrouds at midnight, without anyone saying Kaddish. Even before the gravediggers had thrown the last spadeful of dirt over me, the Angel Dumah opened my grave, spat at me, pierced me with his fiery rod, and dragged me to the very gates of Gehenna. He tried to hurl me inside, but Satan slammed the door and shouted, "It is a disgrace to Gehenna to allow such scum to enter into it."'

"You can be the world's biggest heretic, Zeinvel, but when you see and hear a thing like this, you must admit that there is a God."

"No, you mustn't."

"Then what was all that?"

"Nerves."

"How do nerves know what goes on in the netherworld?" Mottke asked.

"The nerves know everything."

"What are they — prophets?"

"Even better than that," Zeinvel said. "Good night."

"Well, you are talking nonsense."

Zeinvel had fallen asleep and was snoring, but Mottke lay awake. He talked to himself: "Gone to sleep, eh? A dunce, a boob . . . Thinks he knows it all, but to me he's still a fool."

"Mottke, shut up."

"You're not asleep?"

"I am asleep, but I hear every word anyway. I learned this trick in jail. There, if you fall asleep for real they'll strip the shirt right off your back. What became of Freidke?"

"How should I know? I stayed there for three days, then I went my way. I haven't told you everything yet. Neighbors swore to me that Freidke had never sung before. True, a well-brought-up girl doesn't let her voice be heard, so as not to arouse us males; nevertheless, if a girl has a voice she'll sing while rocking a child, or she will join in the Sabbath chants. All of a sudden Freidke started singing droll songs in Yiddish, Polish, even in Russian. She serenaded a bride and made wedding jests, all in rhyme. She mocked the women haggling in the butcher shops, and their splashing in the ritual bath. The hoodlums made snide remarks to her, and she answered each one on his own terms. She fast-talked them so, they were left speechless. All the neighbors said the same — this wasn't Freidke but a wag, a rascal, with a tongue like a razor. His profanities left you rolling with laughter. Brother, I stood by and watched a female turn both into a bull and into a man. Nerves can't do this."

"What can do it?"

"Only God."

"There is no God."

"How did the world form?" Mottke asked.

"It grew from itself like a scab."

11

Zeinvel dozed off again, but Mottke still lay awake. The sick in the poorhouse sighed and mumbled in their sleep. Wasn't Zeinvel right, Mottke reflected. A merciful God wouldn't allow so much misery. People die like flies here. Each day the Burial Society comes with the ablution board to carry out a body.

For a while Mottke listened to a cricket chirping behind the stove. It jingled as if with little bells. It told a tale without a beginning or an end. How was it that it chirped the whole night, Mottke wondered. Don't crickets need sleep too? Or do they sleep during the day? And what do they find to eat among the rags? It was crazy to think that this cricket had a father, a mother, a grandfather, a grandmother, and maybe children too. I'm all befuddled, Mottke mused. I'm dead tired all day, but at night my brain works like a churn.

Sometimes during the day, when Mottke wanted to show off his erudition, he forgot everything, jumbled passages like some ignoramus. But in the middle of the night his brain opened up. He recalled whole chapters of the Scripture, sections of the Gemara, even the liturgies of Rosh Hashanah and Yom Kippur. People who had died so long ago that he no longer remembered their names materialized seemingly alive before him. He remembered names of villages in which he had stayed with Yontche. Chants of cantors and songs of Hasidim came back to his mind. Mottke had been raised in a religious home. His father had taken him along to the wonder rabbi at Turisk. As a boy, he had read Hasidic books, had even dreamed of becoming a rabbi. But his father had died of typhus, his mother had married some boor, and Mottke had slipped into the confidence game with Yontche.

Now Mottke began droning a song that he had heard in Turisk at the Sabbath meal:

> *I'll sing with praise*
> *To open the gates*
> *Of the Heavenly orchards*
> *For their sacred mates.*

Zeinvel got to coughing and sat up. "Why are you singing in the middle of the night? Are you hungry?"

"I'm not hungry."

"You've got a burr in your saddle, eh?"

"Wasted away a life for nothing," Mottke said, shocked at his own words.

"You want to become a penitent like that musician who blindfolded himself so that he couldn't look at women?"

"Too late for that."

"Yes, brother, for us it might have been too late when we were born," Zeinvel said. "That business with Freidke was all stuff and nonsense. It's all made up — the Jewish God, the Christian God. That Chlavna was a clumsy dolt and a miserable coward. Freidke, on the other hand, was putting on an act because he deserted her. Young girls hear old wives' tales, absorb every trifle, and then they mimic them.

"I had a wild female once, a Talmud teacher's daughter. Mindle was her name. She looked like a kosher virgin. I could have sworn she couldn't count to two — a pale little face, big black eyes. It all started when I met her at the pump and filled a pail of water for her. She gave me a pretty thank-you and threw in a sweet smile. I was already a thief by then and I had had more women than you have hairs on your head. At that time, it wasn't easy to get a Jewish girl — not in our parts, anyway — but there was no shortage of shiksas. They don't know any pretenses. They've got Uncle Esau's blood in their veins. Well, but I saw fire in Mindle's eyes. Each time I saw her going with her pail, I ran outside with my pail. I must have pumped a hundred pails for her. I began thinking that it was a waste of time. Suddenly I hand her the pail and she slips a note into my hand. I ran so fast with my own pail that I spilled half of it. I walked into the house and I read, 'Meet me in the cemetery at midnight.'

"One line, that's all — fancy handwriting. I had tasted everything — girls, matrons, young, old — but I grew as rattled as a yeshiva boy. I was scared too. In those days I still believed in the creatures of the night. What kind of girl would meet a fellow in the cemetery at midnight? It was said that corpses prayed in the synagogue at night and that if someone walked by they would call him inside to read from the Torah. Also, a carpenter's daughter had hanged herself in our town because some tramp made her pregnant, and it was said that she climbed out of her grave in the nights and wandered among the tombstones. Just the same, I couldn't wait for night to fall and, later, for the clock on the town hall to toll eleven-thirty. My piece of goods had figured out everything in advance. Her father, a fervent Hasid who wore two skullcaps, one in front and one in back, went to bed with the chickens. He got up before dawn to bewail the Destruction of the Temple. The mother traveled to fairs to support her older daughter, a penniless widow who lived in Krasnystaw with three children. She sold jackets that she padded herself.

"I'll cut it short. Mindle had scheduled our meeting for the end of the month, when the moon wasn't shining and when the mother was off to some fair. The night was hot and dark. The road to the cemetery led through Church Street. The Jews lived close to the marketplace. Farther along, only Gentiles lived — tiny houses and huge dogs. I walked by and they attacked me like a pack of wolves. With one dog you can manage, but with fifty you don't stand a chance. Besides, when the Gentiles hear their dogs bark, they come running outside with cudgels. I thought I was going to be martyred, but somehow I made it to the cemetery. I tapped, feeling my way like a blind man. I was still a believer then, and in my mind I donated eighteen groschen to charity. I stretched out my arms and there she was, as if she had emerged from the ground. When you're scared, all desire leaves you, but the moment I touched her she burned me like a hot coal. She whispered a secret in my ear. There was no need for talk. How can such a firebrand grow up in a pious teacher's house?"

"She satisfied you, eh?" Mottke asked.

"That's not the word," Zeinvel said. "We fell on each other and we couldn't break apart. I took it for granted she was a virgin, but that would be the day!"

"A tasty piece, eh?"

"We lay for hours among the headstones and I couldn't get enough. As hot as fire and as sharp as a dagger. Whenever I began to cool off she said something so spicy that I shuddered and the game started all over again. Where she had learned such talk in our little village I'll never know."

"How is it you didn't marry her?" Mottke asked.

"Eh? I wanted a respectable girl, not a slut. She spoke frankly: one man to her was like an appetizer. She needed many, always new ones. I'm no saint, but I wished a wife like my mother. In my trade, you've got to be ready to do time. To sit in prison and worry that your wife is running around with every bum is scant pleasure. Even as I fondled and kissed her and promised her the moon and the stars, I longed for my Malkele, may she rest in peace. I already knew her by then. She was a friend of my sister Zirel. I wasn't planning to remain a thief. I wanted to amass a stake and become a horse dealer. But man proposes and God disposes."

"That means you *do* believe in God," Mottke said.

"It only sounds this way. What is God? Who is He? No one has gone up to Heaven and come to an understanding with Him. It's all written in the Torah, but what's the Torah? Parchment and ink. Whoever holds the pen writes what pleases him. For nearly two thousand years Jews have been waiting for the Messiah, but he's in no hurry to show up."

"So the world is lawless, eh?"

"Whoever can, grabs. And whoever can't lies six feet under."

"Still, if good people didn't send us groats and soup here we would long since have been flat on our backs," Mottke said.

"They don't do it for us," Zeinvel said. "They think this will reserve them golden chairs in Paradise and large portions of the Leviathan."

"You once said yourself that you believe in fate," Mottke argued. "You said that the last time you went to steal a horse you knew in advance that you would come a cropper and that it was fated this way. Those were your very words."

"God is God and fate is fate. I had stolen a half dozen nags within a few weeks, and the peasants had started sleeping in the stables. They stood guard with axes and rattles. My Malkele begged me: 'Zeinvel, enough!' She knelt before me and warned me to stay home. She spoke about opening a store or, if worst came to worst, of going to America. She demanded that I swear on the Pentateuch that I would begin a new life. But even as I took the holy oath I knew that it wasn't worth a pinch of snuff. It's not in me to stand in a store and weigh out two ounces of almonds or cream of tartar. I don't have the patience for such drivel. Nor was I drawn to the land of Columbus. Everyone who went there ended up pressing pants or peddling from door to door. Letters came telling of a depression in New York, of workers picking food out of garbage cans. I loved Malkele, but she wasn't Mindle. I was faithful to her, God is my witness, but to sit with her days and nights and have her chip away at me didn't appeal to me. She had miscarried twice. She was constantly bewailing her lot and mine too. I wanted once and for all to test my luck."

"You believe in luck?"

"Yes. In good luck and bad luck."

"There is a God, there is!" Mottke said.

"And if there is, what of it? He sits in the seventh Heaven, the angels flatter Him with their hymns, and He cares as much about us as about last year's frost."

"What became of Mindle?" Mottke asked.

"Oh, her father married her off to some dummy, a son of a rich Hasid, a follower of his rabbi's. My little kitten stood with him under the canopy pure and veiled as if she had never been touched. Why she would allow herself to be used this way is a riddle to me. Such females sometimes marry a fool so that they'll have someone to dupe easily. There is a great thrill in cheating — almost as much as in stealing. But you pay for everything. She died two years later in childbirth."

"So that's how it turned out?"

"Yes. Her husband, the lummox, had gone to his rabbi's and he lingered there for months. I was doing time in the Janov jail. Later, they transferred me to Lublin. That time I was innocent. I had been falsely accused. When I finally got out, Mindle was already in the other world."

"It was surely a punishment from God," Mottke said.

"No."

It grew silent. Even the cricket had ceased its chirping. After a while Zeinvel said, "I haven't forgotten her. If there is a Gehenna, I want to lie next to her on one bed of nails."

Khushwant Singh

....

The Mark of Vishnu

"THIS IS FOR the Kala Nag," said Gunga Ram, pouring the milk into the saucer. "Every night I leave it outside the hole near the wall and it's gone by the morning."

"Perhaps it is the cat," we youngsters suggested.

"Cat!" said Gunga Ram with contempt. "No cat goes near that hole. Kala Nag lives there. As long as I give him milk, he will not bite anyone in this house. You can all go about with bare feet and play where you like."

We were not having any patronage from Gunga Ram.

"You're a stupid old Brahmin," I said. "Don't you know snakes don't drink milk? At least one couldn't drink a saucerful every day. The teacher told us that a snake eats only once in several days. We saw a grass snake which had just swallowed a frog. It stuck like a blob in its throat and took several days to dissolve and go down its tail. We've got dozens of them in the lab in methylated spirit. Why, last month the teacher bought one from a snake charmer which could run both ways. It had another head with a pair of eyes at the tail. You should have seen the fun when it was put in the jar. There wasn't an empty one in the lab. So the teacher put it in one which had a Russell's viper. He caught its two ends with a pair of forceps, dropped it in the jar, and quickly put the lid on. There was an absolute storm as it went round and round in the glass tearing the decayed viper into shreds."

Gunga Ram shut his eyes in pious horror.

"You will pay for it one day. Yes, you will."

It was no use arguing with Gunga Ram. He, like all good Hindus, believed in the Trinity of Brahma, Vishnu, and Siva — the creator, preserver, and destroyer. Of these he was most devoted to Vishnu. Every morning he smeared his forehead with a V mark in sandalwood paste to honor the deity. Although a Brahmin, he was illiterate and full of superstition. To him, all life was sacred, even it if was of a serpent or scorpion or centipede. Whenever he saw one he quickly shoved it away lest we kill it. He picked up wasps we battered with our badminton rackets and tended their damaged wings. Sometimes he got stung. It never seemed to shake his faith. The more dangerous the animal, the more devoted Gunga Ram was to its existence. Hence the regard for snakes; above all, the cobra, who was the Kala Nag.

"We will kill your Kala Nag if we see him."

"I won't let you. It's laid a hundred eggs and if you kill it all the eggs will become cobras and the house will be full of them. Then what will you do?"

"We'll catch them alive and send them to Bombay. They milk them there for anti-snakebite serum. They pay two rupees for a live cobra. That makes two hundred rupees straightaway."

"Your doctors must have udders. I never saw a snake have any. But don't you dare touch this one. It is a phannyar — it is hooded. I've seen it. It's three hands long. As for its hood!" Gunga Ram opened the palms of his hands and his head swayed from side to side. "You should see it basking on the lawn in the sunlight."

"That just proves what a liar you are. The phannyar is the male, so it couldn't have laid the hundred eggs. You must have laid the eggs yourself."

The party burst into peals of laughter.

"Must be Gunga Ram's eggs. We'll soon have a hundred Gunga Rams."

Gunga Ram was squashed. It was the lot of a servant to be constantly squashed. But having the children of the household make fun of him was too much even for Gunga Ram. They were constantly belittling him with their newfangled ideas. They never read their scriptures. Nor even what the Mahatma said about nonviolence. It was just shotguns to kill birds and the jars of methylated spirit to drown snakes. Gunga Ram would stick to his faith in the sanctity of life. He would feed and protect snakes because snakes were the most vile of God's creatures on earth. If you could love them, instead of killing them, you proved your point.

What the point was which Gunga Ram wanted to prove was not

clear. He just proved it by leaving the saucerful of milk by the snake hole every night and finding it gone in the morning.

One day we saw Kala Nag. The monsoons had burst with all their fury and it had rained in the night. The earth, which had lain parched and dry under the withering heat of the summer sun, was teeming with life. In little pools frogs croaked. The muddy ground was littered with crawling worms, centipedes, and velvety ladybirds. Grass had begun to show and the banana leaves glistened bright and glossy green. The rain had flooded Kala Nag's hole. He sat in an open patch on the lawn. His shiny black hood glistened in the sunlight. He was big — almost six feet in length, and rounded and fleshy, as my wrist.

"Looks like a king cobra. Let's get him."

Kala Nag did not have much of a chance. The ground was slippery and all the holes and gutters were full of water. Gunga Ram was not at home to help.

Armed with long bamboo sticks, we surrounded Kala Nag before he even scented the danger. When he saw us his eyes turned a fiery red and he hissed and spat on all sides. Then like lightning Kala Nag made for the banana grove.

The ground was too muddy and he slithered. He had hardly gone five yards when a stick caught him in the middle and broke his back. A volly of blows reduced him to a squishy-squashy pulp of black and white jelly, spattered with blood and mud. His head was still undamaged.

"Don't damage the hood," yelled one of us. "We'll take Kala Nag to school."

So we slid a bamboo stick under the cobra's belly and lifted him on the end of the pole. We put him in a large biscuit tin and tied it up with string. We hid the tin under a bed.

At night I hung around Gunga Ram waiting for him to get his saucer of milk. "Aren't you going to take any milk for the Kala Nag tonight?"

"Yes," answered Gunga Ram irritably. "You go to bed."

He did not want any more argument on the subject.

"He won't need the milk anymore."

Gunga Ram paused.

"Why?"

"Oh, nothing. There are so many frogs about. They must taste better than your milk. You never put any sugar in it anyway."

The next morning Gunga Ram brought back the saucer with the milk still in it. He looked sullen and suspicious.

"I told you snakes like frogs better than milk."

Whilst we changed and had breakfast Gunga Ram hung around us. The school bus came and we clambered into it with the tin. As the bus started we held out the tin to Gunga Ram.

"Here's your Kala Nag. Safe in this box. We are going to put him in spirit."

We left him standing speechless, staring at the departing bus.

There was great excitement in the school. We were a set of four brothers, known for our toughness. We had proved it again.

"A king cobra."

"Six feet long."

The tin was presented to the science teacher.

It was on the teacher's table, and we waited for him to open it and admire our kill. The teacher pretended to be indifferent and set us some problems to work on. With studied matter-of-factness he fetched his forceps and a jar with a banded krait lying curled in muddy methylated spirit. He began to hum and untie the cord around the box.

As soon as the cord was loosened the lid flew into the air, just missing the teacher's nose. There was Kala Nag. His eyes burnt like embers and his hood was taut and undamaged. With a loud hiss he went for the teacher's face. The teacher pushed himself back on the chair and toppled over. He fell on the floor and stared at the cobra, petrified with fear. The boys stood up on their desks and yelled hysterically.

Kala Nag surveyed the scene with his bloodshot eyes. His forked tongue darted in and out excitedly. He spat furiously and then made a bid for freedom. He fell out of tin onto the floor with a loud plop. His back was broken in several places and he dragged himself painfully to the door. When he got to the threshold he drew himself up once again with his hood outspread to face another danger.

Outside the classroom stood Gunga Ram with a saucer and a jug of milk. As soon as he saw Kala Nag come up he went down on his knees. He poured the milk into the saucer and placed it near the threshold. With hands folded in prayer he bowed his head to the ground craving forgiveness. In desperate fury, the cobra hissed and spat and bit Gunga Ram all over the head — then with great effort dragged himself into a gutter and wriggled out of view.

Gunga Ram collapsed with his hands covering his face. He groaned in agony. The poison blinded him instantly. Within a few minutes he turned pale and blue and froth appeared in his mouth. On his forehead were little drops of blood. These the teacher wiped with his handkerchief. Underneath was the V mark where the Kala Nag had dug his fangs.

fate *
faith **

Amy Tan

....

Fishers of Men

YES, YES, I'm sure it was 1864. I remember now, because the year sounded very strange. Libby-ah, just listen to it: *Yi-ba-liu-si*. Miss Banner said it was like saying: Lose hope, slide into death. And I said, No, it means: Take hope, the dead remain. Chinese ** words are good and bad this way, so many meanings, depending on what you hold in your heart. **

Anyway, that was the year I gave Miss Banner the tea. And she gave me the music box, the one I once stole from her, then later returned. I remember the night we held that box between us with all those things inside that we didn't want to forget. It was just the two of us, alone for the moment, in the Ghost Merchant's House, where we lived with the Jesus Worshipers for six years. We were standing next to the holy bush, the same bush that grew the special leaves, the same leaves I used to make the tea. Only now the bush was chopped down, and Miss Banner was saying she was sorry that she let General Cape kill that bush. Such a sad, hot night, water streaming down our faces, sweat and tears, the cicadas screaming louder and louder, then falling quiet. And later, we stood in this archway, scared to death. But we were also happy. We were happy to learn we were unhappy for the same reason. That was the year that both our heavens burned.

Six years before, that's when I first met her, when I was fourteen and she was twenty-six, maybe younger or older than that. I could never tell the ages of foreigners. I came from a small place in Thistle Mountain, just south of Changmian. We were not Punti, the Chinese who claimed they had more Yellow River Han blood running through their veins, so everything should belong to them. And we weren't one of the Zhuang tribes either, always fighting each other, village against village, clan against clan. We were Hakka, Guest People — hnh! — meaning, guests not invited to stay in any good place too long. So we lived in one of many Hakka roundhouses in a poor part of the mountains, where you must farm on cliffs and stand like a goat and unearth two wheelbarrows of rocks before you can grow one handful of rice.

All the women worked as hard as the men, no difference in who carried the rocks, who made the charcoal, who guarded the crops from bandits at night. All Hakka women were this way, strong. We didn't bind our feet like Han girls, the ones who hopped around on stumps as black and rotten as old bananas. We had to walk all over the mountain to do our work, no binding cloths, no shoes. Our naked feet walked right over those sharp thistles that gave our mountain its famous name.

A suitable Hakka bride from our mountains had thick calluses on her feet and a fine, high-boned face. There were other Hakka families living near the big cities of Yongan, in the mountains, and Jintian, by the river. And the mothers from poorer families liked to match their sons to hardworking pretty girls from Thistle Mountain. During marriage-matching festivals, these boys would climb up to our high villages and our girls would sing the old mountain songs that we had brought from the north a thousand years before. A boy had to sing back to the girl he wanted to marry, finding words to match her song. If his voice was soft, or his words were clumsy, too bad, no marriage. That's why Hakka people are not only fiercely strong, they have good voices, and clever minds for winning whatever they want.

We had a saying: When you marry a Thistle Mountain girl, you get three oxen for a wife: one that breeds, one that plows, one to carry your old mother around. That's how tough a Hakka girl was. She never complained, even if a rock tumbled down the side of the mountain and smashed out her eye.

That happened to me when I was seven. I was very proud of my wound, cried only a little. When my grandmother sewed shut the hole that was once my eye, I said the rock had been loosened by a ghost horse. And the horse was ridden by the famous ghost maiden Nunumu — the *nu* that means "girl," the *numu* that means "a stare as fierce as a dagger." Nunumu, Girl with the Dagger Eye. She too lost her eye when she was young. She had witnessed a Punti man stealing another man's salt, and before she could run away, he stabbed his dagger in her face. After that, she pulled one corner of her headscarf over her blind eye. And her other eye became bigger, darker, sharp as a cat-eagle's. She robbed only Punti people, and when they saw her dagger eye, oh, how they trembled.

All the Hakkas in Thistle Mountain admired her, and not just because she robbed Punti people. She was the first Hakka bandit to join the struggle for Great Peace when the Heavenly King came back to us for help. In the spring, she took an army of Hakka maidens to Guilin, and the Manchus captured her. After they cut off her head, her lips were still moving, cursing that she would return and ruin their families for one hundred generations. That was the summer I lost my eye. And when I told everyone about Nunumu galloping by on her ghost horse, people said this was a sign that Nunumu had chosen me to be her messenger, just as the Christian God had chosen a Hakka man to be the Heavenly King. They began to call me Nunumu. And sometimes, late at night, I thought I could truly see the Bandit Maiden, not too clearly, of course, because at that time I had only one yin eye.

Soon after that, I met my first foreigner. Whenever foreigners arrived in our province, everyone in the countryside — from Nanning to Guilin — talked about them. Many Westerners came to trade in foreign mud, the opium that gave foreigners mad dreams of China. And some came to sell weapons — cannons, gunpowder, rifles, not the fast, new ones, but the slow, old kind you light with a match, leftovers from foreign battles already lost. The missionaries came to our province because they heard that the Hakkas were God Worshipers. They wanted to help more of us go to their heaven. They didn't know that a God Worshiper was not the same as a Jesus Worshiper. Later we all realized our heavens were not the same.

But the foreigner I met was not a missionary. He was an American general. The Hakka people called him Cape because that's what he always wore, a large cape, also black gloves, black boots, no hat, and a short gray jacket with buttons — like shiny coins! — running from the waist to his chin. In his hand he carried a long walking stick, rattan, with a silver tip and an ivory handle carved in the shape of a naked woman.

When he came to Thistle Mountain, people from all the villages poured down the mountainsides and met in the wide green bowl. He arrived on a prancing horse, leading fifty Cantonese soldiers, former boatmen and beggars, now riding ponies and wearing colorful army uniforms, which we heard were not Chinese or Manchu but leftovers from wars in French Africa. The soldiers were shouting, "God Worshipers! We are God Worshipers too!"

Some of our people thought Cape was Jesus, or, like the Heavenly King, another one of his younger brothers. He was very tall, had a big mustache, a short beard, and wavy black hair that flowed to his shoulders. Hakka men also wore their long hair this way, no pigtail anymore, because the Heavenly King said our people should no longer obey the laws of the Manchus. I had never seen a foreigner before and had no way of knowing his true age. But to me, he looked old. He had skin the color of a turnip, eyes as murky as shallow water. His face had sunken spots and sharp points, the same as a person with a wasting disease. He seldom smiled, but laughed often. And he spoke harsh words in a donkey bray. A man always stood by his side, serving as his go-between, translating in an elegant voice what Cape said.

The first time I saw the go-between, I thought he looked Chinese. The next minute he seemed foreign, then neither. He was like those lizards that become the colors of sticks and leaves. I learned later this man had the mother blood of a Chinese woman, the father blood of an American trader. He was stained both ways. General Cape called him *yiban ren,* the one-half man.

Yiban told us Cape had just come from Canton, where he became friends with the Heavenly King of the Great Peace Revolution. We were all astounded. The Heavenly King was a holy man who had been born a Hakka, then chosen by God to be His treasured younger son, little brother to Jesus. We listened carefully.

Cape, Yiban said, was an American military leader, a supreme general, the highest rank. People murmured. He had come across the sea to China, to help the God Worshipers, the followers of Great Peace. People shouted, "Good! Good!" He was a God Worshiper himself, and he admired us, our laws against opium, thievery, the pleasures of the dark parts of women's bodies. People nodded, and I stared with my one eye at the naked lady on the handle of Cape's walking stick. He said that he had come to help us win our battle against the Manchus, that this was God's plan, written more than a thousand years before in the Bible he was holding. People pushed forward to see. We knew that same plan. The Heavenly King had already told us that the Hakka people would inherit the earth and rule God's Chinese kingdom. Cape reported the Great Peace soldiers had already captured many cities, had gathered much money and land. And now, the struggle was ready to move north — if only the rest of the God Worshipers in Thistle Mountain would join him as soldiers. Those who fought, he added, would share in the bounty — warm clothes, plenty to eat, weapons, and later, land of their own, new status and ranks, schools and homes, men and women separate. The Heavenly King would send food to their families left behind. By now, everybody was shouting, "Great Peace! Great Peace!"

Then General Cape tapped his walking stick on the ground. Everyone grew quiet again. He called Yiban to show us the gifts the Heavenly King had asked him to bring. Barrels of gunpowder! Bushels of rifles! Baskets of French African uniforms, some torn and already stained with blood. But everyone agreed they were still very fine. Everybody was saying, "Hey, see these buttons, feel this cloth." That day, many, many people, men and women, joined the army of the Heavenly King. I could not. I was too young, only seven, so I was very unhappy inside. But then the Cantonese soldiers passed out uniforms — only to the men, none to the women. And when I saw that, I was not as unhappy as before.

The men put on their new clothes. The women examined their new rifles, the matches for lighting them. Then General Cape tapped his walking stick again and asked Yiban to bring out his gift to us. We all pressed forward, eager to see yet another surprise. Yiban brought back a wicker cage, and inside was a pair of white doves. General Cape announced in his curious Chinese that he had asked God for a sign that we would be an ever victorious army. God sent down the doves. The doves, General Cape said, meant we poor Hakkas would have the rewards of Great Peace we had hungered for over the last thousand years. He then opened the cage door and pulled out the birds. He threw them into the air, and the people roared. They ran and pushed, jumping to catch the creatures before they could fly away. One man fell forward onto a rock. His head cracked open and his brains started to pour out. But people jumped right over him and kept chasing those rare and precious birds. One dove was caught, the other flew away. So someone ate a meal that night.

My mother and father joined the struggle. My uncles, my aunts, my older brothers, nearly everyone over thirteen in Thistle Mountain and from the cities down below. Fifty or sixty thousand people. Peasants and landowners, soup peddlers and teachers, bandits and beggars, and not just Hakkas, but Yaos and Miaos, Zhuang tribes, and even the Puntis who were poor. It was a great moment for Chinese people, all of us coming together like that.

I was left behind in Thistle Mountain to live with my grandmother. We were a pitiful village of scraps, babies and children, the old and the lame, cowards and idiots. Yet we were happy, because just as he had promised, the Heavenly King sent his soldiers to bring us food, more kinds than we could have ever imagined in a hundred years. And the soldiers also brought us stories of great victories: How the Heavenly King had set up his new kingdom in Nanjing. How taels of silver were more plentiful than rice. What fine houses everyone lived in, men in one compound, women in another. What a peaceful life — church on Sunday, no work, only rest and happiness. We were glad to hear that we now lived in a time of Great Peace.

The following year, the soldiers came with rice and salt-cured fish. The next year, it was only rice. More years passed. One day, a man who had once lived in our village returned from Nanjing. He said he was sick to death of Great Peace. When there is great suffering, he said, everyone struggles the same. But when there is peace, no one wants to be the same. The rich no longer share. The less rich envy and steal. In Nanjing, he said, everyone was seeking luxuries, pleasures, the dark places of women. He said the Heavenly King now lived in a fine palace and had many concubines. He allowed his kingdom to be ruled by a man possessed with the Holy Ghost. And General Cape, the man who rallied all the Hakkas to fight, had joined the Manchus and was now a traitor, bound by a Chinese banker's gold and marriage to his daughter. Too much happiness, said the man who returned, always overflows into tears of sorrow.

We could feel in our stomachs the truth of what this man said. We were hungry. The Heavenly King had forgotten us. Our Western friends had betrayed us. We no longer received food or stories of victory. We were poor. We had no mothers, no fathers, no singing maidens and boys. We were bitter cold in the wintertime.

The next morning, I left my village and went down the mountain. I was fourteen, old enough to make my own way in life. My grandmother had died the year before, but her ghost didn't stop me. It was the ninth day of the ninth month, I remember this, a day when Chinese people were supposed to climb the heights, not descend from them, a day for honoring ancestors, a day that the God Worshipers ignored to prove they abided by a Western calendar of fifty-two Sundays and not the sacred days of the Chinese almanac. So I walked down the mountain, then through the valleys between the mountains. I no longer knew what I should believe, whom I could trust. I decided I would wait for a sign, see what happened.

I arrived at the city by the river, the one called Jintian. To those Hakka people I met, I said I was Nunumu. But they didn't know who the Bandit Maiden was. She was not famous in Jintian. The Hakkas there didn't admire my eye that a ghost horse had knocked out. They pitied me. They put an old rice ball into my palm and tried to make me a half-blind beggar. But I refused to become what people thought I should be.

So I wandered around the city again, thinking about what work I might do to earn my own food. I saw Cantonese people who cut the horns off toes, Yaos who pulled teeth, Puntis who pierced needles into swollen legs. I knew nothing about drawing money out of the rotten parts of other people's bodies. I continued walking until I was beside the low bank of a wide river. I saw Hakka fishermen tossing big nets into the water from little boats. But I had no nets, no little boat. I did not know how to think like a fast, sly fish.

Before I could decide what to do, I heard people along the riverbank shouting. Foreigners had arrived! I ran to the dock and watched two Chinese *kuli* boatmen, one young, one old, walking down a narrow plank, carrying boxes and crates and trunks from a large boat. And then I saw the foreigners themselves, standing on the deck — three, four, five of them, all in dull black clothes, except for the smallest one, who had clothing and hair the shiny brown of a tree-eating beetle. That was Miss Banner, but of course I didn't know it at the time. My one eye watched them all. Their five pairs of foreign eyes were on the young and old boatmen balancing their way down the long, thin gang-plank. On the shoulders of the boatmen were two poles, and in the saggy middle a large trunk hung from twisted ropes. Suddenly, the shiny brown foreigner ran down the plank — who knew why? — to warn the men, to ask them to be more careful. And just as suddenly, the plank began to bounce, the trunk began to swing, the men began to sway, and the five foreigners on the boat began to shout. Back and forth, up and down — our eyes leapt as we watched those boatmen clenching their muscles and the shiny foreigner flapping her arms like a baby bird. In the next moment, the older man, at the bottom of the plank, gave one sharp cry — I heard the crack, saw his shoulder bone sticking out. Then two *kulis,* one trunk, and a shiny-clothed foreigner fell with great splashes into the water below.

I ran to the river edge. The younger *kuli* had already swum to shore. Two fishermen in a small boat were chasing the contents that had spilled out of the trunk, bright clothing that billowed like sails, feathered hats that floated like ducks, long gloves that raked the water like the fingers of a ghost. But nobody was trying to help the injured boatman or the shiny foreigner. The other foreigners would not; they were afraid to walk down the plank. The Punti people on the shore would not; if they interfered with fate, they would be responsible for those two people's undrowned lives. But I didn't think this way. I was a Hakka. The Hakkas were God Worshipers. And the God Worshipers were fishers of men. So I grabbed one of the bamboo poles that had fallen in the water. I ran along the bank and stuck this out, letting the ropes dangle downstream. The *kuli* and the foreigner grabbed them with their eager hands. And with all my strength, I pulled them in.

Right after that the Punti people pushed me aside. They left the injured boatman on the ground, gasping and cursing. That was Lao Lu, who later became the gatekeeper, since with a broken shoulder he could no longer work as a *kuli*. As for Miss Banner, the Puntis dragged her higher onto the shore, where she vomited, then cried. When the foreigners finally came down from the boat, the Puntis crowded around them, shouting, "Give us money." One of the foreigners threw small coins on the ground, and the Puntis flocked like birds to devour them, then scattered away.

The foreigners loaded Miss Banner in one cart, the broken boatman in another. They loaded three more carts with their boxes and crates and trunks. And as they made their way to the mission house in Changmian, I ran behind. So that's how all three of us went to live in the same house. Our three different fates had flowed together in that river, and became as tangled and twisted as a drowned woman's hair.

Alice Walker

....

The Welcome Table

FOR SISTER CLARA WARD

I'm going to sit at the Welcome table
Shout my troubles over
Walk and talk with Jesus
Tell God how you treat me
One of these days!
— Spiritual

T HE OLD WOMAN stood with eyes uplifted in her Sunday-go-to-meeting clothes: high shoes polished about the tops and toes, a long rusty dress adorned with an old corsage, long withered, and the remnants of an elegant silk scarf as headrag stained with grease from the many oily pigtails underneath. Perhaps she had known suffering. There was a dazed and sleepy look in her aged blue-brown eyes. But for those who searched hastily for "reasons" in that old tight face, shut now like an ancient door, there was nothing to be read. And so they gazed nakedly upon their own fear transferred; a fear of the black and the old, a terror of the unknown as well as of the deeply known. Some of those who saw her there on the church steps spoke words about her that were hardly fit to be heard, others held their pious peace; and some felt vague stirrings of pity, small and per-sistent and hazy, as if she were an old collie turned out to die.

She was angular and lean and the color of poor gray Georgia earth, beaten by king cotton and the extreme weather. Her elbows were wrinkled and thick, the skin ashen but durable, like the bark of old pines. On her face centuries were folded into the circles around one eye, while around the other, etched and mapped as if for print, ages more threatened again to live. Some of them there at the church saw the age, the dotage, the missing buttons down the front of her mildewed black dress. Others saw cooks, chauffeurs, maids, mistresses, children denied or smothered in the deferential way she held her cheek to the side, toward the ground. Many of them saw jungle orgies in an evil place, while others were reminded of riotous anarchists looting and raping in the streets. Those who knew the hesitant creeping up on them of the law, saw the beginning of the end of the sanctuary of Christian worship, saw the desecration of Holy Church, and saw an invasion of privacy, which they struggled to believe they still kept.

Still she had come down the road toward the big white church alone. Just herself, an old forgetful woman, nearly blind with age. Just her and her eyes raised dully to the glittering cross that crowned the sheer silver steeple. She had walked along the road in a stagger from her house a half mile away. Perspiration, cold and clammy, stood on her brow and along the creases by her thin wasted nose. She stopped to calm herself on the wide front steps, not looking about her as they might have expected her to do, but simply standing quite still, except for a slight quivering of her throat and tremors that shook her cotton-stockinged legs.

The reverend of the church stopped her pleasantly as she stepped into the vestibule. Did he say, as they thought he did, kindly, "Auntie, you know this is not your church?" As if one could choose the wrong one. But no one remembers, for they never spoke of it afterward, and she brushed past him anyway, as if she had been brushing past him all her life, except this time she was in a hurry. Inside the church she sat on the very first bench from the back, gazing with concentration at the stained-glass window over her head. It was cold, even inside the church, and she was shivering. Everybody could see. They stared at her as they came in and sat down near the front. It was cold, very cold to them too; outside the church it was below freezing and not much above inside. But the sight of her, sitting there somehow passionately ignoring them, brought them up short, burning.

The young usher, never having turned anyone out of his church before, but not even considering this job as *that* (after all, she had no right to be there, certainly), went up to her and whispered that she should leave. Did he call her "Grandma," as later he seemed to recall he had? But for those who actually hear such traditional pleasantries and to whom they actually mean something, "Grandma" was not one, for she did not pay him any attention, just muttered, "Go 'way," in a weak sharp *bothered* voice, waving his frozen blond hair and eyes from near her face.

It was the ladies who finally did what to them had to be done. Daring their burly indecisive husbands to throw the old colored woman out they made their point. God, mother, country, earth, church. It involved all that, and well they knew it. Leather bagged and shoed, with good calfskin gloves to keep out the cold, they looked with contempt at the bloodless gray arthritic hands of the old woman, clenched loosely, restlessly in her lap. Could their husbands expect them to sit up in church with that? No, no, the husbands were quick to answer and even quicker to do their duty.

Under the old woman's arms they placed their hard fists (which afterward smelled of decay and musk — the fermenting scent of onion skins and rotting greens). Under the old woman's arms they raised their fists, flexed their muscular shoulders, and out she flew through the door, back under the cold blue sky. This done, the wives folded their healthy arms across their trim middles and felt at once justified and scornful. But none of them said so, for none of them ever spoke of the incident again. Inside the church it was warmer. They sang, they prayed. The protection and promise of God's impartial love grew more not less desirable as the sermon gathered fury and lashed itself out above their penitent heads.

The old woman stood at the top of the steps looking about in bewilderment. She had been singing in her head. They had interrupted her. Promptly she began to sing again, though this time a sad song. Suddenly, however, she looked down the long gray highway and saw something interesting and delightful coming. She started to grin, toothlessly, with short giggles of joy, jumping about and slapping her hands on her knees. And soon it became apparent why she was so happy. For coming down the highway at a firm though leisurely pace was Jesus. He was wearing an immaculate white, long dress trimmed in gold around the neck and hem, and a red, a bright red, cape. Over his left arm he carried a brilliant blue blanket. He was wearing sandals and a beard and he had long brown hair parted on the right side. His eyes, brown, had wrinkles around them as if he smiled or looked at the sun a lot. She would have known him, recognized him, anywhere.

There was a sad but joyful look to his face, like a candle was glowing behind it, and he walked with sure even steps in her direction, as if he were walking on the sea. Except that he was not carrying in his arms a baby sheep, he looked exactly like the picture of him that she had hanging over her bed at home. She had taken it out of a white lady's Bible while she was working for her. She had looked at that picture for more years than she could remember, but never once had she really expected to see him. She squinted her eyes to be sure he wasn't carrying a little sheep in one arm, but he was not. Ecstatically she began to wave her arms for fear he would miss seeing her, for he walked looking straight ahead on the shoulder of the highway, and from time to time looking upward at the sky.

All he said when he got up close to her was "Follow me," and she bounded down to his side with all the bob and speed of one so old. For every one of his long determined steps she made two quick ones. They walked along in deep silence for a long time. Finally she started telling him about how many years she had cooked for them, cleaned for them, nursed them. He looked at her kindly but in silence. She told him indignantly about how they had grabbed her when she was singing in her head and not looking, and how they had tossed her out of his church. A old heifer like me, she said, straightening up next to Jesus, breathing hard. But he smiled down at her and she felt better instantly and time just seemed to fly by. When they passed her house, forlorn and sagging, weatherbeaten and patched, by the side of the road, she did not even notice it, she was so happy to be out walking along the highway with Jesus.

She broke the silence once more to tell Jesus how glad she was that he had come, how she had often looked at his picture hanging on her wall (she hoped he didn't know she had stolen it) over her bed, and how she had never expected to see him down here in person. Jesus gave her one of his beautiful smiles and they walked on. She did not know where they were going; someplace wonderful, she suspected. The ground was like clouds under their feet, and she felt she could walk forever without becoming the least bit tired. She even began to sing out loud some of the old spirituals she loved, but she didn't want to annoy Jesus, who looked so thoughtful, so she quieted down. They walked on, looking straight over the treetops into the sky, and the smiles that played over her dry wind-cracked face were like first clean ripples across a stagnant pond. On they walked without stopping.

★   ★   ★

The people in church never knew what happened to the old woman; they never mentioned her to one another or to anybody else. Most of them heard sometime later that an old colored woman fell dead along the highway. Silly as it seemed, it appeared she had walked herself to death. Many of the black families along the road said they had seen the old lady high-stepping down the highway; sometimes jabbering in a low insistent voice, sometimes singing, sometimes merely gesturing excitedly with her hands. Other times silent and smiling, looking at the sky. She had been alone, they said. Some of them wondered aloud where the old woman had been going so stoutly that it had worn her heart out. They guessed maybe she had relatives across the river, some miles away, but none of them really knew.

Daly Walker

....

I Am the Grass

ECAUSE I LOVE my wife and daughter, and because I want
them to believe I am a good man, I have never talked to them
about my year as a grunt with the 25th Infantry in Vietnam. I
cannot tell my thirteen-year-old that once, drunk on Ba Muoi Ba beer,
I took a girl her age into a thatched-roof hooch in Tay Ninh City and
did her on a bamboo mat. I cannot tell my wife, who paints watercol-
ors of songbirds, that on a search-and-destroy mission I emptied my
M-60 machine gun into two beautiful white egrets that were wading
in the muddy water of a paddy. I cannot tell them how I sang "Happy
Trails" as I shoved two wounded Viet Cong out the door of a medevac
chopper hovering twenty feet above the tarmac of a battalion aid station. I cannot tell them how I lay in a ditch and used my M-60 to gun
down a skinny, black-haired farmer I thought was a VC, nearly blowing his head off. I cannot tell them how I completed the decapitation
with a machete, and then stuck his head on a pole on top of a mountain called Nui Ba Den. All these things fester in me like the tiny fragment of shrapnel embedded in my skull, haunt me like the corpse of
the slim dark man I killed. I cannot talk about these things that I wish I
could forget but know that I never will.

Twenty years have passed since the summer of 1968, when I flew
home from the war and my "freedom bird" landed in the night at
Travis Air Force Base, near San Francisco. I knew that in the city, soldiers in uniform were taunted in the streets by flower children. So I
slipped quietly into a restroom and changed from my dress khakis into
jeans and a flannel shirt. Nobody was there to say, "Welcome home,

soldier." It was as if I were an exile in my own country. I felt deceived and confused, and most of all angry, but I wasn't sure at whom to direct my anger or where to go or what to do, so I held everything inside and went about forming a life day by day.

After I was discharged from the Army, I went home to Chicago and hung around there for a couple of years, haunted by memories and nameless faces. Devoid of hope or expectations, smoking dope and dreaming dreams of torment, I drifted from one meaningless endeavor to the next. I studied drawing at the art academy, cut grass with the grounds crew at Soldier Field, parked cars at the Four Seasons. Nothing seemed to matter; nothing changed what I was. I was still fire and smoke, a loaded gun, a dead survivor, a little girl on a bamboo mat, a headless corpse. I was still in the killing zone.

Gradually I grew weary of my hollowness, ran out of pity for my own self-pity. I wanted to take my life and shake it by the hair. I decided to use the GI Bill and give college a try.

I enrolled at the University of Wisconsin at Madison, the headquarters of the Weathermen and the SDS. I lived in a run-down rooming house on Mifflen Street, among all the longhaired war protesters and scruffy peaceniks. During the day I went to classes and worked as an orderly at a Catholic hospital, but at night, after work, I went back to my room to study alone. Through the window of my room I could see mobs of students marching through the streets, chanting, "Ho, Ho, Ho Chi Minh," and, "Bring home the war." What did they know about war? I watched them, and I wanted to kick their hippie asses.

It was in caring for the patients at the hospital that I seemed to find what I had been searching for. While bathing or feeding a patient I felt simply good. It was better than my best trips with Mary Jane. I decided to apply to medical school, and I was accepted.

One night when I was a senior med student, a couple of radical war protesters blew up the Army Mathematics Research Center on campus. The explosion shook my bed in the hospital call room like the rocket that blasted me out of sleep the night of the Tet Offensive. I have never been a brave man, and I lay there in the dark with my heart pounding, thinking I was back in Firebase Zulu the night we were overrun. A nurse called me to the emergency room to help resuscitate a theoretical physicist who had been pulled from under the rubble. His chest was crushed and both his lungs were collapsed. He didn't need resuscitation. He needed a body bag. The war I was trying to escape had followed me home.

Now I practice plastic surgery in Lake Forest, a North Shore Chicago suburb of stone walls, German cars, and private clubs. On my arm is a scar from the laser surgery that removed a tattoo I woke up with one morning in a Bangkok whorehouse. The tattoo was a cartoon in blue and red ink of a baby in diapers, wearing an Army helmet and a parachute with the inscription "Airborne." I feel that I am two people at once, two people fighting within myself. One is a family man and a physician who lives a comfortable external life. The other is a war criminal with an atrophied soul. Nothing I do can revive it.

Even as a surgeon I have a split personality. I sculpt women's bodies with breast augmentations, tummy tucks, face-lifts, and liposuction. I like the money, but I'm bored with these patients and their vanity, their urgent need for surgical enhancement. I am also a reconstructive plastic surgeon who loves Z-plastying a scar from a dog bite on a little girl's cheek or skin grafting a burn on the neck of a small boy who fell against a space heater. I love reconstructing a lobster-claw deformity of the hand so that a child can hold a spoon and fork. I'm no Albert Schweitzer, but every summer I spend a couple of weeks in Haiti or Kenya or Guatemala with Operation Smile, repairing cleft palates and lips. Removing the bandages and seeing the results of my skill sends a chill up my neck, makes me feel like something of a decent man, a healer.

Today, in late September, I am sitting in a window seat in a Thai Airways jet on its way from Bangkok to Ho Chi Minh City. I am headed to the Khanh Hoa Hospital, in Nha Trang, for two weeks of my own little Operation Smile, repairing the cleft palates and lips of children on whose land I once wreaked havoc, whose parents and grandparents I murdered and whom, somewhere deep inside me, I still hold in contempt.

I stare out the airplane window at tufts of white clouds that look like bursts of artillery flak, and I break into a sweat, remembering the descent of the airliner that flew me, a machine gunner, an Airborne Ranger, an eighteen-year-old pissed-off, pot-smoking warrior, cannon fodder, to Vietnam. The pilot lurched into a steep, spiraling dive to minimize the plane's exposure time to ground fire. I pitched forward in my seat, the belt cutting into my belly, my heart pounding. Until that moment I had felt immortal, but then fear came to me in an image of my own death by a bullet to the brain, and I realized how little I mattered, how quickly and simply and anonymously the end could come. I believed that I would never return home to my room with the old oak dresser and corner desk that my mother dusted and polished with lemon oil. Tears filled my eyes.

With the plane in a long, gentle glide, I gaze out the window and search for remnants of the war. I see a green patchwork of paddies and fields of grass, dirt roads whose iron-red dust choked me, whose mud caked my jungle boots. A sampan floats down a river. Smoke curls lazily from a thatched-roof shack. An ox pulls a cart. The land seems asleep, and the war only a dream. I drop back in the seat and close my eyes. Stirring in my chest is the feeling that a dangerous demon is setting itself free inside me.

I spend the night in Saigon at the Bong Song Hotel, a mildewing walk-up not far from the Museum of American War Crimes. The toilet doesn't flush. The ceiling fan croaks so loudly that I turn it off. Oily tropical heat drenches the room, and I can hear rats skittering across the floor. I feel as I once did trying to grab a little shut-eye before going out on ambush patrol. I can't sleep. My mind is filled with the image of myself dragging the lifeless body of a kid named Dugan by the ankles through mud.

In the orange light of dawn I board an old minivan that will take me north to the hospital in Nha Trang. The tottering vehicle weaves through streets teeming with bicycles, three-wheeled cyclos, motorbikes, an occasional car. People gawk at me as if I were a zoo animal of a breed they have never seen before. The driver is Tran, a spindly man with wispy Ho Chi Minh chin whiskers. He has been assigned to be my guide and interpreter, but he is really the People's Committee watchdog. When I was here before, I would have called him a gook or a slope, a dink motherfucker, and those are the words that come to me now when I look at Tran. I picture his head on a pole.

We cross the Saigon River on Highway One, Vietnam's aorta, the artery connecting Hanoi with Saigon. The French called Highway One *"la rue sans joie."* We called it "the street to sorrow." During the war I often traveled this road in convoys of tanks and half-tracks whose treads pulverized the pavement. I was always high on Buddha grass. Armed to the teeth. Frightened and mean. I was so young. I didn't know what I was doing here. A few miles out of Saigon, Tran slows and points to a vast empty plain overgrown with olive-drab grass and scrub brush.

"This Long Binh," he says.

"Stop," I say.

He pulls off the road and parks by a pile of rusty wire and scrap metal. I climb out of the van and stand, looking at acres of elephant grass blasted by the tropical sun. I think of Long Binh when it was an enormous military base, a sandbag city of tents, barbed wire, and bunkers. We called it LBJ, for "Long Binh Jail." It was where I spent my first night "in country," sweat-soaked on a sagging cot, listening to the distant chunk of artillery, fear clawing at my chest. Now all I see is emptiness. Nothing to verify my past, nothing to commune with. How hot it is. How quiet.

Since Nam, I have spent a lot of nights with bottles of wine, reading the poetry of war — Homer and Kipling, Sandburg and Komunyakaa. Through the haze of my thoughts, words by Sandburg are moving. The words are about grass and war and soldiers in Austerlitz and Gettysburg and Waterloo, but they are about this place too. *Shove them under and let me work — I am the grass; I cover all.* I gaze out at Long Binh's grass. It ripples in hot wind like folds of silk.

I climb back into the van, and we jostle on through paddies and rubber plantations, green groves of bamboo and banana trees. I have the strange feeling that my life has shrunk, that just around the bend an ambush will be waiting. I lean forward in my seat and ask Tran if he remembers Long Binh when the American soldiers were here.

"Vietnam believe it better not to remind of the past." He speaks looking straight ahead through aviator sunglasses. "We live in present with eye on future." The words sound rote, as if he is quoting from a propaganda paper. "Vietnam want to be thought of as country, not war, not just problem in other country's past."

On a berm old women in conical hats spread rice and palm fronds to dry in the sun. Charcoal fumes waft from cooking fires. White-shirted children with red kerchiefs tied around their necks march to school. Two men, brown and bent like cashew nuts, face each other over a big teak log and pull a crosscut saw back and forth slowly, rhythmically. For a brief moment the smell of gunpowder comes back to me, and I see little Asian men running headlong through tall grass, firing weapons and screaming. I see GIs running through smoke with green canvas stretchers.

The arrangements for my mission in the coastal city of Nha Trang were made through Dr. Lieh Viet Dinh, the director of Khanh Hoa Hospital. The morning after my arrival, Dinh sends word to my hotel that he wants to meet me for a welcoming meal at a restaurant on the South China Sea. I have been told that Dinh was once in the North Vietnamese army and now is a high official in the province's Communist Party. What does he want? For me to say I'm sorry?

I hire a cyclo driver to pedal me to the restaurant. Mopeds with their exhaust tinting the air blue and bicycles piled high with cordwood tangle the streets. The Sunday-afternoon sun is so bright it hurts my eyes. But there is a cool ocean breeze and the scent of bougainvillaea in the air. Under flame trees with brilliant-orange blossoms barbers trim hair and clean wax from ears. Street vendors hawk flowers and loaves of French bread. Everywhere I look, I see Vietnamese getting on with their lives. I marvel at their serenity. They are no different from the people that I was taught to distrust, that I once machine-gunned. This street is no different from streets that I once helped to fill with rubble and bodies. A man on a Honda raises his index finger and calls, "Hey, Joe. U.S. number one." But I look away from him.

The restaurant is a rickety tile-roofed pagoda perched on stilts over a beach of sand the color of crème brûlée. Below, in a natural aquarium, sand sharks and tropical fish dart among the rocks. In the distance a soft vapor hangs over mountain islands in the bay. The restaurant is empty except for a gnarly little man sitting alone at a table with the sun splashing off turquoise water behind him. He is a militant figure with penetrating black eyes and hollow, acne-scarred cheeks that give him a look of toughness, a look that says, You could never defeat me no matter how many bombs you dropped. I know he is Dinh. The contempt that boiled inside me during the war bubbles up. I can feel it in my chest.

He calls to me to join him. I settle into a wooden chair across from him and extend my hand for him to shake, but he ignores it and offers a stiff little bow of his head. Nervousness dries up the saliva in my mouth. A waitress in a blue ao dai brings us bottles of Ba Muoi Ba beer. With her lustrous black hair and slim, silk-sheathed figure, she is beautiful and exotic like a tropical bird. The shy young girl with a dimple in her cheek that I took on the bamboo mat in Tay Ninh would be about her age now. I wonder what became of her.

In English that I have to listen to closely to understand, Dinh talks for a while about the Khanh Hoa Hospital, the only hospital for the one million people of his province. He tells me that my visit has been advertised on television, and that thirty children with cleft lips to be repaired will be there. His jaw tight, his voice intimidating, he tells me that the hospital has trouble getting medicine and equipment because of the American embargo. I pick up my bottle of beer and press it to my lips and tilt it. The liquid is warm, with the slight formaldehyde taste that I remember from the war. I look at Dinh's slanty black eyes and stained teeth, thinking how easy it would be to kill him. I've been taught to do it with a gun or a knife or my hands. It would come back to me quickly, like sitting down at a piano and playing a song that you mastered a long time ago but haven't played in years. Suddenly the thought of operating on little children in all this heat and dirt, with archaic equipment, jolts me back into the present. I ask him who will give the anesthesia.

"My doctors," he says. "Vietnamese doctors as good as any in the world."

The waitress brings a plate of lightly fried rice paper, bowls of rice and noodles, and a platter of sea bass smothered in peppers, onions, and peanuts. She gives me chopsticks and Dinh a metal spoon. When we begin to eat, I see Dinh's hands for the first time. I am startled. Now I know why he didn't shake with me. His thumbs are missing. I watch him spoon rice onto his plate, clutching the utensil in his thumbless hand. He has learned a pinch grip between his second and third digits, like children I have operated on who were born with floating thumbs or congenital absence of the first metacarpal bone. Using his fingers as if they were tongs, he wraps some fish in a sheet of the rice paper and dips it in nuoc cham sauce. The sauce smells rancid, and a sourness rises up my esophagus.

"I hear you in Vietnam during war," Dinh says between bites of fish and rice.

"Yes," I say. I can't take my eyes off his hands.

"Where?" he asks.

"South of here, along the Cambodian border near Tay Ninh."

"You see Nui Ba Den," he says. "How you call it? The black virgin mountain. This fish good. Dip your fish in nuoc cham."

I picture that black-haired man's head skewered on a bamboo pole.

"Yeah, I've seen Nui Ba Den," I say, feeling as if he must somehow know what I did on top of the mountain.

"Were you Army surgeon?"

"No. That was before I went to medical school. I was with the infantry." I take a gulp of beer. "That was a long time ago."

"Not so long ago," Dinh says. His lips curl into a smile that is filled with crooked yellow teeth. "Americans always think time longer than it is. Americans very impatient. Vietnamese very patient. We believe life is circle. Everything comes and goes. Why grasp and cling? Always things will come around again if you give them time. Patience is why we win victory."

In the filthy little village across the bay I can see tin-roofed shacks, teeming streets, the haze of smoke from cooking fires — the thick stew of peasant life.

"How about you?" I ask. "Were you a doctor during the war?"

He wipes his mouth with his shirtsleeve and says, "In war against French colonialists, I was Vietminh infantry man. Fifteen years old."

He raises a maimed hand and, with a wave motion to demonstrate high altitude, tells how he twice climbed the mountains of Laos and Cambodia on the Ho Chi Minh Trail — once to fight the French and once to fight the Americans and their Vietnamese puppets. He was wounded at Dien Bien Phu. I wonder if that was when he lost his thumbs. I'm fascinated by his thumblessness. The ability to oppose a thumb and a finger is what sets us apart from lemurs and baboons.

"We have little to fight with," Dinh says. "After we shoot our guns, we pick up empty cartridges to use again. We eat nothing but tapioca roots and half a can of rice a day. For seven years I fight hungry."

I listen to him tell of his wars, and it takes me back to mine. Cold-sweat nights peering out of a muddy bunker through concertina wire at tracers and shadows. Waiting. Listening. Grim patrols through elephant grass and jungle greased with moonlight. I can hear screams, see faces of the dead. What is memory and what is a dream? When it comes to the war, nothing seems true. It seems impossible that something that tragic, that unspeakable, was once a part of my life. Suddenly I'm overwhelmed with emotion. I wonder if Dinh ever feels like crying. In the shallows below the restaurant a sea turtle snaps at silver fish trapped in a net.

"How about in the war against America?" I ask. "Were you a doctor then?"

"I was surgeon in the war against you and your South Vietnamese puppets."

"Where did you serve?" I ask. "Were you in a hospital?"

"My hospital the forest. My operating table the soil of the jungle." He holds up both hands and rotates them for me to see. "I have thumbs then. I clever surgeon. I operate on everything from head to toes." He looks up at the ceiling as if an airplane were circling overhead. "Your B-fifty-twos drop big bombs. They make earth shake. They scare hell out of me."

Dinh flashes a smile that makes me uncomfortable. He takes a drink of beer.

"Were you wounded?" I ask.

"You mean my hands?"

"Yeah. What happened?"

He rests them on the table, displaying them as he talks. He tells me that he was captured in the central highlands, not by Americans but by South Vietnamese Special Forces in their purple berets. When they learned he was a doctor, they chose him for torture. They tied him to a stake under merciless sun and every day pulled out one of his fingernails with a pair of pliers. At night they locked him up in a tiger cage. He speaks softly. On the eleventh day they cut off his thumbs. Then they cooked them in a soup and told him to drink it. He hadn't eaten for two weeks, so he did.

"How did you survive?" I ask. "Why didn't you go crazy?"

"I pretended to be somewhere else. Somewhere at a time after our victory. I always knew we would win."

Dinh looks at my hands.

"You lucky," he says. "You have thumbs to do surgery. I can't even eat with chopsticks." He raises his hands, flexing his fingers. He glares at me with eyes as hard and black as gun bores. "This should happen to no one."

We finish our meal in silence. Under the afternoon sun the restaurant is stifling, and I feel queasy. I can get down only a little rice. But Dinh eats hungrily, shoveling in the food with his spoon as if to make up for all those years of rice and tapioca roots. When his plate is clean, he rinses his hands in a bowl of hot lime water with tea leaves floating on the surface.

He looks up at me and says, "To take the smell of fish from your skin."

In the morning I walk from my hotel through steamy air, on streets boiling with people, to the hospital. Around the entryway dozens of crippled peasants and ragged children with skin sores squat on the powdery earth. Everything is dusty. I understand why Vietnamese peasants call themselves "the dust of life." A boy with weight-lifter arms calls to me in English from a bicycle that he pedals with his hands. He wants me to fix his paralyzed legs.

Khanh Hoa's pale-yellow facade gives me an impression of cleanliness and light, but inside, the wards are dim and grungy, with no glass or screens in the windows to keep out flies and mosquitoes. Often two patients occupy a single narrow bed, with family members sleeping on the floor nearby to assist with the feeding and bathing, the emptying of bedpans. A tiny, toothless woman with skin like teakwood waves a bamboo fan over a wasted man on a mattress without sheets. She gazes at me with longing. Everywhere I go, someone with sorrowful eyes looks at me as if I were Jesus.

During my first week I don't have any more conversations with Dinh, but I see him every morning when he comes in his white lab coat to the surgery suite to watch me operate. At the door he slips off his sandals and pads barefoot into the room, where he stands at the head of the table, his black eyes peering at the children whose lips are like hook-ripped fish mouths. He rarely speaks, and when he does, it is usually to address the Vietnamese doctors and nurses in a tone that suggests sarcasm.

It is impossible to know what his silence toward me means, but I become immersed in my work, and I don't worry about him. Once the operation starts, my concentration is complete, my only concern the child's face, framed in blue towels and bathed in bright light. I have always been gifted at drawing and carving, and with a scalpel in my hand I feel like an artist, forming something beautiful out of chaos. I love mapping out flaps of skin around a child's mouth and then rotating them over the cleft to create a nice Cupid's bow of lip with a clean vermilion border. My sutures are like the brushstrokes of a portrait. Dinh must envy the collaboration of my brain and fingers.

Between cases I rest in the doctors' lounge at a wooden table. I drink a pot of pale-tan tea, eat litchi fruit, and look out into the hospital courtyard that serves as the waiting room. I often see Dinh with his hands hidden in the pockets of his lab coat, squatting in the dust, talking with the parents of the cleft-lipped children who are undergoing surgery. His face, glistening under the hot sun, looks as if it has been oiled. His chronic scowl has become a comforting smile.

At the end of my first week I call my wife and daughter to tell them that all is going well. When I report that I have repaired eighteen cleft lips without a complication, my wife seems proud of me. I am getting to like the nurses and doctors in the operating room. My feelings of guilt and ambivalence are being replaced by a sense of goodwill and atonement, as if Vietnam and I were two bad people who had unexpectedly done something nice for each other. But on Sunday, Dinh sends word for me to meet him in his "cabinet," as he calls his private office. I worry that I have done something wrong.

The room is the size of an armoire and sparsely furnished. A single bookcase contains the medical texts of the hospital's meager library. On the wall is a little green lizard and a yellowed photograph of Ho Chi Minh. From a cassette player on a homemade wooden table comes the music of a symphony orchestra playing Vivaldi's *The Four Seasons*. The hospital sewer system is backed up, and the air smells brackish. My stomach churns. I sit in a straight-backed chair across a metal desk from Dinh. My office in Lake Forest, with its Oriental carpet and polished cherry furniture, seems infinitely far away.

"Vivaldi," I say to break the silence.

Dinh looks up from a journal article in which he is underlining with a wooden pencil. His face, shadowed by years of hardship, is expressionless. He wears a white shirt and a clip-on red rayon tie. He has a small Band-Aid on his chin where, I assume, he nicked himself shaving. I imagine him handling a razor, buttoning a shirt, tying a tie or shoestrings. Without a thumb's ability to pinch and oppose, even simple tasks must be difficult for him.

"Do you enjoy Vivaldi?" he asks.

"*The Four Seasons* is one of my favorites. When did you develop a taste for Western music?"

"When I was in medical school in Hanoi, French doctors play music in surgery room. Music only good thing about Frenchmen. Music good healing medicine. I play music to calm my patients."

He clicks off the tape and hands me the article he has been reading. It is a reprint from a French journal of hand surgery. I leaf through its pages, scanning illustrations that depict an operation in which a toe is transferred to the hand to replace a missing thumb.

"Can you make thumb?" Dinh asks.

I sit for a moment, remembering my last toe transplant, performed a couple of years ago. It was on a young farm boy who had lost his thumb in a corn picker.

"Yes," I say. "I've done this operation. Not often, but I've done it."

"I want you do this to me," Dinh says.

"Here? Now? You want me to make you a thumb?"

"Yes. I want you make me new thumb."

It is as if, fighting a losing battle, I suddenly see the enemy waving a white flag. For a moment I look at his narrow, bony hands with the red ridges of scar tissue where thumbs once protruded.

"It's a very hard operation," I say. "Quite delicate. A microvascular procedure. Even under perfect conditions it often doesn't work."

"I watch you operate." Dinh lowers his eyes and his voice. "You very careful surgeon. I know you can do."

"Let me see your hand."

He extends his right hand toward me. I rise and move around the desk. I take his hand in mine and turn it slowly, studying skin tone and temperature. His radial pulse bounds against my fingers. His nail beds are pink with good capillary circulation. The skin of the palm is creased and thickly callused.

"Thumb reconstruction must be carefully planned," I say. "You don't just jump into it. There are several techniques to consider."

In my mind I review them: using a skin flap and a bone graft from the pelvis; pollicization, in which the index finger is rotated to oppose the third finger; and my favorite technique, which uses a tube graft of abdominal skin — but it has to be staged over several weeks.

"The new thumb must be free of pain," I say, carefully palpating the bones of his hand, searching for the missing thumb's metacarpal. I find it intact. "It has to have sensation so it can recognize objects. It has to be long enough to touch the tip of opposing digits. It must be flexible."

"You don't have to teach me," Dinh says gruffly. "I know about this. I read everything in literature. Toe transplant best for me."

"I'm not so sure about that."

"Toe transplant best."

"Maybe so, but you're the patient this time. I'm the doctor. Let me decide."

I bend over and lift his dusty foot into my lap. I slip off his tire-tread sandal. His foot is the size of my daughter's, the toenails poorly cared for. My fingers find strong dorsalis pedis and posterior tibial pulses at the ankle. I would prefer to transplant the second toe, but his is very small; I decide the big toe would make a better thumb.

"What you find?" he asks anxiously.

"You have good circulation and a metacarpal bone."

"So what you think? Toe transplant?"

I look up at Dinh's face. It is pale yellow, contrasting with the density of shadowed books and wall behind him. His haughty eyes have softened into a look of hope and longing.

"I agree," I say. "A toe transplant would be best for you."

"You must do it, then," he says.

"Maybe you could come to the States and have it done."

"I no rich American. No can get visa."

"There's a good chance the graft won't take. I don't have an operating microscope or some of the instruments I use."

He flexes and unflexes the four fingers on his right hand and smiles.

"Do it here tomorrow. I want to hold chopsticks again. I tired of eating like a Frenchman."

"Look," I say, "you don't realize how many things could go wrong."

"It work. I know it work."

I think how the fortunes of the Vietnamese always seem to be in the hands of others.

"Okay," I say. "I'll do it. A local anesthetic would be safest. Would that be all right?"

"Pain no matter. You do it."

"You're on. But don't be surprised if it doesn't work."

That night I lie awake under the mosquito net on my bed, reviewing the technique of toe transplantation, suturing in my mind tendons and tiny digital nerves, minute veins and arteries. Tropical heat drenches me. The bark of dogs comes in from the street. When I finally fall asleep, I dream again of the man whose head I severed and stuck on the end of a pole. We meet in the Cao Dia temple in Tay Ninh, a vast, gaudy cathedral with a vaulted ceiling, pillars wound with gilded dragons and pink serpents, and a giant eye over the altar. He stands naked in front of me, holding his head with its sheen of black hair in the crook of his elbow.

The surgery suite is high-ceilinged, with dirty windows and yellow tile walls, like the restroom in an old train station. The air is drowsy with the odor of ether that leaks from U.S. Army surplus anesthesia machines. Outside the operating room I attach magnifying loupes to a pair of glasses. I focus the lenses on the lines of my fingertips and begin scrubbing my hands in cold water at an old porcelain sink.

Through the door I see Dinh sedated and strapped to the operating table. Bathed in fierce white light, with his arms extended on boards at right angles to his body, he looks as if he has been crucified. I have sent an orderly to his office for his cassette player, and *The Four Seasons* plays softly at the head of the table.

For a moment I rinse my hands, designing in my mind skin incisions and tendon transfers. In the past, to decrease operating time and diminish my fatigue, I used a second surgical team to prepare the recipient site in the hand while I removed the donor tissue from the foot, but here I am alone.

With water dripping from my elbows, I step into the room. Suddenly I feel a surge of force, a sense of power that has been mine in no other place but surgery, except when my finger was on the trigger of an M-60.

The instruments I have brought with me lie on trays and tables. My weapons are tenotomy scissors and mosquito hemostats, atraumatic forceps and spring-loaded needle holders. A scrub technician, who worked as an interpreter in a MASH unit during the war, hands me a towel. Two masked nurses prep Dinh's foot and hand with a soap solution. The surgery team's spirits are high. Listening to them talk is like hearing finches chirp.

Gowned and gloved, I sit on a stool beside Dinh's right hand. I adjust the light and begin the numbing with an injection of Xylocaine. The prick of the needle rouses him from his narcotized slumber, and he groans.

"Everyone ready? Let's go. Knife."

The nurse pops the handle of the scalpel into my palm. A stillness settles over me and passes into my hand.

Dissecting out the filamentous vessels and nerves that once brought blood and sensation to Dinh's thumb is tedious and takes more than an hour. While I work, a nurse sits at Dinh's head, murmuring to him and wiping his forehead with a wet cloth. I wonder what Dinh is thinking. Is he remembering the men who cut off his thumbs? Is he dreaming of what he might do if he met them again? When all the digital nerves and vessels and tendons are isolated and tagged with black-silk sutures, I cover the hand with a sterile towel. Before I move to Dinh's foot to harvest his spare part, I step to the head of the table.

"It's going well," I say. "You all right?"

The day before I am to leave Vietnam is the day of atonement, the time of truth, the moment to unwrap Dinh's hand and see if his thumb is viable. It is also the end of the rice harvest, and the farmers are burning off the fields to the west of the city. As I walk to the hospital, I can see a gray haze of smoke hanging over a horizon curtained with flames. It is a scorched-earth image, reminiscent of napalm and war.

In the surgery clinic I meet Dinh, sitting in a wheelchair with his bandaged hand in a sling and a confident smile on his face. Hoa, a petite nurse with a pretty smile and pearl earrings, places his hand on a white towel. A hush hangs over the room. My heart gallops. I cut the cast with heavy scissors and begin carefully unwinding the dressing. The gauze is stuck with dried blood, so I moisten it with saline and let it soak for a few minutes while I re-dress his foot. I am pleased to find the donor-site incision clean and healing well, but when I peel the last layer of gauze from his hand, I smell the faint odor of necrosis. Dinh's new thumb is the cold clay color of mildewed meat. I feel his eyes on me. I want to leave now, get on an airplane and fly home, let someone else amputate the dead thumb, let someone else clean up my mess. I glance up at his face. He is staring at the dead toe. Goddamn this dirty little Job of a country. Nothing turns out right here. I look out the window. The monsoon season is only a few days away, and already it is raining. Big drops kick up dust like rifle fire.

"It doesn't look good," I say. "Maybe I should re-dress it and give it a little more time."

"Gangrene," he says. "It dead. Take it off."

In the operating room everyone works in silence. On the table Dinh looks small and fragile, exhausted, as if he had just climbed one of those mountains on the Ho Chi Minh Trail. I pull the Kirschner wires from his hand with a hemostat and snip the nylon sutures. It is a bloodless operation. The necrotic transplant falls off onto blue drapes, stiff and cold, no longer a thumb or a toe. Looking at it, I can scarcely believe my childish hope that it would survive. I pick it up with sterile forceps and drop it into a stainless-steel pan. I think of Dinh's torturers in their purple berets chopping off his thumbs with a big knife. I see him drinking soup made with his own flesh and bone.

The day of my departure Dinh sends a driver in an old Toyota to take me to the airport. I am disappointed that he isn't riding with me, but something tells me he will be waiting for me in the terminal. I want to apologize to him because the transplant didn't work, and then have him laugh and say no problem, that in his next life he will have thumbs.

I check my bags at the ticket counter and hurry to the lounge, hoping that Dinh will be waiting there in a rattan chair with his bandaged foot propped up while he drinks a cup of green tea. Over the door to the sunny room a sign announces, NHA TRANG A GOOD PLACE FOR RESORT. With my heart hammering high in my chest, I step inside. No Dinh. The lounge is empty and silent except for the groan of a ceiling fan that churns warm, viscous air.

I move heavily between tables and out glass doors onto the tarmac. Silence surrounds me. The sun. The quiet blue sky. I stand for a while, gazing at tall brown grass and prickly pears that sprout through cracks in the airstrip. Concrete revetments built during the war to shelter American F-4 fighter jets from rocket attacks are empty and crumbling, like mausoleums of an earlier civilization. Beside the runway rests the rusty carcass of a U.S. C141 Starlifter. I watch an old F-4, now a Vietnamese fighter jet with rocket launchers riveted to its wings, practice a touchdown. The plane bounces on the concrete, its tires screeching like the cry of some fierce predator. The gray gunship rises into sparkling blue sky. My eyes follow its flight until it disappears into the glare of the sun.

Soon an Air Vietnam passenger plane lands on the runway and taxies to the tarmac, where it shimmies to a stop. It is an old Russian turboprop with a dented skin and chipped blue-and-white paint. I have heard that Air Vietnam's planes are in poor repair because the airline has trouble getting parts, and that Japanese businessmen refuse to use it.

I mount the steps into the aircraft. Inside the fuselage, heat and the oily odor of fuel squeeze the breath out of me. Only two other travelers are on board, a mamasan in a conical hat and the baby she carries in a broad sling around her waist. She stands in the aisle, swaying back and forth to rock the infant. I choose a window seat with tattered upholstery. Soon the engines on the wings cough and sputter to life. I try to buckle my seat belt, but the clasp doesn't work. I shake my head and smile. In Vietnam danger has always been ubiquitous, life tenuous. For some reason I welcome the risky ride. It makes me feel a part of the land.

Jessamyn West

....

Music on the Muscatatuck

NEAR THE BANKS of the Muscatatuck where once the woods had stretched, dark row on row, and where the fox grapes and wild mint still flourished, Jess Birdwell, an Irish Quaker, built his white clapboard house. Here he lacked for very little. On a peg by the front door hung a starling in a wooden cage and at the back door stood a springhouse, the cold spring water running between crocks of yellow-skinned milk. At the front gate a moss rose said welcome and on a trellis over the parlor window a Prairie Queen nodded at the roses in the parlor carpet — blooms no nurseryman's catalogue had ever carried and gay company for the sober Quaker volumes: Fox's life, Penn's *Fruits of Solitude*, Woolman's *Journal*, which stood in the parlor secretary.

Jess had a good wife, a Quaker minister, Eliza Cope before she was wed, and a houseful of children. Eliza was a fine woman, pious and work-brickel and good-looking as female preachers are apt to be: a little, black-haired, glossy woman with a mind of her own.

He had a good business too. He was a nurseryman with the best stock of berries and fruits west of Philadelphia; in the apple line: Rambo, Maiden Blush, Early Harvest, Northern Spy, a half dozen others; May Duke cherries; Stump the World, a white-fleshed peach; the Lucretia dewberry, a wonder for pies and cobblers. Pears, currant bushes, gooseberries, whatever the land could support or fancy demand in the way of fruits, Jess had them.

There were extras to be had too, there on the banks of the Muscatatuck: black bass; catfish that weren't choosy, that would come out of the water with their jaws clamped about a piece of cotton batting.

Pawpaws smooth and sweet as nectar, persimmons with an October flavor, sarvice berries tart as spring.

In spring, meadow and roadside breathed flowers; in summer there was a shimmer of sunlight onto the great trees whose shadows still dappled the farmland: sycamore, oak, tulip, shagbark hickory. When fall came a haze lay across the cornfields, across the stands of golden-rod and farewell summer, until heaven and earth seemed bound to-gether — and Jess, standing on a little rise at the back of the house, looking across the scope of land which fell away to the river, would have, in pure content, to wipe his eyes and blow his nose before he'd be in a fit state to descend to the house.

Yet, in spite of this content, Jess wasn't completely happy, and for no reason anyone could have hit upon at first guess. It certainly wasn't having Eliza ride every First Day morning to the Grove Meeting House, there to sit on the elevated minister's bench and speak when the spirit moved her. Jess knew Eliza had had a call to the ministry and was proud to hear her preach in her gentle way of loving-kindness and the brotherhood of man.

No, it wasn't Eliza's preaching nor any outward lack the eye could see that troubled Jess. It was music. Jess pined for music, though it would be hard to say how he'd come by any such longing. To the Quakers music was a popish dido, a sop to the senses, a hurdle waiting to trip man in his upward struggle. They kept it out of their Meeting Houses and out of their homes too. Oh, there were a few women who'd hum a little while polishing their lamp chimneys, and a few men with an inclination to whistle while dropping corn, but as to real music, sung or played, Jess had no more chance to hear it than a woodchuck.

What chances there were, though, he took. He'd often manage to be around the Methodist Church when they had their midweek ser-vices and he felt a kind of glory in his soul that wasn't entirely reli-gious when the enthusiastic Methodists hit into "Old Hundred." And when on the Fourth of July, Amanda Prentis soared upwards on the high notes of "The Star-Spangled Banner" only Eliza's determined nudgings could bring Jess back to earth.

This seemed for some time about the best Jess would be able to do in the way of music without having Eliza and her whole congregation buzzing about his ears, the best he could do anyway until he took that trip to Philadelphia and met Waldo Quigley; though of course he had no way of knowing when he was planning the trip that it would turn out as it did.

Jess had been hearing for some time about a new early cherry and he'd made up his mind to go to Philadelphia, and if they were all he'd heard, order some for the Maple Grove Nursery. There wasn't, perhaps, any real need of his going as far as Philadelphia, but to a Quaker, Philadelphia was the place to go if nothing more than a pocket handkerchief was needed. So Eliza packed his valise for him, drove him to Vernon herself, and saw him on the train.

The first word Eliza had from Jess was a letter mailed a couple of days after he left. He didn't mention Waldo Quigley in that letter, though as a matter of fact he was already hand in glove with him as Eliza discovered later. The letter was short: health good, scenery pleasant, that was about the whole of it with the exception of a postscript saying, "Thank thee, dear Eliza, for the little packet thee put in my nightshirt pocket."

The "little packet" contained peppermints, and it was through offering one of these to Waldo Quigley that Jess made his acquaintance. Jess was always sociable when he traveled. He used to say that sun, moon, and stars were the same everywhere and only the people different and if you didn't get to know them you'd as well have stayed home and milked the cows.

After Waldo Quigley put the peppermint in his mouth he settled his big, portly, black-suited frame onto the seat opposite Jess.

"Well, sir," he said, "you a Hoosier?"

Jess said he was and the big man went on, "Got a president shaping up out your way. Got an up-and-comer there on your prairies, a man who can out-talk a trumpet and out-see a telescope. He's a little giant. Man to elevate somewhat and he'll set our country on its feet. He's the man we need."

Jess sniffed. He was a fiery Republican, as fiery at least as a Quaker's apt to be. "Friend," said he, "the man we need is no little giant, but a big one. Not a man busy rousing up the countryside, setting state against state, but a man with the interest of all at heart, little farmer as well as plantation owner, black as well as white."

Jess could see, "That's Stephen A. Douglas," work up Waldo Quigley's gullet as far as his back teeth but there he stopped the words, said, "Them's my sentiments precisely, Brother Birdwell, them's my very thoughts, only better said."

Jess wrinkled up his big nose. "I see thee's a man of harmony, friend."

"Brother," replied the big man, "you put your tongue to the right word. Harmony's what I preach and harmony's what I practice."

Jess listened to these words, took another look at the big man's black suit, and decided that he was a preacher of some sort.

"Is thee, perhaps," he asked mildly, "a minister of the gospel? Though thy habit for a man of the cloth is perhaps a mite unorthodox."

Mr. Quigley cleared his throat, swallowing the last of his first peppermint. "I can't say as I've ever been ordained," he admitted, "but my work's been so much with them that has that I've fallen into a sedate manner of dressing. It strikes me as being a more seemly thing to do. Helps business too," he added.

"Business?" asked Jess.

"You named it yourself, Mr. Birdwell. Harmony is my business. Do-re-mi. Also la-ti-do. Not forgetting fa-sol. Harmony. The music of the spheres. God's way of speaking to his children. The power that soothes the savage beast, the song that quiets newborn babes and eases the pangs of the dying man. In a word, music."

"In several words in fact," ruminated Jess. "Is thee then, Brother Quigley, a musician?" he asked.

"Musician? Yes. But I," said he frankly, "am that rather unusual combination, a musical businessman, or perhaps more truly a businesslike musician. There's plenty of men can keep a double entry set of books and there's a number more, though fewer, can tell a grace note from a glissando, but I," handing Jess a card, "can do both."

Jess took the card and read aloud, "Professor Waldo Quigley, Traveling Representative, Payson and Clarke. The World's Finest Organs. Also Sheet Music and Song Books."

Brother Quigley reached out, took the card from Jess, and wrote "Personal Compliments" on it.

"I note from your speech you're a Quaker, and knowing the way that sect — not that it ain't the finest in the world," he said politely — "feels about music I wouldn't want you to think I was trying to work against your prejudices — convictions rather. So," he said, handing the card back to Jess, "I write 'Personal Compliments,' to show I'm free of any profit-making motives; that we meet man to man. Pays to be delicate-like where religion is concerned. Pays every time," he said, nodding to Jess.

Jess tried Payson and Clarke over once or twice on his tongue. "Payson and Clarke," he said. "So thee sells Payson and Clarke's.

They've got one unless I disremember in the Methodist meeting house at Rush Branch."

"Sure they have," said Brother Quigley. "Sure they have." He took a little red book from an inner pocket and flipped a few pages. "Yes, sir. I sold them that organ three years ago April 19. One more strawberry festival and they'll have it paid for."

"Thee sells a good instrument then. I've heard that organ now and again in passing."

"Good? Mr. Birdwell, it's better than good. Three years ago after them Methodists at Rush Branch heard my concert and song recital, they said to me, 'Professor Quigley, we don't ever calculate to hear the voice of God any more plain while here on earth.'"

Jess said, "That's carrying it a little far, mebbe," but he was really burning to hear more about the Payson and Clarke.

"Well, of course," Brother Quigley reminded him, "you got to remember they's Methodists. Tending toward the shouting order. But this organ, Methodists aside, is pure gumbo, absolutely pure gumbo."

"Gumbo," Jess repeated.

"Rich. Satisfying. Deep. Gumbo, pure gumbo."

Jess knew a thing or two about organs though it would be hard to say how: perhaps from reading Chalmer's *Universal Encyclopedia*, perhaps from an inspection of the Methodist organ. Perhaps in neither way. Knowledge of what you love somehow comes to you; you don't have to read nor analyze nor study. If you love a thing enough, knowledge of it seeps into you, with particulars more real than any chart can furnish. Maybe it was that way with Jess and organs.

So he asked, "How many reeds in a Payson and Clarke?"

"Forty-eight, Brother Birdwell, not counting the tuba mirabalis. But in the Payson and Clarke, number ain't what counts — it's the quality. Those reeds duplicate the human throat. They got timbre." And he landed on the French word the way a hen lands on the water, skeptical, but hoping for the best.

"How many stops?" Jess asked.

"Eight. And that *vox humana*! The throat of an angel. It cries, it sighs, it sings. You can hear the voice of your lost child in it. Did you ever lose a child, Brother Birdwell?"

"No," said Jess shortly.

"You can hear the voice of your old mother calling to you from the further shore."

"Ma lives in Germantown," said Jess.

If the conversation had followed in this direction, Jess would never have come home with a Payson and Clarke; but in every nerve Brother Quigley could feel a prospect retreating and he changed his tack.

"The Payson and Clarke comes in four different finishes," he said. "Oak, maple, walnut, and mahogany. Got a cabinet that's purely elegant. Most organs got two swinging brackets. This one's got four. Two for lamps, two for vases. Has a plate mirror over the console. There's not a square inch of unornamented wood in the whole cabinet. No, sir, there's not an inch of dingy, unembellished wood the length and breadth of the cabinet. But, Brother Birdwell, you're a musician yourself. You're not interested in cabinets. You're interested in tone. Tone's what the artist looks for. Tone's what Payson and Clarke's got."

He began to hum under his breath. Low at first, then louder, with occasional words. "Tum-te-tum — the riverside — tum-te-tum — upon its tide."

"That's a likely tune," Jess said.

"Can't do justice to it singing."

But he stopped humming, launched into the words. He had a fine baritone. Flatted a little, Jess thought, but not bad. When he exhaled heavily on a high note, Jess was sorry to find he'd had a nip or two, but before the piece was finished Jess was beating time with his forefinger on the red plush arm of the seat, completely forgetful of the spirits Brother Quigley had surely had.

"What's the piece called?" Jess asked.

"'The Old Musician and His Harp.' It was written to be played on an organ. Mortifies me that you have to hear it first time sung, merely."

"Thee's a good voice," Jess said.

"Fair to middling. Fair to middling, only."

He sank a fat hand in one of his big black pockets and brought up a leather-covered flask. He wiped the mouth carefully on his coattail and held it toward Jess.

"Wet your whistle and we'll sing it through together."

Jess shook his head.

"Well, I didn't suppose you would, but it's a pity. Cleans your pipes. Extends your range. Gives you gumbo." He took a long swig himself.

"Try it with me, Brother Birdwell."

Jess said afterward he didn't have the slightest intention of making a show of himself in a B&O parlor car singing "The Old Musician and His Harp," or any other song, for that matter. But that tune was a hard thing to give the go-by; the mind said the words and the toe tapped the time; with the whole body already singing it, that way, opening the mouth to let the words out seemed a mighty small matter and before Jess knew it he was taking the high notes in his fine, clear tenor. Jess had the nose for a really first-class tenor — there never was a first-class tenor with a button nose, and Jess, with his, high-bridged, more Yankee than Quaker, had just the nose for it. Before he and Brother Quigley had finished a couple of verses half the parlor car was joining in the chorus.

> Bring my harp to me again,
> Let me hear its gentle strain;
> Let me hear its chords once more
> Ere I pass to yon bright shore.

When they finished Brother Quigley had another nip. "Got to cool the pipes," he said. "Now, Brother Birdwell, when you get to Philly, when you get them cherries located, you stop in at Payson and Clarke's and hear that the way it was meant to be heard. Hear it on the organ. No obligation whatever. Privilege to play for a fellow artist."

Jess hadn't a notion in the world of buying an organ when he went into Payson and Clarke's. He'd got the cherry stock he'd come after, had had a nice visit with his mother, and was ready to start homeward when he thought he'd as well hear "The Old Musician and His Harp" on a Payson and Clarke. Brother Quigley had been clever to him and it was no more than humanly decent to let the man show him what the organ could do. That was the way he had it figured out to himself before he went in, anyway.

When he'd walked out, the organ was his. He didn't know what he'd do with it; he didn't think Eliza would hear to keeping it; he thought he'd like as not slipped clean away from grace, but he had the papers for the organ in his pocket. He'd paid half cash, the rest to be in nursery stock. Clarke of Payson and Clarke was an orchardist.

As soon as Jess heard Waldo Quigley run his fingers over that organ's keys with a sound as liquid as the Muscatatuck after a thaw he'd known he was sunk. And when he'd found he could chord "The Old

Musician" himself, when Waldo Quigley said, "Never knew a man with a better tremolo," when he pumped the air into the organ with his feet and drew it out with his fingers, sounding like an echo of eternity, he began casting up his bank balance in his mind. He was past figuring out the right and wrong of the matter; all he was interested in was getting it, having that organ where he could lay his hands across it, hear whenever he liked those caressing tones.

He managed to get home a few days before the organ arrived. He didn't say a word to Eliza about what he'd done. He figured it was a thing which would profit by being led up to gradually. He talked a good deal in those few days about music; how God must like it or He wouldn't have put songbirds in the world, and how the angels were always pictured with harp and zither.

Eliza was not receptive. "Thee's neither bird nor angel, Jess Birdwell, and had the Lord wanted thee, either singing or plucking a harp, thee would be feathered now one way or another."

There'd been an early snow the day the organ arrived; a foot or two on the level, much more in the drifts. Jess himself brought the organ home from Vernon on the sled.

Eliza knew what it was the minute she laid eyes on the box, for all Jess's care in covering it over with an old rag carpet. Jess's talk about birds and angels had made her fearful of something of the kind, only she hadn't thought it'd be as bad as an organ; a flute, or maybe a French harp he could go down cellar and play had been the worst her imaginings had pictured for her. But she knew it was an organ before Jess had got the covering off the crate, and was out in the snow by the time Enoch had the horses out of the traces.

"What's this thee's bringing home, Jess Birdwell?"

Though she knew well enough. She just wanted to hear him put his tongue to it.

"It's a Payson and Clarke," Jess said, still trying to be gradual.

But it was no use. "It's an organ," Eliza said. "Jess, Jess, what's thee thinking of? Bringing this thing here? Me, a recorded minister and the house full of growing children. What's the neighbors to think? What's the Grove Meeting to think?"

If she'd kept on in this sorrowful strain Jess would like as not have got shut of the organ, but Eliza didn't stop there.

"Jess Birdwell," she said, "if thee takes that organ in the house, I stay out. Thee can make thy choice. Thee can have thy wife or thee can have that instrument; but both, thee cannot have."

Jess had a heart as soft as pudding, and if Eliza'd said Please, if she'd let a tear slide out of her soft black eye, that organ would have been done for; but commands, threats, that was a different matter entirely.

Jess called to the hired man who'd taken the horses to the barn, "Come and give me a hand with this organ, Enoch."

A heart soft as pudding, till someone took it on himself to tell Jess which way to turn, then the pudding froze, and if you weren't careful you'd find yourself cut to the bone on an ice splinter. A mild man until pushed, but Jess solidified fast with pushing.

Eliza saw the granite coming, but she was of martyr stock herself and felt the time had come to suffer for the right. She sat flat down in the snow, or as flat as petticoats and skirts would let her. There in the snow she sat and said, "Jess Birdwell, here I stay until that organ is taken away."

Jess said, "We'll uncrate it where it stands, Enoch, then carry it up to the house. No use having the weight of the crate to move too."

So they went to work on it, got it out of its case and the excelsior packing. Enoch kept his eye on Eliza sitting there in the snow. She made him feel uncomfortable, as if the least he could do would be to give her his coat to sit on.

"Well, let's not dally here, Enoch," Jess said, seeming not to even see Eliza. "Let's get it up to the house."

As they went up the path to the house, straining and puffing through the snow, Enoch said, "Ain't she liable to catch her death of cold there?"

"I figure," said Jess, "that when the snow melts through the last petticoat she'll move."

He was wrong about that. Eliza was wet to the skin before she came up to the house. She had sat there casting up the matter in her mind, but she knew that when Jess was set he was a problem for the Lord. And she had enough respect for both to leave them to each other. There was nothing ever to be gained, she thought, by dissension. Peace, she could at least have. Jess had just finished dusting the organ when Eliza came in, went to the stove, and stood there steaming.

"Jess," she asked, "is thee set on having this organ? Remembering thy children and my ministry, is thee still set?"

"Yes, Eliza," Jess said, "I'm set."

"Well," she said, "that's settled"; and being on the whole a reasonable as well as a pious woman, she added, "It will have to go in the attic."

"I'd thought of that," Jess said, "and I'm willing."

So that's the way it was done. The organ was put in the attic and from there it could be heard downstairs, but not in any full-bodied way. It took the gumbo out of it — having it in the attic — and besides Jess was careful not to play it when anyone was in the house. He was careful, that is, until the day the Ministry and Oversight Committee called. He was careful that day too; it was Mattie who wasn't careful, though unlucky's more the word for it.

Jess had noted right off that Mattie had a musical turn. She'd learned to pick out "The Old Musician" by herself, with one hand, and when Jess discovered this, he taught her the bass chords so that she could play for him to sing. That was a bitter pill for Eliza to swallow, and just what she'd feared: the children becoming infected with Jess's weakness for music. Still, she couldn't keep herself from listening when the deep organ notes with Jess's sweet tenor flying above them came seeping down through the ceiling into the sitting room below.

But in spite of Jess's being careful, in spite of Eliza's being twice as strict as usual, and speaking at the Hopewell Meeting House with increased gravity, the matter got noised about. Not that there was an organ at Birdwells': there wasn't anything definite known, anything you could put your finger on. It was just a feeling that Friend Birdwell wasn't standing as squarely in the light as he'd done at one time. Perhaps someone had heard a strain of organ music coming out of an attic window some spring evening, but more than likely it was just the guilty look Eliza had.

However that may be, the Ministry and Oversight Committee came one night to call. It was nearing seven; supper had been over for some time, the dishes were washed, and the table was set for breakfast. Jess and Eliza were in the sitting room resting after the heat and work of the day and listening to the children who were playing duck-on-rock down by the branch.

The Committee drove up in Amos Pease's surrey, but by the back way, leaving the rig at the carriage house, so that the first sign Jess and Eliza had of visitors was the smell of trodden mint. Amos Pease wasn't a man to note where he put his feet down when duty called.

Eliza smelled it first and stepped over to the west window to see who was coming. She saw, and in a flash she knew why. "It's the Ministry and Oversight," she said, and her voice shook, but when Amos Pease knocked at the door she was sitting in her rocker, her feet on a footstool, one hand lying loose and easy in the other.

Jess answered the knock. "Good evening, Amos. Good evening, Ezra. Good evening, Friend Hooper."

The Committee said its good evenings to Jess and Eliza, found chairs, adjusted First Day coattails — it wasn't First Day, but they'd put on their best since what they had to do was serious. But before they could even ease into their questions with some remark upon the weather or how the corn was shaping up — Jess heard it — the faint kind of leathery sigh the organ made when the foot first touched the bellows. That sound was like a pain hitting him in the heart and he thought, I've sold my birthright for a mess of pottage. For Jess was a Quaker through and through, no misdoubting that. For two hundred years his people had been Quakers, sometimes suffering for that right, and now he thought, I've gone and lost it all for a wheezing organ.

It was Mattie at the organ and Jess knew her habits there: they were like his own. She never began to play a piece at once, but touched the organ here and there, slowly pumped in the air, then lovingly laid her fingers across upon keys. After that the music. Jess looked across at Eliza and he saw by the way her hands had tightened round each other that she'd heard too. I'm a far worse man than Esau, he thought, for he sold only his own birthright, and I've sold my wife's as well as my own.

Jess remembered how Eliza loved to bring the Lord's message to the Lord's people and how his own love for pushing air through a set of reeds was going to lose her all this. And before his lips moved his heart began to pray, "Lord, deliver thy servant from the snare of his own iniquity."

By the time Mattie was ready to touch the first key he was on his feet saying, "Friends, let us lift our hearts to God in prayer." This was nothing startling to a gathering of Quakers. They'd any of them take to praying at the drop of a hat. So some knelt and others didn't, but all bowed their heads and shut their eyes.

All except Jess. He stood with face uplifted to the ceiling, facing his God and his sin. By the time Mattie had got into "The Old Musician," and a few faint wisps of music were floating into the room, Jess was talking to God in a voice that shook the studding. He was talking to Him in the voice of a man whose sins have come home to roost. He was reminding Him of all the other sinners to whom His mercy had nevertheless been granted.

He went through the Bible book by book and sinner by sinner. He prayed in the name of Adam, who had sinned and fallen short of grace; of Moses, who had lost the Promised Land; of David, who had looked with desire on another man's wife. He prayed in the name of Solomon, his follies, of Abraham and his jealousies, and Jephthah, who kept his word in cruelty; he made a music of his own out of his contrition; his revulsion mounted up in melody.

He left the Old Testament and prayed for them all, sinners alike, in the name of Paul, who what he would not, he did; and of Peter, who said he knew the Man not, and of Thomas who doubted and Judas who betrayed and of that Mary who repented.

He stood with his red head lifted up while his long Irish lip wrapped itself around the good Bible names. He prayed until the light had left the room and his hair in the dark had become as colorless as Amos Pease's dun thatch. He prayed until all the mint smell had left the room and the only smell left was that of a penitent man seeking forgiveness.

Now Jess was no hypocrite and if his prayer swelled a little, if it boomed out a little stronger when Mattie pulled the fortissimo stop, it was through none of his planning; it was the Lord's doing entirely. And if his prayer wasn't finished until Mattie'd finished playing after going five times through "The Old Musician," that was the Lord's hand too, and nothing of Jess's contriving.

Finally, when he'd made an end, and the visiting men had taken their faces out from behind their hands and looked around the dark room with dazed eyes, Jess dropped down into his chair and rubbed his forefinger across his lips, the way a man will when he's been speaking. Eliza lit them a candle, then went out to bring in the lamps.

Amos Pease picked up the candle and held it so the light fell onto Jess's face. "Friend," he said, "thee's been an instrument of the Lord this night. Thee's risen to the throne of grace and carried us all upwards on thy pinions. Thy prayer carried us so near to heaven's gates that now and again I thought I could hear angels' voices choiring and the sound of heavenly harps."

And with that he set the candle back down, put his hat on his head, and said, "Praise God." Friend Griffith and Friend Hooper said, "Amen, brother. Amen to that," and with great gravity followed Amos Pease out of the door.

When Eliza came back in with the lamp, Jess was sitting there alone in the candlelight. There was a smell of trod-on mint again in the room and the children had stopped playing duck-on-rock and were whooping after lightning bugs to put in bottles. Jess was huddled over, his eyes shut, like a man who has felt the weight of the Lord's hand between his shoulder blades. But before Eliza could clear her throat to say "Amen" to the edifying sight he made, down from the attic floated "The Old Musician" once again, and Jess's foot began to tap:

> Tap, tap — the riverside,
> Tap, tap — upon its tide.

Kate Wheeler

....

Ringworm

I'T'S BEEN TWO YEARS since I left Pingyan Monastery, but every time my head itches I still think it's that ringworm. It was the blind cat's fault, or mine for getting distracted and feeding her and having a special feeling about her, as if her eyes full of blank green fire could see something beyond what there was — white stucco walls stained with red mud from the monsoon, beautiful brown people walking slowly up and down, meditating. Dust, mud, garbage, jasmine. Every single thing, different from here.

She first showed up at the end of the hot season, gray and black tiger, like a cat I used to have in California. I couldn't tell where she'd come from; she was obviously from outside the orange-and-white gene pool of the monastery cats. Maybe she'd wandered in from the Muslim slum next door. She was so weak she fell down the steps into the basement that was given to us foreign women as a meditation hall, down under the dorm for Burmese women over fifty. There was a special building for older women, mostly devout widows who came to meditate after their familial duties were accomplished. We six Foreigner Women, all younger than that, had to walk through their quarters to get to the toilet. In the long oven of the hallway, there was mutual inspection. I'd peek sidelong into their rooms and see the grandmothers oiling their long hair or resting after lunch, always lying on their right sides because this was the posture in which the Buddha slept. They lay very still, often with their eyes open. Were they thinking of anything? Maybe not. They frequently offered me bananas or a little dish of fermented tea leaves fried with garlic and peanuts. They felt sorry for the foreigners, I think, because we had no families to come and visit us and bring us nice things to eat.

I was a nun, with a shaven head and four layers of pink, vaguely Grecian robes. I'd gone to Burma on recommendation from travelers I met in India. They said that Burma was a fragment of an older world, that in isolation it had worked out the world's strictest, most effective technique for spiritual enlightenment. I waited a year and a half for a special visa, and when it finally arrived I was ready, primed: I told Pingyan's abbot that I wanted nothing but complete freedom of the heart and mind. Because I'd meditated quite a lot in the past, he offered me the robes, a nun's ten rules of conduct, and the name Sumanā, meaning "Open Mind" or "Open Heart" (Burmese don't make a distinction), and also, "Queen of Jasmine."

The monastery covered forty acres in a suburb near the British consulate, and had enough buildings to accommodate the entire bourgeoisie of Rangoon as well as devotees from places like Mandalay, Sagaing, and the Shan and Karen states. There were usually a thousand people meditating, both ordained and lay; four thousand during the Water Festival. As in any religion, females predominated in number, but there was a good minority of monks who were the authorities, as well as a dozen foreigners. We foreign women lived and meditated by ourselves and saw the men only at meals. After a while my eyes turned Asian, and Western males began to look like the barbarians on a Chinese plate, hairy and coarse, their naked pink skin like boiled shrimp.

Breakfast was at five and lunch at ten-fifteen. There was no solid food, then, until the next breakfast. The monks said eating at night causes lust. We woke at three to the clanking of an iron pipe. Each day there were seven one-hour sittings, interspersed with six or seven hours of formal walking meditation, pacing slowly up and down. At eight P.M. the abbot discoursed to the foreigners; Burmese got sermons only on Saturday. Every other day we had an interview, a completely formalized affair in which we described our meditation and the abbot instructed us about how to proceed. Bed was at eleven.

We didn't talk, nor make eye contact with anyone. We were told to keep the mind protected like a turtle in its shell, but to notice everything occurring in that field. Thus, when not sitting with eyes shut, we moved very slowly, minutely attending to sensations and avoiding complex, rapid movements. If strong thoughts or emotions came, we noticed their presence but discarded their content. This practice was intended to lead to the famous and misunderstood Nirvana, which the Burmese call Nibbāna, Liberation, the end of suffering — *cessation* was the word the Burmese used. I believed I could experience cessation because I was in Burma where, it was said, lots of people had psychic powers and the young girls would attain their first cessation during summer holidays from school.

Possibly my great faith contributed to slackness in my practice. I was fascinated with everything. My notebook was stuffed with observations that I knew the monks would disapprove of. "Toothpaste tube still hot at nine P.M.," "Burmese girls grow their toenails long and paint them." I was constantly enmeshed in situations with other Westerners, or with Burmese who wanted to get visas to the States, practice English, teach me Burmese, or donate things to me because gifts to a nun would generate good karma. It didn't matter that I intended to disrobe whenever I reached Nibbāna or the government quit extending my visa — I could have been a nun for a single day and still deserved the same respect. The merit gained by paying respect to ordained people is gauged by what they represent, rather than anything personal. Once I comprehended this, it was easier to let the young girls kneel in the dirt and bow, or simply take off their shoes as they handed me a banana or a sack of boiled cane-juice candy. Giving to a male monk would have been precisely ten times better, but my Westernness seemed to give me an extra value not included in traditional calculations. I got lots of presents; I had a fan club of twenty young girls. One medical student told me I must be a very pure being indeed, for having first merited, and then forsaken, the sensual pleasures of the "United State."

At interviews the abbot said I was progressing and that I should keep a relaxed attitude. So I had little incentive to change, except perhaps the example of my senior nun, Sīlānandī, "Bliss of Morality." She was French, and had done PR for a ritzy yacht club before firmly renouncing the world. Her posture, the result of a childhood in Parisian ballet classes, impressed the girls in my fan club as evidence of deep meditative powers.

I was taking a break, standing at the row of sinks in line with the other women, all of us mixing up glucose tea, which we drank in the afternoon to keep from getting dehydrated. My feet were bare and dirty on the hot black boards, the sinks were giving off their intense slime smell, and my four layers of robes were stuck to my skin with the heat, as usual. Now I heard a thin mew, turned, and saw this pathetic creature, all bones, tottering then falling down the steps.

Next to me, Sīlānandī slowly turned her head to look, slowly turned

with its dark, cool tank of water. My equipment was a mirror, a thermos of hot water, a bar of blue Chinese soap, and a Gillette Trac II cartridge razor I'd brought in from Bangkok. Shaving took an hour, and except for the bliss of leaving behind the hall and my companions, suddenly comical in their diligence, I hated it. The textures put my teeth on edge — cheap lather like saliva, sandpapery stubble, sticky smoothness of my scalp. Next day, the back of my head always erupted in a thousand tiny pimples. Irritation, I suppose. Eventually I learned that a hot washrag cured this.

One shaving day I found a small, red patch on my right temple. By then I was used to various grossnesses of my flesh and found this one interesting. When I pulled my skin a little, it jumped into a perfect circle. There were few perfectly made things in that environment, and this roundness pleased me. But now it itched.

A few nights later, after the abbot's discourse, I went to ask the monastery nurse about it. She was Warden of the Foreigner Women's Dorm, and so she lived downstairs from us.

Saya-ma Aye Shwe, Nurse Cool Golden, was sitting under her mosquito net. As she was deaf, I had to walk into her room and touch her on the shoulder.

"It 'tis a sunburn," she breathed, in English. "Leave it." Her voice was deceptive, as soft as a baby's sigh.

Though she'd trained as a nurse in East Germany and in Australia, Nurse Aye Shwe ascribed most physical ailments to faulty concentration, heat, or cold. She'd cured herself of stomach cancer by meditating alone in a forest hut, vowing not to come out until she died or attained enlightenment. Now it was her right to despise infirmity; one visited the clinic only in a mood of boldness. Westerners were too soft, always sick, always wanting pills. The body is good only for practice, we must learn that it is full of sufferings! To Sīlānandī, who had severe edema in her arms and legs, Nurse Aye Shwe refused any medicament. "It is very good to die in meditation," she reminded.

I retired from her presence that night without a murmur, even though I knew I had no sunburn. It wasn't bothering me much, yet.

A week later the spot was the size of the rubber ring on a Mason jar and itched so much I couldn't sleep. I returned to the nurse's quarters, tilted my head to the light from her barred window.

"Is it ringworm?" I asked, but she didn't have her hearing aid on. "Ringworm?"

It was often hard to tell what Nurse Aye Shwe had understood.

Where deafness came to an end, there some obscurely motivated will-fulness took over. "You are not used to our water," she said sadly. "Try with Go-Min."

"Go-Min!" I laughed, throwing my head back for Nurse Aye Shwe's benefit. In all fairness, it was very difficult to get Western medicines in Burma, especially for one such as a nurse who disapproved of the black market. But Go-Min was made in Burma, and very cheap, a rude little jar of pig fat mixed with aromatic oils. I had heard the nurse pre-scribe it for swollen gums, varicose veins, abdominal bloating, scabies, and mosquito bites. Weeks ago, she'd given me a jar of it for hemor-rhoids; the most I can say is that it burned as if it were having a radical effect.

"Sister Go-Min, they call me," Nurse Aye Shwe said with a smirk. "If your meditation is good, Go-Min will be very effective."

Later that day I was doing walking meditation next to the Hall of the Diamond, where the Burmese women meditated. It looked like a cinema and was fixed up inside like Versailles, with mirror mosaics and a giant aquarium up front, enclosing an enormous white enamel Buddha with a gold-leaf robe and red smiling lips. Foreigner Women were forbidden to meditate there, which was a disappointment to me. Our basement hall smelled of rotting mud and had no Buddha. Often it was invaded by fleas from the Warden's pissing tomcats. More im-portantly, the Burmese women seemed to have more fun than we did. Every morning they chanted in a haunting minor key. Young girls did their walking meditation arm in arm, and no one was terribly serious about the rule of silence. When sad thoughts or terrifying visions came, the women groaned and wept aloud. "Oiyy! Oiyy!" Sometimes their entire hall would erupt in these lugubrious sounds, like a pack of she-wolves howling, and I'd wish desperately to be there, not cooped up with the grim Calvinists in the Foreigner Women's Basement.

Suddenly I was at the center of a bunch of teenaged nuns who were giggling and rapidly speaking Burmese. They pulled me around the corner, out of sight of the women's supervisor or any passing monk. I nearly fainted with delight. I regularly got crushes on these temporary nuns who came, like me, to ordain for a few months or a year. Physically they were lovely — supple bodies in the narrow elegant pink robes, faces exquisite in concentration. I imagined them uncorrupted creatures, isolated in medieval Burma from the evils of the world.

One tall girl pointed at my ringworm, crying, "Pwe! Pwe!" It was so big now, they must have seen it from afar. A pudgy lay girl explained in English, "She bring med-cine fo' you." As we stood there, an old woman came up, as stout as a gnome and dressed in the brown lay-women's uniform of sash, sarong, and jacket. She had diamonds in her ears, rims of gold around all of her incisors. She pulled a tube out of a ratty vinyl purse.

"My son," she said, showing me the tube. TRIMOXTRIM, it said, USE ONLY UNDER THE DIRECTION OF A PHYSICIAN. "Put," she said, shaking the tube toward me. When in Rome, I thought. I put on a tiny dab.

"Tomorrow, fie o'clack," the fat girl said, pointing at the ground.

The next day they were waiting, the dry, brown gnome amid garde-nias. To meet them I had to cross the Burmese women's walking ground, a no-man's-land of hard, barren dirt. Slowly, slowly, eyes downcast — I was in sight of the elder monks' cottages. My shadow flew over dull rocks, smashed brick, eroded asphalt, struggling weeds. Two monks swished past on important business, as fast as Jaguars on a freeway.

The tall nun's name was Nandāsayee, "Expert of Delight." She car-ried a long, flexible branch in her hand. "Lady gah-din, she *find*," the fat interpreter announced. Nandāsayee pulled off seven leaves, rolled a cylinder, tore off one end. She whispered to it quietly; then, puh, puh, puh, she breathed on it.

"'Life, not life,'" the interpreter offered. "She tell to leaf."

Cradling my head, Nandāsayee now rubbed the leaves onto the ringworm, carefully following its outline counterclockwise. This stung a little. Later I learned that the leaves were from a hot pepper bush. Her finger pads were slightly moist and soft, like frogs' palps. I could smell the green crushed leaf, and her body, scorched where mine was sharp.

This could cure me of anything, I thought. I'd been there six months then, physically touched by no one.

Finished, Nandāsayee walked a few paces off and threw the leaves over her shoulder. She came back grinning.

"Tomorrow three time," the plump girl said. "Aftah brehfass, aftah lunch, fie o'clack." I pointed to the Foreigner Women's Hall, and the nuns giggled mischievously. Not long before, a man had come from the office and pounded a sign into the ground just at our door, three rows of Burmese curlicues. I'd gone to the office to ask what the words meant.

"Foreigner Women Are Practicing Meditation," the monastery vice president importantly said. Before assuming this duty he'd been Minister of Finance for all of Burma. "Do Not Stare, Do Not Go In, Do Not Try to Start a Conversation."

Before we all dispersed, the woman in brown anointed me again. Methophan was this cream's name. READ CIRCULAR DIRECTIONS CAREFULLY.

Nurse Aye Shwe was in a mood of laxity. That night she beckoned me into her room.

"I have got! Burmese medicine for ringworm. When you are finish, please return me, unused portion." It was a whitish, grainy cream in a hot pink plastic tub. I made the first application right away. It stung fiercely, satisfactorily. Its job must be simply to kill infested flesh.

Nurse Aye Shwe offered me hot plum concentrate in an enamel cup. "I teach meditation now, in Rangoon Asylum," she remarked. "Soon cure." Her face was a mask of satisfaction; I was filled with nostalgia for such certainty as hers, the same feeling as when I wish to have been born in some past century.

"Today I select my patient," she went on, proudly. "One man present himself. 'Take me!' he say. But he is naked! I say, 'You, never.' Another man come. Ol' man. On his head, hat. Under hat, plastic bag. Under plastic bag, paper bag. Under paper bag, leaf! This one, I say, 'Please come with me.'"

"The Swiss woman has strange thoughts," I suggested. "*Swiss woman, very strange!*"

"I know," Nurse Aye Shwe said. "I am so sorry for the Western people."

That night I couldn't sleep. I lay under the mosquito net's stifling canopy, too dizzy to sit up and meditate. Everything was breaking into particles, the itching at my temple, the passionate sounds of the night. Crickets sawed away, lizards croaked like colliding billiard balls; in the Muslim slum, a woman sang endless Arab vowels, the very voice of unfulfilled desire. I knew I'd miss these serenades, whenever I went home.

Before the dawn mists burned off, Sister Nandāsayee slipped into our basement and closed the door behind her. In the half dark, we Foreigner Women were making our postbreakfast cups of milk tea. Nandāsayee came at me with her leafy branch. I bent my head; she performed the little ritual of treatment. I felt like the birthday girl.

Even Sīlānandī was intrigued enough to stand and frankly watch until Nandāsayee receded out the door, a finger to her lips.

The Swiss woman surged toward me, an ocean liner beaming, beaming, beaming sympathetic joy. Her eyes were two blue lamps. "So beautiful this Burmese nun," she breathed.

I tore a leaf from my notebook and posted a general notice. "I am being treated for ringworm with herbal medicine."

Next time Nandāsayee was more forward. She hovered over each of us in turn, frowned, and pointed at Sīlānandī's tea bags and milk powder. Obviously she'd never seen either. All of us stood around while Sīlānandī, with perfect art, showed how she prepared her tea in an old Milo jar. At the end she offered the jar to Nandāsayee, who made a suspicious face. She barely touched the liquid with her tongue's tip and scowled. All of us laughed. Dour Cathy from western Scotland presented her with a chewable vitamin C, which Nandāsayee tucked into her sash before rushing out the door as if chased by demons.

This was the beginning of my friendship with Sīlānandī. That day I found a note under my cushion in her spiky European hand. "Will the pink angel rub my swollen ankles too? Mmm."

Last night, sir, I felt strange. Objects appeared as streams of particles dissolving. When I observed the abdomen, I found no physical sensations. I was disoriented until I discovered a subtle sense of space. Happiness arose, then images of an event during the day.

How long did you dwell on the images?

Ten, fifteen minutes.

Too long.

Yes, sir.

When objects are subtle, be aware of their pleasantness or unpleasantness. If no objects appear, do not try to find them. Do not ponder, do not ask yourself, "What is this, how is this, why is this?" If you think a thousand ways, you will find a thousand answers. Only direct awareness will show you the nature of the world.

Thank you, sir.

Good. Try to sleep only four hours.

Bigger now and not so weak, the kitten reappeared in the breezeway next to the Foreigner Women's Quarters. I brought back food for her from lunch in a thick white teacup. Chicken gizzards, hunks of pork fat; I barely had time to get my fingers out of the way of her teeth.

A circle gathered. The older women frowned, the girls seemed delightedly scandalized. "*Wet'tha*, pig meat. *Chet'tha*, chicken meat," they chanted. I realized this was better food than they'd had at lunch. Foreigners and monks at the best foods — pork, eggs, mango, durian, birthday cake, ice cream — donated by the pious. Burmese nuns and laywomen ate in a separate dining room, directly beneath the monks'.

Tomorrow I'd bring only bones and scraps.

Nurse Aye Shwe flew out, a dark, screeching gryphon. "No yogi must have pet! This cup for monks, not animal! Very bad *kamma* for you."

The watching crowd laughed as it dispersed. For two days, the nurse's face was thunder. I persisted in feeding the cat but soon found occasion to donate my last bar of Thai disinfectant soap to the dispensary.

"Sumanā is capitalist," Nurse Aye Shwe said sourly, tucking the soap into her cabinet. But that afternoon she gave me half a coconut shell to use as the cat's dish. "Pussy very t'in. Blind." I wondered why I hadn't noticed. The way she picked her way across the monsoon gutters, shaking her paw, surprised when she stepped in puddles near the outdoor bathing tank.

Soon Nurse Aye Shwe began to scrape her own rice bowl into the cat's. I still brought food from lunch, even though it was a major complication in the closed and narrow circuit of my life. Choosing the scraps, wrapping the cup, finding the cat, enduring the watching, washing cup and napkin, remembering to return them the next day — it all stood out as tedious labor. Our teachers said there were three kinds of suffering. The suffering of pain itself, the suffering of the alternation of pleasure and pain, and the suffering of the cumbersomeness of life. I reported to my teacher that I understood this now. He laughed and said to be more continuous.

But I was bad, bad. I began doing my walking meditation under the shaded breezeway where the cat liked to sit for hours on end, her paws hidden under her chest. "She is meditating," I told myself. When no one was looking, I would carry her the length of my twenty-pace walking track, cradled in my arms. She was developing a belly, a hard little ball; though it didn't look exactly healthy, it seemed an improvement, a justification for feeding her.

The breezeway fronted on another Burmese dorm, this one for

younger girls and several women who were permanent residents. Walking there, I learned many new unnecessary things. I saw the wrist motion with which the women beat their laundry on the flat stone; learned that some of the young girls were lazy and would lock themselves in a room all afternoon, giggling and eating cookies. The woman who lived at the end was some sort of witch. I'd see her on a patch of waste ground at the end of my walking track, making strange passes with a twig broom and singing softly to the air. At first I thought her saintly, but one day it struck me that her face was as hard and primitive as an alcoholic's. I guessed her family had abandoned her, or died. In return for her keep, she swept the leaves from the broad cement walkways on the monks' side of the compound.

One day she gave me a boiled egg, the poorest egg I've ever tasted. The white was blue, translucent; the gray yolk tasted of fish. As I should not have done, I imagined the hen it must have come from.

The Swiss woman was deteriorating. Some days she would not come to the meditation hall at all but stayed inside her room with the door closed. Slowly pacing the breezeway, I watched and worried but didn't intervene. She blocked her transom with a cotton blanket. Ten times a day, with a great rattling of the latch, she raced to the bathroom and flung water over herself. Our tank was always empty. I wondered what she reported in her interviews, whether the monks were capable of understanding her condition. Maybe the heat was getting to her, I thought, or just the isolation.

My ringworm was a pale ghost. Who knows which treatment was responsible? I used the Burmese ointment hourly; at ten, as I waited to join the lunch procession, the gnome in brown accosted me with frightening Western creams, halting tales of her son in L.A. And of course, Nandāsayee, my goddess, came three times each day. We were all in love with her. We gave her mint tea, sugar, and chocolates, and she reciprocated with jasmine and frangipani. Once I brought down my camera and got Scottish Cathy to document the treatment. Nandāsayee demanded formal portraits of herself holding hands with each of the Foreigner Women yogis. She stood very still, unsmiling, as if her image were a sacrifice she offered to the camera. I had several sets of prints made by the monastery photographer at fabulous expense and gave one to her in return for the treatment.

The next day she didn't come, nor the next. I began to see her in the company of senior nuns.

"Your friend, small nun, very successful meditation," Nurse Aye Shwe said.

Now I was galvanized by spiritual urgency. I felt I had been wasting my time in Burma, socializing and feeding a cat, when I could have been saving myself from endless rebirths in the ocean of suffering, the eighteen vivid Buddhist hells. It was all right for Nandāsayee to giggle and laugh; she was Burmese, a fish in water. Circumstances rearranged themselves conveniently: the hot season was coming to an end, and the young nuns were disrobing one by one to go back to Rangoon University.

Even as her contemporaries vanished, Sister Nandāsayee was to be seen, still in pink, running about the nuns' quarters. Her experience must have been especially profound, I thought. Yet, in my new mood, I was glad she came no more to our hall. The healing leaves withered, and I threw them into the monsoon gutter. In a spirit of divestiture, I gave the Burmese cream back to Nurse Aye Shwe and avoided the brown gnome of the squashed tubes. My ringworm must be dead by now, and if it wasn't, I would keep the pain dancing in my hand.

I even stopped feeding the cat.

The first Rains fell, thundering on the galvanized roofs with a heart-stopping roar. My mind settled along with the dust.

As I notice objects, sir, I feel deep stillness, like a forest early in the morning. I am not looking for any particular object. Sensations are mixed with calmness. Then I find nothingness as an object, more subtle even than space. Afterward I try to remember it. I think there was some kind of knowing, but very subtle. When walking I feel light, barely existing.

Stay with what is present. If your awareness vanishes, be with that too.

Am I close to cessation?

Ha, ha, maybe so.

Walking on the breezeway, I feel sun's heat transmitted through iron roof. Ancient cracked cement. Crows dump over the garbage basket, rifling through fruit peels, cawing. Left foot, right foot. I am trying to concentrate because, in an hour, I have an interview.

A brown hand appears, waving in my field of vision: here are Nandāsayee's wide feet in red velvet thongs.

I look into her dancing eyes, this tall, strong, young woman. "My mother," she says, indicating a vast coarse hag in brown. I smile and shake hands. Mother grins back genially. She must have come to celebrate Nandāsayee's finishing her meditation, from their home village a day's ferry ride up the Irrawaddy, that village I had tried to imagine.

"Potograh," Nandāsayee insists, miming a snapshot. I go up to my room and load my last roll of fresh film into the Japanese idiot camera for this occasion in my friend's life. I expect to take one or two pictures of the family, but she grabs the camera and I have no heart to refuse her. I am still trying to keep my mind like a turtle in its shell. I pretend nothing is happening, stalk up and down in a fury while Nandāsayee poses her mother with a book, asks bystanders to photograph the two of them. Girls come out and learn to push the button, laugh at the automatic flash. I learn a new thing from the gross, grinning mother, that Burmese women wipe themselves on their sarongs and hide the wet spot in the front pleat. I see this while she is rearranging herself for a portrait.

"Sistah!" I sit on the steps with my eyes shut, feigning meditation. Nandāsayee pushes my chin up a little, then stands back and clicks the shutter. When all thirty-six frames are shot, she brings me the camera; I remove the film and hand it to her, wondering how she will find the cash to develop it.

Nandāsayee explains that she will be a nun for life. I am happy for her. Her family is poor and she will now have the chance to go to the Thilashinjaun, nuns' school. Maybe she'll even become fully enlightened and die, when it will be her time, into the unnameable beyond the suffering of name and form; maybe when she is cremated, her bones will reveal the tiny crystals.

"Sister, give me bow-peh," she says angrily, plucking at my notebook. "Bow-peh, bow-peh!" She wants my ballpoint pen. Her soft features gather at the center of her face.

"No," I finally say. "I need this for myself."

Time is moving slowly, sir.
For one who cannot sleep, the night seems long. For a lazy meditator one hour seems long.
I have been trying to make an effort.
Then there should be more activity in your practice.
This little nun came just now and disrupted my walking period.

You find many objects of interest in the body. Then you see that what is in the body is boring, of no interest.

"Pussy has deliver," Nurse Aye Shwe announced.

"What?"

"Your cat, is mother now."

I had given up walking in the breezeway. When in the evenings I didn't see the cat, I restrained myself from asking the nurse where she had gone. Now I was sent to peek under the stairs, where my cat crouched in awkward defensiveness over two orange kittens nearly as big as she was. Aha. Now I understood her belly's sad, hard bulge. One of the orange toms had often visited her on the breezeway. She'd snarled at him and cowered in the rain gutter. No wonder, I thought. But now I had to admit she seemed happy and fulfilled, as she curled herself, purring, round her suckling children.

At once I resumed stealing fat pork and giblets from lunch. I gave her Thai milk powder, full-fat. My effort to be perfect had lasted two weeks. Now, I rationalized, if I couldn't make it to enlightenment acting normally, I didn't want to get there.

Sīlānandī wrote me a note, which I tore up. "I think I'm close! Subtle lights! *Espace!*" Her arms were sticks.

In the middle of the Rains, the Swiss woman set fire to a straw mat and was asked to leave. She said she would go to a great Hindu teacher, Sattya Ma, who took your head in her lap as if you were a two-year-old child. I thought it would be good for her to go where she could talk, touch, and spend all day in rituals of devotion.

"I must remain as nun," she said with Swiss determination. "Nothing in the world is good for me."

The kittens made wobbly appearances in our rooms at night, left runny piles in the hall. Their mother left them mewling to resume her vigils in the breezeway. The ringworm came back in two places on my head and one on my left breast. I asked for more Burmese cream, which was slow in coming. In the end, I had to go to a clap clinic in Bangkok and a doctor in Australia, and even now I believe the fungus may be dormant in my skin.

"You will never attain cessation with all your pets," the nurse grumbled. "I will give them to ol' lady. She will feed them, you can forget about."

"All right," I said. Sīlānandī was writing me notes of triumphant phenomena; I was determined to resume my progress.

The nurse took the kittens away in a box and blocked the lower half of the Foreigner Women's Dormitory gate with chicken wire. My little cat was confused; she cried heartbreakingly at the barrier day and night. I hardened my heart and remembered the nurse's threat to report me to the abbot. The witchy sweeper was the new mother and would feed the cat only rice scraps. But walking at night in the breezeway, I watched the cat tease and kill a black scorpion and convinced myself that she could catch the food she needed, despite being blind.

One afternoon she dragged her children back and forth in the pouring rain trying to bring them back to the stairwell. The babies died, Nurse Aye Shwe told me days later.

I had known nothing; I was in the meditation hall.

Their mother forgot the kittens long before I did. I saw her meditating under the breezeway, paws tucked under, vacant eyes afire, as enigmatic as an idol of the East.

I was tortured by guilty thoughts: I never should have agreed to the eviction of the little family; my selfish spiritual desire had cost two infant lives. Finally I realized there was nothing to be done anymore and I tried to follow the cat's example, living on calmly with my share of pain. In a way, I thought, it was better for her not to have those mouths to feed.

It didn't matter what I thought.

I tried to remember what time I sat down. I think it was eleven. I felt as if I had been sitting for two minutes, but actually an hour had passed.

How was your posture?

Straight.

Did you have any dreams?

No dreams.

How did you know the time had passed?

Consciousness came back when the gong sounded midnight.

This is all right. Please continue.

Why is this happening?

Maybe later I will tell you.

Puzzled by this interview, I compared "experiences" with Sīlānandī and found that she had undergone the same sudden, extended vanishing of time. I ran to the abbot's cottage and asked whether this was cessation. He smiled with the utmost pride and indulgence and asked me whether I thought it was. "Yes," I hazarded. The experience repeated itself for shorter periods over the following week; the abbot had me and Sīlānandī listen to a tape that described the progress of meditation and various subtleties of cessation. At the end of the tape it said:

You must look in the mirror of the truth and see whether your experiences conform to this description, whether your cessation is genuine.

My teacher wanted me to work with resolves to strengthen the mind, but I was enervated, jumpy — after so much effort, neither able to make further rules for myself nor, much less, follow them. I asked for something new: the meditation on loving-kindness. He agreed and instructed me to repeat four phrases, constantly, in my mind.

May you be free from danger. May you be physically happy. May you be mentally happy. May you have ease of well-being.

Sir, should I listen to the sound of the sentences? Should I think about the meaning? Should I consider the welfare of all beings, the objects of my good wishes?

Just practice and don't worry. Send your loving feeling.

It was absolutely different. My mind was on rails, a locomotive. The body swung free, unconstrained by perpetual attention. But shortly after I began this blissful practice, I realized that the sounds I'd taken for taxis backfiring in the neighborhood were gunshots.

I went to the nurse and asked her to tell me what was going on outside the walls.

"They break the law," she said, both vague and fierce. "Do not disturb your practice."

No one wanted me to disturb my practice; but I went from one person to another, parlaying one tiny piece of information into the right to hear another. The day a machine gun shattered the air — the loudest sound I'd ever heard — I knew that unarmed demonstrators were being mown down. The people of Rangoon had risen against the military government. During the time I'd sat with my eyes shut inside Pingyan's high, thick walls, the prices of rice and oil had risen four hundred percent, so that a single measure of each now cost two weeks' average salary. Yesterday, in the poor suburb of Okkalappa, men had beheaded two police, cut out their hearts and livers, roasted and eaten them.

May you be free from danger. May you be physically happy.

A column of children, placed at the head of a peaceful pro-democracy demonstration, had been mown down.

May you be mentally happy. May you have ease of well-being.

Curfew: we were forbidden to walk in sight of the main gate after five P.M. The food got worse: gray, thin gruel of rice with a few dried shrimp. Like what most Burmese have been eating, I thought. People went home; Nandāsayee, too, vanished like some spirit, without a good-bye. Pingyan was nine-tenths empty, as lonely as the sky without the moon.

A green viper slithered in the bush next to the water tank; I sent it loving-kindness.

After sundown, bullhorns started squawking lies and threats; the nuns retreated into certain rooms, closed the shutters, and listened to the BBC World Service. I heard that Western embassy personnel were being evacuated; Air Force planes were on alert in Thailand to rescue U.S. citizens in the event of a general emergency.

In the depths of the hot season, I'd taken to waking at two A.M., when the air was cool and I could walk as fast as I liked, wherever I liked, unseen except by the servant who rang the hourly bells. Wrapped in the softness of sleepers, dreamers, my wakefulness was thunderbolt and diamond; I loved to look up at the enormous mango tree near the Western men's quarters, an ink cumulonimbus blocking clots of stars.

Nights were a toxic yellow now, marred by the sound of troop trucks grinding into position for the next day's massacre. Shooting began after lunch, politely at eleven-thirty A.M., and lasted three hours.

The air felt as full of passionate love as of disaster. People were willing to die for better lives. People were dying right next to us, even though we couldn't see them, because of the monastery walls.

Sound is only sound, impermanent, ungovernable, a source of pain. Sound is a material object, a wave that strikes the sensitive consciousness at the ear door. Sound is not a story. It is not your thought, it is not the image you may see in your mind about what produced the sound. For hearing to occur, three elements are needed . . .

Each night, the abbot dryly dissected the process at one of the sense doors: eye, ear, nose, tongue, body, and mind. But his discourse was cut to half an hour; then he disappeared behind the curtain, leaning on his translator's arm. I knew he was going into his bedroom to listen to the BBC.

Then he stopped giving discourses at all. Interviews were left to a handsome twenty-two-year-old monk whose name meant "Uncle Beautiful." He told me he was not qualified to instruct me in loving-kindness practice. I wanted to go to the abbot, but the jalousies and curtains were closed, and Nurse Aye Shwe was visiting the cottage twice a day, carrying a steel kidney pan covered with a handkerchief.

"Heart," she told me. Flicking up the handkerchief, she let me glimpse bottles of medicine, a blood pressure bulb.

"Has he had a heart attack?"

"No, but his heart is sick."

May you be free from danger. May you be physically happy. May you be mentally happy. May you have ease of well-being.

The phrases ground through my brain unlubricated; I began to wonder whether it was appropriate for me to stay in Rangoon. Who could possibly benefit from my presence? I went to the monastery's vice president, who reassured me. "Don't be afraid. Even besieged, we have rice and dried fish to keep you for a year. All Burmese respect a monastery, even the army."

I wasn't afraid for myself, but I imagined some U.S. Marine wading through a sea of blood to reach me, and dying — or the monastery officials gunned down for harboring me, like the doctors and nurses who'd rushed to the doors of Rangoon Hospital in an effort to protect their patients.

At last I went to the abbot's cottage. First I stood on his porch a long time, wavering. His Chinese clock played the first bar of *Eine Kleine Nachtmusik*. The house was dark, forbidding, thick with the smell of an unwashed body.

When I pushed open the door, I'd forgotten that a bell would jangle. *Come in*, he said in Burmese.

He was alone, staring at the inner side of the monastery's high, thick outer wall. "They kill those children," he said.

He spoke in English; I hadn't known he could.

But he'd spoken English to me once before. One morning, early in my stay at Pingyan, he'd come up quietly behind me as I was doing walking meditation.

"Sumanā?" he asked, gently prolonging the syllables. He always said my name so, as if in indulgent reproof.

I turned to look at him, a shaven old man a foot shorter than I was, leaning on his telescoping aluminum alpenstock. It had been a gift from some European student.

"Anything?" he'd said. Meaning, anything you need?

"Anything?"

"Anything?"

How will anyone believe in us now?

No one disbelieves in one person because of another person's unrelated crimes. As for me, my mind cannot be changed. It's settled now, because of the meditation.

Good . . .

But I want to leave.

You want to give back your robes and your precepts of morality?

I don't want anyone getting killed on my account.

That will never happen.

My parents are surely worrying.

I cannot stop the waterfall.

Thank you. I'm sorry.

We have not offered you a proper atmosphere.

No! You've influenced your students deeply — for life. Me, for example. I know there is no happiness to be found in outward things now. It's something deeper than mere belief. I've seen it for myself.

Then it should be easy for you to remain celibate. For life?

I don't know . . . maybe a year.

One year. Okay!

Wily old fisherman.

I held a meeting with the Foreigner Women and explained that I would leave on the first day it was safe to do so. No one wanted to come: they were in deep, practicing without regard for body or life. They didn't want to lose their time. Sīlānandī was making resolves, finding that her mind obeyed her automatically.

As it turned out, the shooting soon stopped: the army had suppressed the uprising, with four thousand dead.

But I'd already ridden to the airport with the British vice consul's wife and daughter. We were driven in a white Land Rover down a deblockaded road, lined with gray trucks full of terrified fifteen-year-old conscripts. This was the murderous army. Its helmets slid over its eyes, its rifles trembled at the ready. Even if I'd had film, I wouldn't have dared raise my camera into view.

Soon I was fingering the thick, slick paper of the airline magazine, gazing at a color photo of two women leaning across a grand piano in identical, black, backless silken gowns, advertising the state of mind that could be induced by perfume.

I took the long way home, stopping for a rest on the beaches of South Thailand, where the world's most avant-garde sybarites go to play. There I ate well and lay in the sun, my body slowly thickening into concreteness. I didn't know whether I was ahead of the game or behind it. Milanese women played in the surf, the tops of their bathing suits rolled down.

There'd be no kamikaze operation: I'd smuggle no boxes of medicines to Rangoon Hospital.

I could not stop the whirling of this world.

Was moving myself not, truly, the best that I could do? So the Burmese taught.

The Buddha said, *Long have you wandered, and filled the graveyards full. You have shed enough tears on this long way to fill the four great oceans.*

On my last day on Koh Samui, I spotted another woman with hair as short as my ex-nun's fuzz. Blond sparks in the sunrise: she picked her way across the hummocky white sand as delicately as my cat crossing rain gutters, leaning heavily on her boyfriend's arm. She wore a baggy, faded purple dress; she looked wonderful.

I was sitting cross-legged, facing the pale coralline sea from which a cooked red ball was rising. Exquisite light. The world was as delicate as baby skin.

Sister, my mind called out.

Suddenly I realized she was mind-blown, blitzed, so high on acid or the much-advertised local mushrooms that she could hardly walk.

European chocolate. Fresh fish. Green salads. Long before arriving in the "United State," I had confirmed Nurse Aye Shwe's prediction: "Now your virtue will go down. You will eat at night, you will eat whenever you like." Generous, she was. But I kept the promise I gave to the abbot of a year's celibacy, and I dedicated any merit that might arise to the Burmese people.

I also followed his injunction not to describe cessation. There could have been a way to talk about it, but really there was nothing to describe, for there had been no experience, nothing on which to base a statement. Afterward I felt different, but not in any way I could grasp.

This bothered me, subtly, pervasively. I might say it was as if I now had a hole at the bottom of my consciousness rather than any solid foundation; but this was difficult to assess.

Difficult to build any sense of achievement, even of event, on no basis. Why had I gone to Burma? What had I done there?

For a year I embodied the qualities the tape had said would reveal themselves as signs of a true cessation. I never lied, I didn't drink a drop, I had no interest in sex or money. I lived in an apartment as small and dark as Nurse Aye Shwe's rooms on the first floor of the Foreigner Women's Quarters. I felt happy to think that I no longer was a candidate for hell or rebirth in the animal realm.

And I wrote letters to my senators, asking them to remember the plight of Burma.

One night my father came to my city and took me out to a very good restaurant. He is a Republican businessman, but he'd found a way to be proud of my exploits in Burma by comparing me to some of the grand Victorian women travelers who "dressed in burnouses and went everywhere on camels." At this dinner he proposed a toast to me and my adventures. I didn't stop him from filling my glass with French wine. After he raised his glass to me, I took an experimental sip, just to see if I was capable. The first drop told me I was capable of anything.

That drop would have brought my kittens back to life; as I drank it, the monastery gates closed behind me. The most rigorous enlightenment system in the world shut me out. Or so I felt that night, not understanding my own rigorousness.

"Here's to you, too, Dad," I said, and drank the rest of the glass. I didn't quite know how I'd go on living, but I knew that I must.

Biographical Notes

Elizabeth Cox (1942–) was raised in Chattanooga, Tennessee, and studied creative writing at the University of North Carolina, Greensboro. She has completed three novels and a book of short stories (*Bargains in the Real World*, in which "Saved" was first published) and has won a North Carolina Fiction Award, an O. Henry Award, and a Lillian Smith Award for the novel *Night Talk* (1997). She taught creative writing at Duke University for seventeen years and now lives and teaches in Massachusetts. Her next novel is due for publication in 2004.

Gabriel García Márquez (1928–) was born in Aracataca, Colombia, in 1928. He attended the University of Bogotá and later worked as a reporter for the Colombian newspaper *El Espectador* and as a foreign correspondent in Rome, Paris, Barcelona, Caracas, and New York. He is the author of many novels and collections of stories, including *One Hundred Years of Solitude* (1967), *The Autumn of the Patriarch* (1976), *Chronicle of a Death Foretold* (1982), and *Love in the Time of Cholera* (1988). García Márquez was awarded the Nobel Prize for Literature in 1982. A resident of Mexico City, he is currently working on his much-anticipated memoir. "A Very Old Man with Enormous Wings" was first published in *Leaf Storm and Other Stories* (1972).

Mary Gordon (1948–) has written several best-sellers — the novels *Final Payments* (1978), *The Company of Women* (1981), *Men and Angels* (1985), *The Other Side* (1990), and *Spending* (1998) and a memoir, *The Shadow Man* (1999). She has published a book of novellas, *The Rest of Life* (1995); a collection of stories, *Temporary Shelter* (1987); and two books of essays, *Good Boys and Dead Girls* (1992) and *Seeing Through Places* (2000). Her most recent work is the biography *Joan of Arc* (2000). Winner of the Lila Acheson Wallace Reader's Digest Award, a Guggenheim Fellowship, and the 1997 O. Henry Award for best short story, she teaches at Barnard College and lives in New York City. "The Deacon" first appeared in *The Atlantic Monthly.*

Nathaniel Hawthorne (1804–1864) was born July 4, 1804, in Salem, Massachusetts. One of America's most important nineteenth-century writers, he was educated at Bowdoin College and lived most of his life in New England. "Young Goodman Brown" first appeared in *New England Magazine* in April 1835 and was included in his first book, *Twice Told Tales* (1837). Other collections followed, but Hawthorne achieved popular acclaim only after the publication of his two classic novels about New England and the New England character: *The Scarlet Letter* (1850) and *The House of Seven Gables* (1851). Hawthorne died near Plymouth, New Hampshire, at the age of fifty-nine.

Marjorie Kemper (1944–) has published stories in *The Atlantic Monthly, New Orleans Review,* and *Greensboro Review.* Her first novel, *'Til That Good Day,* was published in 2003 by St. Martin's Press. "God's Goodness" first appeared in *The Atlantic Monthly.*

Hanif Kureishi (1954–) was born in Bromley, England, the son of a Pakistani father and an English mother. He studied philosophy at the University of London. His novel *The Buddha of Suburbia* (1990) won a Whitbread Book of the Year Award, and his screenplay for the 1985 film *My Beautiful Laundrette* was named best screenplay by the New York Film Critics Circle. Kureishi has written short stories in addition to novels and screenplays, and his work has been translated into more than fifteen languages. *Gabriel's Gift* (2001) is his most recent novel.

John L'Heureux (1934–) is the author of sixteen books of poetry and fiction. His stories have appeared in *The Atlantic Monthly, Esquire, Harper's Magazine,* and *The New Yorker,* and they have frequently been anthologized in *Best American Stories* and *Prize Stories: The O. Henry Awards.* Since 1973 he has taught at Stanford University, where he has twice received the Dean's Award for Excellence in Teaching. His recent publications include a collection of stories, *Comedians* (1990), and the novels *Having Everything* (2000) and *The Miracle.* "The Comedian" was first published in *The Atlantic Monthly.*

James A. Michener (1907–1997) was born in New York City and graduated from Swarthmore College. Prior to becoming a writer, he worked as an academic, an editor, and a U.S. Navy lieutenant commander during World War II. His first book, *Tales of the South Pacific* (1947), won a Pulitzer Prize and became the basis of the award-winning Rodgers and Hammerstein musical *South Pacific.* Over the next forty years Michener wrote such monumental best-sellers as *Sayonara* (1954), *The Bridges at Toko-Ri* (1953), *Hawaii* (1959), *The Source* (1965), and *Chesapeake*, from which "Voyage Four: 1661" was excerpted. Michener was decorated with America's highest civilian award, the Presidential Medal of Freedom, and held honorary doctorates in five fields from thirty leading universities. He died in his Texas home in 1997.

Yukio Mishima (1925–1970), born in Tokyo, Japan, produced forty novels, thirty-three plays, two travel books, and countless short stories and poems. Several films have been made from his novels, including *The Sound of Waves* (1956); *Enjo*, which was based on *The Temple of the Golden Pavilion* (1959); and *The Sailor Who Fell from Grace with the Sea* (1965). Among his other works are the novels *Confessions of a Mask* (1970) and *Thirst for Love* (1969) and the short-story collections *Acts of Worship* (1989) and *Death in Midsummer* (1966), in which "The Priest and His Love" was first published. On November 25, 1970, the day he completed *The Sea of Fertility*, Mishima committed ritual suicide at the age of forty-five.

Joyce Carol Oates (1938–) is a prolific writer of fiction, poetry, drama, and criticism. Among her many awards and honors are the National Book Award, the Pushcart Prize, three O. Henry Awards, the Rea Award, and the O. Henry, PEN/Malamud, Bobst, and Bram Stoker lifetime achievement awards. Her most recent publication is her thirtieth novel, *I'll Take You There* (2002). Born in upstate New York in 1938, Oates received her B.A. from Syracuse University and her M.A. from the University of Wisconsin. She is the Roger S. Berlind Distinguished Professor of Humanities at Princeton University. "At the Seminary" appears in her collection *Where Are You Going, Where Have You Been?* (1974).

Edna O'Brien (1936–) was born in a rural Catholic village in the west of Ireland. Her novels include *Johnny I Hardly Knew You* (1977), *The High Road* (1988), *The Country Girls Trilogy* (1986), and, most recently, *In the Forest* (2003). Among her half dozen collections of stories are *A Scandalous Woman* (1974), *A Fanatic Heart* (1984), and *Lantern Slides* (1990), which won the Los Angeles Times Book Prize for Fiction. O'Brien's stories have appeared in magazines such as *The New Yorker* (where "Sister Imelda" was first published), *Ladies' Home Journal*, and *Cosmopolitan*. She has taught creative writing at City College of the City University of New York.

Katherine Anne Porter (1890–1980), born Callie Russell Porter in Indian Creek, Texas, was raised by her father and grandmother, whose name she adopted in early adulthood. Despite her humble upbringing and lack of formal higher education, Porter became learned in the ways of the world through extensive travel. Her first book of stories, *Flowering Judas* (1930), received immediate recognition and critical acclaim; it was followed by *Pale Horse, Pale Rider* (1939) and *The Leaning Tower* (1944). Her first long novel, *Ship of Fools*, was published in 1962 and became a best-seller. Porter's crowning literary achievement was the publication of *Collected Stories* (1965), which received the National Book Award and a Pulitzer Prize. She died at the age of ninety after several debilitating strokes.

Reynolds Price (1933–) was born in Macon, North Carolina, and was educated in the public schools of his native state. He graduated from Duke University and later studied literature at Oxford University as a Rhodes Scholar. His 1962 novel, *A Long and Happy Life*, received the William Faulkner Award for a notable first novel and has never been out of print. Since then he has published more than thirty books, including the novel *Kate Vaiden*, winner of the National Book Critics Circle Award in 1986; *Collected Stories* (1993); and *Collected Poems* (1997). He has recently published his first novel for young readers, *A Perfect Friend* (2000). Price lives in Durham, North Carolina, and is the James B. Duke Professor of English at Duke University. "Full Day" first appeared in *Harper's Magazine*.

Tova Reich (1942–) is the author of the novels *Mara* (1978), *The Jewish War* (1995), and *Master of the Return* (1988), which won the Edgar Lewis Wallant Award for fiction. Her stories and reviews have appeared in, among other publications, *The Atlantic Monthly*, *Harper's Magazine*, and the *New York Times*. "The Third Generation" first appeared in *The Atlantic Monthly*.

Rémy Rougeau (1953–) is a cloistered monk living in the upper Midwest. He holds an M.F.A. from Emerson College and has published parts of his novel in *The Atlantic Monthly* and elsewhere. His first novel, *All We Know of Heaven*, was published in 2001.

Salman Rushdie (1947–) was born in Bombay, India, and educated in Britain at the Rugby School and Cambridge University. He is the author of numerous works of both fiction and nonfiction. His second novel, *Midnight's Children*, won the Booker Prize in 1981, as well as the James Tait Black Prize. The publication of his controversial fourth novel, *The Satanic Verses* (1988), led to the issuing of a *fatwa* against him in 1989 by the Iranian leader Ayatollah Khomeini for alleged blasphemy against the Koran. Since then, Rushdie has vigorously campaigned for the right of freedom of expression and continued to write. Recent publications include *Haroun and the Sea of Stories* (1990), *The Moor's Last Sigh* (1995), and *The Ground Beneath Her Feet* (1999).

William Saroyan (1908–1981), born in Fresno, California, created a literature based on his Armenian background. His many short-story collections include *The Daring Young Man on the Flying Trapeze* (1934) and *My Name Is Aram* (1940). In addition to novels and memoirs, he wrote several plays, notably *My Heart's in the Highlands* (1939) and *The Time of Your Life* (1939), for which he was awarded a Pulitzer Prize in 1940.

Isaac Bashevis Singer (1904–1991) is considered by many to be the greatest postwar writer of Yiddish literature. Born in Leoncin, Poland, he was the son of a pious rabbi, who considered secular writing heretical, and a more skeptical, rationalist mother. He began to write as a young man, first in Warsaw and later in New York, where he moved in 1935 to be near his brother, the eminent writer I. J. Singer. Among Singer's best-known works are *Gimpel the Fool and Other Stories* (1957), *The Family Moskat* (1950), *Satan in Goray* (1955), and *The Magician of Lublin* (1957). Most of his work was first published in serialized form in the *Jewish Daily Forward*, a Yiddish newspaper based in New York, and many Singer stories have yet to be translated into English. In 1978 Singer received the Nobel Prize for Literature. He died at the age of eighty-seven.

Khushwant Singh (1915–), novelist, historian, and editor, was born in Hadali, India (now in Pakistan). He was educated at the Government College, Lahore, and at King's College, Cambridge University, and the Inner Temple in London. He practiced law for several years before joining the Indian Ministry of External Affairs; later he would have a distinguished career as a journalist and editor. Among his published works are a classic two-volume history of the Sikhs, several novels — including *Train to Pakistan*, which won the Grove Press Award for the best work of fiction in 1954; *I Shall Not Hear the Nightingale* (1969); and *Delhi* (1991) — and a number of books about Delhi, nature, and current affairs. His autobiography, *Truth, Love, and a Little Malice*, was published in 2002.

Amy Tan (1952–) was born in Oakland, California, to Chinese immigrant parents. Her father was a Baptist minister. She is the author of *The Bonesetter's Daughter* (2001), *The Joy Luck Club* (1989), *The Kitchen God's Wife* (1991), and *The Hundred Secret Senses* (1995), from which "Fishers of Men" was excerpted. Her essays and stories have appeared in numerous magazines and anthologies, and her work has been translated into more than twenty-five languages. Since earning a master's degree in linguistics from San Jose State University, Tan has worked as a language specialist with programs serving children with developmental disabilities. She lives with her husband in San Francisco and New York.

Alice Walker (1944–) was born in Eatonton, Georgia. She won the Pulitzer Prize and the American Book Award for her novel *The Color Purple* (1982), which was preceded by *The Third Life of Grange Copeland* (1970) and *Meridian* (1976). Her other best-selling novels include *By the Light of My Father's Smile* (1998), *Possessing the Secret of Joy* (1992), and *The Temple of My Familiar* (1988). She is also the author of two collections of short stories, three collections of essays, fives volumes of poetry, and several children's books. Her books have been translated into more than two dozen languages. A new poetry collection, *Absolute Trust in the Goodness of the Earth,* was published in 2003.

Daly Walker (1940–) is a surgeon and Vietnam veteran. His stories have appeared in a number of literary magazines, including *The Atlantic Monthly,* where "I Am the Grass" was first published. Originally from Indiana, he now lives in Boca Grande, Florida, where he practices medicine and is at work on a novel.

Jessamyn West (1902–1984), born in Indiana of Quaker parents, grew up and was educated in California. She was the author of nineteen books, including novels, memoirs, short stories, and poetry. Among her best-known works are *The Friendly Persuasion* (1945), from which "Music on the Muscatatuck" was excerpted; *Except for Me and Thee* (1969); *The Massacre at Fall Creek* (1975); *Cress Delahanty* (1953); *The Life I Really Lived* (1979); *The Woman Said Yes* (1976); and *A Matter of Time* (1966). Her work appeared in many distinguished and popular periodicals, including *The New Yorker, The Atlantic Monthly,* and *Harper's Magazine.* Until her death in February 1984, she lived with her husband in Napa, California.

Kate Wheeler (1955–) was born in Oklahoma and grew up in several countries in South America. She graduated from Rice University and the creative writing program at Stanford, and was ordained as a Buddhist nun in Burma. Her debut collection, *Not Where I Started From* (1993), was a finalist for the PEN/Faulkner Award and was also named a New York Times Notable Book. She has also written a novel, *When Mountains Walked* (2000). Wheeler is the recipient of a Whiting Award, an NEA fellowship, and a Guggenheim fellowship, and she was named by *Granta* a Best Young American Novelist. Wheeler is on the adjunct faculty at Southwest Texas State University and lives in Massachusetts. "Ringworm" first appeared in *The Gettysburg Review.*

Faith: Stories

Edited by C. Michael Curtis

FOR DISCUSSION

1. In the stories by James Michener and Jessamyn West, conflicts arise between faith orthodoxies: in the Michener, Quaker convictions are taken as a challenge to Puritan stringencies; in the West, the music-loving husband of a Quaker minister brings an organ into their household, thus directly challenging a deeply ingrained Quaker distrust of music and its ability to divert believers from businesslike piety.

In what way, in the Michener story, does Kenworthy's Quakerism threaten the reigning community belief system? And what explains its appeal to his cellmate, Paxmore? How does the unidentified but vengeful "woman" function in the story's final page?

How would you characterize the accommodation to Jess Birdwell's organ reached first by his minister-wife and then by members of the Ministry and Oversight Committee? Does the accommodation represent a weakening of resolve?

2. In the stories by Khushwant Singh, Hanif Kureishi, and Salman Rushdie, articles of faith are explored ironically. In all three, true believers are portrayed unsympathetically, though in all three the workings of fate appear to underline the potency of their convictions.

In the Singh story, how considered does Gunga Ram's treatment of

Kala Nag, the cobra, seem to be? Why does Gunga Ram pay the ultimate price for the violence of "we youngsters," one of whom narrates the story?

In the Kureishi story, to what extent is the behavior of Parvez's son fanatical? What justifies the son's use of the term to describe his father's behavior at story's end? How does Bettina function in the story?

In the Rushdie story, do events appear to confirm a belief that the prophet's hair has magical properties? To what extent could the behavior of all the characters in the story be said to have intensified, to have taken each to an extreme but logical consequence of impiety? What does Rushdie appear to be saying about the perils of faith commitment? Or of its absence?

3. In what sense can Josie Wire, the heroine of Elizabeth Cox's "Saved," be said to have succeeded in her effort to "save" the man who speaks to her from the Wagon Wheel? What, in the story's seduction scene, seems to have influenced Samuel Beckett/Bob Hunnicut's change of heart?

4. In "The Deacon" by Mary Gordon, how important is Gerard Mahoney's misreading of Sister Joan Fitzgerald's remark, "You know that you are greatly beloved"? How does that misreading affect Sister Joan's wish to order a Scotch and soda at Gallagher's restaurant?

5. In what sense does Cello, the visiting Tibetan monk in "Cello" by Rémy Rougeau, provide an example for Brother Antoine? What evidence does the story provide that Antoine might profit from such an example? How do you feel about the visitors' decision to conceal their companion's gender?

6. Ling Tan, the heroine of Marjorie Kemper's "God's Goodness," describes herself as a "good Christian," and her faith, at story's end, appears unshaken. During the course of the story, has that faith been tested? In what way? Can Mike's view of Ling's religiosity be said to have changed by story's end?

7. In "The Third Generation" by Tova Reich, Nechama, the granddaughter of Holocaust survivors, decides to become a Catholic nun in a convent built on the outskirts of Auschwitz. Why, apparently,

does Nechama make that choice? Why does Arlene, her mother, not "recognize" the language of "suffering and salvation, martyrdom and redemption"? Where, at story's end, do Arlene and Nechama stand with regard to their differing views of a purposeful life?

8. Kate Wheeler's narrator in "Ringworm" says that she went to Burma and sought admission to a Buddhist monastery in order to achieve "complete freedom of the heart and mind." To what extent, by story's end, does she appear to have been successful? How might the experiences and disciplines described help her achieve her goal? Why, at story's end, does a sip of French wine close "the monastery gates" behind her?

9. "A Very Old Man with Enormous Wings" by Gabriel García Már-quez may be read as a comic allegory. Should it be? Insofar as it seems to challenge a number of faith responses, what appear to be the au-thor's targets? Why is the appearance of an angel, even one in ragged condition, such a puzzle to the villagers? To Father Gonzaga? To Rome? What would you assume to be the author's attitude toward the Catholic Church? How would an angel fare in *your* backyard?

Also edited by C. Michael Curtis

God: Stories

"A provocative and delightful tour through the varieties of religious experience." —KATHLEEN NORRIS

T HE COMPANION VOLUME to *Faith: Stories*, this fresh approach to an age-old discussion collects twenty-five dazzling short stories by eminent writers about spiritual experiences. Including John Updike, Philip Roth, Louise Erdrich, James Joyce, Flannery O'Connor, James Baldwin, Alice Munro, and more, *God: Stories* offers insight, solace, and pleasure not only to the faithful but to the seekers — and to those who simply love fine stories.

ISBN 0-395-92971-7